A Married Man

Also by Catherine Alliott

THE OLD-GIRL NETWORK
GOING TOO FAR
THE REAL THING
ROSIE MEADOWS REGRETS . . .
OLIVIA'S LUCK

A Married Man

—CATHERINE ALLIOTT—

Ballantine Books • New York

A Ballantine Book
Published by The Random House Ballantine Publishing Group

Copyright © 2002 by Catherine Alliott

All rights reserved under International
and Pan-American Copyright Conventions. Published in
the United States by The Random House Ballantine Publishing Group,
a division of Random House, Inc., New York.
Originally published in Great Britain by
HEADLINE BOOK PUBLISHING IN 2002

www.ballantinebooks.com

Library of Congress Control Number: 2003090451

ISBN 0-345-46280-7

Text design by Holly Johnson
Cover design by Royce Becker
Cover photo © Yuen Lee/Photonica

Manufactured in the United States of America

First American Edition: May 2003

2   4   6   8   10   9   7   5   3

A Married Man

Chapter One

"SHE'LL HAVE YOU FOR BREAKFAST," OBSERVED JESS TARTLY, rubbing a bit of grime off a Spode jug and setting it down on the trestle table in front of us.

"Who will?" I broke from my contemplation of the assorted bric-a-brac and antiques before us to glance up defensively.

"Your mother-in-law, of course. Talk about strolling back into the lion's den. You didn't actually say you'd go, did you?"

"Of course I did," I said hotly. "Christ, Jess, if someone offered you two sets of school fees and a converted barn over your head in a picturesque rural idyll, don't tell me you'd pass it up! Don't tell me you wouldn't leap at it, too, and anyway, she's my *ex*-mother-in-law—that makes all the difference."

"Rubbish," she scoffed as she arranged a fistful of silver spoons on our faded velvet tablecloth. "Not in her eyes. As far as she's concerned you'll always be the mother of her grandchildren, and that, my dear Lucy, is entirely the point. That is precisely *why* you've been offered such a mouthwatering package down in Netherby-sur-la-ancestral-pile with all its crumbling turrets and sod-off acres. It has absolutely nothing to do with your well-being or your welfare, and certainly nothing to do with your undoubted charms." She beamed past me as a customer loomed. "Yes, madam, it *is* Royal Worcester and you're quite right, there's just a teeny bit of damage to the spout, but otherwise it's in wonderful condition for such a rare piece, don't you think?"

She bestowed a radiant smile on Madam, who, swaddled in ethnic knits on this flaming cold June day and with all the hallmarks of a seasoned Portobello Road aficionado, was peering doubtfully over her spectacles. She ran a practiced eye over the rest of the collectibles on our stall, sniffed, and put the teapot down. She looked far from convinced.

"No," she snapped. "I think it's in rather ropy condition actually.

1

And I also think that all these tags you've put on everything are very misleading. Who are you to tell me that's a 'very decorative piece of early Meissen?' Surely I should be the judge of whether it's decorative or not, and I fail to see why that bit of old lace is so 'absurdly pretty' or why that rusty old oil lamp so 'quintessentially important in the molding of eighteenth-century France.' "

"It's to help some of our less discerning customers," purred Jess obsequiously. "To point them in the right direction, lead them, antiquarily speaking, to the right century, right country even, so they don't feel foolish asking. Clearly you don't need any pointers, but golly," she rolled her eyes expressively, "you should see some of the types we get round here."

I smiled down into my plastic mug of hot chocolate, lacing my cold fingers around it and reflecting that Jess's labels had indeed gotten more and more outrageous as the weeks had gone by. We'd temporarily taken over the antique stall from my mother, Maisie, who'd had a stall in the Portobello Road since the beginning of time, and certainly since I was a little girl. In the last couple of weeks, though, her chronic arthritis had almost forced her to give it up, so I'd stepped into the breach to keep it going until she was better, roping my oldest friend, Jess, in with me. For Jess it made a welcome diversion from changing her small son's nappy at the weekend, and for me—well, antiques were my passion, so I was happy. Happy just soaking up the atmosphere of this famous street, gazing at the stalls crammed haphazardly along it, silver next to clocks and watches, old farm implements next to yellowing books, starched Victorian christening gowns billowing in the breeze beside pop memorabilia, and, of course, my mother's own eclectic offerings, which included anything from French café ashtrays, to exquisite porcelain, to faded sepia postcards. I'd even added a few choice pieces of my own, which I'd priced ridiculously high and watched like a hawk, hoping secretly that they wouldn't sell but knowing I needed the money.

I needn't have worried. As we'd sat there, three Saturdays in a row now, surrounded by what we thought were the most delicious and interesting bits of other people's domestic history, we'd sold very little. Even more galling was having to look on incredulously whilst Fat Ronnie at the next-door stall—peddler of crap, both verbal and antique, and with a special interest in flatulence, his own and other people's—sold shedfuls.

"Orright, gels?" he'd yelled over last week as he popped yet another sensationally ugly toby jug into a plastic bag and handed it to its proud new owner. "Need any help over there? Blimey, you won't sell much wiv that heap of rubbish!"

He chuckled and fanned theatrically behind his backside to let us know that he'd broken wind for the millionth time that day. "Surprised you've got any customers at all!"

"Surprised you've got any trousers," Jess had muttered, but then, with characteristic zeal, had whirled into action.

"It's his labels," she hissed, swinging round to me, "that's all. His stuff's rubbish, we know that, but it's the way he sells it. That's where we're going wrong, Lucy. You can't just bung it all down on a trestle table and hope for the best. It's all in the marketing!"

"I'm not sure you really market bric-a-brac, do you?" I said doubtfully. "I mean, surely—"

"Of course you bloody market it, and don't call it bric-a-brac for heaven's sake. Some of this stuff is priceless!"

I stared doubtfully at the array before us, but she was off, frenziedly slapping *beautifully restored* onto a horribly cracked chamber pot and *breathtakingly pretty* onto one of our major mistakes, a hideous piece of Coalport bought from another stallholder after a liquid Saturday lunch. I have to say, the bits of tartan ribbon Jess tied them on with did improve the look of our offerings and we didn't do too badly that week, but not so today.

Today, tartan ribbon notwithstanding, business was disastrous, and as Fat Ronnie leered across, hands deep in pockets, jingling his change around his privates, we gave in.

"Come on," muttered Jess. "Let's pack it in."

"Business a bit slow is it, gels?" he called. "Can I offer you a loan?" He jingled some more.

"No thanks," said Jess, eyeing his crotch with distaste. "Not when we know where it's been."

He chuckled. "Ah well, all the more for me then." Suddenly he frowned, sniffed the air. "Dear God, who's dropped one? That you, Lucy?"

"Shut up, Ronnie," I said wearily, getting up to wrap some brass candlesticks in newspaper.

"Well, someone let one go." He sighed, shook his head. "I don't know, you girls with your educated accents and your silk shirts and your violin lessons, and you can still belt them out like that. Frightening." He shuddered.

"How did we do?" I asked, ignoring him as Jess shook the little velvet bag of money onto the table.

"Twenty-two pounds and . . . six pence."

"That's our worst yet."

"I know." She sighed, pouring it all back in again. "Oh well," she said grudgingly, "I suppose at least you'll be taken away from all this. But I still think you're selling your soul."

"Oh, don't be so melodramatic!" I snapped. "What option have I got? I can't afford to send Ben to a good school—and he hates the one he's at—and I can't stay in that tiny little flat any longer, either. Even if I could afford it, which I can't, the three of us are bursting at the seams, and I certainly can't move back in with Maisie and Lucas and cramp their style forever. And anyway, Jess, what could be nicer than living in the country?" I demanded. "The children walking across the fields to school, ponies to ride," I said wistfully, "streams to dam, daisies to, um, you know . . ."

"Chain," she said dryly, "prior to rattling them. Come on, Lucy; you're a city girl through and through and you know it. You'll miss all of this, for heaven's sake!" She swung her arm around at the bustling street full of traders and tourists, alive with cheerful banter and laughter and haggling and eating on the hoof. "You'll miss the buzz. I mean, I'm willing to accept that fresh air is wonderful for the cheeks, but it doesn't do much for the brain—you'll stagnate down there. Christ, you don't know one end of a cow from another! And you said yourself when you married Ned that the one thing you'd never do was go and live near his ghastly parents—and now look at you. He's not even here anymore, and down you go."

"Jess, I have to cut my cloth," I warned tersely.

"Yes, to go and live on your parents-in-law's estate, *totally* at their mercy, *completely* beholden to them, and *absolutely* at their beck and call. There you'll be with Lady Horse-Face lording it over you, Lord Tit-

Face pinching your bum at every conceivable opportunity, the tragic Lavinia drinking herself to a standstill, Pinkie-Pie, or whatever she's called, gleefully bonking stable boys in haylofts, drippy Hector dithering ineffectually around trying to convince his father he's got what it takes to take over All This one day, and all the time surrounded by the memory of your dead husband, who'll stalk in and out of the plot like Banquo's ghost!" Her normally pale face was pink and her eyes shone. I blinked at her in silence.

"Sorry," she said abruptly, averting her eyes. "I mean—that last bit. But you know what they're like, Lucy," she urged. "God, at least you've faced up to it, coped with it, and brilliantly, too, but four years have gone by and they haven't even started. Haven't even begun to accept he's dead. That house is like a shrine to Ned—everywhere you go there are photos of him; his childhood fossil collection still sits in the hall; cricket bats he once owned are stuck up on the walls; even paintings he did as a *child*, for heaven's sake, are pinned up in the kitchen. His room is untouched up in that godforsaken turret, and the way they *talk* about him! *Constantly*, as if he's still there, sitting at the table with them, and not in a nice, relaxed way like dropping his name into the conversation, but long and hard, for hours, like they've been taught to do in *therapy* or something. There's just no getting away from him. I'm surprised they haven't got him embalmed in the cellar." She stopped when she saw my face.

"OK," she muttered hastily, hoisting a sackful of china onto her back and picking up one end of the table we'd speedily collapsed, "that was tasteless, I agree. But you must admit, Luce, it's going to set you back about three years, and you were doing so well. You've got those four mornings a week in your beloved porcelain department at Christie's, you've got this stand on a Saturday—"

"This stand," I said witheringly, swinging another sack onto my shoulder and picking up the other end of the table.

She swept on regardless. "The kids are doing well, and *you're* so much better. God, Luce, you're finally out of the loop." Like a couple of paperhangers we picked up our table and plunged into the heaving, drizzling depths of the Portobello Road, dodging through the crowds, loaded down with goodies.

"I mean, OK, the money's tight," she yelled back at me through the noise, "but give it a couple more years and you'll be fine; you'll be through it. But to give up on London, on your flat, and go down there, to be *swamped* by that wretched family again . . ."

"The money's not tight, Jess." I stopped suddenly in the street, jolting her to a standstill. "It's bloody nonexistent! I get paid a pittance by Christie's for busting a gut—"

"But you love it!"

"Yes, *and* I can keep on doing it."

She gaped. "From Oxfordshire?"

"Course I can! God, people do commute from there, you know; it's not entirely the back of beyond. And I'm going to change it to two full days, which will suit me much better," I said confidently. "And anyway," I sighed, picking up the table and moving on again, "I told you, even if I wanted to stay in that flat, I can't. I can't afford it; the mortgage is crippling."

"So why don't Lord and Lady Po-Face offer to pay it for you?" she demanded. "Or . . . or why don't they offer to set you up somewhere else, in London? Why does it have to be down there with them?"

"Because Ben starts prep school soon and they've offered to pay the fees," I began patiently. "And because he needs somewhere that can cope with dyslexia."

"And because they want him to go to the Right One. The school of their choice, not Highfield Road where he is now—"

"Where he's bullied and they sniff glue—"

"But somewhere much more traditional, somewhere where they can make a *man* of him, mold him into a nice little Grenadier Guard like his grandfather. They want control, Luce, control of you for a start—God, word might even have got back that you've had a few hot dates; well, they'll want to knock that *right* on the head for starters—but more important, control of the children. They want to monitor them, choose their friends, organize their social lives—of *course* they want you down there in their tastefully converted barn in their back garden!"

"Oh, don't be absurd," I said hotly. "You're so cynical, Jess. It's the whole class thing with you, isn't it? The shooting and the striding round in breeches, that's what you hate, and that's just small-minded, prejudicial, and snobbish. That's like talking against ethnic minorities because they smell of curry."

She snorted with derision at this but didn't instantly come back at me.

"And OK," I went on, encouraged by her silence, "Ned's mother can be," I hesitated, "a bit tricky at times. . . ."

"Tricky!" she scoffed. "Needs smothering with a pillow, you once said."

"But you know recently," I hurried on, "well, Rose and I have sort of," I licked my lips, "bonded."

"What!"

"And even if we hadn't," I went on defiantly, "there's simply no way I'd look this gift horse in the mouth, complete with financial security for me and *total* security for my children. You don't know what it's like, Jess, eking out a flipping widow's pension. I've been beside myself with worry. God, this is like manna from heaven! When I got Rose's letter I cried, if you must know, wept, I was so bloody relieved. So just back off and stop taking the wind out of my sails, OK?"

She made a face but looked slightly contrite. We walked on in silence.

"*And* you'll have the mad aunts next door to contend with," she reminded me, at length.

I smiled. "I *love* the mad aunts."

She sighed as we threaded our way precariously down another heaving backstreet. "Yes, well, I suppose they will be something of a diversion, and at least they've got the measure of Rose. Hmmm . . ." she said thoughtfully, "perhaps *they* could smother her."

I sighed, stopped, and made her face me again. "Thanks, Jess; this is really, really helping."

She opened her mouth and pretended to look astonished, but then her eyes slid away. "Sorry," she mumbled, scuffing her toe. "It's only 'cos I care. And I'll miss you. Selfish, really. But I can't help feeling . . ." she puckered her brow and wrestled with herself for honesty, "well, that there's nothing *down* there for you."

"No man, you mean," I said darkly as we picked up our load and dodged through the crowds again.

"Well, you must admit, it's a social wasteland where they live. I mean, correct me if I'm wrong, but don't they even own the bloody village and everyone in it?"

"Used to," I muttered.

"What?"

"Used to," I yelled wearily above the noise. "Only half of it now."

"You see? Half a flaming village! Stuffed full of aged old retainers who still get beriberi and cholera and whom Rose no doubt visits graciously with rabbits and poultices in her basket. Probably dispenses maundy money, too, as she mops those wrinkled, fevered old brows. God, you'll be lucky if you run into anyone under eighty. You can bet your life anyone younger fled to Milton Keynes long ago."

I gritted my teeth and trudged on, ignoring her.

"I suppose you might meet the odd blacksmith or two," she conceded grudgingly. "All red-hot irons and rippling biceps, but you'll never meet anyone cerebral, whereas here—hey!" She broke off suddenly. "Whatever happened to that nice solicitor chappie you were seeing?"

"Oh God no, not him. Too full of Chablis and self-belief."

"Well, OK, that guy you mentioned last week, Charles or something. Fantasy man in the office?"

"Charlie." I colored instantly, glad she couldn't see. Crikey, had I said "in the office?" Perhaps I had.

"Ah, you see! Charlie. Well, you won't see him, will you?"

"I might. Apparently he's got a place near Oxford," I said, unable to resist it.

She halted suddenly, yanking the table and obliging me to stop behind her.

"Right," she said slowly, watching me carefully. "And did you know that when Rose asked you?"

"Asked me what?" I said, pathetically playing for time.

"Asked you to go and live down there, for heaven's sake!"

"Well, I . . ." I hesitated. Oh God, I knew I shouldn't have mentioned Charlie. Why had I mentioned him?

"Forget Charlie," I said quickly, aware that I was still flushing. "The truth is, Jess, I don't even know him, and even if I did, he'd be out of the frame, out of the equation."

"Why?"

"Because . . . he's out of my league."

"Bollocks," she scoffed. "No one's out of your league, Lucy, you're flaming gorgeous! It's just you got married so young no one else ever got the chance to tell you, to stare at you, flirt with you. You were snapped up by Ned at university in about ten seconds."

"Nonsense." I gazed past, beyond her.

"Oh yes, quite right, nonsense. Waist-length blond hair, green eyes, and a voluptuous figure to die for, *very* unattractive. *Very* wince-making. I'm surprised you can look at yourself in the mirror in the morning. Do me a favor—out of your league? You're just so unused to men looking at you, you don't know they're doing it." She peered at me from under her dark fringe. "God, you're *still* red. Purple! Who is this guy, anyway?"

"I told you, Jess," I snapped, "he's no one. Just leave me alone and live your own life, can't you? Why have I got such bossy friends?" I made to move on, but she stuck firmly to the pavement. Stared.

"So what's wrong with him then?"

"There's nothing *wrong* with him."

"Oh yes, there is. You're being really cagey, and I know you, Luce." She narrowed her eyes thoughtfully. "He's married, isn't he?"

"Of course he's not married!" I blustered. "Would I mess around with a married man?"

"You bet your sweet life you would, and you know why?"

I stared down, bit the inside of my cheek.

"Bit older, no doubt, bit wiser, so security in that, but also, *also*, security in the fact that he's not *quite* available, so no real emotional output. At the end of the day, you don't have to commit yourself, don't really have to take the plunge. Ooh, yes, ideal." She rubbed her hands together gleefully. "Perfect!"

"Just get off my case, Jess," I said angrily. "I told you, there's nothing in it. I have a minor crush on him, OK? A harmless, pathetic, long-distance crush, like sitting in the hairdresser's and gazing wantonly at Hugh Grant's picture in *Hello!* He's just someone who makes my heart beat faster when I walk past him in the stree—office," I said quickly. "That's all."

"Well, it bloody better be," she said darkly. "You know how I feel about married men. It's a sacred institution, Luce, and don't you forget it."

"I'm hardly likely to with you ramming your perfect marriage permanently down my throat, am I!"

Suddenly we stared at each other, aghast.

I swallowed. "Why are we fighting?"

"I don't know." Jess scratched her head sheepishly. "My fault, I think. Anyway," she shrugged, "you know as well as I do my marriage isn't perfect. Half the problem is that Jamie would love to be your man in the office, love to have women gaze openmouthed at his chiseled features as they stand beside him at the photocopier, but because they don't, he just stares at their tits instead."

"All men look, Jess," I said generously, knowing she was magnanimously knocking her own life now in the hand of friendship. "You've just got to accept that. And you know jolly well he doesn't touch," I added staunchly.

Jess sighed, and I knew she was wondering what might have been. Bright as a button and armed with a First from Newcastle and a fistful of job offers, Jess had cruised seamlessly into a merchant bank. A few years later she'd been on the brink of partnership, seemingly with the world and a host of arrogant City men at her feet, when—oops! She was pregnant. Unfazed, she'd swiftly married the perpetrator—who, happily, she was in love with—and then smartly lined up a nanny, determined she'd be back at work nine months later in her size 10 Armani suit and her Miu Miu shoes. But then a bizarre thing happened. When the baby was born, Mother Nature roared in, too, and amidst many tears and much heart searching, Jess had been unable to do it. At the *moment critique*, on that fatal Monday morning, she'd clutched her baby to her breast, sacked the nanny, slammed the front door on the world, and, with tears streaming down her face and still in her cheesy dressing gown, gone back to bed with her son. It had shocked everyone, particularly Jamie, who was understandably alarmed at this sudden loss of her income. Nevertheless, he'd taken it on the chin and, somewhat bemused, gone off to work, only that much harder, and that much later, it seemed, now that he was the sole breadwinner and had a wife and child to support.

Jess, though, having lived the life, was unable to look at his long hours rationally and dispassionately. She was plagued with doubt as to her lovely twinkly-eyed journalist husband's whereabouts and the bizarre phone calls she claimed she was receiving.

"It was some horse of a girl last night," she seethed as we trudged on, "asking for Jamie's mobile number. Still got her bloody bridle on as far as I could tell, but spat the bit out to whinny, 'Air hellair, Jess, Spunky Bunky here. Arm, listen, Jamie's got a bit of a prob with a deadline and if I catch him, I might j-a-rst be able to help, OK?' I felt like saying the only 'prob' he'd have would be pulling the carving knife out of his shoulder blades when he finally walked through the front door at midnight."

"Journalists keep odd hours," I soothed, "and with the strangest people. You knew that when you married him."

"I suppose," she said listlessly. "It's just—well, it was a level playing field then. If he said, 'I'm off to Bognor for a conference next week,' I could trump it with, 'Well, I'm off to New York to do a deal.' Now all I do is put my hands on my hips and bellow, 'Oh, *are* you indeed!' Then when he comes back, I rifle through his pockets when he's asleep, looking for a hotel bill with 'breakfast in bed for two' stamped on it."

As we finally turned the corner into my parents' road, more or less dragging our heavy load now, she sighed. "All I'm saying, Luce, is don't forget this Charlie character has a wife, that's all."

I dropped the table with a bang, I hope on her foot. She swung round. "Could we please get this into perspective, Jess! I told you, he doesn't even know I exist, for crying out loud; that's how close I am to wrecking his marriage. Forget it, OK? God, I wish I'd never told you." I tore my hair briefly, hopelessly. "*Why* did I tell you?"

"Because," she said as we picked up the table and lobbed it expertly over the small wall and into my parents' tiny front garden, "until you tell your friends your dreams, they lack an important dimension."

"Oh yeah?"

"Yeah, if they're not out there, they're not real," she said, smiling wisely. "Surely you know that?"

I was about to protest, but she swiftly leaned forward and gave me a quick conciliatory peck on the cheek. "Bye, got to get back to the animals."

"You're not coming in?" I gestured to the front door.

"Better not, better get Jamie and Henry some lunch. Golly," she boggled, "wouldn't it be nice if they really *were* animals. In a pit, and I could just toss them a bun occasionally." She grinned. "Give my love to Maisie and Lucas and—listen, sorry if I banged on a bit."

"Forget it. You were just flexing your argumentative muscles because you don't get to use them at work anymore. Luckily I still sharpen my wits four mornings a week." I was rather pleased with this little sally. I hadn't expected it to sail out of my mouth quite so confidently.

She laughed and turned off down the street, giving me a brief backward wave. I waved back, then puffed on up the steps with the two sacks of loot, shoulder barging my way through the bright blue front door at the top.

My parents' house was a classic case of buying well. Amazingly well, as it turned out. Forty years ago, five years after he'd come over from Poland to study at Oxford, Lucas, my dad, had snapped up number 36 Burlington Villas—a rather crooked, skinny town house in a grotty area full of rolling dustbins and billowing litter—for pretty much next to nothing. Even then, it was more than he could afford on his choirmaster's salary, but needing a house for his wife and small children, he'd taken the plunge and got by renting out the top floor. Now, of course, the entire area had Up and Come, and in estate agent's parlance, number 36 was an "elegant terraced house in a much sought after area." Aside from painting the outside a joyful color every year—apple green at present—Maisie made little effort to keep up with the media whiz kids on one side and the dot.com millionaires on the other, with their shiny front doors and burgeoning window boxes, as the dazzling array of dandelions in her own front garden bore testament. But if she made no effort on the outside, she made even less within.

Shut your eyes and push was the only way to squeeze down the dark, narrow hall of death, as my brother called it, stacked floor to ceiling with Lucas's books and Maisie's accumulated antique clutter. Battling on through the darkness, arms outstretched, praying for safe arrival somewhere, anywhere, one eventually stumbled left into a sitting room. This was a narrow, overly long room, since the one concession Lucas and Maisie had made to modern living had been to turn two rooms into one and knock the partition wall down—together, in their dressing gowns, one Saturday morning after breakfast, amidst gales of laughter from us children. All it meant, in effect, was that yet more clutter could bowl joyously through, as ancient chandeliers, Georgian commodes, and Art Deco girls holding balls of light aloft jostled for space with three-legged Victorian balloon-back chairs, enamel pitchers, bundles of knives and forks, and ancient mixing bowls. Any conceivable floor or table space was taken up with these assorted curios, and only the top of the piano, it seemed, was sacrosanct. Here, in splendid isolation, lay a large ginger tomcat, whose one compromise was to share his instrument with another instrument, Maisie's precious violin.

A violinist by profession—and a damn good one, as Lucas would point out gruffly to anyone who cared to listen—my mother could, on occasion, still be persuaded to get the old fiddle down and play. Then, without much prompting, Lucas would happily reminisce . . . about dashing out of the school chapel where he'd taught as a young man, past rows of small boys in cassocks, up Birdcage Walk, arriving at St. Martin's in the Fields just in time to hear her play a lunchtime recital, marveling at her exquisite bowing action, her wonderful straight long legs.

Fifty years on and here she was, despite her arthritis, on all fours in the sitting room, amidst the clutter, with her youngest grandson on her back. A light flex had been slung around her neck for reins, and an old lampshade was on her head, since clearly, this neddy wore a hat. Her long legs were still good, with not a knot to be seen, but the bright copper hair was now a faded gold. The Celtic blue eyes that she turned on me now were a little misty but still huge, and still with the power to break portentous news. These were the eyes that, four years ago, without her having to utter a word, had informed me that my husband was dead. These days, her fatal equipment was more used to telling me that Woolworth's had closed down in the High Street or that the fish she'd bought for lunch was off, but the force was still with them.

Max, my younger son, squealed with delight as I came in now, and Maisie sat up on her haunches to let him slide off her back.

"You're back early, love—no luck? Not got any pennies for me then, my beawty," she wheedled, aping Fagin, hunching her shoulders and rubbing her hands together. "How was business?"

"Terrible," I groaned, chucking the velvet bag of money on the floor and collapsing into an armchair. I pulled Max with me, who grabbed my handbag and proceeded to disembowel it, searching for sweeties with all the thoroughness of the Drugs Squad.

"Here: Smarties." I delved in and handed them to him. I rubbed my eyes. "No, it was just a really, really bad day, Maisie. Probably the weather. But thanks for having them for me. I enjoyed it. Were they OK? Where's Ben?"

"Gone to the new Howard Hodgkin exhibition at the South Bank with Lucas," she said. "But Max didn't want to go, did you, love?"

"Too cold," he said, sucking a Smartie. "An' I seen a picture before," he informed me importantly.

" 'Course you have, my darling," I said, giving him a cuddle. "Seen one picture you've seen them all, haven't you?" I looked over his head at Maisie. "Howard Hodgkin, eh?" I grinned. I loved the way my dad, at seventy-odd, still had his finger on the artistic pulse and, not only that, took his eight-year-old grandson along to feel the beat with him as well.

"Cup of tea, darling? There's one in the pot." Maisie got to her feet and brushed herself down, smoothing the old blue painter's smock she wore on pretty much a daily basis and slipping on her beaded Bohemian mules.

I looked at her fondly. No prizes for guessing where I got my love of secondhand clothes, my crushed velvet waistcoats, my fringed scarves, and my embroidered peasant shirts. I wore them pretty much on a daily basis, too, although, in order not to look too much like a sixties reject, tended to team it all with black jeans and high suede boots.

"Please," I said gratefully, hauling myself to my feet and following her into the kitchen. I noticed, with a pang, that she trod slowly and tentatively, holding on to the banisters as she went and causing me to hang around behind in order not to rush her.

As we reached the kitchen, the back door flew open, and in came Ben, at a run, breathless and pink-cheeked. He was followed by his grandfather, tall, slightly bowed, and as usual sporting his rather dashing felt hat.

"Mum! Guess what? We went to the National because the other one was shut—and we saw loads of fat naked ladies! Didn't we, Lucas?"

"We did, my love, although sadly not in the flesh. No actual WI contingents peering at the pictures in the altogether, starkers but for handbags and spectacles." Lucas winked at me and dropped a National Gallery catalog onto the table as he sank into a chair with a sigh. "Ahh, cup of tea," he murmured, his Polish accent still faintly discernible. "Lovely."

"And some of them had huge, *huge* bottoms." Ben seized the catalog and riffled through to show me. "Really white and flabby, Mum, and bosoms as droopy as yours—look! And it was really fashionable then. Just think, you'd have been cool, Mum, in the old days."

"Excellent news, my love. Born just a couple of centuries too late then, eh?"

"Important the lad doesn't grow up just having skinny women as role models, don't you think?" Lucas murmured.

"No danger of that," I said darkly. "Ooh, thanks, Maisie." I smiled as she set a cup of tea in front of me. "I'll drink this and then we'll be out of your way."

"No rush, love, stay as long as you like. You're not in our way."

"I know, but still . . ."

I was all too aware of how exhausting small children could be, particularly as my parents were not young. Having had two children in quick succession in their twenties, brought them up, sent them out into the world, and then settled back, child-free to enjoy their forties, they must have been somewhat aghast when I'd appeared when Maisie was forty-five. If they were, I never knew it. It never showed. To me they were the most loving, laid-back parents, and the envy of all my friends as I was growing up. So relaxed were they, in fact, that when my brother, aged about ten, had referred to them by their Christian names as a joke, Maisie and Lucas hadn't even noticed. It had stuck, long before I was born.

Seventy-five-year-olds though, in my opinion, need to see their grandchildren for a few hours a week, in short, sharp blasts. Then, after we'd gone, and after a quiet lunch, Maisie might tune up her violin and Lucas would accompany her on the piano; in the evening, they'd leave it to the CD player to do the work, dozing in chairs and letting the Mozart wash over them. Together and in peace, which was entirely how it should be.

"Come on, you two." I crouched down and began bundling Max into a jumper. "Back to the flat. But only for a few more days and then my darlings, we're away!"

"Oh!" Maisie swung around and clapped a hand to her head. "That reminds me. Rose rang."

"Oh yes?" I looked up.

"Says she's expecting you on Thursday?"

"That's right."

"And then something about a nanny."

"A *nanny?*" I sat back on my heels and abandoned Max with one arm up his jumper. "What? What about a nanny?"

"Oh, just something about how she thought it would be much nicer if you took your evening meal up there with them, rather than sitting all alone in the barn," said Maisie vaguely. "Said she couldn't possibly have all the family sitting around at supper and not you, so she's organized a girl—a lovely girl, she said—to come and baby-sit the boys." She paused. Frowned over at her husband. "That was it, wasn't it, Lucas?"

Lucas slowly raised his brown eyes from the newspaper he'd picked up. They met mine. "Yes, love," he said softly, "that was it. That was about the size of it. Evening meals to be taken up at the house."

His gaze was steady, looking to hold mine, but I slid my eyes away, down toward my tea. I took a hasty gulp. It was colder than one would wish.

Chapter Two

NED DIED IN CHILDBIRTH. MINE, OF COURSE, NOT HIS. Not even Ned, who could turn his hand to most things, could stretch to popping out an offspring. No, it happened while I was giving birth to Max. While I was straining and sweating, swearing and cursing, pushing the child out and yelling at the medical team, because where *was* my wretched husband? Digging my nails hard into Maisie's hand, shrieking, "Just *get* him here someone, please! I don't want him to miss this! *He* doesn't want to miss this!" And all the while, being beaten up from the baby within. Riding the waves of pain with clenched teeth and eyes shut, every contraction a new agony, and *still* Ned wasn't there, so . . . where was he? Why was he missing this? How *could* he miss this?

And then suddenly—suddenly it didn't matter. Suddenly a computer beside me, the one that had been monitoring the baby's heartbeat throughout, started beeping urgently. The pen recording the printout slowed, did some crazy disconnected marks, and anxious heads scrummed down in alarm. I remember urgent mutterings about the baby being distressed, about the cord being around its neck, perhaps, and a no-nonsense hand thrusting up to sort things out.

Sheer panic, now, on the faces around me. It *was* around his neck. Had he lost precious oxygen? Should they rush me down to theater for a cesarean? No, too late, he was coming, the baby was coming, the head had crowned, and—oh God, just save my baby, my precious baby! And then that sheer white pain as the head emerged. That ghastly final push—and out he slipped, like a seal.

I leaned back weakly on the pillows, eyes wide with shock to the ceiling, the agony over. Someone scooped him up joyfully, whisking him up in the air and over my head. She paused to let me see.

"Look, dear, you've got a baby boy!"

I gazed up expectantly, a weak smile forming on my lips, awaiting

17

my precious moment, longing to hold him in my arms. I stared. My
mouth fell open in horror. I couldn't speak for a second, then—

"Christ!" I gasped. "He's black!"

My fuddled mind whirled, struggling to take it in. But—I hadn't, I
thought desperately, I hadn't! I'd remember a thing like that, I—

"No, dear," soothed the midwife quickly, "he's just blue. Very *dark*
blue in this case, but his color's coming back already, see? It's lack of air
to his lungs."

"Oh! Oh God, I thought—"

I gazed around, surrounded as I was by Jamaican nurses. Not a
white face amongst them. Four pairs of huge dark eyes regarded me over
their masks.

"Sorry," I gasped. "I didn't mean—but is he OK?"

"Fine," one chuckled, "just fine. A very bonny boy." She took off
her mask and handed him to me, a huge grin splitting her face.
"Thought you were gonna have to call him Winston, didn't you, honey?"

They all burst into cackles of laughter, slapping their thighs and
clutching one another. I grinned sheepishly, gazing down at my little
bundle, who was indeed getting pinker by the minute.

"Just going quietly crazy," I murmured. "As I think one does after
that sort of labor. After any sort of labor, come to that. And Maisie,
where's Maisie gone?" I glanced around, suddenly feeling very euphoric.
Needing to share it with someone. "Crikey, I'd like some sort of birthing
partner round here if you don't mind," I laughed.

"Over here, my love," came a quiet voice from the corner. I twisted
my head the other way. Maisie was indeed in the room, but behind me, in
the shadows, stuffing a hanky up her sleeve, blue eyes huge and horrified.

"No, no, he's fine, Maisie, absolutely fine," I reassured her, one
hand cradling the baby, the other reaching out to pull her in. "Don't
worry, he just lost a bit of air, but he's OK!"

She nodded, coming forward, taking my hand, fighting tears. "I'll
go and tell Lucas then," she muttered. "He's outside."

"Yes, yes—and Ned," I urged, as she made to go. "Maisie, did you
get hold of Ned? Try his mobile again or—"

And that's when I knew. As she turned back to face me. Knew
something truly horrendous had happened, when her eyes met mine.
Full of foreboding, full of fear.

She shook her head. "No, well, no, I haven't done that. But, yes. I'll—I'll try again."

As I let her fingers slip through my mine, a terrible fatalism rose up from my soul and stilled me. Something too horrific to contemplate had happened. Something she couldn't tell me about, not now, not with this newborn baby in my arms. Not within minutes of his birth.

I felt numb and terrified, had already started to tremble. Half an hour later, they wheeled me into a private room and whisked Max away to the nursery. I lay there, paralyzed with fear, thinking the unthinkable, so that when it happened I was almost, ridiculously, prepared.

Maisie and Lucas came in. They sat, side by side, on those gray plastic chairs, white and harrowed, and Lucas told me. In a steady, low voice, twisting his felt hat in his hands, ashen-faced, he told me how Ned had lost control, it seemed, rushing to get here. How he'd taken a shortcut from the editing suite where he worked and how, mobile phone in hand, he'd taken a bend too sharply, colliding with a lorry. No belt on, he'd gone straight through the windscreen and had died instantly.

I remember being unable to breathe for a moment and thinking, That's how Max must have felt with that cord round his throat. I felt— suffocated. Strange, almost inappropriate thoughts whirled around my head, too. It occurred to me, for instance, quite matter-of-factly, that whilst the son was taking his first breath, the father must have been taking his last.

Memory, kindly, becomes something of a blur after that, but I do remember the trembling turning to uncontrollable shakes and someone whisking a blanket around me, swaddling me like a small child. I remember, too, that Maisie kept a constant vigil, a constant grip on my hand, never letting go, and looking about ninety.

My abiding memory of that time, though, is that they wouldn't give me Max. Maybe they thought I wouldn't want him. That it would be too much for me. Or maybe the received psychobabble was that I'd reject him, take it out on him in some way. Eventually, though, I sat up in bed and screamed the place down. He was rushed back into my arms from down a long corridor.

Ben, four at the time, had to be told, and Lucas and Maisie did that. He came to see me. I have, in my memory bank, snapshots of that time, but absolutely no footage. I have a snap of Ben, for instance, lying on my hospital bed and of me cuddling him and Max. Then I have another of Lucas driving us back to the flat, me holding Max in the back, one arm around Ben, white-faced, silent. There's another, too, in the communal hall as we prepared to walk up four flights with the carry-cot, Maisie opening the flat door at the top and, beside her, my sister, Dee, over from Italy, where she lived, their faces taut with worry.

People say to me now, "Oh, it must have been so much worse for you with a new baby," but actually, that made me cope. That, combined with an overwhelming incredulity that numbed my mental processes, slowing them almost to a halt. In those early days I didn't recognize my life as my own. I felt detached from it; I had no thoughts, made no plans, I just existed in a bright inner glare, disoriented, as if in the aftermath of a huge explosion. I didn't have the luxury of going to pieces, either, because I had Max and Ben to look after, and I was aware, all the time, of Maisie and Lucas hovering, wondering if we'd be all right.

My parents were my lifeline at that time, and when we weren't in the flat we were over there, but friends were extraordinary, too. Grief has a way of sorting the men from the boys. Some steered clear "until she's ready"—and I haven't seen much of them since—whilst one or two, like Jess, got it spot on. Not overdoing it but nevertheless wading in when I needed her, getting drunk with me into the small hours, railing when I railed, crying when I cried.

I had grief counseling, too, on a Monday night, just like an upholstery class or something, when, armed with a loo roll, I'd sob and rant at a perfectly sweet middle-aged woman with a twitch. I even punched her walls on one occasion, which sent the twitch berserk. She didn't seem to mind, but she didn't seem to help, either, and it was after that occasion that one of my neighbors met me on the stairs and said, "Well, for God's sake, come and punch *our* walls instead!" So I did.

I had five neighbors in all: Teresa, Carlo, Theo, Ray, and Rozanna, and they were all, to a man or woman, spectacular. In fact, in those early days, when their walls took quite a battering, I'd swear I could look up on occasion and see Ned's face, beaming down from the heavens, swear I could hear his delighted voice saying, "See? Look who I found for you, Lucy! Look at the people I surrounded you with! We made the right decision, didn't we?"

"The decision," taken just before he died, had been where to live. At the time we were living in a basement flat in Fulham that was small, dark, and all we could afford, but light was beginning to filter through in the form of a promotion for me at Christie's and the promise of an art-house film for Ned to direct at his production company in Soho. Now whilst this wasn't necessarily going to get the money flowing, it wasn't going to be so cloyingly stagnant, either, and since we'd recently received a ludicrously high offer for the flat and there was another baby on the way, we decided to move.

Armed with sound advice and in the wake of all our friends, we dutifully trekked south of the river, to find "a bit of space." Putney, Clapham, and Wandsworth beckoned, along with rows of Victorian terraced houses in tree-lined streets. One of them, a four-bedroom semi in a quiet location, held our attention. It had a large en suite bathroom, a family bathroom, a knocked-through drawing room, a bright conservatory, and an airy kitchen billowing onto a huge garden. Ned and I stood, I remember, on the back step, gazing down and admiring that garden. The lawn was bordered by neat flower beds, the wooden shed stood sentry at the bottom, and a vast climbing frame loomed importantly in the middle.

"It really is one of the nicest roads around here," our vendor confided, sotto voce, as she stood beside us on the step. "And full of *such* lovely people."

"Really?" I smiled across at her. She was a few years older than me, blond and pretty, with neat Boden clothes, a light tan, and expensive highlights.

"Oh yes, totally like-minded." She flicked back her hair. "I mean, next door for instance, he's with Morgan Stanley and she's a solicitor, and then on the other side, he *was* at Goldman's—gardening leave at the moment—and she's in advertising. Then opposite—well, four children poor thing, so complete nightmare, doesn't work, but he's a barrister. Tax, I think, or shipping. Anyway, the point is, you won't be short of friends."

"No. No, I can see that," said Ned thoughtfully, his thin, intelligent face taking it all in, his eyes narrowed down the garden. "And there? At the back?" He nodded to a house that vaguely overlooked.

"The Waters. Both doctors," she purred happily.

"Right. And everyone," he glanced up and down, over the fences, "has the same climbing frame?"

"I know; isn't it uncanny?" She laughed. "We call ourselves the Tommy Tonka set. *We* got one, then the Waters, then the Pickthorns, and the great thing is, you know precisely when it's drinks time, because we all raise the slides like drawbridges to stop them getting soaked with dew, and then it's children to bed, a glass of Sancerre with a neighbor, and a *lovely* moan about our husbands or the au pair! Usually the au pair. We could leave it with you if you like; we need a new one."

Ned blinked. "The au pair?"

"No! The climbing frame."

"Ah, right. Yes."

He met my eye, which wasn't hard, because we were both much the same height. Both five-foot-eightish. Ned, spry and wiry, with soft fair hair, and me, constantly fighting a fuller figure, and in those days a light mouse, because Ned liked me natural.

He turned back to her, his face creasing up as it did for even the most social of smiles. "Well, thank you so much, Mrs. Foster. We'll be in touch if we may." Studiously polite, as ever.

Once outside, on the quiet pavement at the front, he gazed around at the rows of tastefully draped windows, at the terracotta pots on the doorsteps, the NEIGHBORHOOD WATCH signs in every door. He sighed, thrust his hands deep in his pockets.

"I suppose we'd better take the plunge."

I scuffed my toe. Nodded. "Yep. You're right: we should."

"I mean," he struggled, "it's easy to mock, to call it suburban and wonder why we should choose to live in a buzzing cosmopolitan city if it comes down to—you know, all professionals in a row, brolly and *Telegraph* under the arm . . . easy to say where's the color, the variety, and why the hell are we living in London if we're missing out on all of that, but—" He broke off, considered. "Well, for Ben, and the baby? Cricket stumps in the garden? Bikes, tents, all of that? Bit of conforming for a change? What d'you think?"

I glanced up. Smiled. "I agree. Time to grow up."

I didn't know then that there was no such thing, and we went home to Fulham, *ad idem*. The next morning he rang me at work.

"Meet me on your lunch hour," he said excitedly. "I've found something."

"What sort of thing?"

"A flat?"

"A flat! But I thought—"

"Twenty-four Royal Avenue, SW3. Twelve-thirty. Just be there, Luce."

And I was. Running hotfoot from work, which, from South Ken, wasn't far, down to the Fulham Road, across to the bustling King's Road, and then left, toward the Royal Hospital and the river. My pace slowed as I approached, and I checked my A to Z in surprise. I seemed to be walking into the most perfect London square imaginable. It was broad and long and lined with tall white wedding-cake houses, all with black and white checkered steps and all with glossy black front doors and brass knockers that glinted in the sunlight. I stopped and caught my breath. The square itself had an almost Parisian feel to it, with gravel instead of grass, so I felt that at any minute now a few old men in berets might materialize and play *boules*. Instead, some Chelsea pensioners shuffled helpfully into frame, complete with medals and sticks, and sat on a bench in the spring sunshine. I swallowed excitedly. At one end, crowds of people thronged, but the glittering shops of the King's Road held them in thrall, and they never peeled off past the flower seller who marked the corner. At the other end, the Hospital Gardens formed a warm, tranquil pool of green.

A cab drew up and Ned jumped out, bright-eyed.

"You're mad," I called as he flashed me a grin, simultaneously shoving fivers at the driver. "What is it, anyway. A shoe box?"

"Practically," he said cheerfully, "and more than we can afford, but look at the location." He swung his arm around demonstratively.

"I'm looking, but, Ned—"

"Come on; I'll show you!"

Keys in hand he dragged me protesting up the grand stone steps and into the communal hall. The door closed softly behind us. On we went, up the wide stairs, up and up, actually, until we eventually arrived, panting, at the fourth floor.

"With small children?" I gasped. "Prams? Bikes?"

"Good exercise." He grinned. "I'd leave the pram at the bottom."

"Oh, would you. And the oxygen cylinders?"

"Don't be wet," he scoffed, and put the key in the door. He led me into a tiny white hallway, which in turn led into a corridor.

"Down here," he insisted, leading the way, and since two abreast would be tricky, I followed. He turned left into a bedroom.

I looked around. Shrugged. "Not a bad size, I'll give you that, and—ooh, look at that view."

"Uh-uh, not yet. I'm saving that. In here first." He ushered me out, across the passage, and into another bare room.

"Boys' bedroom," he breezed. "Bunks here, in the corner."

"Boys?" I said, hand on the small bump of my stomach. "How d'you know?"

"Trust me; I'm a budding film director." He grinned. "And then back here." He disappeared. "Well, a bit of a kitchen."

" 'A bit' is right. So . . ." I swung back. "You mean we've finished with the bedrooms? Just the two?"

"That's it, cuts down on the housework. But the kitchen, Luce, look. *Very* neat and tidy and, um, clean . . ."

"Oh, bog off, Ned. Is that all you can say?"

"And the French range, terrific! Very fancy, very *à la mode*, and cupboards galore!" He swung one open. Shut his eyes and swooned. "Mmmm . . . *lovely* hinge action, and—no, *not* the window, Luce, not yet." He put a hand over my eyes and hustled me away, to face a pair of double doors. "Terribly Jane Austen, don't you think?" He grinned, reaching down for both handles and opening them with a flourish. "Ta-dah!"

I gasped. Because I had to admit, this room was a joy. Large, lofty, empty—which helped, of course—and with acres of pale wooden floor. Tall sash windows marched all the way down one side, except in the middle, where the windows went right to the floor and issued onto a balcony. Someone had artfully left them wide open, so that the wisps of ivory muslin that passed as curtains blew in the breeze. And then, of course, there was the view. I walked across as if pulled by a string and stepped out onto the balcony, gazing over the rooftops. A fair old chunk of London town looked back at me, with the King's Road to the right and to the left the river and the hospital gardens.

"Perhaps they could ride their bikes in there," I mused. "If it's allowed."

"Of course they could. And in the square—which we have a key to. And Luce, there's a bathroom—"

"I should jolly well hope so, Ned," I said, following him back in. "I'm not peeing in the river." I peered inside. "Tiny," I sighed, "and no shower. And still only two bedrooms." I bit my lip. "If only there was just one more."

"We only need two bedrooms, Lucy, and look, come and see this."

"More?" I followed hopefully.

"No, but . . ." He held my arm and led me out of the front door. Still holding on, he bundled me across the hallway and banged on the green front door opposite.

"Ned!" I drew back in horror. "What the hell are you doing?"

The door opened almost immediately, and a pretty, Continental-looking girl stuck her head around.

"Aha!" She swung the door open wide. "You back. You say you be back and you are." She put her hands on her hips and beamed delightedly at my husband.

"Of course." Ned grinned. "I always keep my promises."

I shot him an incredulous look as she reached out and pulled us across her threshold, simultaneously calling over her shoulder, "Carlo! *Non indovinerai mai, è ritornata!*"

"Making promises to pretty girls whilst the mother of your unborn child toils?" I muttered in Ned's ear.

"And you bring your lovely wife, too." She beamed back at me. "And pregnant! Lucky you."

I smiled back. Impossible not to like her.

"Lucy, this is Teresa," Ned introduced us, "who has a shop in the King's Road which sells . . .?"

"Oh, you know." She waved her hands about airily. "Lovely beady scarves and belts and silky bits and bobs which I buy for nothing back home in Italy and sell for fortunes over here!" she said cheerfully. "And thees," she swung her arm back, "is my husband, Carlo, who don't have a shop, but who try to tell me what to do with mine!"

A small, swarthy man got up from a table at the far end of the living room where he'd been playing backgammon with two older men. He gave a small bow, then grinned.

"You theenk she letta me tell her what to do? Huh? 'Ello, Lucy."

"And thees," Teresa went on, "is our good friends Theo and Ray, who live on first-floor level in much tidier flat—smarter, too—and who are so much delighted to meet you!"

They got to their feet politely, a pair of immaculate well-preserved elderly gentlemen, with pressed jeans, pastel Polo shirts, and cashmere jumpers slung artfully around their shoulders. Little leather pouches dangled from their wrists as they simultaneously swept back their gleaming silver hair. Clearly an item. They stepped forward together and shook hands.

"We gather you're moving in. How absolutely marvelous," boomed Ray in a theatrical John Gielgud voice.

"Well, I—"

"And so much more marvelous because you have a Ben and I have a Pedro!" broke in Teresa. "Four years old together, see?" She lunged for a photograph on a crowded sideboard. A little dark-haired boy with a snub nose and mischievous eyes smiled back at me. "So they be matey, yes?"

I smiled. "Well, that would be lovely. Obviously, though, Ned and I will have to discuss—"

"Of course! So many things."

I glanced at Ned, who was looking inordinately pleased with himself. He wasn't meeting my eye but finding a great deal of charm in the carpet.

"And soon," went on Teresa, "you meet Rozanna, our other good friend. She come up for a sharpener most days, but she not here today." She frowned. "I don't know why. She live down on first floor and—"

"What d'you mean, she's not here today?" purred a silky voice behind us. "She's very much here, and quite ready for her sharpener, thank you. My usual please, Carlo, there's a love. Sorry I'm late, darlings," she breathed as she whisked by, "but I got waylaid by a ghastly prospective client. He wanted to relive his toddlerhood, but I told him my days of dressing up as Little Miss Muffet were over, and he could take his eyes off my tuffet. He took a bit of persuading, but I lost him eventually. Hello my dears," she drawled, turning deep blue eyes on us.

"Teresa told me you were moving in, and I couldn't be more pleased. Heterosexual *and* English. Such a rarity round here, surrounded as I am by foreigners and poofters." She rolled her eyes as her friends laughed. "And a baby!" She beamed, looking down at my stomach. "What heaven."

I blinked at this very beautiful girl, blond, tanned, and swathed from head to toe in silk and suede. She swept her pashmina dramatically around her shoulders and rolled her eyes again. "God, I love babies; when's it due?"

"In May."

"Lovely. A spring baby, so we can all take turns to push it round the square, show it the daffodils. Stopping for a game of backgammon, my dears?"

"No, no, we really must be going," we said, and finally, *finally*, with many good-byes, thank-yous, promises to return and—oh yes, *definitely* to stop for a drink next time—we made our exit.

We clattered downstairs.

"Bastard," I muttered.

"What?" Ned laughed.

"You stitched me up."

"Not at all! I simply wanted you to see some local color. And you must admit, it's a bit more vibrant than Cranborough Road, Clapham."

More vibrant, yes, and more eclectic, definitely, but it was the warmth that really knocked me out. I'm quite sure the stockbrokers south of the river would have been equally kind, but all I know is that when the shit hit the fan six months later and there I was, in Royal Avenue, with a newborn baby and no husband, these people weren't just kind; they were my family. Which is why I wondered if Ned was watching.

In those dark early days after Ned's death, I'd take to my sofa in that lofty airy room for hours at a time, a tiny baby asleep on my tummy, a sea of screwed-up tissues around me. And left to my own devices, that's where I'd have stayed. All day. Until Ben came back from school. Except that I found I couldn't. Because inevitably around mid-morning there'd be a soft tap at the door, and it would be Teresa, wondering if I'd like to see her new collection of scarves, or Theo, saying no pressure, but they needed a fourth for whist. They were kind, never pushy, but also immediate. I didn't have to make arrangements or promise to be somewhere later; I'd just force a smile, heave myself off my sofa, and totter downstairs. Then an hour or so later, I'd totter back up. It was enough.

No one was ever asked to Rozanna's flat, and of that I was glad. Ben and Pedro, who'd become inseparable, once knocked on her door, giggling, but she'd shoed them away, carefully shielding the cabinet minister in his dressing gown from view. "Not in here, my darlings," she'd said gently, turning them around. "Not in Rozanna's little *salle d'amour*."

True to her word, though, she regularly took the baby to the park.

"Of course he's mine," she'd snap to anyone silly enough to ask. "Just look at those eyes, for heaven's sake!"

When she returned him, I'd rise drowsily and sometimes woozily from my sofa, and she'd linger, concerned, making endless cups of tea, chattering gaily, waiting until she was sure I could take over the reins again.

Later, when I felt stronger, Teresa and I would walk the boys to school and I'd go on to the shop with her, with Max in a sling around my neck. I'd stay for an hour or so, perched on a stool, helping her pop scarves in bags, hang cardigans back on hangers. I'd watch the customers come and go and then totter back to the flat again, feeling I'd had a sliver of life.

And so there I was, at my most vulnerable, surrounded by the most fiercely protective: my parents and Jess on one side of London and my new friends in Chelsea on the other. All of them were magnificent, and all of them did their damnedest to assuage my grief. And then, of course, there was Ned's family, the Felloweses, who, as far as I could tell, did their damnedest to augment it.

I DIDN'T MEET NED'S FAMILY UNTIL THE SUMMER OF 1993, just before Ned and I were married and a whole year after we'd begun going out together, as students, at Oxford. Too long, I'd decided, one bright April morning as we'd cycled to lectures together. Crikey, I reasoned, he'd met Maisie and Lucas loads of times, been to stay with Dee in Florence—my brother in India was somewhat harder—and by now was practically part of the family. So how come I'd never set eyes on any of his lot? What was the problem, for heaven's sake? Was he ashamed of them? Or of me?

"Of them," he'd assured me firmly as I wedged his front tire in the bicycle stand, refusing to let him go to his lecture until he'd told me.

"They're not like me, Lucy, and they're not like you. Or Maisie and Lucas. They're not normal."

I laughed. "Why—how so? Hairs on palms of hands? Eyes in the middle of foreheads? I'm up for any of that. In what way not normal, Ned?"

He smiled wryly. "Trust me. You're going to get a terrible shock."

"Oh yeah?" I said defiantly. "Try me. In fact, try me this weekend. Let's go and see them, Ned. I'll put on a frock and buy some flowers for your mum, and you can take your washing home like any normal student. Come on; I want to rattle all the skeletons in your cupboard!"

"Big mistake," he said, shaking his head ruefully. "Really, big mistake." But I was insistent, so we went.

Two days later I emerged, wide-eyed and reeling. Hairy palms would have been lovely. Cyclopes perfect. Instead, it transpired that, far from dating a bog-standard member of the proletariat, as I'd rather assumed, I was actually dating Prince Charles. Ned's father was Lord Fellowes, ennobled for services rendered during the Thatcher government, and his mother, naturally, Lady Fellowes but actually Lady Rose, too, since, as the daughter of an earl, she had a serious gong in her own right. So far so scary. Second, home, if you could call it that—and clearly Ned didn't—was Netherby Hall, a majestic Georgian mansion, surrounded by two thousand acres of prime Oxfordshire farmland, which included in its portfolio two farms, six cottages, three lodges, and, as Jess had so rightly pointed out, half the flaming village, thank you very much. And there they all lived. The entire Fellowes clan—with the exception of Ned—under one roof. A sort of ménage I'd previously only encountered in a popular eighties TV drama based on an oil baron's family.

Ned's father, Archie—Eton, Oxford, Grenadier Guards—was pop-eyed but amiable and quiescent. Lady Rose, by contrast, was gimlet-eyed, had a smile that could freeze the marrow in your bones and a tone of voice similar to that employed by our first lady prime minister. She certainly scared the pants off me. Hector, the elder brother and therefore crown prince and heir apparent, was flaxen-haired, pink-faced, and easily embarrassed, whilst his sister Lavinia was formidable, forthright, and liked a drop. Pinkie, the indulged younger sister, was flighty, oversexed, and probably not a lifer in that house like her siblings, although, unlike Ned, more on course for Tramps than Oxford. Finally, there were two maiden aunts who shuffled on- and offstage periodically, neither of whom was the full shilling. Phew.

"I see," I'd said faintly to Ned after a long silence in the car on the way home.

He grinned across. "Still fancy me?"

"Ask me again in the morning," I said as I leaned my weary head back, shut my startled eyes.

He did, and actually, he asked me to marry him, too, to which I happily agreed, and then he accused me of gold digging because I'd seen his house.

"It's that family crest that's got you all excited, isn't it, you little hussy," he hissed as we rolled around giggling on his futon in his Oxford bed-sit. "You can't wait to get your hands on my motto."

"That's it," I squeaked. "I want coronets on my matchboxes and monograms on my napkins. And it's not just your ancient lineage I'm after, either. You'd better get the family vaults prised open pronto. I want a socking great rock for my finger, too!"

Instead, he decorated it with a dear little garnet that we found together in Bermondsey Market the following weekend. I can still remember smiling uncontrollably at it, twisting it round on my finger, and admiring it from every angle, as we headed off on a bus across London to see Maisie and Lucas, to make plans.

The wedding, we decided, would be soon, in the summer, at my parents' local church in London. We'd follow it up with a quiet lunchtime reception in their back garden. A few mutual friends from Oxford would be there, Jess, of course, all my family, naturally, but apparently, and rather unnaturally, none of Ned's.

"Ned, this is crazy!" I said, banging my fist on my parents' kitchen table, Maisie and Lucas having tactfully withdrawn. "For Christ's sake, write to them. Ask them to come. They can always say no."

"But that's just it: they *will* say no. To this, anyway. What—a low-key do in a local church and then back here to your parents' house for lunch? It's hardly the Guards Chapel and a reception at the House of Lords, and that, my dear Luce, is what they'll want. Either that or something equally grand with a sodding great tent in the grounds at Netherby, and I don't want that, either. I'm just not up for it, Lucy; it's not my style."

It wasn't mine, either, but I couldn't help feeling we were sneaking around, which I wasn't comfortable with, either. I bit my lip for a couple of days, then steeled myself and wrote to them; guiltily and fearfully, one Saturday morning when Ned was at a seminar. I told them where and when it was happening, invited them, if they'd like to come, and popped the letter in the post. It sparked our first row. I can see him now, as I told him what I'd done, standing over me as I sat on the edge of his bed, white-faced and with a terrible clenched calmness.

"Don't ever interfere with my family again," he seethed. "You know nothing, Lucy, nothing. If I say I don't want to tell them about my bloody wedding, then I don't want to bloody tell them! They've had a damn good crack at messing up most of my life, but they're not going to balls up this bit, OK?"

He was trembling with emotion. I'd never seen him so angry. Never seen him angry at all, actually.

"OK, OK," I whispered. "I'm sorry."

Nonetheless, far from forbidding me to marry her son and drawing up affidavits to keep me out of the family coffers, Rose wrote back immediately, clearly touched:

> . . . *You were so sweet to let us know. Of course it was a shock, but you know, I always had an idea that Ned would get married like this. Quietly, privately, and to a clever, bright girl like you. Thank you so much for writing to us, my dear.* . . .

I showed it to Ned, waving it triumphantly in his face as he woke up that morning.

"You see? Perfectly sweet. Couldn't be nicer. And she approves of me, too."

"Oh, I knew that wouldn't be a problem," he muttered sleepily, not deigning to raise his head from the pillow.

"Oh, why so? Lucas and Maisie are hardly landed gentry."

"No," he opened one eye, "but they're intellectuals, and here in Oxford, where my parents live, that counts. Hundreds of years of respectable ancestry is all very well, Luce, but when your pile is on the doorstep of a famous seat of learning, it ups the ante. Adding a little gray matter to the breeding mix helps. It lends *gravitas*."

"But . . ." I puzzled.

"Forget it, Luce," he sighed. "It's complicated. But genius, being unbridled, is very upper-class. And take it from me: my mother's as upwardly mobile as the next person." He turned over and shut his eyes. "Can't help noticing they're still not coming, though," he murmured.

I blinked and read the letter again. Oh. No. Clearly not.

And so the wedding went ahead, quietly and simply as planned, and with lunch afterward in my parents' back garden. Trestle tables overflowed with food, flowers brimmed from urns and vases, friends crammed into the tiny garden, shrieking with laughter, and aside from a lovely cousin of Ned's called Jack, we didn't trouble the Felloweses. In fact, we didn't trouble the Felloweses again for—ooh, the next couple of years.

Periodically, though, as time went by, I felt guilty. Particularly when Ben was born. With another rare show of courage, I insisted we go and see them, just occasionally, to show them their grandson. These forays were never a great success. Ned was mute and stony-faced as we ate lunch in the huge paneled dining room at Netherby, with its pendulous chandelier, sea of glassy mahogany, and array of dazzling silver, and I was always terrified that Ben, in his high chair beside me, would misbehave. Archie sat at one end and Rose at the other, but quite often there'd be scores of other friends and family, too, because Rose, it seemed, being terribly social, couldn't sit down without at least twenty people around her. Or maybe she felt, as Ned constantly consulted his watch, itching to go, that it diluted a potentially tricky situation. Either way, we'd finally drive home exhausted, with Ned gripping the wheel, his knuckles white, vowing, "Never, *never*, again."

Ironically, after that particularly torrid occasion, we never did go again, because six months later he was dead. And whereas before they'd always kept us at arm's length, suddenly I couldn't move for Felloweses.

Rose was beside herself, naturally—her son, her beloved boy—and wept so loudly at the funeral, she had to be restrained by Archie at the grave. I couldn't help wondering why she hadn't shown more emotion when Ned was alive. She then went into overdrive and a few weeks later arranged the most extravagant memorial service in the Guards Chapel, which Ned would have loathed. Numb with grief and not caring anyway, I went along with it, sitting quietly in the front with Ben, hoping it would soon be over.

"It's only right," Maisie had assured me, squeezing my arm as we'd left, crossing the forecourt at Wellington Barracks. "They're an important family, Lucy; these things matter in their circles."

I'd nodded dumbly. Ned wasn't just my husband; he was their son, and I had to remember that. Had to remember not to hog the grief. To be considerate. To include them.

I did include them, but then suddenly Rose wouldn't leave me alone. She was on the phone constantly, day and night—mostly night— and always at my worst time: when the children were in bed and I allowed myself the luxury of breaking down. The telephone would ring, and I'd hear her voice, quavering, breaking slightly: "Hello, Lucy?" Then: How was I coping? How was I finding the strength to carry on? Didn't I miss him dreadfully? She knew she did. How on earth did I get through the days?

Finally, I realized she was doing me no good. I was trying my damnedest to be strong, and three times a week, regular as clockwork, she was breaking down my defenses. I went to see her, taking Jess with me for moral support, hoping a personal appearance might do the trick, but still the phone calls continued. After a while, gradually, guiltily, I let things slide. I left the answer machine on and I rarely returned her calls. Cruel? Perhaps, but I knew it was for the best.

At first she persisted, baffled by my silence, but then she, too, went quiet. I heard nothing for months, by which time it was stalemate. I was too nervous to ring out of the blue, and she, I think, was too proud. I kept meaning to write, but I never did. Christmas cards were exchanged, presents arrived in the post on the boys' birthdays, but no contact. No words exchanged. Four years went by, in fact. Until I got her letter:

My dear Lucy,

Forgive me for writing to you after such a long silence, but this letter has been written and rewritten many times. So much to explain, and so hard to know where to begin. Firstly, my un-shackled behavior at the time of Ned's death must have un-nerved you, and I feel I should go some way to explaining what must have seemed like a disproportionate outpouring of grief. Grief is discouraged in this family; Archie dismisses it as a weak-ness and the children bottle it up, but I was incapable of doing either. You see, my dear, despite all the differences Ned and I had in later life, when he died, I felt as if I'd died with him.

Does that shock you, Lucy? Of course it does, but then how little you know. And I don't say that in a patronizing way, because why on earth should you? After all, Ned and I never seemed close when he was alive, and yet did you know, for instance, that when he was a child he and I were insepara-ble? Did you know that he was laughingly known as "Rose's shadow," always trotting around the garden after me, trowel in hand, hating me to be out of his sight? You wouldn't think so, would you? You wouldn't think that, up until he was fifteen, he and I would fish for salmon most weekends, walk the dogs to-gether, read the same books, discuss them, enjoy each other's company.

One should never admit to having them, of course, but he was my favorite. My only cerebral yet lighthearted child, my darling boy. Perhaps that goes some way to explaining why, when he had a classic teenage rebellion at fifteen, it came as such a terrible shock to me. He wore such strange clothes, be-came obsessed with music and the film world, smoked and drank—all natural progressions, of course—yet instead of ac-cepting them as such, I felt as if I'd been slapped in the face, and told him so, too.

We rowed horrendously, as only people who love each other can, and some terrible things were said, mostly by me. The memory makes me go hot with shame. I behaved like a spoilt child whose best friend has chosen to play with someone else. I broke down and smothered him with ghastly maternal tears, for which I'm sure he never forgave me. I wanted my little boy back, and he was rightly repulsed.

Lucy, what strange ways we have of showing our love, especially mothers to their children. I know you felt uncomfortable about coming to see us here, but perhaps you now understand the depths of emotion only shimmering on the surface, and how hard it was for both Ned and me.

Still, the years have gone by, four, now, of course, and I'd like to make it up to Ned's memory. Like to go some way to making it right, for you and the boys. I gather from Maisie that things are hard in London, that money is tight, so here it is: would you do me the honor of letting me help? Archie and I would love you to have Chandlers Barn—you know, the pretty old timbered one at the top of the meadow where the Jacob sheep are. It's been beautifully converted and would make a wonderful home for you and the boys, with a pretty garden and the lake at the bottom. We *are* close by, of course, but not entirely on your doorstep, and your privacy would be respected and paramount. The barn would be made over in your name, and we'd also like to pay for the boys' education, until they're eighteen, at schools of your choice. Do let us know if you feel you could accept our offer; we would so love to have you amongst us. At any rate, and whatever your decision, please count on my love and support, at whatever distance.

With best love,

Rose.

I showed it to Maisie. "Lovely," she said finally. She took off her glasses and looked surprised. "Really lovely. She's come clean at last. I always thought there was a heart lurking in there somewhere. What are you going to do, love?"

"I don't know," I said quietly, taking the letter back as she handed it to me. I narrowed my eyes thoughtfully. "I really . . . don't know."

But I think I did, even then. I think I'd made up my mind the moment I'd read it. Ben was unsettled at school, Max was riding his bicycle around our minuscule flat and driving me insane, and Netherby was only a couple of miles away from Hexham. Hexham? Where the hell was that? And what the hell difference should that make to anything, anyway?

Oh. Well. Hexham was the village where Charlie lived. And I had to do something about Charlie. I tucked the letter back into the pocket of my jeans, gazed reflectively over my mother's shoulder and out of the window behind her. Yes, I had to do something about Charlie. It was just getting ridiculous.

Chapter Three

I FIRST MET—NO, SAW—CHARLIE ABOUT SIX MONTHS AGO. He was standing on the end of my road talking to Ricky, the flower seller, who marks the corner. Not buying, just chatting, passing the time of day, newspaper under one arm, dark head thrown back, laughing loudly. He had an athlete's physique, tall, broad, and powerful-looking, and I just remember thinking, What an attractive man. That's all, just, What an attractive man. When I came out of the newsagent's, my own paper tucked under my arm, he was still there. He caught my eye, smiled, and I smiled back. He said something, too. I couldn't quite catch it, but I think the gist of it was that Ricky would keep you talking all day if you weren't careful! I laughed, and he held my eye. Briefly, but long enough for me to know that he'd noticed and wasn't disappointed.

I'd gone home slowly, thoughtfully, gripping my paper tightly under my arm, but when I reached my door I ran straight up our four flights of stairs, taking them two at a time without pausing. I went quickly down the passage to my bedroom, shut the door, and sat down at my dressing table, my heart pounding. I stared at my reflection, curious. Fascinated, even. My cheeks were pink, but no pinker than they'd be under normal circumstances if I'd just run up four flights, and my eyes sparkled a bit, but there was something else, too. Something stirring within me that was making me glow, entering me somewhere around my toes and sweeping through me in a great wave, and which I recognized as pure sexual attraction. Something I hadn't experienced since Ned, hadn't felt for four years.

And not for want of trying, either. Oh no, I knew the rules, knew what was expected of me after all this time. "Can't mope forever, Lucy, life goes on," et cetera—and so I'd played the game. I'd been out with one or two guys, mostly at Jess's instigation and mostly friends of Jamie's. Nice guys, too. Journalists, mostly. I'd been to the theater a couple of times, been out for dinner, and once I'd even asked a guy in for coffee and gone for a full-blown snog on the sofa. We'd almost got to the bedroom door when—

"God, I'm so sorry; it's me, I know. So awful, but I just can't seem to . . ."

"No, no, don't worry. It's fine. I'll go."

And he had. Whoever he was. Shutting the door quietly behind him. Nothing, you see. Not a spark, not a flicker of interest, either lustful or romantic, and yet, just now, after the briefest of exchanges on a pavement with a man I'd never seen before . . . something.

I picked up my brush and swept back my hair—hair Ned wouldn't recognize now with its honey blond highlights—hooking it back behind my ears in firm, swift strokes. I lifted my chin and gave a sudden smile, challenging my reflection. Well, whaddya know, Lucy. Progress. Definitely progress. Perhaps there's hope for you yet?

After that, I kept an eye out for him. Only on a terribly casual basis, you understand. I certainly wasn't tailing him or anything creepy, but I was alert. I checked on the corner shop, for instance, walked slowly past Ricky with his flowers, peered into the Italian deli—any sign? No. But then a few days later—bingo. As I walked into Mr. Khan's Seven-till-Eleven, there he was, wire basket in hand. In the basket, a solitary pack of Brillo pads suggested domestic ritual but did nothing to diminish his shine, particularly since his legs were on display, too. It was summer, so he was wearing khaki shorts, and a blue sailing sweatshirt, bleached and worn. His black hair was a little damp around the edges, particularly at the back of his neck, indicating a recent shower. I could hardly breathe, I was so excited. Ridiculous! Joyfully I snatched a basket and, head down, scurried over to the chilled cabinet where he was browsing, reaching for a pint of milk.

"Ooops, sorry!" I said as our hands clashed over the semiskimmed. I flashed up a smile.

"Here," he laughed, handing me a carton. "You're obviously in dire need."

"Thanks." I flashed some more.

"Thirsty work, this weather, isn't it?" He grinned.

"It certainly is."

And that was it. Two seconds later he'd paid and left the shop, and I was still standing there, with one pint of milk in my basket.

Must follow, must follow, I thought desperately, scurrying to the till. But Mr. Khan was on the telephone. I tapped the counter impatiently, willing him to hurry, but he was talking fast and furiously in Hindi, and I had to watch, helplessly, as my man strode past the plate-glass window, drinking his milk straight from the carton, disappearing into the crowd.

By the time I'd emerged, he'd gone. Hopeless, Lucy, hopeless. Oh, and riveting repartee by the way. "Thanks," and, "It certainly is." Really memorable. He'll ponder that for hours.

The next time, I was slightly more prepared. I had Max with me, which wasn't necessarily a godsend, when I saw him nip into Mr. Khan's again.

"Come on!" I seized Max's hand in the street and started to run. "Sweeties, Max, we need sweeties, don't we?" I hissed in his ear. "Come *on!*"

Max looked startled but rose magnificently to the occasion, and we were in that shop in seconds. I grabbed a magazine from the rack and nipped in behind my man in the queue, almost elbowing an old lady out of the way in my excitement. Well, all right, *actually* elbowing an old lady out of the way.

Sanjay, Mr. Khan's son, was serving behind the counter, one eye on the television.

"Orright, Charlie?" He chewed gum laconically.

Charlie! Now I knew. I gazed rapturously at Charlie's back. It seemed to me to be entirely composed of erogenous zones. My heart was beating in my fingertips. Sanjay's gum rotated rhythmically round his mouth as I listened intently.

"Not bad, Sanjay, and you?"

"Yeah, orright. Thrashing you in the test. A hundred and three for four."

"Early days, my friend, early days."

"Dream on; you're playin' wiv schoolboys! Couldn't bat their way out of a paper bag. There you go." He handed him some change. "Yeah?" This to me, because of course Charlie had been served and was walking away from the counter reading his paper, whilst I gazed, slack-jawed, after him. I snapped to.

"Oh! Oh yes. Come on, Max, hurry. What d'you want, fruit gums?"

God, he was going. He was going! I shoved some sweets into Max's hand, but he screeched and threw them back again, determined to choose for himself. The door was opening. Quickly I swung around. Smiled, as if surprised.

"Oh, hi there!"

Almost out of the shop, he glanced around. Blinked. Clearly didn't recognize me, then either did or pretended he did.

"Oh, hi."

Sanjay cleared his throat. "Just the fruit gums and *Caravanning Weekly* then, love?"

I glanced down at the magazine, horrified. Charlie looked, too, then up at me in surprise.

"Oh! Oh no, I thought it was . . ." I dropped it hurriedly. Sanjay was grinning widely, and when I glanced around, Charlie had gone.

I flushed to my roots. Stupid. So *stupid*. And so adolescent, Lucy. God, what was I *doing*, picking up strange men in corner shops? And with my four-year-old son in tow, too! I rooted miserably in my purse for some change.

"He not with it today." Mrs. Khan smiled kindly at me, elegant in her sari as she slid off her stool in the shadows. She came forward to take over from her uncouth son, who sidled closer to the television, picking his nose.

"Sorry?"

"Charlie. He lost in his work. He not recognize anyone when he like that."

"Oh!" I stared. "No, that's right. He does get very involved, doesn't he. Um, does he say how it's going?"

"Oh, he nearly finish, he say. But then, you know, he also say when is it ever finished." She laughed. "Always he say he can play with it, you know?"

I gulped. "Yes. Yes, of course he can."

"OK?"

"Hmmm? Oh." I startled. "Yes, OK. Just the sweets."

And that was that. I walked slowly back to the flat, wondering what on earth it was Charlie was playing with.

The next day I breezed back in again. Walked confidently up to the counter. Oh, good, Mrs. Khan. I smiled at her as I handed her a *Daily Mail.*

"Charlie looks well. I've just seen him in the street. Says he's nearly finished."

She looked surprised but recovered. "Oh, good." She smiled. "So he can go home soon. He like that."

"Home?"

"Yes, somewhere near Oxford. He only here to work, and he miss his wife, I know. Thirty-six pence, please."

I left, shattered. In pieces. *Married.* And he didn't even *live* here. Only here to work. Oh well, that was it. Definitely it. Married. Hopeless!

Except that it wasn't it. Short of breath and almost having palpitations, I stepped off the bus behind him the very next day. Then, two days later, without even looking for him at all, I was in the deli with him. Only this time he was behind me and I was at the front of the queue, choosing some cheese. I dithered wildly, gazing desperately at the display.

"That," he said, leaning past me and tapping on the glass cabinet, "is delicious." He pointed to the Epoisses.

"Oh!" I breathed as his shoulder brushed mine. "Is it?"

"Strong, powerful, really mature, and when you get it out, it just oozes . . . everywhere."

Well, I nearly lost control of my legs.

"I'll take the Epoisses!" I gasped, holding on to the counter.

"How much, madam?"

"All of it!" I squeaked.

I made my purchase and turned to thank him, but found I couldn't. Couldn't speak. Pathetic. Then just as I'd cranked up the vocal cords, he turned to someone I realized he was with, an older man, and continued his conversation. I gaped, stupidly. As I left, I was just lucky enough to hear:

"Yes, sir?"

"A piece of Epoisses, please."

"Oh, I'm awfully sorry, that lady just bought the lot."

I stopped, horrified. Shut my eyes and groaned. Then walked on, shaking my head.

This is absurd, I thought a few minutes later as I headed down the road to Safeways, to do the proper shopping. I hadn't behaved like this for years, not since I was about sixteen. And not with Ned, certainly, because he'd chased me. All around Oxford, in fact. So had I ever—I thought back. . . . No, I decided. Never. Never chased a man in my life. So this was what it felt like, eh? I savored it, rolled it around in my head reflectively. Predatory—definitely. Controlling and powerful, yes, because no one knew. He certainly didn't, and I hadn't told anyone, so no one could belittle it. No one could pour scorn, mock it, spoil it. I was the only one. I straightened my shoulders. Smiled. And I felt invigorated, too, better than I had for weeks, months, even though at home—well, at home I was barely with it. Barely had a grip on the household at all. Why, only yesterday I'd forgotten to put Ben's recorder in his bag, left his homework undone on the kitchen table, and neglected to put anything in Max's sandwiches.

"Jus' butter, Mum?" he'd said indignantly when he'd come home from school, outraged. "Jus' butter, in my samwidges?"

And all the time, all the while that I was absently putting the shoe polish in the fridge and the rubber gloves in the oven, I was inflating my fantasies to pneumatic proportions. Rewriting history, too. So that instead, for instance, of staring mutely at him after that cheese episode, what I'd actually done, what I'd *actually* said, was something scintillating like:

Me: "Oh yes, of course—Epoisses. It's from the Buleric region in southern France, isn't it?"

Him (delighted, turning to look at me properly; momentarily mesmerized by my beauty): "Yes! Yes, that's right. Have you ever been there?"

Me: "No, never, but I hear it's wonderful."

Him: "Oh, it is. Enchanting. Would you like to go?" (Yes, I *know*, but this is the stuff that dreams are made of.)

Me: "What, to the Buleric hills?"

Him: "Yes! Come on!"

And off we'd go. It was the work of a moment. So that instead of trolleying dreamily around Safeways as I was now, reaching for the Cheerios, what I was actually doing was climbing those enchanting Bulimic—or whatever—hills, hand in hand with the tantalizing Charlie. Past the goats and the sheep we'd stroll, through the daisies, like Heidi and her grandfather—no, *not* like Heidi and her grandfather. Charlie wasn't that mature. More like—well, Heathcliffe and Cathy, only not Yorkshire.

Likewise, the milk episode in Mr. Khan's had swelled to:

Him (handing me the milk): "Here. You're obviously in dire need, so—hey. Are you all right? You look a bit pale. Let me get you a—Mr. Khan! Have you got a chair?" (Mr. Khan bustles over with chair, then bustles away again, leaving us to it.)

Him (hovering anxiously): "Is it the heat?"

Me (hand to brow, looking fragile and very beautiful): "No no, I'm fine, really." (Brave smile.)

Him: "My house is literally down the road; why don't you come back and lie down? I've got cold compresses and all sorts."

Cut to me, lying on his sofa, not exactly undressed, but he'd had to remove a few garments, naturally, lest I expire. Him, hovering anxiously and—no. He'd hovered anxiously in the shop. Plucking a guitar at my feet? No, stupid, Lucy, much too cringey and—

"Damn!"

A jar of Branston slipped from my distracted grasp, smashed on the supermarket floor, and splashed up, all over my jeans. I gazed down at the mess. I appeared to be up to my knees in pickle. Was this symbolic? I wondered.

Apologizing profusely to the girl on the till, I finally lugged my carrier bags out of the shop and home. Was this all getting out of hand? I asked myself as I strolled along. And if so, did it matter? After all, I was happy, and in some ways, it was so uncomplicated. So much easier than having a real man. I didn't need one, you see; my dreams were enough. In my head, he was already mine. I walked up the checkered front steps and smiled at my reflection in the hall mirror. The black front door closed softly behind me. Yes. Mine. I could see why people did it. I stared at my reflection, horrified. Did what, Lucy? Stalk? Jill Dando's face on the ten o'clock news sprang terrifyingly to mind. Clutching my Safeways bags, I bolted upstairs, aghast.

Teresa was at the top, just trying my door handle.

"Ah, you back! Good. I brought you a present, see?"

She drew a beautiful moss green scarf from a plastic bag. "The supplier sent too many, and it so pretty. See, it suit you! Go with your eyes." She wrapped its silken swathes around my neck and stood back, eyes narrowed to appraise. "Yes!"

I grinned and let us both in. "Thanks, Teresa, it's lovely, and lovely to see you, too. I think I've been on my own too much recently. Going quietly crazy. I've got a present for you, too. Here." I handed her the Epoisses.

"For me?" She sniffed, then shut her eyes ecstatically. "Aahhh! Proper cheese!"

"Well, you know I can't take anything stronger than Dairylea, and I was—well, talked into buying it. Come on; come in. I need a drink, and I hate drinking alone."

"Me, too, my feet are killing, but it only five o'clock, Luce. Bit early, no? You get boys from school or me?"

"I'll go, but later; they've got football club, remember, so we've got at least half an hour. And anyway, since when did Italians have any truck with that stupid sundown rule? It must be six o'clock somewhere."

I poured a glass of wine from the fridge and handed it to her. She walked with it to the window. "Ah yes," she murmured. "Somewhere. In Rome, no doubt."

She leaned her forehead pensively on the glass and we were silent for a moment. I pushed the cork back in the bottle, turned away.

"Teresa, d'you think it's healthy to daydream?" I asked tentatively, putting the bottle back in the fridge. "I mean, constantly? As if . . . well, as if reality's some kind of unwelcome intruder, always barging in on your thoughts?" I frowned. Turned back. "Teresa?"

"Hmmm?" She lifted her head off the window. "Sorry, Luce, I was in another world. Just opening my third shop in the Piazza del Navona, just down the road from the Duomo. Quite an opening party actually; all the glitterati were there, spilling out of my shop onto the pavement, all in their finery. . . ."

I smiled. "Quite normal then. And clearly I'm not a patch on the real, hardened escapists. Except," I paused, running my finger reflectively round the rim of my glass, "your dreams are about your career, your ambitions. About bettering yourself, which is all very laudable. Whereas mine . . ."

"Yes?" she prompted as I broke off. She was gazing at me intently now, her dark eyes steady.

"Well, mine . . ." I bit my lip.

"Lucy, these past few weeks, I never seen you look so well," she said softly. "Your eyes, they sparkle now, and your face has lost that dead, defeated look. You look like you did when I first met you, that day when Ned banged on our door." She smiled. "If I didn't know better, I'd say you were in love."

I laughed nervously. "No, not in love, because there's nothing real about this, and never will be. You see, it's all in my head."

I must have looked anxious, because she came across and hugged me.

"It's got to start somewhere. It's fine; let it grow; work with it. It's good, you know? You're coming back to life."

Chapter Four

THE WEEKS WENT BY AND THE SUMMER BLOSSOMED. I saw Charlie—ooh, probably once a week, because I was careful not to overdo it and, anyway, that was enough. He'd hop on a bus and I'd spot him and hop on, too. God knows where I was going, but I'd sit behind him for a few euphoric minutes, then get off at the next stop and walk home, smiling. It was ridiculous. I felt . . . possessed, almost—but I loved the feeling. Hugged it to myself and told myself it was harmless.

I was learning more about him, too. I knew which paper he read, which brand of cereal he liked, and which cigarettes he smoked, but I still didn't know where he lived. He was clearly local, but I hadn't actually had the courage—or the audacity—to tail him home. On the weirdo scale of things I thought this was quite promising, though I have to admit the opportunity had never really presented itself. One of the peculiarities of the King's Road is that it can bustle to bursting point, with people literally jostling one another off the pavement, but pop down a side street and *wham!* It's empty. Silent. So quiet and rarefied you can almost hear the pavements squeak. Even the pigeons look snooty in these areas of Chelsea, and this, of course, was where Charlie disappeared to.

I did pluck up the courage to follow him one day, but it was so quiet, I could hear myself breathing. Nervously. Heavily. Great gusts of it. Any minute now, I thought, he'd turn and say, "Oh, hi, it's you! Where are you off to?" And I'd billow away like the Atlantic, blushing horribly, and then the game would be up. He'd know I was following him and I'd never be able to do it again. I had to be so careful.

A few days after that little episode, I had a thought. I borrowed Theo and Ray's dog.

"He's had a walk today already, Lucy," Ray insisted in the hallway as I put Bob on a lead. Bob was a rather scrawny Yorkshire terrier who wore his fringe in a bow, poor chap, and looked permanently startled. He looked even more alarmed than usual today.

"And he does get awfully puffed," added Theo. "He's not so young now, rather delicate."

"I'll carry him if he gets tired," I promised with a smile. "Trust me, boys; I grew up with dogs. He'll be fine." And with a tug of the smart tartan lead, we were off, Bob and I. Off to wander those smart, slumbering backwaters, off to those elegant squares and mews where Bob, I reckoned, was my passport. My perfect excuse, as looking—I hope—rich and nonchalant, I searched for the most fragrant lampposts, the most manicured squares, in order for Bob to do, what was for a small dog, quite a bit of business.

We trailed for miles, Bob and I. Up and down those discreet, bleeding backwaters, round and round those oh, so elegant squares, and yes, one day we did see Charlie. Just as I was bending down to scoop the poop. Just as I was groaning, "Oh God, not, *another* one, Bob!" Just as—as luck would have it—twenty Marlboros and a pair of sunglasses fell out of my shirt pocket and plopped right into it.

"Arrrggh!" I screeched. "No! Oh God, now it's all over my hands! *Bastard* dog!"

Naturally, Charlie didn't linger. He gave a brief nervous smile of recognition, neatly sidestepped my crouching form, and walked smartly on.

At times like this, as I straightened up from my pile of ordure, I'd swear I could hear Ned laughing at me. And not just laughing but guffawing and holding his sides. "You idiot, Lucy," he'd hoot. "What on earth are you doing?"

"Oh, I don't know," I sighed, trying to wipe my hands on the grass. "What *am* I bloody doing?"

And I didn't feel guilty, either, about chasing a man in the presence of my husband's ghost. No, that wasn't the problem at all. You see, I knew that's what he'd want. Not the chasing, necessarily, but the man. Because for the last four years, as I'm sure, periodically, I've mentioned, I'd been so deeply unhappy. Sometimes I'd even given in. And on those occasions, when I'd stolen back to bed as soon as the boys had gone to school, wept silently, stared at the ceiling, hating him for having left me, on those occasions I'd swear Ned had come to me, crouched down beside me.

"Lucy," he'd said gently. "Come on, Luce; get up. Don't *do* this to yourself. You'll be fine; you'll see. There'll be someone else for you, I promise."

You smile, but two or three times I actually felt him there, too. Felt his presence. Smelt him even, beside the bed, urging me on.

I was thirty-one years old. Twenty-seven when he'd died. Would he want me to be alone forever? No. Did he want the boys to have another daddy? Oh, harder, much harder. He would always be their daddy. And he'd loved Ben so. . . .

But there. Enough. He was laughing at me now. Pleased perhaps that I was having a go, but—God, what a *mess*, Luce. What a Horlicks! I could hear him sigh.

"Yes, I know," I muttered to the clouds, tucking the hapless, exhausted Bob under my arm. "I know, Ned, and I know he's married, too. But I'm not actually interested, OK? I'm just interested in the way it's making me feel; that's all. The way it's making me better." I hoped I could sense him nod approvingly, but I couldn't be sure.

And then one day, he disappeared. Charlie, I mean. A week went by and I didn't see him, and then another, and another, and although I told myself not to panic, after four weeks I was distraught. I could feel myself sinking down again. Saw those dark pools of despair rising up to meet me, found myself reaching for too many paracetamol, too much Night Nurse. And I didn't want to go down that black alley again. I knew I was missing my weekly relief, and I felt like a junkie with a terrible habit. Desperate for a fix.

Mrs. Khan at the corner shop couldn't help.

"Golly, I haven't seen Charlie for absolutely ages; have you?" I breezed brazenly one morning, no pride now, clutching her counter anxiously.

"Charlie?" She frowned.

"Yes, you know—tall, dark, married. Lives near Oxford. Buys milk," I added desperately. It was all I knew.

"Oh, Charlie." She paused. Looked at me carefully. "No, no, I not seen him."

I waited, willing her on.

"Maybe he go home," she said eventually, unnerved by my silence.

"Yes! Yes, maybe," I agreed, raising speculative eyebrows, as if this thought hadn't occurred to me, every waking moment. "And that is?" I asked shamelessly, despising myself but out of control now. As if my lips were moving without my mind.

"Sorry?"

"And home is? Charlie's . . . home is?"

She blinked. "No idea. Like I say, he say Oxford but—ah, Rozanna, she know. Rozanna, where Charlie Fletcher live?"

I swung around to see Rozanna behind me, holding half a bottle of gin and looking gorgeous as usual, swathed in lilac cashmere.

"Charlie Fletcher?" she drawled. "Well, around the corner somewhere, but in the country? Oh, some farmhouse near Woodstock, I believe. Why?"

"Because Lucy was—"

"No reason," I interrupted, flushing. "How—how d'you know him, Rozanna?"

"I shag him, darling."

I stared, horror-struck.

She gave a throaty laugh. "No, no such luck. I just get the has-beens and the wanna-bes. No, everyone knows Charlie; he's quite famous. Writes TV scripts. Wrote that arty little film a while ago—*Coming Up for Air*, I think it was called. It was on Channel 4. Hollywood's after him now, I gather."

My mind was assimilating all of this greedily, stashing it away in the golden archive for later but simultaneously reeling in horror. Surname: Fletcher. Occupation: Scriptwriter. Status: Relatively famous. Damn. Too much, *far* too much for me. Why couldn't he be an aspiring porter, desperate for a job at an auction house? Desperate for a peek inside a porcelain department? I could have helped him there, been his salvation.

"And married to a lovely girl called Miranda, who runs a very successful business from the country, but I can't quite remember what it is." She frowned. "Catering, I believe, or something domestic. I was at school with her actually. Sweet little thing—and as you know, Luce, I'm not mad about sweet little things as a rule, but she's awfully nice. Stunning, too, a bit younger than me. You've gone terribly pale, Lucy. Why d'you need to know all this?"

Need, not want. At least, as she was banging nails into my heart, she'd given me an escape clause, too.

"Oh, because I . . . need . . . to send him some mail. For some reason it got sent to me, addressed to Charlie Fletcher. So I need to know his address."

She frowned. "How bizarre. At your flat?" She regarded me for a moment. I didn't answer. She shrugged.

"Oh well, here, darling. I've got it in here, somewhere."

She rooted around in her Gucci bag and found her address book. Flicked through to the *F*s. "This . . ." she showed me, pointing, "is London, Langton Villas, which is literally round the corner, and this"—I scribbled away frantically on the back of an old envelope—"is where I presume he's hanging out now. In Oxfordshire, in the country."

Chapter Five

"HAVE YOU GOT EVERYTHING, BOYS?" I YELLED, CLATTERING downstairs with a box full of saucepans. "Because I'm not turning round with that trailer on the back!"

"Can I take this?"

I swung around to see Ben at the flat door, dragging an ancient wicker chair with exploding arms out onto the landing.

"Oh, darling, no, not really. I thought we'd leave it. I did say I'd leave it fully furnished, and I won't have room in the trailer."

"But it's my special chair. Where am I supposed to sit and read in my room then?"

"Granny will have masses of chairs, you'll see, lovely ones."

"But this is *my* chair, where all my animals sit, and where I listen to my tapes and things, and—"

"I'll take it," said Teresa, quickly coming to the rescue from across the hallway. "And when you come and see us, you take it then. We put it in Pedro's room for the minute, yes? It's just Mummy's got no room."

He gave it up sulkily, then went trudging back inside, slamming the door behind him.

I caught Teresa's eye and she smiled sympathetically. This wasn't going quite as smoothly as I'd hoped. Ben, whom I'd talked to at length about the benefits of the move, whose opinion I'd canvassed, and who initially had been thrilled to bits at the idea of streams and woods and badgers and barn owls, was suddenly getting very cold feet. Catching the vibes and loving a drama, Max was rapidly coming out in sympathy. When I went back up to collect the pair of them, they were sitting on the top bunk together, Ben staring moodily into the distance and Max sucking his thumb defiantly, eyeing me resentfully. They reeked of solidarity.

"Come on, boys," I cajoled softly. "I know it's a wrench, but we really have to get a move on, you know. Got to hit that road. And it'll be great when we get there; you'll see. You'll be tickling trout and whit-tling sticks and wondering why on earth we didn't go sooner."

"No, I won't," said Ben, jumping off the bunk but snapping his Walkman firmly to his head. "I'll be wondering why I can't go to the Science Museum anymore, or to Peter Kelly's party at the ice rink on Saturday, and why you always decide things without thinking about us."

"Yeah," added Max for good measure, glaring at me. "Finkin' 'bout us."

As Ben brushed past me with his henchman beside him, I caught my breath at the injustice. Did I deserve this? Did I? As they stamped out to the landing, I made to follow, to lock the door behind me, then paused. Turned. Slowly, and alone, I walked around that tiny flat one last time. It was tidy—in fact, it was immaculate—and it seemed to me it was reproachful, too, as it waited poised for its next occupant.

A company had bought it and paid me a fairly decent whack for the privilege of having their thrusting young executive move in, but perhaps I should have rented it out, I wondered nervously, as I fingered the muslin curtains. Perhaps I shouldn't have burnt my boats entirely, because what if Oxfordshire . . . No. I bit my lip, standing at the win-dow gazing out across the familiar rooftops. No. It *would* work out, and anyway, this was the home I'd had with Ned, and Ned was no longer in it. Too many memories, too much clinging to the past. I had to make a new life for myself, elsewhere.

"Come on then, pickle; let's go," I said, forcing a smile as I encoun-tered Max, staging a last sit-in on the landing. I picked him up like a sack of potatoes, feeling a pang of sympathy for the police at Greenham Common but noting with relief that he did at least flop obligingly over my shoulder. Ben, preternaturally obedient, was trailing miserably down the stairs behind us, despite his misgivings.

I'd said my good-byes to everyone else in the block last night—couldn't bear to be doing it on the doorstep this morning—and had told them so in no uncertain terms. Pedro had gone to school so that it wouldn't be too emotional for Ben, and only Teresa was hovering help-fully, the other flat doors remaining discreetly closed. Teresa hugged me hard on the pavement, tears in her eyes.

"You'll come back?"

"Of course I'll come back, you idiot. God, I'm only in Oxfordshire.

Anyone would think I was going to the moon! We'll be back all the time, and you'll come and stay. Think of all the weekends away you'll have; we can be your very own country retreat. Pedro will love it, and it'll be fab for you and Carlo to get out of London."

"For me, maybe, but I worry about you, stuck down there. And no job now."

I sighed. Teresa had a happy knack of not pulling her punches, and this one caught me low. She was quite right, of course. This particular blow to morale had fallen quite unexpectedly—last week, in fact, as I'd finally plucked up the courage to ring my head of department at Christie's and find out what the hell was going on. Find out what sort of headway he'd made in changing my four mornings a week to two full days. Had he swung it for me? And if so, why hadn't he called? After all, it made far more sense if I was coming all the way up from the country, didn't it? Well, didn't it, Rupert?

There'd been an awkward pause and then a fair bit of throat clearing on the other end.

"Rupert? Is it OK? Are you still there?"

"Um, yes, still here, Lucy. It's just . . . well, the thing is, it's all been a bit tricky. You see, I've been instructed by the powers that be to implement one or two changes in the department. One of them, I'm afraid, is to cut down on all the part-timers."

"Cut down? Part-timers? But, hang on, I am the *only* part-timer!"

"Er, well, precisely. And, um, the thing is, Lucy, they're being a bit sort of all-or-nothing about it. A bit sort of total commitment on all fronts."

"Which means?"

"Basically, five days a week plus overtime if needs be and trips abroad if necessary."

"Trips abroad? But I can't possibly do all that with two small children and a god-awful commute from Oxfordshire!"

"Er, no. Quite." Silence.

"So it's the nothing option, is it? Is that it, Rupert?"

"Well, Lucy," he struggled, "you know, what can I say?" I could sense him shifting uncomfortably in his chair at the other end. "I don't make the rules. Just implement the bloody things," he said miserably.

I opened my mouth to explode, then abruptly caved in. Oh God, it wasn't his fault. And actually, he was a thoroughly decent man. I sighed.

"It's OK, Rupert. I've felt the vibes for a while, actually. I expect that's why I was so nervous about asking."

This much was true. For some time now I'd felt guilty about sliding home at lunchtime, knowing jealous eyes were upon me and knowing, too, that there was heaps to do and no one to do it. At times I'd talked airily of arranging a job share with some fictitious character, but it hadn't materialized and the reality was resentful colleagues, who were still there at six-thirty picking up my workload. I swallowed.

"Sorry Lucy," he muttered. "You know I'd do anything to keep you, especially . . . well."

After all you've been through was the unspoken phrase, left hanging in the air. Rupert had been brilliant when Ned had died, had probably kept me on out of loyalty, I thought now, with a sudden guilty pang, but I couldn't be carried forever. And now, here I was, gaily trying to re-arrange my schedule to suit myself again. Suddenly I was embarrassed to have asked, to have put Rupert in that position. But I felt sick, too, as I put down the phone. My lovely job. My buzzy South-Ken lifeline, my slice of London, my *money*, for crying out loud. But—no matter. I turned a brave smile on Teresa now, aware of Ben's anxious, knowing little face turned up to me, too.

"Oh, I don't mind about that," I lied breezily. "It paid peanuts any-way, and it would have been such a slog, coming up from the sticks. I'll find something down there; you'll see. Anyway, Teresa, you'll have a string of shops soon. Perhaps I can manage one in Oxford for you. Mus-cle in on your fortune!"

She hugged me hard. "You being brave," she muttered in my ear.

"What choice do I have?" I muttered back. "I've made the decision now. If everything conspires against me and taunts me at the last minute, what can I do?"

"I won't mention the Kyshogi boys, either, then, eh? That taunt you, too?"

"Oh God," I groaned. "No, don't! Isn't it just bloody typical? Christ, what am I doing, Teresa?" I clutched my hair.

One of the other key motivating factors for making this momentous break was that Ben was having a tough time at school. Twin boys in his class, Bobat and Rahu Kyshogi, had taken it upon themselves to make his life a misery, picking on him, calling him a wimp, waiting for him when he came out of school, so that I had to make sure I was there, at the school gates, on the dot every day, to intervene. True, Pedro had been on the receiving end of the same sort of treatment, but although small, Pedro was much more savvy and streetwise and quite handy with his fists, whereas Ben, tall, skinny, sensitive, and who'd never hit another child in his life, was an easy target to take the brunt of their bullying.

Teresa and I had arrived to pick the boys up yesterday afternoon, to be told, by a beaming headmaster at the gates, that the Kyshogi brothers had ripped their last blazer, kicked their last victim, and spat in their last school dinner. They were being expelled. I'd gaped, speechless, at the man.

"But why couldn't you have done that six months ago, when I told you it was unutterably bloody? When I brought Ben in to see you for heaven's sake, with a cut lip, bleeding knees, pencil case ripped to shreds. Why now?"

He shifted awkwardly, scratched his chin. "I suppose I didn't know the full extent of the Kyshogis' behavior then, Mrs. Fellowes. Now, of course—"

"Now that they've beaten up Andrew Krugar," Teresa interrupted sweetly behind me, "it's been brought to your attention."

I swung around. "Have they? Andrew Krugar?"

She nodded. I turned back. "Ah, I see. Ah yes, well, the dawn comes up, Mr. Brightman."

Andrew Krugar's father was head of the school governors and a pretty *grand fromage* locally. A lot of school funds came winging that way.

"I'm sorry, Mrs. Fellowes," he was hopping nervously from foot to foot now, "but I really didn't realize it made such a difference to your taking Ben away. His place is still here, you know, and he's such a lovely intelligent boy. I really don't see why—"

"Oh, it's a bit late now, Mr. Brightman," I snapped. "We're moving tomorrow! The telephone's been disconnected; the papers have been stopped—the die is cast, as it were."

I turned on my heel, furious, with Ben trailing anxiously behind.

"Is that why we're going, Mummy? Because you thought I was unhappy?"

"But you were unhappy, Ben," I fumed.

"Yes, but I'm not now," he said eagerly, trotting to keep up. "The Kyshogis are going, all my friends are still here, and Mr. Brightman says I can stay, so . . . so can we stay?"

"No," I groaned, stopping abruptly in the street. I clenched my fists. "No, we can't. Plans have been made, Ben. Granny's expecting us—the flat's been sold, for heaven's sake!"

"But you weren't going to sell it! At first you were only going to let it!"

"Yes, but, Ben, I told you. The offer we got was too good to turn down and I no longer have a job to finance everything, so—"

"Everything's too good to turn down, except the things *we* want!" His voice broke and he ran on ahead, without me.

I sighed, rubbed my forehead wearily with my fingertips. It was true, I had been seduced by the money. I hadn't intended to sell the flat, but the estate agent had persuaded me that renting was a hassle and since he had a cash buyer dangling . . . "Far easier to let the thing go, Mrs. Fellowes. Far easier, hmm?" Now, though, I felt as if I'd let everything go. I felt I was witnessing a landslide, with everything slipping inexorably away from me, all the handholds I'd subconsciously put carefully in place, just in case, crumbling before my eyes as my fingernails slipped on the scree.

I gave Teresa one last hug and snapped Max into his seat. Ben got in beside him and I hopped, with forced jollity, into the front.

"Bye then! Come and see us soon, won't you? Give my love to the others."

My heart lurched as I suddenly spied "the others," patently disobeying orders. Rozanna, Carlo, Ray, and Theo were peering sheepishly around the curtain in Theo and Ray's flat. They saw me look; then broad grins broke out all round, as, waving madly and blowing kisses, they were unable to resist. I blew them all a quick kiss, swallowed hard, and shunted into first. Then, beeping my horn cheerfully, I took off. With the trailer piled high behind us and all our worldly goods rattling around in the sunshine, we roared down the road, plunged into the depths of the King's Road, and headed for the M4.

It didn't help of course, I thought, blinking furiously and brushing a few stray tears away with the back of my hand, that I was grotesquely hungover this morning. That didn't add to the gaiety of nations, and that was all down to last night. Yes, last night had been send-off night in Royal Avenue, and in the first-floor flat—since that was the largest— the usual suspects had gathered; Theo and Ray, the hosts, together with Rozanna, Teresa and Carlo, Jess and Jamie, Lucas and Maisie, and Pedro and Ben falling asleep in front of a video.

Theo and Ray, being the most marvelous cooks, had prepared a feast fit for kings. After much stirring and muttering and shooing us out of the kitchen, they'd whipped off their pinnies—and lo. A mountain of *ceps* risotto, together with bowls of salad, had appeared. We'd fallen on it ravenously, having pretty much drunk their drinks cupboard dry, and then had happily frittered the night away and drunk more. Lucas, Maisie, Ray, and Theo had talked music and theater; Teresa, Jess, and I were predictably on schools; whilst Jamie, in thrusting *Daily Mail* mode, had swung his chair around and cornered Rozanna, probing her for a scoop on her latest liaison with a well-known captain of industry. Their heads were close and their voices low, and Jess, naturally, got the wrong idea. Eyes glazed by this stage and mouth drooping dramatically, she bent in close to me.

"You see?" she'd whispered furiously in my ear. "Just look at him flirting with her, Lucy; he's completely shameless. And look at her, too, smoldering away under those heavily made-up lids. She looks like a high-class tart, for heaven's sake!"

"But that's exactly what she is," said Teresa, surprised. "Didn't Lucy tell you?"

Jess's jaw dropped to her chest. "No! No, she *didn't*. God, how gripping! Is she really? Why didn't you tell me, Luce?"

I shrugged. "Because she's always wanted to maintain the fiction, I suppose. So I have, too, for her sake. Rozanna's quite vulnerable, you know, for all her supposed toughness."

Rozanna turned at her name. Smiled fondly. "All right, darling? Lovely party. Did you manage to get that stuff off to Charlie, by the way?"

Jess's ears pricked up like greased antennae. "Charlie? The guy in your office?"

I caught my breath. "Yes. Yes, that's right."

Rozanna frowned. "In your office? At Christie's? But—no, I told you, darling, he writes film scripts and things. He—"

"Yes, yes, I know," I gabbled, "but he . . . just came in one day. To view an auction. English furniture, I think."

"Hang on." It was Jess's turn to frown. "You said he worked with you. I thought you said he was in your department or something. In fact I could have sworn—"

"Oh, *that* Charlie!" I said quickly, wondering why on earth I hadn't killed Jess months ago. Stabbed her to death in our stall with an antique letter opener, popped the body in a black bin liner, and dropped it in the Thames. "No no, that's Charlie . . ." I glanced around wildly for inspiration. My eye snagged on Ben and Pedro's video. "Bond. Charlie Bond."

There was a surprised silence. Jess blinked. "Charlie Bond?" she said dryly. "What, as in 'licensed to kill'? Please don't tell me you're Pussy Galore."

I flushed. "Don't be silly; it's a perfectly common name, Jess. It's just Rozanna's talking about a completely different Charlie, that's all. One who lives round here."

"Ah." Jess shut her eyes in mock exhaustion. "Lordy, silly me. I'm losing track of all the Charlies. Not the one you've got the hots for then."

I colored dramatically and could feel Rozanna's eyes on me. "I haven't got the hots for any Charlie, actually, Jess," I sputtered.

"Just as well in Charlie Fletcher's case, daahling," purred Rozanna softly, reaching for her drink. "Because believe me, you'd be going down an awfully blind alley there." She eyed me carefully over the rim of her glass as she sipped from it.

As I gripped the steering wheel now, steaming down the M4, I knew just how blind she meant. She was warning me off, of course. And I knew why. He wasn't just married, he was happily married, and naturally, in my head, I'd always entertained dreams that it was otherwise. Imagined that his wife was perfectly ghastly, vile. Much older than him, probably, forty-five at least, and she'd trapped him by—yes, by getting pregnant. He'd had to marry her. There he'd stood, young and white-faced at the front of the church, as she'd ballooned down the aisle, smug and triumphant, forcing his hand and his destiny. Other days I fancied something entirely different, that they'd married very young, when she was sixteen, gormless, and spotty, that he'd been pushed into it by overzealous parents, to amalgamate family fortunes, that it was practically an arranged marriage.

Either way, young or old, she was totally unsuitable. I imagined she drank heavily and had indiscreet affairs. I saw her prowling around Tesco's looking for loose-limbed youths stacking shelves, dragging them back to her lair by their polyester ties. I imagined Charlie's distress, his embarrassment. After a while, though, this particular fantasy began to bother me. If she was such a goer, might she not be tempted to go with her husband, occasionally? When there weren't any shelf stackers available? Instantly she became a downy-lipped librarian, timid and shy, with swirls of dark hair showing through her American Tan tights. Naturally she was allergic to sex—terrified, in fact, following a nasty experience, years back, in the reference section—and now a glimpse of the naked male body was enough to make her vomit.

He was miserable, of course, *miserable*, but he kept up a pretense for—who? The children? Did he have any children? This tormented me for hours. On the one hand, yes, lovely, because that made him a sweet and caring father, just as I was a sweet and caring mother, and what a big happy family we'd make one day, de-dah de-dah, but on the other hand, no. No, ghastly, because it tied him to her. Some days it was impossible to resolve, but either way, I decided, the marriage was a sham and it was only a matter of time before I cruised in, saved his bacon, and became the second Mrs. De Winter, as it were.

I sighed. But no, according to Rozanna, she was lovely. Beautiful, talented, successful, and he loved her dearly, as Ned had loved me. I swallowed, and tears of self-pity welled in my nose. And imagine if it *were* Ned and me, I thought in sudden horror. Imagine some predatory hussy prowling around Soho with a ridiculous dog under her arm, waiting for my husband to emerge from his editing suite, waiting to hustle him downstairs and pin him to the cutting-room floor.

Suddenly I felt ill. And not only that but dirty, cheap, and low. As I sped off at the motorway exit, I resolved not to even look up Hexham when I got there, not to gaze, wistfully, at the village on the Ordnance Survey map, not even to go past the place in the car. No, I'd find someone else, I determined, squaring my shoulders. Someone single and available. Find a bloody blacksmith, if needs be, bonk the living daylights out of him.

I swept a despairing hand through my hair and glanced in the rearview mirror. God, I'd been so impulsive, what sort of a madness had gripped me? I'd followed my heart and my hotheaded instincts and now here I was, hurtling down country lanes with two unhappy boys in the back, no job, no prospects, and destined to live with my mother-in-law, for crying out loud. And I'd have to *get* a job down there, of course, I thought savagely. In a farm shop or something, selling cabbages, or . . . or saddles. Muck spreading, perhaps . . . Christ!

"Mummy, why are you doing that?" Ben removed his earpiece for a moment and looked at me in the rearview mirror.

"What, darling?"

"Banging the steering wheel and making faces? Grinding your teeth?"

"Oh, was I? Well, because I'm so excited, I suppose." I ground a bit more to persuade him. "This is all so terrifically exciting, isn't it? Such an awfully big adventure!"

"Is it?"

"Of course!"

"Oh."

"Just look at all this lovely scenery, Ben. All that lovely . . . grass. Those, you know, hedges, and things."

He sat up. "Are we nearly there, then?"

"Nearly there?" I swung nervously down a little lane, perilously close to another car, palms sweaty on the wheel. "This is Granny's lane, Ben. Don't you recognize it?"

Ben peered out of the window. Max unstrapped himself and knelt up beside him. A colossal twenty-foot wall surrounding the estate was making it impossible to see anything, actually.

"I'm not sure. It's ages since we've been." Ben sounded nervous. "Is that their house?"

He pointed to a little lodge as we finally found a gap in the wall and swept through the gates.

"Um, no, darling, that's Mrs. Shilling's house. You know, who's married to the woodman? The man who does the logging for Grandpa."

It occurred to me to wonder if Ben remembered anything at all about this setup. It was indeed ages since we'd set foot in the place.

As we purred slowly up the long drive, through the parkland, rattling periodically over cattle grids, my sons fell silent in the back. As I did, too. As one, we took in the sylvan scene: the well-tended acres that spread to either side of us, the trees neatly encircled by deer protectors, the sheep that grazed contentedly, crossing our path occasionally, so that we had to slow down to let them pass.

"Is this still their road, then?" asked Max, at length.

"Their drive," muttered Ben.

"Still?" Max repeated in awe, a few minutes later.

"Still."

"So . . . where's the house?"

"Hang on, my darling; hold your horses," I tinkled merrily. "It's right around this bend, I think."

Except it wasn't.

"It goes on forever," said Ben. "We'll never escape."

"And why should you want to, silly? Ah—here it is!"

As we turned a corner, Netherby finally unfurled itself, rearing up at us out of the manicured green in all its Palladian glory. Banks of windows glinted in the sunlight from the golden sandstone façade, and balustrades and porticoes frowned down. Halfway up, a front door loomed, and from it a huge bank of steps swept down and then divided into two, to meet the sweep of gravel below. Beyond the house, beyond the parterres, the lavender walks and the rose gardens, immaculate parkland rolled to a glassy lake, then up again to wooded hills in the distance.

"Oh! It's like a castle!" breathed Max, suddenly excited.

"Isn't it," I agreed, crunching to a halt on the gravel. And there, I thought with a gathering sense of dread, was the Queen.

Rose, who'd clearly been waiting, came, not from one of the many side doors I knew the house boasted but out of the front door, which was rarely used, except for very formal occasions. She threw it wide and tripped dramatically down the hundreds of steps to meet us. Halfway down, she was overtaken by a pair of bounding lurchers, who raised their heads, baying out a welcome. Behind her, slowly, came her elder son, Hector, gangly and blond, corduroys billowing in the breeze, blinking away like billy-oh behind his glasses, clearly under orders to attend.

I glanced at my watch as I got out. We were over an hour late. They must have been waiting for ages, poised in the morning room perhaps, at the table in the window, sipping coffee together silently, waiting for our car. Rose muttering, "Where *is* the wretched girl?" and then finally, as we came into view, putting her cup down abruptly. "Here they are, Hector. Right, action stations. Come on, quickly now, out we go, and don't forget to *smile*, for heaven's sake."

Skipping lightly down the last few steps, she came toward us across the gravel, arms outstretched, beaming, a tiny spry, energetic figure, neat in a lovat green twin set and smart trousers. Her navy shoes had horse bits on the front, and her immaculate gray hair was swept back and curled neatly round her ears.

"Darlings! You're here!" she called, still from some distance.

"Hello, Rose."

As I helped Max out of his seat, I glanced up at the house and caught a glimpse of Lavinia's pale face at an upstairs window. She quickly shot back behind the heavy drapes, clearly wanting to spy but not wanting to be seen.

I clutched my two boys by their hands, one on either side, and steeled myself. Then I strode confidently toward the welcoming committee, a smile fixed firmly in position.

"Hello there."

"Lucy! Ben! Max!" Rose called lightly. Her hands lit briefly on my shoulders and she gave me a swift kiss. "Isn't this wonderful?" she purred. "Isn't it just marvelous?" She crouched down between the boys. "And let me look at you both. My goodness, you've grown. Look at the pair of you—huge!"

She straightened up, smiling. As she did, her pale blue eyes traveled comprehensively over my jeans and T-shirt and finally came to rest on my face. They glittered intently.

"So! Lucy, what a treat. Isn't this perfect? Here we all are, together again. At long last. All present and correct!"

Chapter Six

"COME IN; COME IN!" SHE CRIED, TURNING ON HER HEEL and leading the way toward the steps. She was, as ever, I noticed, dauntingly thin. "I'm sure you'll want a cup of something after your journey," she said, striding on, "and then I'll show you Chandlers Barn. But first, come and say hello to everyone. Lavinia! Lav-in-ia! Yoo-hoo, they're he-re! Follow me, Lucy."

I would, of course, but first I thought I might just pause to greet Hector, whom she'd brushed past rather dismissively.

"Hi, Hector, how are you?" I reached up and bestowed a quick kiss on his cheek.

He blushed predictably. "I'm well, thank you, Lucy," he muttered, spectacles flashing in the sunlight as he glanced nervously at his mother's back. "Shall we . . . ?"

I took the point and we obediently fell in behind the great lady, speedily following her up the mountain of steps, the boys, nimble as goats, behind us.

As we crossed the threshold and went through into the vast vaulted black-and-white flagstone hall, heavy with the scent of orchids, which rose from urns poised on columns, Rose paused—for effect, I couldn't help thinking. The boys and I dutifully gazed about us, adjusting our eyes to the gloom, silently succumbing to the hushed opulence of our surroundings. Above the magnificent stone fireplace a stag's head bore down with dead eyes, and from the walls yellowing, faded faces gazed out from the ancestral oils. Dotted about sparingly was the sort of furniture one normally only views from behind a rope, and in the distance I heard the familiar stately ticking of a large and ancient clock. The faded rose drapes at the windows, like everything else, bore the pall of antiquity and, more important, the touch of generations of Felloweses.

"Wow," said Ben shortly.

Rose said nothing but smiled and raised her chin in appreciation.

63

There was a proud gleam in her eye, a certain dihedral to her nose. Timing it to a nicety, her daughter chose that moment to trip lightly down the grand staircase. One hand brushed the rail, and her dark, straight hair bobbed and shone behind her, held back still, I noticed, by an eighties velvet hairband. She was wearing a sensible Liberty print shirt and skirt I knew of old. What was new, however, was the broad, bright smile and the light in her dark eyes.

"Lucy! You're here at last!" she cried. "How marvelous; we've been absolutely dying for you to come."

"Have you?" I said, wrongfooted slightly and trying to keep the surprise from my voice. "Gosh, how sweet of you, Lavinia."

And what a cow I was for thinking she was spying on us up there. She was probably just waiting at the window. I hid my embarrassment in her hair as she pecked me on the cheek.

"And you're going to just love the barn," she gushed. "Everyone who's seen it is so impressed. I can't wait to show you round. I have to say, Mummy and I have worked jolly hard in there, and now it's finished, I'm even just a teeny bit jealous. Quite tempted to live in it myself!"

"Don't be silly, Lavinia; it's much too big for a single person," said her mother crushingly, comprehensively taking the wind out of her sails.

"Oh well, Mummy, I didn't really mean—" She turned anxiously.

"I'm sure it's wonderful," I assured her quickly, "and I can't wait to see it. As for you . . ." I looked her up and down approvingly. "Am I allowed to say . . ."

"That I've put on some weight?" She laughed. "You are. Two stone actually, although admittedly most of it's up here." She indicated her huge bosom. "But I feel marvelous. Loads better."

"You look it." I smiled, relieved.

Poor Lavinia, jilted two years ago by Piers, the fiancé whose feet had frozen solid just as the invitations were going out and the presents were rolling in. She'd never quite got over it and, whilst not exactly Miss Havisham–esque in her grief, had nevertheless gone into a steep decline. White as a sheet, she'd wandered this house like a ghost, quite unable to eat or sleep for months, poor girl. Her whole life had been a preamble to getting married to the right man, living in the right house and in the right county, like some throwback from a Victorian novel, but once she had snared her totally harmless and charmless suitor, he'd glimpsed the future and done a runner. Never mind that he brayed like an idiot, wore his trousers under his armpits, and had all the prepossession of a duck; he was also in possession of a pile that, whilst not comparable to Netherby, was still "a house one wouldn't be ashamed to entertain in," she'd once confided breathlessly to me. Lavinia was devastated by her loss.

I remember being lost in secret grudging admiration for Piers at the time. I wouldn't have thought he'd had it in him, to snub the Felloweses like that, but I was also deeply sorry for her. She'd suffered the most unimaginable indignity of her tribe; a huge wedding had been planned, the tiara was out of the vault, half the county were ready to assemble, and then . . . total, naked humiliation. I wondered, then, if she'd ever get over it, but looking at her now, her hazel eyes shining in a face that was still a bit pale—but then that was her particular pallor—I thought with relief that she had. She looked better than I'd seen her for years.

"And look at you, you great big boys!" She bent down to greet them. "My, you've grown—haven't they grown, Hec?"

"They certainly have," said Hector, straightening up. "Little men, now." He cleared his throat importantly. "And may I say, Lucy, how pleased we all are that you decided to come and live here. We couldn't be more delighted to have you and the boys amongst us, and we hope you'll be very happy."

This was quite a speech for Hector, and his glasses all but steamed up with the effort. His mother and sister gazed at him in astonishment.

"You sound like an alderman, Hec," giggled Lavinia. "You'll be growing a paunch next!"

Hector palpitated a bit behind his glasses, but I was touched. And, suddenly, thoroughly ashamed of all my doubts and misgivings. I looked at the three faces smiling anxiously at me and realized that actually, they were all perfectly sweet and it was all going to be fine. In my mind I'd stupidly let them balloon into grotesque, pompous caricatures, blue-blooded ogres, which they weren't at all, just simple country people who couldn't be more welcoming.

"Thank you, Hector." I smiled. "That's so sweet of you. I'm sure we're going to be really happy here." I squeezed his arm, knowing anything more effusive would send a rush of blood to the cheeks again.

"So." Rose clapped her hands happily. "Come on then, let's take you boys through to the sitting room for an orange juice and a biscuit, and we'll get Mummy a cup of coffee. Oh. Where's Max?"

I swung about. God, where was Max? He was here just a moment ago, but it would be just like him to disappear to the farthest turret and stone the peacocks the moment we arrived.

"Here," said a little voice behind us as he appeared from down a long corridor. "I went to the toilet."

"Loo, darling," I breathed nervously. "They say that at school," I muttered.

"Well, clever boy for finding the right place," said Rose, which made me quake again. God, what exactly *had* he found to pee in? A priceless commode? Archie's gun cabinet?

"And did you wash your hands?" she tinkled merrily, leading him off down the corridor.

He gazed at her solemnly. "No, but I licked them."

Rose dropped his hand hastily.

"Max!" I squealed.

"Ah, well," Rose purred, "you'll soon get used to our funny little ways. I'll introduce you to the delights of Wright's Coal Tar tomorrow."

"But, Rose, he—"

"But for the moment," she swept on, ignoring me, "refreshment! Here we are." She hung a left down the paneled corridor. "In here, I thought; it's cozier. And let's hope the dogs haven't scoffed all the Jaffa Cakes!"

Still smarting with embarrassment, I followed her into the sitting room. A long stool in front of the fireplace was laden with coffee, juice, and biscuits, which the boys fell on instantly.

"Steady." I gripped Max's wrist just a little too tightly as it flew to the plate.

"Ow!" He turned on me. "That hurt!"

"Just behave," I breathed, fixing him firmly with my eyes, then adding brightly for Rose's benefit, "Oooh, Jaffa Cakes, Max. How lovely."

I perched apprehensively beside him on the club fender. Rose had indeed chosen one of the few cozy rooms in this vast mausoleum of a house for our induction, and Jaffa Cakes out of a packet with the boys kneeling on a rug and patting the dogs whilst they ate would never have been allowed when I'd first met Ned. I had a feeling Rose had planned the consciously casual ambience rather meticulously, even down to the newspapers strewn about on the floor, but so what? That in itself was considerate, designed to make us comfortable. And perhaps, too, I was being cynical and they really had relaxed a bit. They certainly looked less tucked up, I thought, watching Lavinia laugh with Ben. I glanced about the room. Family photos as usual abounded, but it seemed to me that the serried ranks featuring Ned had gone. I peered. Yes, just one or two. Rose caught my eye.

"I put them away," she murmured. "Can't live in the past forever, can we? Time to move on."

She regarded me over her coffee cup and I smiled gratefully back. I made a mental note to check out the fossil collection and the cricket bats tomorrow and phone Jess triumphantly if they, too, had disappeared.

"What's this one called?" asked Ben, hugging a huge shaggy lurcher and sharing his biscuit with him.

"That's Hoover, and you can see why," remarked Rose as he slavishly licked the carpet clean of crumbs.

Ben laughed. "Better than a hoover!"

"And that," said Rose pointing to the one sitting in front of Max, quivering with excitement as she watched him for tidbits, "is his daughter. So guess what she's called?"

"What?"

"Dyson."

The boys were delighted with this. "And is she going to have puppies?"

"Yes, if we can find a suitable mate."

Ben instantly ransacked his memory bank for more household suction appliances to cover this eventuality.

"Electrolux! If she had puppies you could call one Electrolux! Or . . . or just Vacuum, that'd be good."

"Or Dildo," said Max thoughtfully.

"Max!" I gasped, horrified. "Where did you hear that word!"

"Pedro told me. Rozanna's got one in her flat. He went in one day and saw it by her bed. You turn it on and it shakes."

"Well, that's not a hoover then, is it?" demanded Ben. "That's no good; it's got to be a sucky thing."

"More Ribena, boys?" murmured Lavinia, getting up to pour and shooting me a faintly hysterical look. Hector gazed, puce-faced, at his shoes, whilst Rose looked thoughtful.

"Hmm, Dildo. Pretty name. Why not? I'll put it to Archie."

"How—how is Archie?" I managed, hoping to God she'd forget or that finding a suitable mate for Dyson would prove as difficult as it was for her children.

"Fine," she beamed, "in peak condition, as he would say. Fishing, naturally, at the moment, or supervising the restocking of the river, but longing to see you. He sends his regards and you'll see him at supper. I thought we'd have an early supper, incidentally, so that the boys could join us. Or," she added anxiously, "or maybe you'd prefer to be on your own the first night?"

"An early supper would be fine," I soothed. "Thank you for including us."

"Excellent." She looked relieved. "So, let's go and see the barn." She rose abruptly and stood before me, sovereign and motionless.

"Oh! Right." I startled. Threw a cup of hot coffee down my throat.

The others jumped up, too, quite skippy with excitement, and it dawned on me that this was quite an event. Even Hector was hopping about a bit, and I prayed the boys would react well, enthuse madly, that we could all come up with some kind of reciprocity of scale.

I needn't have worried. As we trooped out of a side door, followed a gravel path past a number of formal beds, skirted the old kitchen garden and orangery, and headed for the most parklike fringes of the place, I suddenly spied it across the lake.

"Oh!" I stopped in my tracks. Shaded my eyes. "Is that it?"

I was genuinely surprised. Where once had stood a fairly grotty dilapidated barn on the far bank now stood a very smart, timbered and whitewashed affair, complete with a reclaimed slate roof, a weather vane on top, and surrounded by a riotous jumble of cottage garden.

"Oh, but it's gorgeous. Look, boys, isn't it heaven!"

But they were off already, running down to the water's edge, thundering across the wooden bridge that crossed the narrowest part of the lake and up the bank toward the little picket fence that surrounded it. It was closer to the main house than I'd remembered, I thought, glancing back at Netherby with a secret qualm, but at least we were separated by the water, I consoled myself rather guiltily.

By the time we'd got there, the boys were already thundering up the path and throwing back the front door.

"Look, Mum; it's huge!"

I peered inside. Blinked. It was. Because true to the natural aesthetics of a barn, it had been left open and cavernous inside, with no obvious partitions. I walked into the most magical room I had ever seen. The floor was of seasoned wood, the walls whitewashed and beamed but hung with Navajo-style stripy blankets, and the sitting area a square of colorful, squashy sofas and armchairs covered in kilim tapestry; all flowed effortlessly into a dining area with a robust wooden table that faced the garden, and beyond it a small wooden kitchen. Up above, and running all around, was a gallery, and up higher still exposed rafters supported the roof, huge ones that had been stripped back to their natural pale pine. It looked like the ultimate log cabin, where a person could snuggle down in one of the deep cushion-strewn sofas and not emerge for days.

"Oh, Rose, it's wonderful," I breathed, meaning it, and delighted I could mean it, too.

"Do you like it? Do you really like it!" Lavinia was beside herself with excitement, rushing to the windows to fling them open. "Look at the view, Lucy. You can see all the way up through the meadow to the old folly, and then right up to the woods!"

I went across to admire. Outside, a sillful of wisteria snaked about. I smiled with pleasure. "It's fab, Lavinia. Really fab."

"Up here, Mummy! Look!"

The boys had clattered up to the gallery and were leaning over. "There are some rooms up here, Mum, bedrooms, and—ooh, look!" They disappeared into one. "This is ours, must be, because it's blue with two beds in it and—oh! A train set! Hey, Mummy, there's a train set! A Hornby one!"

"Hector's old one," explained Rose. "And I put them in together because I knew that's what they were used to in London." She sounded anxious. "There *is* another bedroom, only it's much smaller and I didn't know if Max might feel aggrieved."

"No, together is perfect," I said. "Just perfect. And just as they'd want. Thank you, Rose. Thank you so much!"

As Rose dispatched Hector to supervise the bringing round of my luggage, I wandered around touching everything, taking it all in.

Stroking the backs of the sofas, running my hand along the granite work surface that divided the kitchen, feeling the soft, thick curtains, admiring their warm stripes of ocher, gray, and spicy red, soft, unpretentious, expensive.

"But the money," I breathed, "I mean, to convert this place. The plumbing, the lighting, and then . . . then putting in a proper fireplace, and all these furnishings!" I knew it was unutterably vulgar to mention the subject in this family, but I simply couldn't help myself.

"Now don't you worry, Lucy," said Rose, quickly coming over and putting a hand on my arm. "I wanted to do this for you and the boys, but . . ." She hesitated. "Well, I wanted to do it for Ned, too," she finished softly.

I hung my head. Waited. This would normally be the cue for a hanky to come out of a sleeve, for a small sniff, a dab at the eye, and then a reminiscence; a story of the day she'd taken him to the village fête and he'd won the best-kept-rabbit competition or the day he'd accompanied her to the sheepdog trials, and then the sniff would turn into a full-blown weep, and Lavinia would rush up to console her. I steeled myself—but nothing. Instead, she smiled, shook her neat gray head impatiently.

"Anyway, it's what I wanted to do, and it's given me an aim, a project. We've loved it, haven't we, Lavinia? Every second. Had real job satisfaction. Don't quite know what I'm going to do with myself now."

"I'm not sure I do, either," I said nervously. "You see, I'm afraid they've ditched me at Christie's. Couldn't cope with me being quite so temporary, apparently. I'll have to look for something else. Something round here."

"Oh, what a shame." Rose looked genuinely concerned. "You loved that job."

"But quite nice to have a break from it, surely?" suggested Lavinia. "I mean, you're not exactly desperate to work, are you?"

"Well, I'll need the money, obviously."

"Oh, but, my dear, I intend to pay for everything here," said Rose in surprise. "You know that, surely? All your bills, your gas and electricity, telephone—you won't actually need much money."

"I couldn't possibly let you do that!" I said, horrified.

"Nonsense. I do it for all the other children. I do it for Lavinia, in her flat, and Hector in his cottage on the estate, and Pinkie in her rooms here; why on earth wouldn't I include the barn? Of course I would. And it would be quite wrong of me not to," she added firmly. "Quite wrong. And actually, Lavinia's right. Now that the school fees are covered and what with the money you got for the flat in London . . . well, you won't need to work."

They regarded me squarely. I felt a bit like Lear, trying to explain his frivolous need for soldiers to Goneril and Reagan. *Reason not the need*. But she was right. If she was covering all my bills and all I had to do was find the wherewithal for food and clothing for me and the boys, the Royal Avenue money would easily cover it. I was grateful, overcome even, but panicky, too. I took a deep breath.

"You're very kind, Rose," I said carefully, "but you know, I will have to do something. Find some sort of employment, just—well, just for me. To satisfy myself. I also have to have some sort of financial independence. Because although I'm obviously going to be here for quite a while, who knows, maybe one day . . ." At this point my courage failed me. It seemed so churlish to mention it. To mention moving on, buying my own house, standing here as I was in her luxurious barn, her wide, anxious blue eyes upon me.

"Well, one day, who knows." I finished lamely. "You've all been so incredibly kind, but I do feel I'd like to do something."

Lavinia seized my arm urgently and brought her face close to mine. "Prison visiting," she hissed. "That's what I do. Honestly, Lucy, it's marvelous, and quite, quite gripping. You should hear some of the stories they tell me." Her bosom began to heave rather alarmingly. "Quite unprintable! And I really get through to them, too," she added earnestly. "Those poor, poor misguided men. I really," her bosom lurched again, "you know—communicate with them. It's so spiritually uplifting, I can't tell you."

I had an idea it was the prisoners' spirits that were supposed to be lifted, but I let it pass. "Er, yes, well, prison work would be lovely, or—"

"NSPCC?" Rose swooped, with a quick, hawklike plunge of the nose. "I always did the NSPCC when I was younger, remember, Lavinia? And we had a super committee. Hugo Ashworth was chairman then, of course." She looked wistful. "He had the most marvelous balls."

"Oh!" I blinked.

"Yes, huge. In his old barn. We used to get at least three hundred in there, plus a jazz band. Or Cancer Relief? That's very rewarding, if you get the right people."

What—dying? I wondered wildly. Or just on chemo?

"Er, yes, maybe. Or," I plowed on bravely, "or, you know, perhaps something in an office? Or a shop?"

Rose looked thoughtful. "I believe Save the Children has a shop in Oxford."

Lavinia nodded slowly. "It does. Secondhand clothes, books, home-made marmalade, tea towels, that sort of thing. I could ring Patricia Mc-Govern; she's very big in Save the Children."

"No, I meant, you know, proper work. For money." God, that word again.

"Oh!" Rose looked startled. "For you?"

"Well, yes, you know, like a career," I said desperately. "Like I had before. Not just for the money, but—well, something for me!" I flushed. Awful. Like some jumped-up little arriviste in a Noël Coward play. Except this wasn't a Noël Coward play, dammit, this was the twenty-first century, and why was I being made to feel like a grasping parvenu, demanding even more largesse?

"But you're quite right," I mumbled. "I could do some charity work as well. It would be . . . terribly good for me."

"Excellent!" Rose beamed. "I'm sure Lavinia can think of something suitable. The NSPCC are always looking for volunteers, even if it's just rattling a tin outside Waitrose, and there's always the church flower rota, of course. Mimsy Compton-Burrell usually does the altar, but you could take the pews, and we're always short of people to make new kneelers. Do you do tapestry, Lucy?"

"Not . . . terribly well."

"Oh well, never mind. The cleaning rota then. Anyone can do that, rub-a-dub-dub! And don't forget, it's not all work and no play around here. There's always a tennis four somewhere, isn't there, darling?"

Lavinia nodded enthusiastically. "Oh, absolutely. And in the winter of course the hunt meets twice a week, here sometimes, which is jolly convenient, but—oh. You don't, do you, Lucy?"

"Not as such," I said weakly.

"Oh well. Masses of girlie lunches and dinner parties galore, then. You won't be short of things to do!"

"Super," I breathed faintly.

"Now. Hector's gone to make sure that your luggage is brought straight round here by Ted and put *exactly* where you want it. Don't take any truck from him, incidentally," warned Rose. "We're having a bit of trouble with him at the moment. He doesn't think Archie pays him enough, which is ludicrous. *And* I gave his wife my old pashmina the other day."

"Not your lavender?" Lavinia raised her eyebrows.

"Absolutely. So watch him, Lucy; he can be rather . . ."

"Uppity," finished Lavinia firmly.

"Exactly," her mother agreed. "So. We're going to leave you in peace now to unpack, and we'll see you for an early supper, my love. Drinks at six, and I'll introduce you to your new au pair! Don't take any truck from her, either. Quite a little madam. *Too* exciting! Toodle-oo!"

And off they both scurried, arm in arm, out of the barn and down the bank to the lake, chattering animatedly.

I walked to the door and watched them go, leaning rather feebly on the door frame. I felt exhausted already. Faint, even. No breakfast, of course, which didn't help, and this vile hangover, but—something else, too. I narrowed my eyes across the parkland, watching their figures hurrying up the hill to the yellowing glory of Netherby. Something to do with turning over a new page in my sketchbook, expecting to see a fresh sheet—only to find someone else had already started a picture. A picture I wasn't sure I liked. I quickly averted my eyes from the house and gazed instead more proximately, at the myriad of flowers at my feet. The sun, high in the sky, beamed benevolently on the phlox and roses and lupins that spilled over the little path, urging me to forget my misgivings and feel the pulse of nature. I breathed in deeply, shutting my eyes and savoring the heady scent. Lovely. Suddenly, though, I shivered. When the sun went behind a cloud, it was cooler than one imagined. I turned and went inside to phone Maisie and Lucas. Let them know I'd arrived. It seemed to me I missed them already.

Chapter Seven

BEFORE THE BOYS AND I FINALLY PANTED UP THE HILL TO Netherby on the dot of six that evening, we were to endure a faintly hysterical afternoon. It had started soberly enough with Ben and Max playing quietly with the train set whilst I unpacked, then gravitating to bouncing on every bed and sofa in the place yelling their heads off, to them finally going awfully quiet as they discovered a long coil of rope at the bottom of the garden.

When I came down from making up the beds, someone whizzed past my ear.

"Hey!"

It was Ben, who, having climbed onto the kitchen table, slung the rope over the lowest beam, and tied it fast, had launched himself off the gallery. He was now swinging, Tarzan-style, from one side of the room to the other, shrieking and grinning from ear to ear. It looked great fun and not as dangerous as it sounds, as the rafter was low and immensely strong, but I couldn't be persuaded to join them.

"Come on, Mum! It'll easily hold you—look, we're both on it!" He swung across with Max holding on to his legs, whooping madly.

"No thanks," I said unpacking a box full of tins and cereal. "I don't particularly relish the thought of Granny popping down to see how we're getting on and finding me flying around the room, flashing my knickers."

"Why not? It's our house, isn't it?"

"Yes, but it just looks a bit, you know. Cavalier."

"What's that?"

"Well, you know, a bit ungracious and flippant. Like pop stars trashing a hotel or something."

"I'm not trashing it!"

"I know, you're fine, but—oh, crikey. I don't know why I've brought all this food; come and look at this!"

They slid down the rope and ran over.

"Cupboards," I cried, flinging them open, "literally *full* of stuff. Soup, cereal, pasta—she's catered into the next century. And blimey, look at the larder!"

I held open the door for them to see and we gazed upon not just a pint of milk and some Mother's Pride to keep us going, but shelves full to bursting with cakes, fruit, biscuits, pork pies, pâté, cold sausages, salami, children's yogurts, and bars of chocolate.

"Yum!" drooled Max.

"How kind," I murmured as the boys fell upon it. "She really has thought of everything."

"I know: let's take it outside and sit by the lake." Ben was already grabbing some Scotch eggs and a packet of biscuits.

"We could, I suppose," I said doubtfully. "As long as we remember to be back in time for drinks. It's quite late already. . . ."

But Max was already disappearing out of the door with fistfuls of chocolate and bananas.

"Hey, hang on. Here!" I seized a wicker basket Rose had left on the bottom shelf of the larder and we piled the stuff into it. Convenient, I thought, as I packed the basket. And there was a rug on the larder floor, too, and a checked tablecloth. I picked them up slowly. Was this what she'd planned, then? And if so, why hadn't she just said, "Oh by the way, I've left you a picnic?"

Nevertheless, we dutifully set off down the hill to the lake and picked a spot just before the grass got too long and the bulrushes started. On the other side, the moorhens dipped and the mayflies were gathering. The lake had that perfect, peaceful flow, without turbulence, silent but for the dragonflies and butterflies adding their delicate hums and flutters to the shimmer. All very idyllic, but—I glanced up warily—there, too, was Netherby, looming on the hill, windows glinting in the sun. We were incredibly visible. Max already had his shoes and socks off and was dangling his feet in the water, his toes large and bleached against the bronze pebbles of the shallows. Ben grabbed the rug and made to throw it up in the air, but as he did, I held his arm.

"Actually, no, not here, Ben. Tell you what, why don't we go round the other way? Toward the folly?"

"Oh, M-u-m!" Max protested. "I'm all wet!"

"But it's just fields and things up that way," reasoned Ben.

"I know, but—so? We could explore."

I turned and set off determinedly. Off in the opposite direction, up and around the back of the barn. After a few moments, I heard the boys complaining but nevertheless following on behind.

The sun was strengthening now, but up the hill we trudged in the heat, toward the old folly, traipsing through fields of watchful sheep, until finally we pushed open a gate and arrived in a glorious meadow full of tall grass and buttercups. I had a quick look around to ensure it was stock-free.

"I haven't the faintest idea where we are," I panted, pretty much on my chin strap now, "but what d'you think? Will this do?"

I glanced back to see that the boys had already flung themselves into the buttercups with the air of travelers who'd reached their journey's end. Flat on their backs, arms and legs spread like a couple of starfish, they gazed up at the sky. I grinned and knelt beside them, setting out the picnic. Yes, I thought, eyeing them as they sat up and guzzled the Coke I handed them in cans, yes, this *will* do. This is good. Thank You, God. This is precisely what I had in mind for them this summer.

We ate our picnic, and then I watched as they tickled buttercups under each other's chins, measuring their mutual regard for butter. Building poignant memories, I told myself. And this was how it should be. Miles from the city and with world enough and time, for once, to enjoy one other.

I laughed as the boys tried to flop backward in the grass without their knees buckling and then, the grass being so high, hiding from me as I pretended I couldn't find them. Later, we lay on our backs in the meadow, peacefully counting butterflies; Max was burping on purpose and pretending he couldn't help it and Ben and I were doing our best to be outraged—"Max!"—but giggling, too, when suddenly a shot rang out.

We sat bolt upright in horror. Then—*peoww!*—another one came winging over our heads.

"Shit!" I grabbed the boys and shoved them down in the grass.

"Get off my land, you bastards, or I'll blow your brains out!"

Keeping the boys' brains firmly in the dirt, I sat up and swung about, terrified. I couldn't see anything, but the voice had come from up near the folly. I narrowed my eyes. Away in the distance, I spotted a tweedy figure, in breeches and a hat.

"Go on! Bugger off!"

"I don't believe we're trespassing," I squeaked back nervously. "My parents-in-law, Lord and Lady Fellowes, own this land, and they—" *Peoww!* "Shit!"

There it went again, another shot, only this time I didn't hang around to argue.

"Come on, boys," I muttered, grabbing the basket, which happily I'd pretty much packed. "We're leaving. OK, we're going!" I yelled as, seizing our bundles but still leaving a certain amount of detritus behind, we fled.

"Keep your heads down!" I hissed as we raced across the field.

"And don't come back!" came the warning shot as we raced down the hill to the barn.

We flew inside.

"Was he going to kill us?" breathed Ben, wide-eyed with terror as we slammed the front door shut behind us.

I leaned back on it, eyes shut, heart racing. "No, darling, not kill," I gasped, clutching my chest. "Just trying to frighten us, that's all. Probably the gamekeeper, who has no idea we're here yet." I staggered weakly to the sofa and flopped down. "Grandpa probably forgot to tell him. Although I could have sworn . . ."

"What?"

"Well, I just thought the voice was familiar, that's all." Suddenly I sat up with a jolt. Looked at my watch. "Oh, Christ, you two, look at the time! It's ten to six already. Granny's expecting us in ten minutes."

"But were they real bullets, Mummy?" persisted Ben.

"No, darling," I soothed, snatching a hairbrush and raking it through my hair. "An airgun probably. People don't shoot each other out here. This isn't the Wild West."

I hurriedly brushed their hair and rubbed dirt off their faces with spit before running up to change. Ben, tailing me the while, was clearly still unnerved by the experience, whilst Max, exhilarated, kept popping up behind sofas with an imaginary gun, yelling with homicidal glee, "*Peeeow! Peeeow!* Go on, bugger off, you bastards!"

"Max!" I came running down in what was hopefully an appropriately chaste skirt and top, fiddling with some beads around my neck. "That'll do. Now forget it, please. Come on, let's go—oh God, *look* at me!"

I caught sight of my flushed cheeks and tousled hair in a mirror by the door and seized the brush again.

"You look lovely, Mummy." Ben's brown eyes were still anxious as he stood beside me.

I hugged him hard. "Thank you, my darling. And listen, don't worry about what happened in the field, OK? I'll talk to Granny. There's bound to be a perfectly reasonable explanation."

"But . . . maybe we shouldn't ask her immediately?" He looked worried. "I mean, she's been so kind and everything, she might think we're complaining, if it's the first thing we say when we go up there."

I regarded this serious, sensitive child of mine. Wondered how many years of him putting me to shame there were ahead of me.

"Quite right," I agreed. "We won't march up there, guns blazing, demanding to know who the devil ruined our picnic." Even if we were threatened with decapitation, I thought privately. "I'll bring it up later, quietly, to Grandpa, when the evening's got going."

The evening got going fairly promptly, actually, with what could be described as a flying start. As we walked up through the park on what was turning out to be the most blissful summer's evening, I noted with surprise that everyone was gathering on the huge balustraded terrace at the back. It was well known that Archie loathed eating outside, considering it continental, uncomfortable, and basically for poofters only, but a table under a vast umbrella had been laid.

"How nice," I said in surprise as Rose came scurrying across to meet me, as ever on her tiptoes, nose up, like a little squirrel.

"I thought the boys would prefer it out here. It's much less formal. The dining room has a way of making people feel ill at ease, don't you think? And the kitchen's so hot."

"It's perfect," I assured her. "And the boys will love it. Oh, Archie." I turned. "How lovely to see you."

Archie, a huge man with bristling eyebrows, was bearing down on me, brigade tie strangling him in an uncompromising knot. As Rose slipped away to supervise dinner, his rheumy brown eyes roved over me lasciviously.

"Lucy, my dear. Looking quite ravishing as usual, if I may say so. Quite delicious!" He kissed me, quite close to my mouth, and then quickly rubbed his thigh with the palm of his hand, which he did when he was excited. "I can't tell you how delighted we are to have you here amongst us, and with these young whippersnappers, too! Grrrrr!" He ruffled the boys' hair so energetically Max nearly fell over. "Little horrors, eh? Grrrrr!" Max's hair took another battering. Archie clasped his hands gleefully. "So! Quarters all right? No complaints? Rose has been fannying around down there for months, so it should be up to scratch. Obsessed, she's been. Sliding off at a moment's notice to iron napkins or some such rot—so much so that I thought she might have a lover down there. But no such luck—*haw haw*!"

I joined in nervously. It had long been tacitly accepted that relations had fizzled out years ago between Rose and Archie. Rose, after four children, had determinedly hung up her negligee, leaving Archie to "sort himself out," as she delicately put it, as if he were simply fixing his own breakfast. Whether her offhand attitude was genuine or face-saving was hard to tell, because the "sorting out" apparently involved a mistress, a rather bosomy blonde called Wanda in the next county, who hunted hard with Archie twice a week, before tumbling into bed with him for some energetic sex. "Boots, hunting stocks, an' all" was the rumor that went tartly round the kitchen staff, with Rose, one assumes, happy enough to turn a blind eye and hand over the reins on a twice-weekly basis.

It was clear that this didn't entirely satisfy Archie, though. There were rumors of further liaisons in London, and I have an idea he was fabulously oversexed. He was quite capable, for instance, of listening to some old crony hold forth at a party whilst absently stroking the bottom of the woman beside him, murmuring, "Lovely, lovely," with the poor woman, eyes huge with horror, too taken aback to slap him.

One took for granted that his gaze pretty much got stuck at bust level during mixed conversation, and he made little attempt to disguise it. Female anatomy was his hobby; he was interested so, de facto, he stared. This evening, however, I noticed his brown eyes were focused on bigger and better distractions.

To my left, a very pretty girl with auburn curls, a wide smile, and a Gap T-shirt strained across her ample bosom was talking to Hector, who looked fit to expire, so flummoxed was he by the attention. Her Antipodean accent drifted across the York stones, and by the way she was dressed I guessed she was the au pair. As I talked distractedly to Archie, it occurred to me to wonder if Rose had selected her deliberately. There had long been some frustration in the Fellowes camp at Hector's inability, at thirty-six, to produce a girl, any sort of girl, of any description and from any background, just for a cup of *coffee*, for heaven's sake, Rose would lament. He went to dinner parties, she reasoned, was always the spare bloody man, and met plenty of women but never brought anyone back. "And he's got so much to offer!" she'd wail, waving her arms around to indicate, one felt, rather more than just his personality.

Ned and I had always maintained that Hector wasn't gay, as some suspected, but just incredibly shy and possibly a bit asexual. I wondered, too, if this recent ploy of Rose's, to pluck a really pretty one, a really voluptuous one, and dangle her under his nose like a fat, wriggling worm as if to say, "There now, matey, resist *that* if you can," wasn't actually a high-risk strategy. In the first place, Hector, being the sensitive soul he was, was quite likely not to get his rocks off but fall madly in love with the girl, which wouldn't be what Rose had in mind at all, and second, I couldn't help feeling that Archie might be keen to have a go, too. His mouth was fairly watering at the prospect now, and he was rubbing his thigh like billy-oh. But then again, Rose was no fool. She'd probably thought of that and decided, So bloody what?

"Have you met Trisha yet?" Archie hissed abruptly, cutting me off in mid-sentence and dragging me across the terrace. "I'm not supposed to perform the introduction because Rose wants to spout some ridiculous tommyrot about insisting she's not foisting her on you or something, but you simply must meet her. Hell of a filly. *Hell* of a filly. I say, Trisha!"

She broke off from talking to Hector, which gave the poor boy a chance to mop his brow, catch his breath, and rearrange his trousers. Just then, Rose came bustling up.

"Oh, Lucy, have you met Trisha yet?"

"Well, no, but Archie was just—"

"Only I simply wanted to say that I don't want you to think I'm interfering and arranging everything without consulting you, but, my dear, we've been *so* lucky. Trisha here is over from Australia for a year, and although primarily engaged to help Joan in the kitchen, she's also kindly agreed to look after the boys, if and when you need her. No pressure at all though, Lucy. She knows you're pretty much a full-time mum; it's just . . . well if you *do* want to take off to London for the day or—I don't know get your hair done . . ."

"It would be marvelous," I broke in, "to know I could leave them in capable hands. Thank you, Rose; you're quite right. It would give me such a lifeline."

Rose beamed in relief as Trisha and I shook hands.

"Hi!" Trisha grinned, flashing perfect pearly whites at me. "And these are the boys? Ben and Max? Archie's told me all about you two." She crouched down. "We're going to have such a good time. D'you know how to play canasta?"

"No, I don't," said Archie eagerly as the boys blinked shyly. "Sounds fun. Cana—?"

"It's a card game, Archie," she laughed, straightening up. "And you're probably a bit old for it."

"Rubbish!" he snorted. "Not too old for anything. Fit as a fiddle, me. Keep going for hours—I mean, miles!" He rubbed his thigh feverishly. Lowered his voice. "Incidentally, I thought I'd, um, show you around the place a bit later on, my dear. Make sure you know your way around. Don't want you getting lost in the raspberry canes, do we?"

"Aw, cheers, Arch, but Rose already did that. When I arrived yesterday."

He winked broadly. "I'll warrant she didn't show you everything though, did she? Hmm?" He lowered his voice to a gravelly growl. "Might I, for instance, be permitted to show you my ha-ha?"

Trisha's eyes widened. "You dirty old devil, Arch! Is that what you call it? What, because it's so small it's a joke, or something?"

"Certainly not," he bristled. "It's enormous! Stretches the entire length of the park."

Trisha stared. "Jees, you've got some gall, Archie!" She suppressed a giggle. "Sure it doesn't go all the way round the block?"

"No, no, not that far." Archie looked perplexed but delighted to have clearly impressed her with his outré humour.

I smiled and left them to their cross-purposes, disappointed not to witness Trisha's astonishment as Archie confided that his ha-ha also played tricks on the eye, but I'd spotted Pinkie, tripping across the terrace to greet me, resplendent in kitten heels and cropped jeans.

"Hi, darling," she squealed. "God, I'm pleased to see you. Couldn't believe it when Mummy said you were coming back. Is this wise?"

"Time will tell." I grinned, kissing her.

"Won't it just, but I for one am delighted. God, we simply must have a goss; I'm dying to hear all your news. And that fab barn! What d'you think?"

"Amazing," I agreed.

"We could spend all day wallowing around on those sofas, couldn't we? Probably will." She took my arm and lowered her voice confidentially. "Tell you what, why don't I come down tomorrow? We'll sink a bottle of Chardonnay between us and I'll tell you all about Ludo."

"Ludo?"

She rolled her eyes. "Heaven. Sheer, unadulterated heaven. You'll love him, Luce. Daddy will hate him, of course, call him a filthy dago and kick him out of the house or something horrible, but I don't care; he's the most terrific lover. But it's not just the bed bit, Lucy, I swear. This time it's much more than that. He's terribly talented, has the most marvelous hands."

"A pianist?"

"No, a plumber. He can mend anything. You'll adore him."

"I'm sure I will." I found it hard not to like Pinkie, unlike Jess, who was diverted only by her name. "So . . . what are you up to these days, Pinkie?"

As her eyes went blank, I wished I hadn't asked. Opening gambits of this nature were generally a mistake in this household, as I'd found out to my cost, years ago. The first time I'd met Hector, seated between him and a pink-faced buddy of his at dinner, I'd lobbed up a polite, and seemingly innocuous, "So, what do you do?" There'd been a flummoxed silence. At length, Hector had frowned, cleared his throat, and said, "Well, I suppose I farm." His friend had regarded him with astonishment for a moment, then blinked, too, and said with some surprise, "Yes. Yes, I suppose I do, too."

Naive as I was, I'd imagined the pair of them astride gleaming tractors, straws in mouths, trusty sheepdogs at their sides, but as I got to know Hector I realized the reality was rather different. Occasionally he'd wander timidly into the estate office to inquire how the farm was going, which was rather like a green young officer straight out of Sandhurst asking his sergeant of twenty years' service how the battle was coming along. I have no doubt Hector was met with a respectful response, at least until his back was turned.

"Up to?" Pinkie repeated, her eyes still fuddled with unaccustomed concentration.

"Well yes, you know. Um, courses, or anything?" I helped.

"Oh! Oh yes, well, I did do the most marvelous Pilates course a couple of months ago. Sweet local girl. I'll give you her number if you like?"

"Thanks," I said faintly. "I'll bear that in mind. But I thought you were living in London now, Pinkie?"

"I was, but I ran out of money," she said cheerfully. "Much cheaper to live here for a bit and sponge off Mummy and Daddy."

"Right." I blinked, taken aback by her candor. But actually, who was I to feel superior, I thought uncomfortably. We were all doing the same—me, Pinkie, Hector, and Lavinia, too, of course, who, having almost got married, had somehow managed to confer Married Woman with at Least Three Children status on herself, which left her far too busy to even go through the motions of doing courses like Pinkie.

And where was Lavinia? I wondered. We all seemed to be drifting toward the table. Joan was bringing out plates of melon and Parma ham, which luckily, the boys loved, I thought with relief, and Archie was marshaling Ben and Max to sit on either side of him, Ben shooting me a nervous glance. We'd been in our seats some minutes when Lavinia finally appeared through the French windows. She held a large tumbler in one hand—ice and lemon clinking at a dangerous angle—and a rolled-up magazine in the other.

"Am I late?" she sang loudly, staggering about a bit, I noticed, as she negotiated the step.

"No, darling, not a bit," said Rose with a touch of ice in her voice. I caught her eye, but she betrayed nothing.

Ah, I thought, picking up my fork. So Lavinia *was* better, on the whole, but the little problem still existed. Even if it only materialized in the evening.

"I'll sit next to you," she murmured, slipping into a spare space beside me. "Because I've got something to show you." Her mouth drooped dramatically at one corner, and she had lipstick all over her teeth. "I've been lying on my bed all afternoon, looking at this," she slurred, stabbing a finger at the magazine she'd hustled under the table. "Absolutely salivating. And I have to tell you, Lucy, there are some dreamy ones in here this month. Absolute whoppers."

My eyes popped and I swallowed a bit of Parma ham whole. "Really?" I coughed.

"Massive," she trembled, breathing heavily. "Mummy gets totally livid of course," she confided, "so I have to be really careful. But when I say *now*, glance across."

I shot a horrified look down the other end of the table where, sure enough, my mother-in-law's glacial eyes were firmly upon us.

"Um, Lavinia, maybe later," I said nervously. "I really think—"

"*No!*" she insisted, her voice horribly loud. "You simply *must* see this one. OK—*now!*"

Against my better judgment and to shut her up, I shot terrified eyes down into her lap and found myself gazing at a double-page spread—of a huge Jacobean mansion.

"Look at the gables on that one," she purred. "Pure Grade One Elizabethan, and with all the original features. And look—look at this one!" She flipped feverishly through the pages of *Country Life*. "William and Mary," she murmured caressingly, "listed, of course, and with two hundred acres and fishing on the Test thrown in for good measure. Not as big as Netherby, nothing comes close, but still . . . don't you just salivate?"

"That'll do, Lavinia. Put it away, please," Rose's silken tones cut icily across the table.

Lavinia pouted and let the magazine fall with a thud to the floor. "I'll show you later," she promised.

"Now why," her mother went on smoothly, "has poor Lucy still got a spare place on the other side of her? And—oh heavens, look over there, another one next to Ben! That wretched girl Joan's laid too many as usual. How very boring of her. Ben, be a love and hop inside and ask her to clear them, would you?"

Ben, looking understandably nervous at the prospect of hopping inside this huge house and finding someone called Joan in its depths, was saved by Archie, who put a restraining hand on his arm.

"No no, that's all right, old chap, at ease." He turned to Rose. "I invited the aunts, my dear," he explained. "Saw them this morning in the village and asked them to come for supper, seeing as how it's a family do. Didn't think you'd mind, just forgot to mention it."

Rose opened and shut her mouth. "The aunts!" she squeaked. "Oh, good grief, Archie, you might have said! I don't think we want to subject the poor girl to that pair on her first night, do we?"

"Oh, but I've met them before," I assured her. "And I liked them."

"Liked them?" She eyed me incredulously.

"Don't worry, old thing," soothed Archie. "They were a bit distracted at the time, so they've probably forgotten."

"Distracted?" Rose's left eye began to twitch. "In what way?"

I smiled into my plate. Archie's aged sisters, Cynthia and Violet, lived in a cottage on the estate. They were variously described as "mad" by Rose and "eccentric" by kinder critics. Cynthia, older by a few years and rather butch and scary, had certainly retained some of her marbles, although it was a bit hit-and-miss when she paraded them, whilst Violet, the younger, had surely lost most of hers years ago. She had, I believe, been regarded as a great society beauty and, as the first female jockey to ride at Ascot, been rather dashing with it. She still rode, apparently, at eighty-two, and also owned a herd of cattle, of which she was incredibly protective. I remember meeting the two women years ago with Ned and finding them hugely entertaining.

"What were they doing in the village, anyway?" Rose swooped suspiciously. "They never go near the place if they can help it, say they're allergic to the fumes now that the traffic's so heavy."

"Collecting their pensions, I believe," Archie said casually. His mouth twitched. "Had a pot of white paint with them, too, which was causing a bit of a diversion."

"White paint? Why?"

"By all accounts they couldn't get across the road to the post office. Apparently they'd written to the local council to get a zebra crossing put there, but nothing's happened, so Cynthia told me they were going to paint the bloody thing themselves."

Ben looked up, delighted. "What, really? Did they?"

"Had a damn good crack at it, Ben. Violet held up the traffic in some long white evening gloves while Cynthia set to with a paintbrush. Gathered quite a crowd, fair bit of cheering, too. Seems one or two of the locals have had the same problem. But then a member of the local constabulary appeared and spoilt all the fun, I'm afraid."

"Fun!" spat Rose. "God, you're as bad as they are, Archie. You'll probably go the same way, too. It's all in the genes. Oh God." She shut her eyes. "Hear that? Talk of the devil."

I looked around expectantly. There was nothing to see though, just the distant roar of a car traveling very fast. It appeared to be roaring up the front drive, with the speed and accompanying gear changes that one would normally associate with Formula One racing. We waited, spellbound, as seconds later an ancient red Fiesta shot around the side of the house and careered toward the fountain below us, performing a hair-raising hand-brake turn in the gravel, just short of the water. As it lurched to a halt, fumes billowing, gravel flying, we held our breath, waiting for the doors to open. Seconds later it lurched backward though, reversing at speed, straight into an ornamental box hedge. This, apparently, was where they fully intended to park, because the doors opened—as much as was possible—and the sisters squeezed out through the hedge, nonchalantly brushing bits of box off themselves.

Cynthia, the elder, was looking immaculate in a silk jacquard dress and pearls, very Knightsbridge, very elegant, until one looked down and realized she had woolly socks and slippers on. On closer inspection, it also transpired that her lipstick was spread all around the outside of her mouth. She marched purposefully toward us, a handbag in one hand, a packet of sausages in the other.

Violet, her sister, followed behind. She was much smaller and more casually dressed: in a red-and-black silk jockey's cap, a shirt that had lost most of its buttons revealing a black bra, a pair of trousers so covered in mud, manure, blood, and guts, they practically stood up by themselves, and on her feet the biggest pair of black trainers I've ever seen in my life.

As they walked up the flight of terrace steps, Archie found Ben's ear. "Not quite like other budgerigars," he murmured.

Poor Ben's eyes widened even more at this as, totally unfazed, the sisters sat down at the two empty places.

Cynthia put the sausages in the middle of the table. "Thought we'd make a contribution," she said firmly.

"Thank you, my dear," said Rose faintly. "And . . . how lovely to see you. I hope you don't mind, we started without you, so you've rather missed the first course. We'll move on to the duck if—ah. Thank you, Joan." Joan materialized to clear the plates, and a brief silence ensued.

"Now." Rose smiled, regaining her composure. "Cynthia, I don't know if you remember Ned's wife, Lucy? And my grandsons, Ben and Max. They're going to live in Chandlers Barn, you know, on the other side of the lake, near the paddocks."

"I know where the barn is, Rose," snapped Cynthia. "I grew up here, as I keep having to remind you, and of course I remember Ned. He was my nephew, for crying out loud. Died prematurely, as you never fail to remind *me*. The only one of you lot that had any sense." She narrowed her eyes at me. "Ned's wife, eh? I remember, you're Lucy. So that makes you Hetty's girl, doesn't it?"

"Er, well. No, I—"

"*Violet, it's Hetty's girl!*" she yelled across the table at her sister. "Bit deaf," she muttered to me.

"Hetty's girl?" Violet blinked.

"*That's it!*" Cynthia roared, then turned back to me. "How is that trollop of a mother of yours? Still whoring her way around Cadogan Square?"

"Oh! No! No, she—"

"Terrible business with Roddy McLean, eh? His poor wife ended up falling on a fish knife, she was so distressed. Nasty, common way to die. Incidentally, didn't I see you in the field today?" She frowned at me.

"F-field?" I gasped, trying to keep up.

"I thought it was you!" Ben piped up suddenly, cheeks pink. "I was listening to your voice just now, and that's how you shouted at us! It sounded like a man, but it wasn't."

"Ah, that was you, was it?" She raised her eyebrows at him. "Sorry about that, thought you were trespassing, you see. Rose here thinks she owns the whole bloody shooting match, but she doesn't, in point of fact. Pa left us that patch of land and we put our cattle on it, *de temps en temps*. Resting it at the moment."

"Oh." Rose clutched her heart. "Lucy, I'm *so* sorry. Did she—? Cynthia, you didn't . . ."

"Let them have it with both barrels? Of course I did. Would have blown their heads off if they'd come any closer."

"Real bullets?" Ben was impressed. Something to tell Pedro.

"No, darling, blanks," breathed Rose quickly. "Aunt Cynthia wouldn't fire real ones!"

"Don't bet on it," muttered Cynthia darkly. "Particularly in your direction." She smiled down at Ben. "No, my sweet, not real ones, I'm afraid. And I'm sorry if I frightened you."

"You didn't," said Ben staunchly, earning an indulgent smile from Archie.

"Good lad," he growled. "Cool under fire."

The duck appeared and was almost totally raw, arteries still pumping. No one seemed to notice, though, and it was followed by some sort of livid green mousse, which was inedible. The evening lurched on, and as I struggled to eat, coping with Lavinia on my right, who was getting disastrously drunk and muttering on about porticoes and gargoyles, simultaneously trying to keep an eye on Ben, who was making a valiant effort to eat his food, whilst Max, who hadn't even bothered, was falling asleep in his plate, I was all the time aware that Violet, across the table, was eyeing me very suspiciously.

The filthy mousse finally disappeared. I was just clearing my throat to suggest that the boys were awfully tired and could I possibly hustle them away when Cynthia roared across the table, *Do your shirt up, Violet!"*

"What?" Violet took her eyes off me for a split second.

"Do your shirt up! No one wants to see your tits!"

Rose gave a nervous little laugh. "Cynthia, dear, language. *Pas devant les enfants, n'est-ce pas?"*

Max sat bolt upright, eyes snapping open. "I know what that means," he declared. "It means not in front of the children. And I know what tits are, too."

"Shut up, Max," muttered Ben, embarrassed. He flushed.

"Well, I do!"

" 'Course you do," said Cynthia briskly. "Every woman's got them, for God's sake, just as every man's got balls."

"And a willy," added Max. "And Mummy's got a string."

There was a startled silence. I stared, horrified, at my plate.

Archie frowned. "A string . . ." he said thoughtfully at length. "Interesting. Let me have a little chat with you later, eh, young fella? Set you straight on a few things."

"Come on, Max," I said, lowering my burning face and trying to ignore Pinkie, who was crying with laughter into her napkin. "We'll have to go. You're falling asleep in your chair."

"Oh, but won't you stay for coffee?"

"Oh, Rose, I'd love to. But you know, first night and everything, everyone's exhausted. Would you mind awfully excusing us?"

Rose inclined her head graciously showing rather yellow teeth. "Of course. *À demain."*

"And tomorrow," said Lavinia, suddenly coming to from her drunken slumber and snatching my arm, "we'll see about those committees."

"Well, actually, Lavinia, I've decided I'm not really committee material," I said bravely, getting to my feet.

"Not?" She looked up, horrified. Pissed, but horrified.

"I don't mind helping out in some small way for the church, or—"

"Flowers?" she pounced. "Only have to do it on the second Sunday of the month?"

"Flowers," I agreed. "Once a month."

"Perfect." She beamed, satisfied. "We'll go and see Mimsy Compton-Burrell tomorrow. She'll be thrilled to have you on board."

"Fine," I said faintly, thinking even I could shove some dahlias in a jar once a month. "See you tomorrow."

I gathered up the boys and we kissed, smiled, and nodded our way around the table, thanking everyone and making our apologies. As I said good night to Violet, ducking under her riding hat to peck her floury old cheek, she held my arm firmly. Looked me in the eye.

"I want you to know," she said, fixing me with wide pale blue eyes, "that I was riding a cow, yesterday."

I gazed. "Excellent," I said finally. "That's . . . good news."

"I also want you to know," she hadn't finished, her grip tightening on my arm, "that Roddy McLean's wife was my bridesmaid."

I stared. Gulped. Right. Well, she was coming after me, wasn't she? Armed with a fish-knife. Riding a cow.

"Um, Violet, my mother isn't who you think she is. You see—"

"Never mind, Lucy," tinkled Rose. "I'll sort it out. On your way now, darlings, on your way!"

She shooed us away, and for once, I blessed her. I held the boys' hands and we scuttled down the terrace steps. As we skirted the fountain and headed off across the park, away into the night, I realized my heart was beating really rather fast.

Chapter Eight

THE FOLLOWING MORNING LAVINIA WAS ON MY DOORSTEP at what felt like dawn. It was probably more like nine o'clock, but the boys and I were barely awake. There we were, faintly comatose at the kitchen table, blearily shoveling Cheerios into our mouths in our pajamas, when—

"Co-eee! Sorry it's a bit early, but I thought I'd catch you first thing," came winging in though an open window.

"The door's open," I growled from deep in my bowl, not moving from my chair, and grinding my cereal to a pulp.

I wondered, through a foggy blur, if such visits were to be a regular feature. Then realized in a blinding flash that of course they jolly well were. I groaned quietly. She was looking horribly chipper, too, in a bouncy *Fun in the Fourth* sort of way, floral skirt swinging jauntily. Very bright-eyed and no hint of a hangover. A sure sign of an alcoholic, I thought caustically.

"Sorry to intrude," she whispered, tiptoeing through in an annoying fashion, as if being bent double made her less obvious. She sat down purposefully, all set for a cozy little chat. "But we *did* mention yesterday—"

"Yes, yes, I know, and I'll be around this afternoon, Lavinia," I said. "But not until then. The boys and I want to go and have a look at Oxford this morning, have a peep at their new school."

"Oh, but it won't be open. It's the holidays."

"I know that," I said patiently. "They just want to look at the outside, get a feel for the place. See where they're going in September."

"Do we?" Ben looked doubtful.

"Yes, darling, don't you remember, you said?" I glared meaningfully at him over the breakfast table.

He blinked. "Oh. Right."

If I'd had one clear thought that morning as I'd crawled out of bed, it was that what we needed was a plan. We needed to look busy and not as if we were waiting for the Felloweses to come and organize our lives. It was important to look as if we already had one.

"Oh, well, I was going to suggest this afternoon, anyway," she said airily. "Mimsy and I will be in the church from about three, so pop down anytime after that. OK? We'll show you the ropes."

"Right," I promised faintly, thinking, But this is *it*. This is absolutely all I'm doing on the pillar-of-the-community front, and then, when the boys have gone back, I'll see about getting a job. I was *not* going to turn into *her*, I thought grimly, taking the cereal bowls to the sink and banging them down on the draining board with more force, admittedly, than I'd intended. I busied myself guiltily in the sink as she chatted to the boys.

"Oh, but how lovely!" she exclaimed suddenly. "You've put all your china up."

I paused, elbow-deep in the suds, and followed her eyes to my prized collection of Asiatic Pheasant porcelain decorating the dresser. Last night, when the boys had gone to bed, I'd spent a very happy hour unpacking boxes and carefully unwrapping piece after precious piece from their nests of newspaper. I very nearly had a full dinner service, which was quite an achievement considering how hard it was to come by. There was a lovely soup tureen Ned had given me for my birthday, various dishes from Maisie and Lucas—all of whom knew I'd rather have china than cashmere—then some bowls and plates I'd bought myself. Most of it I'd spotted at Christie's, eyed all week, then stood anxiously at the back of the auction room on a Friday night, usually groaning as the pieces went way over my budget but occasionally securing something, Rupert grinning broadly as he waved the hammer in my direction, me waving back triumphantly. Happy days.

"Mummy thought you'd put it all up there," said Lavinia smugly.

I clenched my teeth and took a deep breath. Now why should that annoy me? Last night I'd been delighted to find a huge empty dresser, had filled it happily, standing back to marvel at the delicate faded blue and cream gleaming against the dark, Welsh oak.

"Did she," I muttered savagely. There was a silence.

When I turned around, Lavinia had gone. I walked quickly to the open door.

"Did she hear?" I asked Ben, anxiously wiping my hands on a tea towel and watching her go down the hill.

"Hear what?" He looked up from the *Beano*, marking his place with his finger.

I bit my lip. Oh God, I was such a cow. And she was probably so lonely and only trying to be kind. She was walking back fairly jauntily though, I decided, so she couldn't be too despondent.

"See you later!" I called out impulsively.

She turned, looked surprised. Then grinned back broadly. "Okey-doke!"

No, I thought wryly, it clearly hadn't registered at all. Fellowes skin was thicker than rhino hide, of course, which helped. Particularly if I was going to oscillate between guilt and defiance like this on a regular basis.

As I went to shut the door again, I spotted another figure in the distance and realized my mistake. Silly me, open house wasn't over yet. I had more guests to entertain this morning. I sighed and leaned against the door frame, waiting in the sunshine, as, looking lovely, long-limbed, bronzed and relaxed, Trisha strolled languorously up the hill, no rush, no worries, and just about dressed, in tiny white shorts and a bright pink crop top. She was gaily swinging a bucket full of Omo, J-cloths, and dusters. I couldn't help but smile. And in point of fact, with this little treasure popping in on a regular basis to clean and look after the children, I might avoid all my houseguests altogether and get out amongst the gainfully employed. I'd never in my life had help like this. Yes, well, you've never had the money to pay for it, have you, I reminded myself guiltily. Yep. More guilt.

"Mornin', missus!" she croaked as she came in, affecting a cockney accent and tugging her forelock. "Where d'you want me to start then?"

"Air, hellair, Mrs. Mop," I said haughtily. "Just scrub the floorboards till you can see your face in them and then beat the living daylights out of the carpets, would you? I'll be back to take tea at four."

"Silver service?"

"Naturally."

"Iron yer newspapers? Warm yer loo seats?"

I giggled. "What a revolting thought. No thanks. Seriously, though, Trisha, there's absolutely nothing to be done in this place. Look . . . ." I swung my arm around expansively. "As you can see, it's all brand, spanking new, and without a speck of dust to be seen, Rose has made sure of that. What exactly has she asked you to do for me? Polish inside the teacups?"

"Yeah, something like that, as well as being totally at your beck and call, of course," she said cheerfully. "I tried to tell her you might not want me in the way, but she wouldn't have it."

"It's not so much that I don't want you; it's just that nothing needs doing. I mean, it will later on, when the boys have wreaked havoc, but even then, not every day. Maybe later, when I'm working . . ."

"Exactly. That's what I thought, in which case you'll let me know." She shrugged. "So meantime, why don't I clean the place, say—ooh, twice a week? Do the tub, the kitchen floor, some ironing maybe, and then when you've fixed yourself up in the real world, I'll come down and look after the kids? We don't have to tell Rose I'm not down here constantly, and Joan certainly doesn't want me hanging round Her Kitchen, as she grandly calls it, so maybe I could chill out a bit? Maybe go into town, do a bit of shopping, have my legs waxed, you know?" She smiled winningly.

I shrugged. "Fine by me."

"I mean," she contrived to look serious for a moment, "I *do* feel a bit guilty about being paid to do bugger all and skiving off," she said, without an ounce of moral conviction, "but if you and Joan don't want me," she widened her eyes artfully, "what's a girl to do? I think the woman's barking, actually," she finished darkly.

"Joan?"

"No, Rose. Mad as a box of snakes."

"Quite possibly, although in my experience, there's generally method in her madness. Don't underestimate her; she's no fool." I hesitated for a moment. "OK, Trisha. Let's play it your way for the minute, since it suits both of us." I reached into a drawer. "Here's a key," I chucked it to her, "and if you give me your mobile number . . ."

"Oh yeah! Good point." She scribbled it down. "Then if you need me or, um," she glanced up quickly, "if Rose comes looking for me, you could beat the jungle drums, yeah?"

I grinned. "Will do."

She sauntered out. "Oh, and can I leave my bucket? Not necessarily the smartest accessory to be seen with in Oxford!" She handed it to me with a grin at the door.

I watched as she went back taking a different route, over the lake and up the park but then skirting the parterres, head low, weaving in between the box hedges and making for the stables where the old Renault, which Rose had given her the use of, was kept.

Nice work, if you can get it, I thought admiringly as I listened to her rev up the engine. A spot of shopping in Oxford, then back for a well-deserved rest by the pool, with Rose thinking she'd earned it. I smiled and turned to my offspring.

"Right. Come on, you lot. Let's get dressed and get out of here ourselves, before we have any more visitors."

Half an hour later we were in the car and purring down the back drive, which was more rustic and much less formal than the front. In fact, I thought, gazing at the bucolic scene stretching before us into the distance, but for the fact that Netherby was still visible, perched behind us on the hill, one could easily be in the middle of Devon rather than on a grand estate in Oxfordshire. Halfway down the track we came across the aunts' cottage, a tiny whitewashed affair with bow windows, which, for some reason, had newspaper plastered all over the insides. Presumably so no one could see in, I thought, peering. Well, it worked. No sign of life in the garden, either, except—hello, what was this? I slowed almost to a halt as marching down the lane toward us, dressed exactly as she had been the night before, even down to the dirty black bra, was Violet, and behind her a herd of cattle. At the back I spotted a harassed-looking farmer with a stick, yelling and trying to whip a particularly recalcitrant Jersey into line. I stopped, and they parted around us like the Red Sea, lowing mournfully, heads rocking from side to side.

"We're putting them in the field you were in yesterday!" Violet yelled, sticking her head in my open window, a rather hectic gleam in her eye. "So don't go sunbathing in there today, Popsy won't like it."

"Righto!" I grinned. "Who's Popsy?"

"Pretty one at the back." Violet jerked her head. "White blaze and socks. Dear little thing."

I let them go past, but Popsy suddenly bolted left into the open pasture at the last minute, the farmer belting after her.

"This one could go to market tomorrow for all I care!" he shouted, whipping her into line again. "Make someone a nice handbag. She's a bloody nuisance."

"Nonsense! She's as docile as a lamb," Violet called back imperiously.

"Moving them about from field to field every day like bleeding pets," he muttered. "Drives me mad! I've got better things to do. They have her in the house, you know," he said, gesturing at Popsy. "She craps in the kitchen. They'll have her in bed with them next."

The boys giggled. "She is a bit, you know, odd, isn't she?" said Ben, twisting round in his seat to stare as we went past.

"A bit," I agreed, putting my foot down, "but harmless."

As we approached Oxford, I sighed with relief. This gracious old city where I'd spent three happy years never failed to work its magic with me, and I couldn't wait to show my sons my alma mater, their father's, too. Unfortunately, the traffic was so heavy and the sun so fierce, we were all but melting by the time we reached the center. A mistake, of course, since apparently one Parks and Rides these days, but then I'd only ever negotiated these streets on a bicycle.

"Look," I gasped, wiping the sweat out of my eyes as we finally crawled past Ned's old college. "That's where Daddy went. See, through the archway there, a flash of green—there! Look at the quad!"

"Where?"

"Oh, sorry Ben, the lights went; did you miss it?"

"Can we get out?" moaned Max, clawing at the door.

"No, darling," I said, looking desperately for a space in the tree-lined road. "I can't park. But maybe down here . . ." No. Chock-a-bleeding-block. Disastrous.

"Do look at all these lovely old buildings," I urged as I swerved to avoid yet another clever attractive young person on a bicycle. Had I really ever been one of their number? It seemed like a century ago.

"Looks just like London," commented Max.

"Except we don't know anyone," muttered Ben sulkily.

"Oh no, Max, it's nothing like London! See, the stone's a different color, much mellower, softer, and it's all so beautifully preserved. Look at the belfry up there and . . . and the towering spires and dreaming whatnots and—oh! There's my old college." A pretty blond girl dismounted from her bike and stashed it in the stand. "And that could have been Mummy," I added boldly, "off to a lecture!"

The horror and disbelief on the two faces in the rearview mirror was shaming. That I could *tell* such craven lies. I had, of course, always been a desiccated thirty-two and always would be.

"Oh, and I remember that street," I said, peering down it wistfully. "It's full of bookshops and cafés and antique shops and—"

"No!" they roared collectively. "*Not* antique shops," said Ben.

"No, quite right," I agreed humbly, knowing of old that like most aesthetic tastes, a passion for trawling through bric-a-brac stalls was inappropriate in a mother of young children.

"Mum, we're dying in here!"

"I know, I know," I muttered, "but if we could just find somewhere to flaming well park . . . Jesus, this place is a nightmare."

It occurred to me that in London we'd walked to school and that this drive was going to test our nerves every morning. And anyway, where was this school? In the center, apparently. Well, we couldn't be more flaming central; we'd be in the river in a minute. Finally we parked, miles away, and trudged back, mostly uphill, and now in the heat of the day. Max was folding up and emitting a death rattle, but I would not be beaten. I would find this sodding school if it—"Ah!" I gasped, consulting the prospectus with map they'd helpfully sent me. "This must be it. Yes, St. Michael's."

We teetered to a standstill beneath a redbrick building in a busy street with lorries thundering past, tall and towering with bars on the windows.

"Looks like a prison," said Ben.

"Nonsense, darling. It looks lovely. Look at the playground."

"Where?"

"There, outside the front door."

"That's a paving stone, Mum."

"Well, perhaps there's more round the back." I rattled the gates. "Shall we see if we can open these? Maybe we could—"

"No, come on, Mum. I hate it when you force your way into places. Let's go." Ben bit his nails nervously.

I glanced at him. "All right, my love."

I went to take his hand, but he shoved it in his pocket. We walked silently down the street, Max trailing behind.

"Well, at least we've seen it," I said cheerfully. "Rather attractive I thought, in a Victorian sort of way, with its pediments and, you know, fancy bits and bobs. . . ." I trailed off, realizing I was beginning to sound like my wretched sister-in-law, but also wondering what else Ben hated about me.

Food and drink were crucial now, and Brown's would be lovely, I decided, with its palms and cooling fans. It had been prohibitively expensive when I was student, but old age has its compensations. I headed eagerly in the direction of Woodstock Road. Naturally, the queue to get in went all the way down the street, as, naturally, it did at the next watering hole of my choice. We ended up in a dismal McDonald's, too tired even to talk, the boys draining Coke after Coke in silence. As I nibbled a McNugget, I resolved that the plan for tomorrow might well revolve around lying in a buttercup field again, staring at the sky. And the next day, and the next day . . . right. Lovely. And in the winter, Lucy? Well, who knows.

On the way home, undiluted misery got the better of me. What were we doing here? I wondered with rising panic. Where were my friends? Where were Jess and Teresa? And once the boys had started school, what then? They'd make friends, but what about me? Well, then I'd meet all the lovely mums, I thought staunchly. Have coffee. Shop. That sort of thing, except—no, I was going to work! I wiped my damp forehead, confused. But if I couldn't find work, would I be happy having coffee? Perhaps I would. Perhaps I could join the PTA, be on a committee—a committeeeeeee! I nearly drove into a hedge. Christ, that way madness lay, and speaking of madness, I came to a sudden halt in a country lane. Stared up at the signpost.

"Why have we stopped?" asked Ben, who was map-reading rather efficiently in the back, as he had done on the way over. "It's straight on here."

"Yes, I know; it's just . . ." I licked my lips, then suddenly, on an impulse, reversed back a bit, swung the wheel left, and shot off down a tiny lane.

"No! No, Mum, this is totally, totally wrong! That road back there was the way to Granny's house. You should have just gone straight on." Ben turned around, gazing back at the junction.

"Are you sure? I thought this might be quicker. Oh well, never mind; I'm pretty sure we can get back to that road this way. This lane sort of loops." I was beadily scrutinizing the signs at every junction now. "We'll just go back through the villages, that's all, go the pretty route."

"But this is miles out of our way and you're wrong; the road doesn't loop at all." Ben frowned down at the map.

I breathed deeply and gripped the wheel, wishing he weren't so flaming smart. He was supposed to be dyslexic, for God's sake. Why couldn't he behave like any other educationally challenged child, instead of navigating like a demon?

"So we'll be discerning tourists," I said gaily. "I wonder where this little road goes?"

"It goes to Bartwood, actually," he said sulkily. "Followed by Hexham."

"Really?" I breathed. "Hexham." Oh God, I needed to say it. I rolled it around in my mouth, savoring it. And that lovely little *Hex* bit at the beginning, which sounded so like . . . Mmmm. Lovely. Yes, Charlie Fletcher territory. And I needed my fix. Needed to breathe again.

"D'you know, you're quite right." I feigned surprise. "This *is* Bartwood, and if we go on just a little bit further, down here . . ." There was a stony silence in the back as we cruised along. "Here we are, in Hexham."

I sat up and peered over the wheel excitedly. We purred slowly through a pretty village, complete with Dirty Duck pub and a village green beside it. I glanced feverishly from left to right, scanning the names on the gates. *Apple Tree House, Tudor Cottage,* no . . .

"Why are we going so slowly?" demanded Ben.

"I'm hungry; can we get some sweets?" whined Max.

"We could, my love, although there doesn't appear to be a shop. There is a church, though."

"That's no good."

"So Church Farm," I muttered under my breath, "must be somewhere down . . . bingo."

Right next to the church, of course. I slowed right down. Stared. It was a long, low, ancient-looking farmhouse, seventeenth-century perhaps, whitewashed and beamed, and with what looked like a carefully tended garden at the back and a duck pond at the side. In front was the obligatory crunchy gravel drive, and surrounding the whole thing a white picket fence. Comfortable but not grand and imposing, and utterly, *utterly,* charming. I gave a groan of pleasure.

"Lovely," I breathed, coming to a stop on the opposite side of the road. I gazed out of my window. "Absolutely lovely."

"What is?" asked Ben.

"This village," I said brightly. "Don't you think it's pretty?"

Ben shrugged. Looked around. "It's all right. Why have we stopped?"

"Oh, because I have to post a letter, darling."

Handy. *Very* handy, I thought, spotting the red box across the road and right by the picket fence. I wondered if he was here. It was amazing how good it felt to be close to him again, how, just knowing that he spent time here, lived here, sent the blood racing round the old arteries, arteries that ten minutes ago I could quite cheerfully have slashed. But not now. Now my heart was beating right down to my fingertips, banging away like a bongo drum. I felt alive again; I felt—oops! Hello, the front door was opening. A young woman was coming out.

"Mu-mmmy!" from the back.

"Just a minute," I hissed, ducking my head down. "Shoes have come undone," I mumbled from somewhere around the pedals.

I raised my head an inch, and peered. Yes, a young woman in a denim dress, clutching a purse, with long blond swinging hair was turning back to talk to someone in the doorway, who—shit! It was him. He *was* here! I watched, frozen with guilt and fascination, as he put an arm round her shoulders, giving her a quick squeeze, before she turned and went down the drive to her car. I couldn't keep them both in view and, torn between looking at him or her, settled for him.

He was looking lovely, of course; brown and broad-shouldered, his dark hair tousled, in a navy blue T-shirt and chinos, one hand up supporting the door frame as he watched her get in the car. I couldn't see much of her now and she had her back to me anyway, but I'd seen enough to know that she was slim, blond, and attractive, with that long sheet of shiny hair. She started the engine, then stuck her head out.

"Do we need anything else?"

"You could get a few beers," called Charlie. "And we're running a bit short of milk."

She nodded, then neatly reversed and negotiated the gravel drive, turning in a circle and driving toward me. I instantly shot my head down again.

"I thought you said you wanted to post a letter?" said Ben.

"Yes, yes, I do. It's just these laces. . . ."

"Mum, you've got espadrilles on. Where is this letter?"

I sat up and reached for my bag, realizing Charlie was still in the doorway and that, now she'd gone, was looking rather curiously at our car. Probably wondering who on earth was sitting opposite his house in this empty village street for no apparent reason.

"Quick, Ben, here." I reached in my bag and shoved a letter in his hand. "Run across and post it, quick."

He stared. "But it's already got a postmark. You need a new stamp, Mum."

"Never mind, never mind, just put it in."

"This is an old gas bill, Mum. Addressed to you. This won't go anywhere."

"Just post it, Ben, post it!"

God, Charlie was *really* peering at us now, shading his eyes against the sun to see. I went hot. We had to have a reason for being here, in case he spotted the car later, knew I'd been lurking. He mustn't recognize me, either, or think, Gosh, how odd, I used to see her in London, and now here she is, right outside my house.

"It's open, too, Mum. This is just an old letter you've had in your bag. It won't get there."

I took a deep breath. "Course it will. It's such a big bill they'll pay at the other end, they'll be so delighted to get the check."

"But it's to you," he insisted. "Not to them."

"Just post the sodding thing, Ben, or I'll sodding well kill you!"

There was a deathly hush. After a moment Ben slid out of the car. He walked across the road, posted the letter, and silently got back in again. We sped off down the road at speed, just as Charlie had started to take his first step, out of his porch, down the drive toward us.

There was a horrible silence. Even Max was stunned.

"Sorry, darling," I croaked finally, wiping my brow, which was dripping. "Really sorry."

"You swore at me," he said in a small voice.

"Said 'sodding,' " added Max importantly. "Twice."

"I know, I know, but you know, Ben, sometimes grown-ups do have to—well, let off steam."

"And you deliberately posted an old letter just to give the postman more work," he said coldly. "I'm ashamed of you. You're corrupt."

He turned defiantly to stare out of the window. I groaned inwardly.

Yes, well, I was ashamed of myself, too. Thirty-two years old and stalking a man, with two small children in the back of the car. Christ. And I'd sworn I wouldn't *do* it. Said never again, but oh God, it was so compulsive! *He* was so compulsive. And it gave me such a rush. Gave me a dream, a vision, albeit a totally inappropriate one and so out of reach. I mean, I'd even seen *her* now, his wife—and I knew, deep in my soul and without a shadow of a doubt, that it *was* his wife. Wasn't a friend, wasn't the nanny, I didn't need further and better particulars—but even that little blow to morale didn't stop me, didn't dampen my resolve. What was it about the man? And would it get worse? I wondered. Would I end up with a secret little room dedicated to him? A room that could only be accessed by pushing through a false bookcase or something and that the police would find one day, after I'd boiled up bunnies and pushed his wife off the top of a multistory car park—a room they'd wander round, lips pursed, gazing at the gallery of photos of him I'd plastered all over the walls? "Look at this, sir," grimly, "and this." A stony-faced sergeant showing his DI how I'd stuck a profile of me against one of Charlie, lips locked in a passionate snog. And then a muffled cry from below. Someone finding the trapdoor. And the headlines the next morning:

MOTHER OF TWO ARRESTED FOR LOCKING MARRIED MAN
IN CELLAR FOR TWO WEEKS

Or even—quick rewind to where I hadn't gone quite so insane and was just prowling round villages posting old gas bills:

MOTHER OF TWO ARRESTED FOR BADGERING
HAPPILY MARRIED MAN

I swallowed. You see? Even that was enough. I'd read stories like that before. Read them with horror, thinking, How could anyone be that crazed, that inadequate? And now, was that me? Was I in the grip of an obsession?

I trembled a bit, then squared my frail old shoulders. Nah, I sniffed. Hell, we'd just got a bit lost, that was all. Just driven through his village, for God's sake! How was I to know he'd be there?

I found the main road and headed back to Netherby, slowing down for some traffic lights. Lovely to see him, though, I thought dreamily. And so delightfully unscheduled. Really, really, an unexpected pleasure.

"Lovely to see you," I whispered as we stopped. An old boy on a bicycle beside me glanced in my open window, startled. He didn't wait for the green light and pedaled off furiously, taking his life in his hands. In the rearview mirror I saw the boys exchange horrified glances.

Ah well, I thought, letting out the clutch and a huge sigh. Off to church now. How appropriate. Off to atone for my sins. I glanced at my watch. Yes, nearly four o'clock, so time to meet Lavinia. That was my penance.

Ten minutes later we arrived in the village, the boys still slumped sulkily in the back. As I drew up to the little Norman church, I thought how pretty it was. The square old tower nestled squatly amongst ancient spreading yews, the churchyard was green and well tended, and all was surrounded by a low flint wall. This, of course, was where Ned and I were supposed to get married, had the Felloweses had their way. And the Felloweses had surely had their way in all other respects concerning this church; I should think every kneeler had their family crest embroidered on it, every vault held a member of the clan, every stained-glass window was donated by one or other of their tribe—probably featured one or two of them, too. God didn't get much of a look-in, in here.

I swiveled round in my seat and bestowed a conciliatory smile on my traveling companions.

"I've promised to pop in here for a moment and see Aunt Lavinia, OK? It's really ancient, this church, got dead knights under the floor and all sorts of things. We could look at the bell tower, if you like? Might even be able to climb it."

"I'm staying here," said Ben, staring stonily out of the window.

"Me, too," added Max, but he looked a bit confused, as if he couldn't quite remember what we were arguing about and rather liked the sound of dead knights.

I sighed. "OK, but won't you be a bit hot in here?"

No answer. I shrugged, then got out and went up the path to the main door.

I walked through the flagstone porch, feeling the smooth stones beaten hollow with age through my shoes, and on into the delicious, dark cool. I spotted Lavinia almost immediately. She was just ahead of me in the aisle, talking nonstop and stooping, with her back to me, collecting armfuls of greenery from a huge heap on the floor. Her voice echoed around the place, gushing, ingratiating.

"Oh, so *pretty*, Mimsy—enchanting, in fact! I don't know how you do it. I get in a terrible dither and end up with short ones at the back and tall ones at the front. I'm all over the place."

I knew immediately she was keen to be "in" with whomever she was talking to. She scuttled ahead of me, up to the altar, carrying armfuls of flora and singing "Bread of Heaven" in a breathy contralto. God was in His heaven and Lavinia was in her element. I followed her up. She wasn't aware of me behind, and anyway, her attention was firmly fixed on a pretty girl with short blond hair up at the altar, arranging flowers in vases. Limping around in the background was an old woman, straight out of Central Casting, who despite the heat, was wearing a huge brown overcoat, and sloshing water from overfull vases as she ambled to and fro. Occasionally she stopped, clutched the vases, and stared straight ahead, as if she might be on the verge of a diabetic coma.

"Sorry I'm late, Lavinia," I called as I approached. "And I can't stay long, I'm afraid. I've left the boys in the car."

"Lucy, hi." She turned around looking hot and overexcited. "Oh, don't worry; this won't take a jiffy. Now, Lucy, this is Mimsy Compton-Burrell, a *very* dear friend of mine." She beamed possessively. Then remembering her manners, she waved her hand dismissively. "Oh, and this is Mrs. Barlow."

"Hello." I smiled at both of them. Mrs. Barlow focused somewhere over my head. I wasn't convinced she was all there.

"Hi," said Mimsy. "Come to join the workers?"

"Well, I'm not sure I'll be able to do anything like that," I said, gazing in awe at a truly beautiful and elaborate arrangement of lilies, white roses, and greenery, all clustered together tastefully and held with a long raffia bow.

"Oh, don't worry," Mimsy told me. "Any help is much appreciated, and it really doesn't matter what you do. In fact, it's rather nice to have a contrast every week, isn't it, Lavinia?"

"Oh, absolutely," my sister-in-law fawned.

"Wildflowers surrounded by bulrushes?" I suggested.

"Perfect." Mimsy grinned. "Although I have to warn you, wildflowers may not last the week, so you may find you're up here on a daily basis replacing them."

"Ah," I said hastily. "In that case . . ."

"You'd better nick something more robust from Rose's garden. Red Hot Pokers will last a month. I once covered the church with them, but then the vicar told me, in rather flustered tones, that he thought they were too 'suggestive.' I felt like saying, 'What, you mean too much like throbbing members?' Imagine! All those old dears getting palpitations during his sermon. But seriously, anything goes, doesn't it, Mrs. B.?"

Mrs. B. looked confused. Then suddenly she shuffled up beside me. Found my ear. "I'm a bit of a plonker," she confided in a hoarse whisper.

"Oh!" I started. "I'm sure you're not."

"Just plonk them in any old how," she growled. "Stick a bit of greenery at the back, few pansies at the front, no one's the wiser. You'll be fine." She nudged me hard and gave a toothless smile.

"Oh. Right. Well, thanks for the tip."

"And don't let Lavinia talk you into doing too much," Mimsy muttered as Lavinia hurried off to the pile by the door again, shrieking, "More gypsophila!" "She'll organize the pants off you if you're not careful."

"Oh, I'm well aware of that," I muttered back, thinking how nice Mimsy was. She looked nice, too, with her wide-apart frank gray eyes, floppy blond fringe, and huge toothy smile. How the hell did she get caught up in all this? I wondered.

"Just do the business once a month, and Lavinia will be happy," she said out of the corner of her mouth. "I promise you, it takes ten minutes if you're organized, but do *not*, if you've got any sense, put your name down for Sunday-school rota or agree to contribute to the parish magazine, like I did. Just Say No, as the Drugs Squad says."

"God, poor you, can't you wriggle out?"

She grimaced. "I'm in too deep now, and actually, I quite enjoy it. But it is a bit time-consuming."

"I can imagine."

"More ferns, too?" cried Lavinia musically, from down by the door.

"I rather thought I'd finished, Lavinia." Mimsy raised her voice. "What d'you think?" She turned the vase around to show her. "Can I go now?" She grinned.

"Perfect." Lavinia came scurrying back, clasping her hands sycophantically. "Just perfect. Got the idea, Lucy?" she panted. "Couple of large displays either side of the altar, a few little dinky ones at the end of the pews, and then if you've got time," she puffed out her chest, "a nice big fronty one by the door. Frightfully welcoming. I'll put your name down for two weeks on Sunday, OK?"

"Fine," I said meekly, "only I must dash now, boys in hot car and all that. It was lovely to meet you by the way," I said, turning to Mimsy. "Perhaps I'll see you around," I added hopefully, recognizing a possible kindred spirit.

"Oh, but you will. I'll see you on Saturday, up at the house, surely?"

"Really?"

"Yes, didn't Mummy tell you?" Lavinia turned to me with a frown.

"Tell me what?"

"She's having a big drinks thing for you, quite a bash. You know, to welcome you to the neighborhood, introduce you to everyone."

"For me!"

"Yes, so you can get to know people. Golly, half the county will be there! Such fun."

"But I've made plans for this weekend. Teresa, a friend of mine, and her son might be coming down and—"

"Well, that's wonderful," Lavinia purred. "The more the merrier. Honestly, Lucy, it couldn't matter less. Have a word, but I'm sure it'll be fine. I'm sure Mummy won't mind a bit!"

Chapter Nine

ROSE WRONGFOOTED ME THE FOLLOWING MORNING AND rang before I was ready for her.

"Now. I gather you've got a friend for the weekend?"

"Er, yes." I put my book down and swung my legs out of bed, hastily reaching for a dressing gown. "But listen," I said, struggling into it and trying to hang on to the receiver, somehow feeling she could tell I was nibbling toast in bed in a slovenly manner and that the boys were downstairs watching cartoons. "I was going to ring you, Rose, and say please don't count us in. Only Lavinia said you were having a party, so—"

"Nonsense," she interrupted. "The party's for you, my dear, so you can meet people. Of course I'll count you in. Your friend must come, too. Her name is?"

"Teresa. Teresa Carluccio and Pedro, her little boy."

"Foreign?"

"Well, yes, Italian. But listen, Rose—"

"Hmm . . . better not mention that to Archie. Just in case. Although, I have to say, it's usually the men he objects to. Extraordinary the way some foreign women with the tightest possible skirts and makeup that looks like it's been applied with a high-pressure hose don't offend him at all. How long is she staying, your Italian friend?"

"Oh, just the night."

"Oh, just the night! Oh, fine, fine, not a problem. We'll see you both up here at about seven then, shall we? Oh, and incidentally, *not* half the county, as Lavinia probably indicated, just drinks in the rose garden for about fifty, OK? Bye now."

Not a problem? I thought, putting the phone down. Of course it wasn't a problem; it was my flaming house Teresa was coming to, wasn't it? Surely I could invite who I liked?

As I sat hunched on the side of the bed glaring at the phone, nostrils flaring with annoyance, it startled me by ringing again.

"Hello!" I barked, snatching it up and rather hoping it was her. Hoping to rattle her.

"God, you sound cross. I thought rural idylls were supposed to destress you, not razz you up."

"Oh, Jess, sorry. Hi." I held my forehead.

"What's eating you so early on a beautiful morning, then? Not that hag-ridden old mother-in-law of yours, I hope?" she said gleefully.

"Oh no, no. She's . . . fine. How are you, Jess?"

"You might well ask, my friend. The lines of communication couldn't be quieter, could they? I was thinking of resorting to carrier pigeon soon. Didn't you get the message I left on your mobile?"

"Oh God, yes, sorry. Yes, I did, Jess." Golly, she sounded miffed. "And I've been meaning to ring you, honestly, but I just haven't had a moment."

"Ah. How soon one forgets."

"Oh, bog off. I've only been gone three days, for heaven's sake! And I've been absolutely up to my eyes down here."

"What, in clover or cow poo?"

"Oh, clover, definitely clover. It's really lovely down here," I enthused. "So pretty, with masses of fields and flowers and—"

"Air?"

"Oh yes, loads of fresh air. And flies," I muttered, swatting one absently. "And the barn's amazing, by the way." I sat up a bit straighter, wrapping my dressing gown around me. I was dimly conscious that one of the reasons I hadn't rung Jess back was that I'd slightly wanted to wait until I could say, "Hey, look at me! Look at my house, my job, my man!" The latter two were wildly ambitious, of course, but the point was, I wanted to be on my uppers.

She sniffed. "Yes, well, you've clearly got some space down there, at any rate. I hear Teresa is coming for the weekend. I bumped into her in Harvey Nicks."

Bugger. *Really* miffed. "Did you?" I panicked. "Yes, yes, she is, actually, and I was going to ask you, too, only I thought you'd probably like to come with Jamie, and isn't he still covering that European conference or something?" I said lamely.

"Don't be silly; that finished weeks ago. And why on earth would I want to come with him? No, he's home for a bit, which makes a change.

We had a huge row last night actually, about him always going away and me never going anywhere, and at the end of it he said, 'OK, so why don't I look after Henry this weekend and you go and see Lucy?'"

"Oh, how sweet," I said faintly. "Yes, lovely, well, *do* come down, Jess. I'm sure we can all squeeze in somehow. The only problem is, there's a party up at the house on Saturday night, you know, at Rose's. Quite a smart do, I gather, which may not be your sort of thing, but it's a bit of a three line—"

"Nonsense, I love parties. Life and soul, me. And I do possess a smart dress, Lucy, and can be relied upon to behave in a civilized manner at a swanky gathering. Won't gob in the champagne and goose all the old generals or anything gross."

"No! No, of course not."

"So I'll be down at about lunchtime on Saturday, OK?"

"Fine, fine. Look forward to it, Jess."

I put the phone down and held my head. Oh God, what was I going to say to Rose? Happily, Jess was as English as they come, but she was clearly in cracking, scathing form, and if she continued to flex her argumentative muscles like that, heads would surely roll. I ran to the shower in a panic, turned it on full blast to steady the nerves, and was just working out my plan of action when Ben popped his head round the door, distraught.

"It's Teresa on the phone. She says they can't come on Saturday after all, because Rozanna's got crabs or something. It's not fair, Mummy; please make her come. I want to see Pedro!"

Tears began to stream down his cheeks as, dripping and swearing, I grabbed a towel and ran to the telephone again.

"Teresa, I'm counting on you," I hissed. "Ben's desperate for some company in this godforsaken child-free zone. What d'you mean, she's got crabs?"

"Cramps, not crabs. No, she been getting these terrible pains under her arms, you see, Luce. I don't think she should be left on her own. Yesterday, she suddenly seize up and scream with pain; it awful! I hear her in my flat and think, Oh no! and rush down. I mean, sure, you know, I could bring her along with me, I suppose. She love that, Luce, but it's a lot for you. . . ."

I looked at Ben's white tearstained face beside me, eyes huge and anxious.

"Oh, Christ, bring her," I said resignedly. "God knows where we'll all sleep; there's only one spare room, but if we put the boys on Lilos in the sitting room—"

"And I'll bring Pedro's sleeping bag, too," she said happily. "Oh, thank you, Luce; she be so pleased! She been feeling rather low and down in the tip recently; she love to see you. Only few days gone and we all miss you so much. Theo and Ray, too! They send their love."

"Yes, well, bring them along, too," I said dryly. "Let's make a party of it."

There was a pause. "Well, I could ask, but—"

"No!" I groaned. "I was joking, Teresa. Do give them my love, but please, no more guests."

Oh God, I could just see Archie's face if that pair minced onto his terrace, clutching their purses and oohing and ahing at the balustrade, complimenting him on its nice big balls.

I put the phone down and paced about the house biting my nails, dithering about what to say to Rose. Finally, I lit a cigarette—first for days—and sat down and seized the phone, ready to brazen it out. Pinkie answered and it dawned on me I could just leave a message.

"Oh, sure, Lucy," she said airily. "That's not a problem. The more the merrier. I'll let Mummy know when I see her."

Well, a day went by and then another, and still I didn't hear from Rose, so after a while I breathed again and wondered what on earth I was worrying about. She obviously didn't mind at all. It clearly couldn't matter less. And anyway, in the event, come Saturday, it was so lovely to be seeing the old crowd and I was so excited, I simply didn't care.

BEN AND MAX HAD BEEN WAITING FOR OVER AN HOUR AT the spare room window, which gave a fine view of the drive, and a shriek of glee went up as the car approached. Down they thundered, and we all went outside to meet our visitors as they tumbled out of the car. The boys fell on Pedro and instantly disappeared into the barn; then Jess emerged, blinking in the sunlight. Teresa had given her and

Rozanna a lift, so she was in conciliatory mood as she climbed out of the back, all in black Lycra and looking very London in her dark glasses. She was followed by Rozanna, swathed in cream silk and looking lovely but pale and fragile as she stepped uncertainly from the car, a huge bunch of lilies in her arms.

"Darling, how lovely," she murmured, embracing me affectionately. "So sweet of you to have me."

I had a feeling there were tears in her eyes as I hugged her back. "It's lovely to have you," I assured her, meaning it. "How are you feeling?"

"Better." She smiled. "Teresa forced me to go to the doctor, who assured me I have mild rheumatism and not Parkinson's as I rather feared, since my dear old pa went down with it."

"Oh, Rozanna, that's a relief. You must have been worried."

"I was a bit twitched," she admitted.

"Wow, it's huge!" said Teresa admiringly, getting out of the car and gazing up at the barn.

Jess took off her glasses and peered. She looked tired, I thought. "It's no cowshed, is it?" she commented. "I must say, Lucy, I was expecting something a bit more rustic."

"Were you?" I said, thrilled. "Oh no, it's terribly swish, and look inside." I swung the door right back and they gaped.

"Massive!" said Teresa. "And—ooh," she groaned, "look at the beautiful fabric, on chairs, and curtains! Your Rose have some taste."

"I'd say you could have some fun from those rafters, too," murmured Rozanna, looking up.

"Oh, the boys do. They love it."

"Not entirely what she had in mind, I'd hazard," murmured Jess, shoving a rather hot box of chocolates into my hand. "And where are the rest of the Felloweses?" She looked around suspiciously as we went inside. "Mother Rose, for instance? Can't believe she's not lurking somewhere, trying to get a quick shufty at us, keen to size us up. And the tragic Lavinia? Not waving her bottle as usual?"

Teresa giggled. "We hear all about them in the car," she admitted guiltily.

"Oh no, they very much keep to themselves," I said airily, wishing Jess hadn't met them. "They've been terribly sweet, actually," I added, aware of a slightly heroic quality in my response.

"Sweet?" Jess's eyes widened. "Rose Fellowes? Don't make me laugh. Only as sweet as cold fish, surely? Gravadlax, perhaps?"

"Now, Jess, you are not to be inflammatory!" I hissed, hustling her upstairs to the spare room as she dragged her case. "You're here as a guest in her bloody house, so you can jolly well behave."

"*Her* house?" She stopped on the stairs and frowned. "Some mistake, surely, Luce. I could have sworn this was yours."

She grinned as I ground my teeth, then suddenly dropped her case and gave me a hug.

"Sorry," she said contritely. "God, sorry. I'm being a cow already, aren't I? Really scratchy. I'm just a bit jealous, that's all." She sighed. "Life seems to be such a bloody struggle at home at the moment, if you must know: screaming baby, filthy nappies, broken nights, a tiny flat, and an absent husband. I'm sunk in the mire of shitty despair, and here you are in this palace. . . ." She gazed around wistfully. "Seems you've really fallen on your feet this time, Luce."

I hugged her back, relieved. This was some admission coming from Jess. "Oh, don't worry. It's not all beer and skittles," I assured her magnanimously.

"Glad to hear it. Got to get my cynical teeth into something or I shall have withdrawal symptoms. And don't worry about tonight." She winked. "I shall sing for my supper and be as good as gold. You won't recognize your gracious, socially adept friend. I'll charm the pants off them."

I grinned gratefully and settled them all in their rooms; Rozanna and Teresa sharing, Jess in with me, and the boys downstairs. Later we ate huge bowls of pasta and salad in the garden and drank far too much wine, roaring with laughter about anything at all but particularly a story Rozanna recounted about Theo and Ray having a stand-up row on the corner of the road about which flowers to buy that week, which culminated in Ray hissing, "Well, if we're going to have tulips, you can jolly well give me back my Calvin Klein underpants!"

The boys played happily the while, proudly showing Pedro the lay of the land, whilst the rest of us frittered away the afternoon, draining bottles dry, lying flat on our backs in a soporific haze, and exposing parts of our bodies that hadn't seen daylight for months. Occasionally someone would open one languid eye and murmur sleepily, "So lovely here, Lucy. Just smell those roses!"

"And so quiet," someone would murmur back.

I'd smile to myself, and I must admit to feeling rather smug and proprietorial, but I also occasionally sat up and glanced nervously over my shoulder lest Lavinia should wander into view, keen to join the party, staggering slightly, clinking her ice and lemon, all ready with a jolly, "Yoo-hoo!" to give Jess the thrill of her life. Happily, Lavinia stayed away.

Later that evening when we'd all abluted and changed into our party gear, there was much more to admire. It was a beautiful evening, and as we strolled across the fields and down to the lake, the sun was low in a hazy sky. I'd deliberately taken them a rather convoluted but pretty way, out of the back of the barn, through the buttercup meadows where the willow trees waved their feathery fronds languidly in the evening breeze, and then down and across to the shimmering lake, which even the jaundiced Jess couldn't fail to admire. We crossed the wooden bridge, subtly exchanging nature for nurture as the wildflower meadows turned to manicured parkland, and then strolled up to Netherby, perched proudly on the hillside, bathed in evening sunlight.

"*Dio mio,*" said Teresa nervously, reaching out for Pedro's hand suddenly. "What's this: Balmoral?"

"Don't be silly," said Jess dryly. "Rose wouldn't stoop to showing visitors round like they do at Balmoral."

"You're wrong, actually," I informed her. "On Thursdays and Fridays an orderly queue forms and a little old lady from the National Trust performs the task in precisely forty minutes."

"No! You mean there are staterooms, or something?" said Teresa.

"Certainly there are," Jess assured her. "There's even a throne room, through which the orderly queue has to file, heads bowed, tugging forelocks to Lady Rose, the enthroned one."

Teresa laughed nervously. "Now you kid me."

"I do, but believe me, I wouldn't put it past her."

"And you were going to behave," I muttered as we approached the rose garden. It was thronging with glittering people.

"I know," she sighed, "but she doesn't half bring out the beast in me. Look at all this."

We gazed around at the milling crowd, everyone chattering away at the tops of their voices in the dusky evening light, champagne glasses clinking. Fairy lights twinkled in the trees above, whilst below, roses in curved beds encircled the throng, mingling their heady scent with the musky nicotianas on the terrace.

"You know secretly, Lucy," Jess confided in my ear, "I'm a terrible little suburban snob. I adore queen and country and all that regalia, wouldn't swap it for any grotty little republic, and would biff on the nose any cad who suggested it, but this place makes me want to leap on the nearest chair and sing 'The Red Flag.' "

"For my sake, resist that temptation," I begged grimly as we moved forward and muscled our way in.

I'd deliberately timed our entrance rather late, so that, I hoped, most people had assembled and my few extra guests could mingle with the crowd and not be too noticeable. Thus far this seemed a reasonable ploy, since the garden was indeed awash with people, but none, perhaps, quite so gorgeous as Rozanna, in a simple white linen shift dress, slim arms and legs golden brown, her blond hair tumbling down her back, and none, perhaps, quite so trendy as Teresa and Jess, in their tight little shimmering King's Road dresses and slingbacks.

Rose was upon us in seconds. "Who, my dear, is that beautiful girl?" she murmured as I took a glass of champagne from a passing waiter's tray.

"Hmmm?" Jess had cleverly slipped away, and I gazed about, pretending I hadn't the faintest idea. But there was no escape. Rose was pointing a bony finger now.

"Oh, that's Rozanna," I said.

"Rozanna?"

"Rozanna Carling. She's staying with me tonight," I added bravely, knocking back my champagne for courage. Rose looked startled. Clearly my message hadn't got through, but I took advantage of her silence to call Rozanna over. Surely Rose couldn't be rude to her face?

"Rozanna, this is Rose Fellowes, our hostess tonight."

Rozanna said hello, and Rose inclined her head, just a fraction. She gave a tight little smile and looked like she'd swallowed a lemon.

"My dear, you didn't say you had other guests," she murmured, head still bowed.

"Oh, just one or two," I said brazenly. "And this," I went on, emboldened, as Archie ambled up, "is our host, Archie Fellowes. Rozanna Carling."

Archie's eyes inexplicably popped, and he nearly bit clean through his champagne glass. "Rozanna!" he gasped.

"We've met," purred Rozanna, extending a golden arm. "Archie, how lovely to see you."

"Oh, er, yes. I—er . . ." Archie spluttered as he took her hand, his face quite purple now. Sweat was beginning to bead on his brow.

"You've met?" Rose frowned. "Where?"

"Oh. Now. Let me think. Where was it? Um . . ." Archie stuttered.

"House of Lords," said Rozanna quickly with a smile. "A reception there, back in May. Remember, Archie?"

"Was it?" He looked startled. "Oh! Oh yes, yes, that was it. House of Lords. And you were down here, my dear." He eyed his wife nervously, chewing his lower lip. "Tending to the, um, you know. The roses."

"But . . . what on earth were you doing," Rose turned to Rozanna, "at the House of Lords?"

"Oh, I was with my father. Lord Belfont." She regarded Rose steadily and didn't flinch for a moment.

Rose did, though. "Oh! Really?" She eyed her suspiciously.

Archie continued to nod furiously, staring hard at the ground. "Hmm, yes, Belfont. That was it," he muttered.

"Well, how lovely to meet you, my dear." Rose collected herself at length. "Always a delight to meet Lucy's friends. Do excuse us if you would, though; my husband and I simply must go and talk to the rest of our guests. So many people to get around. Archie, come," she called him sharply to heel, and he followed sheepishly.

"Oh, please don't tell me," I groaned as they disappeared, shutting my eyes. "*Please* don't tell me, Rozanna—"

"That he was one of my clients? Prospective, actually, but I turned him down. Much too old, and anyway, he couldn't afford me. Tight as a drum, old Archie Fellowes, but through him I met a much younger, nicer chap who was a regular for years. His loss, not mine. I must say, I had no idea he was your pa-in-law, Luce. Just think, you could have bumped into him on the stairs of Royal Avenue! Imagine how entertaining that could have been."

"Hugely," I muttered grimly. "And you realize Rose has beetled straight off to the library to look you up in *Debrett's?*"

"Which is precisely where she'll find me," she said sweetly.

"Oh!" I blinked. "Really?"

"Really." She glanced around. Sighed. "Rather a lot of people I know here, actually. Might have to make myself scarce. Can't have too many men biting through their champagne glasses and trying to avoid my eye, can we? I must say, it's a novelty to see them with their wives. Amazing really," she mused. "I could clear this place in seconds."

"Well, please don't," I said nervously. "I shall have to live with the consequences. Oh, look, here's one you hopefully won't know since he doesn't have a wife to cheat on. Hector, this is Rozanna Chambers."

Hector sidled up blushing and shook hands, his enlarged Adam's apple bobbing up and down in his throat. Rozanna, spotting a gauche ingenue, smiled gently and engaged him in what passed, for Hector, for animated conversation, whilst I took the opportunity to wander off. I was vaguely looking for Teresa and Jess, hoping they were OK, but I needn't have worried. As I glanced around I spotted them leaning against the terrace wall, giggling like schoolgirls and being thoroughly chatted up by a couple of older, hearty-looking hunting types, who clearly couldn't believe their luck to come across such a pretty young London duo at one of Rose's bashes. Jess and Teresa, minus their husbands, thank you very much, appeared to be having a whale of time and were flirting their little socks off. I watched as Jess, head back and roaring with laughter, gaily plucked a glass of champagne from a passing tray, apparently having conquered any qualms she might previously have had about consorting with the ruling classes.

I jumped as Lavinia suddenly seized my arm from behind.

"I think you should meet Simon," she hissed urgently, teetering to a standstill beside me and trying to focus her pink road map eyes on mine. "In fact, I think it's imperative."

"Simon?"

"Yes, lovely man. God, Mummy's invited some real duffers this evening, I can't *tell* you how shocked I am at the standard, Lucy, and I'm so sorry, but Simon's sweet. You'll like him. Bit of a rectory."

"Sorry?" I glanced across as she jerked her head in the direction of a pallid narrow-headed man in a shiny dinner jacket.

"That's what he's got. Wouldn't do for me of course; you'd be pushed to even call it imposing." She sniffed and waved her glass in the direction of the pallid man's back. "Handsome, though."

I peered. "D'you think?"

"No, no, the rectory."

"Ah, right." I recovered. "Oh, I see. Oh, well then, no, Lavinia, in that case he wouldn't do for me at all. You see, unless it's Grade One Georgian and moated, with four thousand acres and a safari park in the back garden, I'm afraid I'm simply not interested." I bestowed a sweet smile and moved on.

"Good for *you*," I heard her mutter behind me. Then, rather belligerently to a passing lackey, "To the top, please, young man. Yes, I'm *per*fectly sure. Just pour it, damn you!"

Hector reappeared at my elbow. Alone again, naturally, and looking awkward, as I suspected he always did at these shindigs.

"You look lovely," he said wistfully.

I smiled, surprised. "Thank you, Hector."

"Everyone says so. And everyone keeps asking me who you are. When I say Ned's wife, no one can quite believe it. I suppose they remember you years ago. You know, when you were quite fat. With darker hair."

I giggled. No one could accuse Hector of being a smooth-talking charmer, and with such a seductive line in small talk, was it really any wonder he hadn't found a wife yet?

"You'll be telling me next I don't sweat much, for a fat girl."

"Don't you?"

I sighed. "Oh, Hector . . ."

"And she was a sweet girl, too," he went on, jerking his head back in the direction of Rozanna, surrounded now by admirers.

"Rozanna?"

"Mmmm." He sighed. Looked thoughtful for a moment. "You know," he said suddenly, "it occurred to me the other day, Lucy, that maybe I should just marry you. March you up the aisle and be done with it."

I jumped, horrified. "Me!"

"Yes, what d'you think?"

"Well, Hector, I really don't—"

"You know, do the right thing by Ned and all that. Look after you. For him."

I smiled. Squeezed his arm. "That's really sweet of you, Hec, but I'd say it's above and beyond the call of duty, wouldn't you? That sort of chivalry went out with the Indians."

"Oh, I don't know; it wouldn't be too bad. Just think, you wouldn't have to get to know a new set of in-laws, and from my point of view, you're a known quantity and all that. Pretty, too. And being married of course, you've done it all before. Wouldn't come as too much of a shock. Probably know more than I do, actually."

Suddenly I had a violent desire to be elsewhere. The lavatory, perhaps. Perfect, that would do. I informed Hector of this and scurried away, glancing back nervously over my shoulder as I walked up to the house.

Deciding I might as well take refuge in the loo for a bit anyway, I walked through to the back hall and tried the one by the butler's pantry, knowing it wouldn't be familiar to the rest of the guests. As I rattled the handle, a shriek went up.

"Hang on! Just a moment!"

Two seconds later Pinkie emerged, living up to her name, with a hectic glow about her cheeks. Her hair was tousled, and she was frantically smoothing down a very tight little black dress. She was followed, a moment later, by an equally flushed young man, doing up his flies.

"Oops! Sorry, Lucy." Pinkie giggled.

"Ah," I purred, with what I hoped was cool élan. "This must be Ludo."

"Ludo?" He glanced up from his flies looking blank. "No, no, Peregrine Vesty, actually. Delighted." He smiled toothily and extended his hand.

I took it briefly then disappeared into the sanctuary of the loo, locking the door firmly behind me. God, this *family*, I thought, flicking up my skirt and sitting down with a vengeance. No wonder Ned had avoided them like the plague.

I emerged a few minutes later, looking about cautiously and keeping a wary eye out for Felloweses. Happily, though, the aunts had arrived and were causing a welcome diversion. Having roared throatily up the drive—momentarily scaring the party in the rose garden into silence, as they no doubt imagined the local boy racers were about to careen straight through them, scattering them like skittles—the red Fiesta had then spun around the fountain and paused, leaving everyone in an agony of anticipation. I arrived just in time to see it—not scorch backward into the hedge but spring forward, up onto the lawn, narrowly missing a waiter who had to leap out of the way, tray flying, and skid to a halt. The aunts emerged looking unperturbed. They were resplendent in matching floral frocks of an eye-searing pink-and-yellow combination, emblazoned with a hectic bird-of-paradise design. It came to me that, of course, these were the curtains. Hence the newspaper at the windows. On their feet were huge court shoes the size of boats, again identical, and presumably bought at a job lot in a outsize sale.

As we watched them march determinedly into the middle of the party, I heard Rose whisper to Archie, behind me, "We'll have to get them back to the doctor again, Archie. Get him to *order* them to give up driving. They'll kill someone one day. Betty Partridge says they roar through the village like that every day!"

"Awfully difficult to live in Netherby if you haven't got a car," observed Archie mildly.

"Much harder in live in Netherby if you've killed half the residents!" she snapped back before stalking off.

"Actually, it wouldn't make much difference," said a dry voice in my ear. "Most of the residents round here are half-dead anyway."

I spun around. "Jack!" I said delightedly as I was swept off my feet in a huge bear hug. "Oh, Jack, how lovely! What are you doing here?"

Jack was Ned's cousin, a lovely, irreverent, dissolute man; tall and with the Fellowes blue eyes, but with dark chestnut curls and a disreputably handsome face.

"What d'you mean, what am I doing here? I'm family, aren't I?"

"Yes, but I thought you couldn't bear these bashes!"

"Oh, I wouldn't miss this one for the world. I'm here in a professional capacity, you see, in anthropological mode. Come to watch another world go by. A dim and distant one." He grinned. "And anyway, I'd heard you were here, so I thought I'd come and pester you for a bit."

"You're staying?"

"Oh yes, most definitely. Most definitely on the scrounge for some hospitality, but unlike you, not forever. That would be unscrupulous. No, I'm just here for a month or so while my house is being renovated." He regarded me mischievously over his glass.

"Jack, I am not on the scrounge," I said furiously. "I don't know what you've been told, but I was kindly offered the barn by Rose, and for the boys' sake, simply for the boys' sake—"

"You thought you'd be mad to look a gift horse in the mouth. And quite right, too." He grinned. "Don't worry, Luce. I'm just seeing if you still rise as spectacularly as you always did. Just reeling you in."

"Ah, the Compleat Angler," I observed dryly.

"Absolutely, and keen to do a bit of the real thing, too, while I'm here. The river looks perfect. Still," he mused, glancing around, "be interesting to see if you can stay the course. They haven't driven you to drink then yet, like someone we know?" He raised his eyebrows as Lavinia staggered past, breathing heavily, muttering to herself and clutching a champagne bottle to her breast.

I groaned. "No, but I have a feeling it's only a matter of time. I'd forgotten—well." I stopped, guiltily.

"How ghastly they all are? Ah no, not me," he said, shaking his head, lips pursed. "I only have to walk through that front door and it all comes flooding back in glorious Technicolor. Still, needs must, and I have to say, I am a bit needy at the moment." He drained his glass cheerfully.

I smiled. Jack was a university lecturer of sorts, inasmuch as his wild social life would let him hold down a job at all. He hung on to his post at London University by the skin of his teeth and, when he wasn't being hauled up before the dean for reprehensible behavior, taught English and theater studies. He was a bit of a poet, too, on the sly, but as he always rather ruefully observed, poetry wasn't quite merchant banking, and he always seemed to be lurching from one financial crisis to the next.

"Not in gainful employment at the moment then, Jack?" I inquired sweetly.

He straightened up. "I'll have you know I'm about to have a small volume published, for which I've been slipped a not-inconsiderable advance. Added to which I've also been made head of my department, but it may have escaped your notice, Lucy, that the holiday season is upon us, and as such, my services are not required. I told you, I've come to annoy you."

"That'll be fun," I said, and meant it.

Undeniably wicked, and with an appalling reputation for unsuitable dalliances with beautiful women, Jack, nonetheless, was terrific company. He radiated vitality and was the only member of the family Ned had ever had any time for. The first time I'd met Ned, years ago, at a dance here in Oxford, he'd been with Jack. The pair of them had been propping up the college bar and getting exceedingly drunk—quietly in Ned's case and noisily in Jack's—and Ned had bought me a drink. We'd then danced the night away in something of a euphoric trance—eyes locked in recognition of something really rather wonderful—and didn't see Jack for the rest of the evening. The next morning, however, there was a terrible rumpus when he was discovered in bed with the warden's daughter and had to make a speedy exit, naked but for an apron, from a second-floor window. I smiled into my glass, remembering the scrapes Ned and I had hauled him out of.

"And you, Luce. Are you better?" he inquired gently, breaking into my thoughts.

I startled. "Oh! Oh yes, much better, thanks, Jack." I blushed. Poor Jack had been party to some miserable evenings with me after Ned had died. I'd sobbed all over him, and not just at the time, either. Up until relatively recently he'd been subjected to some very maudlin company in Royal Avenue, when I still hadn't quite recovered.

"It took me a long time," I said ruefully. "As I'm sure you're aware. But you know, Jack," I glanced up, "I think I can safely say that four years down the line I'm as well as I'll ever be." I smiled. "And you? Still the seasoned Lothario? Still hustling your wares around the university, simultaneously breaking undergraduates' hearts and colleagues' marriages?" I glanced around. "Unusual to see you unaccompanied, I must say. What happened to that pneumatic Brazilian beauty I met you with last time? She was gorgeous."

"Two Planks?" His eyes widened.

I giggled. "Oh, come on; she wasn't that bad."

"Oh no, not that bad. In fact, very good, in many respects—mostly horizontal—and very easy on the eye, too, but pretty devoid of gray matter nonetheless. No, I decided her best friend, Ursula the Nord, was more of a challenge. A mistake, as it happened, since Ursula was a big girl, much bigger than me, and I still have the bruises to show for it." He gave a mock shudder. "But actually," he mused, "I'm grateful to old Ursula in many respects. She was the catalyst, you see, Lucy, the turning point in my career. After Ursula I felt drained, exhausted, a mere hulk of a guy, but I rose up, and these days . . . well, I'm a changed man."

"Oh, really? How so?"

"It's quite simple. I've decided to abandon the predatory sexual role I've been forced into all these years. I've grown weary of it, you see." His blue eyes widened innocently.

I chuckled. "I don't believe that for one moment! And who says you were forced into it, anyway?"

"Ah but it's true." He sighed. "All of us unattached males who don't suffer too much from dandruff or gushing armpits do feel a dreary sense of obligation to chase the fairer sex, you know. And sometimes— well, frankly I'm just not in the mood. Haven't got the energy. I sometimes long for the days when the back of a neck, underneath a wimple perhaps, bent to study some charming needlepoint, could keep a chap going for months, before galloping off with your mates to have a bloody good battle in Scotland. Must have been marvelous. So much more restful, and actually," he mused, "more sexy. All that pent-up desire and never actually doing it . . ."

"Except with your whore, of course."

"Oh, of course. Chap's got to let off steam." He drained his glass and sighed. "No, I've had it with women, I'm afraid, and I intend to withdraw from the whole tedious charade. I plan to build myself a nice little Platonic world where I'll have more time to appreciate literature and the arts, because frankly, Luce, I'm just a shagged-out old wreck at the moment." He gazed mournfully into his glass.

I laughed. "You'll perk up."

"Oh, absolutely not. No, I'm past perking. God, you've no idea. It's all so utterly predictable. All that obligatory chasing to sustain your reputation, and then when you do get a night off, that terrible moment when some Lycraed bum slides onto the bar stool beside you and bang goes a quiet evening with a pint and a book as you realize you're committed to yet another evening's full-blown flirtation. Christ, the effort, the brainpower expended, the attempts to be winning and charming and then back to her place to execute some supposedly classy maneuvers and prove your magnificence in bed, and then waking up the next morning, surrounded by cuddly toys, with a sore head and no clean underpants." He shuddered. "I'm too old for all that." He shook his head ruefully and sank into his champagne glass again. "In fact, I sometimes think . . . Hello?" he said suddenly, without quite rising from his glass. "What have we here? Rather pretty."

I followed his gaze to where Trisha, who was supposed to be employed handing round canapés, was roaring with laughter in the middle of a clutch of male guests, dressed in a low-cut top and a sarong skirt.

I laughed. "You see? You *see*! Always on the prowl!"

"Not at all," he said quickly. "I'm merely continuing the anthropological study I mentioned earlier. Merely making observations, because study is, after all, a major part of my new Platonic venture. And speaking of study, young Lucy, what do you intend to do with yourself down here? Thinking of going back to work at all, or are you just going to continue bringing up those two young scamps I ran into earlier? They seemed to have found a friend, incidentally, a certain Pedro, and the three of them set about tackling me and pinning me to the ground in a horribly expert manner. I let them think I was subjugated, then roared like fury and rose up like a phoenix from the ashes, arms flailing as— Lucy?"

But I wasn't listening. I was still watching Trisha, whose conversation was clearly about me. She was nodding and smiling in my direction in an animated fashion, and now she was pulling the arm of her friend, a man who had his back to us. I caught my breath, tightening my grip on the stem of my champagne glass. The man turned his head and looked in our direction. My heart leapt up into my throat and rattled around like some crazed pinball. They were coming toward us now, the pair of them, and the man Trisha had by the sleeve of his jacket . . . was Charlie.

Chapter Ten

THE PAIR OF THEM CAME ACROSS THE LAWN TOWARD US:
Trisha, clearly overexcited, gesticulating wildly, and talking nonstop,
and Charlie, looking even more devastatingly handsome than I remembered. He was wearing an elegant biscuit-colored linen jacket, and his
head was slightly cocked to one side as he listened to what Trisha was
saying. Despite the incline of his head, though, his dark eyes were
bright and focused. Principally on me. I felt the blood drain right
through me, down my legs, and away into my witty little Italian shoes.

"Lucy," Trisha called. She flagged me down with a long brown arm
as she approached. "Hey, Lucy, listen!" She halted breathlessly in front
of me. "This guy's called Charlie Fletcher, right, and—oh boy," she
rolled her eyes dramatically, "are you gonna be thrilled to bits. Are you
gonna just be so pleased I got you guys together!"

I couldn't speak. Had neither wind nor words to draw on. I couldn't
look at him, either. Kept my eyes firmly on her.

"You won't believe this," she swept on, "but I was like prattling
away to Charlie just now about all your antiques and stuff in the barn,
telling him how it had been your thing in London and how you'd like
to get back into it and I'll look after the kids and everything, and suddenly Charlie was like: 'Oh, OK. Well, hang on, Trish; I've got this
friend, right, who's got an antiques place near here, and he's looking for
some help. D'you think that would be her kind of thing?' So I was like,
'Oh, *what*? Her kind of thing? That would be *totally* her kind of thing!'
Well, wouldn't it, Luce?" She beamed. "Lucy? Charlie?"

She glanced back at Charlie, but he was staring intently at me. He
didn't appear to be listening to her at all.

"But how extraordinary," he said finally. "It's you. We know each
other, don't we? Please tell me I'm not going mad."

I could feel my cheeks burning up now. "N-no," I stammered.

"You're not. I mean, you're right; we do. Know each other. From London."

"From London," he said, nodding slowly. "That's it. That's it exactly. How peculiar." He blinked. "D'you know," he said suddenly, taking his eyes off me and turning to Trisha, "it was the weirdest thing. Up until a few weeks ago, I used to see this girl constantly. Practically every single day. It was quite extraordinary. And now—well bugger me." He turned back, ran a bemused hand through his hair. "Here you are again. Down here!"

Trisha frowned, confused. "Hang on; how d'you mean?"

"It was just bizarre." Charlie shook his head incredulously. "Literally everywhere I went in London, every shop I went into, every bus I got onto—there she was!" He paused, gestured toward me. "Lucy, is it?"

"Yes, Lucy," I gasped, horrified and positively dripping with perspiration now. Oh, come *on*, I thought, aghast. Not *every* day, surely, and not *every* bus, and *every* shop—that was a little far-fetched! I was aware of the deep blush spreading down my neck to my chest now and of Jack's eyes upon me.

"But wouldn't you agree, though?" persisted Charlie relentlessly. "We were always bumping into each other. Crowded street, busy supermarket, you name it, there we were behind each other in the queue—and d'you know what's really uncanny?"

I shook my head. Just about managed an uncanny little whinny. Wondered if I could slink away and die without anyone noticing.

"The other day, I could have sworn I saw you somewhere else. It was just a glimpse, and it didn't even register at the time, but I've been wracking my brains ever since to remember where on earth . . ." He frowned, bent his head, and stared at the grass.

Oh God, don't wrack too hard, I thought, allowing myself to breathe as he took his eyes off me—breathe, Lucy, breathe, or you will bloody die. My heart was going like billy-oh, and not just with the effort of preserving my world. I gazed rapturously at the top of his head. I'd forgotten, for instance, the way his dark hair curled on his collar like that, the way he was going very slightly gray at the sides, the way—

"And always with your dog!" he said, jerking his head up suddenly.

"Dog?" Jack frowned.

"Yes, you always had a funny little dog with you, didn't you?" he insisted. "Under your arm, mostly, and you used to walk up and down my street endlessly with him. All sort of red in the face and panting. I was usually working at my desk in the window and I used to feel so sorry for you. You were always staring around, wild-eyed, as if you were looking for something. I almost flung open the window once and yelled, 'What? What are you looking for, tell me!' "

I gasped. Christ! Just as well he hadn't. They were all looking at me expectantly.

"Grass," I croaked finally.

"Grass?" Jack looked startled. "You were looking for grass?" He blinked. "Well, stroll on down. I didn't think you indulged," he drawled. "You were always such a Goody Two-Shoes. And now I find you making a drug-crazed trawl of the London streets, desperate for your next fix."

"No, no, for the dog! So he could—you know, do his business. He was a very fussy little dog, you see, couldn't do it on the pavement. Had to have a bit of soft stuff for, well . . ."

"Antisplash?" offered Jack. "Don't we all, my love; don't we all. I always pop a sheet of Andrex down first to soften the blow." He scratched his head. "How very fascinating, Luce. I didn't know you were such a canine expert. I must admit, I'm only really interested in doggy talk in bedroom situations, but—ooh, hello." He broke off suddenly to gaze down appreciatively at Trisha's bejeweled navel. "Someone's had a tummy job."

"What doggy talk?"

I turned to find Jess at my elbow. Oh God, she was all I needed, although I was relieved to see that Trisha had taken Jack by the arm and was leading him away toward the shrubbery, bent on further acquainting him with her sparkling midriff, which he, in turn, seemed keen to investigate. So much for Plato.

"What dog's this then?" demanded Jess.

"Oh, um, Theo and Ray's Yorkie," I mumbled. "You remember, I used to take it for walks a lot. In London."

"Did you?" She blinked. "I didn't know that. Thought you said it was a ghastly little runt. Hi there." She directed this last at Charlie, flashing him a dazzling smile and clearly thinking he was the furthest thing from a ghastly little runt she'd seen in a long time. She shot me a look and waited expectantly.

"Oh, um, this is my great friend from London Jess O'Connor," I muttered. "And this . . ." I stalled suddenly. Panicked. Oh, bugger. Oh, *big* bugger. "This . . . is Charles," I concluded lamely.

He raised his eyebrows in surprise. "No, no, Charlie's fine. I haven't been called Charles since I was at prep school."

"Charlie," said Jess thoughtfully, rolling it around in her mouth, savoring it as a python would a dormouse. Her eyes narrowed and she dropped the dazzling smile. "Really. And how do you know Lucy, Charlie?"

As another huge bucket of red-hot blood threatened to wash over me, I realized that all I really wanted to do was wake up in a cool hospital bed to find this had all been a ghastly anesthetic dream and that my only task was to tick fruit cocktail or apple crumble on the hospital menu. I couldn't believe I was standing here talking to him. Couldn't believe this fantasy man, this pinup on the bedroom wall of my mind, was here, right in front of me, with my best friend all set to interrogate the pants off him.

"Well, we don't actually know each other," Charlie was saying, "but as I was just explaining, we used to bump into each other an awful lot in London. It was extraordinary; we—"

"Look, this job," I blurted out, desperate to turn the conversation away from chance meetings in London streets and Jess's beady gaze. "I hate to sound grasping or anything, but Trisha did mention something. In an antique shop?"

He looked blank for a second, then came to. "Oh! Oh yes, quite right. We got sidetracked. Yes, well it belongs to a mate of mine called Kit Alexander. He calls it an emporium, actually, rather than a shop, which I suppose is fair, because it's huge. It's in this amazing old manor house in Frampton, takes up about three floors. He's always run it pretty much single-handed, but it's getting too much for him now, and he's looking for some help. Is that the sort of thing you'd be interested in?"

"Oh, definitely," I breathed, hopefully not too gustily and not too much all over him. "My mum has a stall in the Portobello Road, so I know all about selling antiques. Jess and I used to help her with it, didn't we?" I said eagerly.

"We did, but that was just a lark on a Saturday morning," said Jess carefully. She turned to Charlie. "Lucy's not giving you the entire picture here, I'm afraid. She used to work in the porcelain department at

Christie's. She's a specialist in eighteenth-century European china, hardly a shop girl. I thought you said you were going to try the auction house in Oxford, Lucy? Or even approach the Art History Department at the university? Go for something a bit more cerebral?"

"I was," I hissed, wondering what I'd ever seen in this girl and wishing she'd disappear. "But this would be a start, Jess." I grinned, baring my teeth at her.

"Yes, but you don't want to take this job as 'a start' and then leave the poor chap in the lurch, do you?"

And you don't want to find arsenic in your cornflakes.

"Well of course I wouldn't do a thing like that!" I laughed.

"Perhaps the thing to do is to be up-front about it," suggested Charlie. "Say that you'd like the job, but it may not be your final career move. That you might well move on at a later date. Be honest with him."

"Oh, absolutely," I agreed, nodding earnestly, endeavoring to look as honest as the day.

"Because I must say, you do sound a bit overqualified to be serving in a shop. But on the other hand, Kit knows an awful lot of influential people in the antiques world. Particularly around here. He'd be a very good person for you to meet in any event."

"And I'd very much like to meet *him* in any event!" I glowed, gazing into his chocolate brown eyes and thinking, Ooh, yesss, yesss, I would. Any friend of yours. Just go away, Jess; go *away*. She would keep staring at me though, really rather rudely.

"I was going to pop in and see him on my way to Bristol on Friday, actually," said Charlie, scratching his chin thoughtfully. "Why don't I pick you up and take you with me?"

I nearly fainted with pleasure. Those glorious words. Pick You Up and Take You with Me. What, in his arms? Naked but for a wolfskin?

"That would be marvelous," I croaked.

"But isn't it rather out of your way?" persisted the ghastly Jess. "We passed through Frampton on our way down from London. It's hardly en route to Bristol, is it? Surely it's in the other direction?"

"No, no, it's not that far out," said Charlie airily. "And Trisha pointed your barn out to me earlier, Lucy. I'll come by at about ten o'clock, shall I? Would that be all right?"

"Perfect." I smiled happily.

Jess smiled, too. "Perfect," she repeated with a purr. She looked pointedly at Charlie, folded her arms, and tucked in her chin, like someone looking into the eye of a storm. But he wasn't looking at her; he was looking at me. Jess glanced around. "Lovely party, isn't it, Charlie?"

"What?" He took his eyes off me and followed her gaze. "Oh, oh yes. Lovely."

"So many beautiful people," she said wistfully. "Beautiful women, more to the point; makes me feel rather dowdy. Should be the other way round, really, coming from London. Is one of them yours?"

"Sorry?"

"I mean, is one of them your wife? Or are you here alone?"

"Oh, I see. Well, yes, I'm here alone—"

"But you are married?"

"I am as a matter of fact, but—"

"Oh, look, here are the boys!" I interrupted hastily as at that fortuitous moment Teresa appeared with Pedro, Ben, and Max. "Hi, Teresa!" I cried, waving with perhaps more gusto than was strictly necessary.

"They were getting a little out of hand," called Teresa as she came toward us, keeping a tight grip on various small hands. "I thought maybe we take them back, put them to bed. Max—he been a real monkey. Keep asking waiters for Bacardi Breezers!"

Jess laughed. "The little love. So killing at that age. Do you have any children, Charlie?" Out it flicked, faster than a serpent's tongue.

"A daughter, Ellen. She's eight."

My heart lurched. Questions crowded my mind. Why only one? Can't you have any more? Or have you gone off each other in bed? How is your sex life, by the way, and if it's not great, might I offer my services? What is your opinion of open marriages, anyway?

"How lovely," smoothed Jess, not done yet. "And, um, I'm sorry, I forgot what you said—is your wife here tonight?" She glanced around, including me in her glance.

"She's not actually; she hasn't felt very well for a few days. Got a filthy cold, so she decided to give it a miss. Probably putting her feet up in front of the telly with a box of chocolates. And are these yours, Lucy?" He grinned down at Ben and Max who were tussling together on the grass, fighting over a can of Coke.

"Yes, yes, they are. Ben and Max. Boys, um, this is Mr. Fletcher. He's very kindly suggested a place where Mummy might go and work. A sort of shop-type thing. Isn't that lovely?"

"Oh, cool, then you won't be so stressy," said Ben, looking up. "I prefer it when you work."

Max had lost the battle of the Coke can and was peering up at Charlie from the ground. He shaded his eyes with his hand. "We saw you the other day," he said suddenly. "I remember you. You were outside that white house. The one with the pond at the front."

Charlie frowned momentarily; then his face cleared. "That's it!" he exclaimed. "Exactly! God, I was trying to remember where I'd seen you, and you were parked outside my house."

Was it my imagination, or had the world gone a little darker? Had God inadvertently hit the toner button on the remote control?

"Yes, because Mummy wanted Ben to post a letter," went on Max, standing up. "Except it wasn't a real letter. It was an old gas bill."

"Don't be silly; it wasn't an old gas bill, Max! It was just a bit scruffy!" I chortled. "Got crumpled at the bottom of my bag. Now, are you boys ready to go?"

"And then they had a fight 'cos Ben said it wouldn't get there and Mummy said she'd sodding well kill him if he didn't sodding well put it in."

"Ah, ha ha!" I tinkled merrily as Jess raised her eyebrows. "Yes, well, I'm sure Mr. Fletcher doesn't want to hear all our domestic trials and tribulations. Come along, Max." I damn near dislocated his shoulder as I yanked him around.

"Oh, but on the contrary, it all sounds remarkably familiar," said Charlie with a grin. "I have a similar sort of brown envelope syndrome, in that I simply can't open them. Leave them rotting away in the bottom of drawers. I must say, I've never thought of sending the buggers back. That's inspired!" He smiled down at Max. "I was just telling your mum, I have a daughter not much older than you. She's eight."

"Then that's much older than me. I'm only four and a half. But I'm very mature for my age." He straightened up. "Very well developed."

"Of course you are," Charlie chuckled. Then in an aside to me—"I believe that's what's known as a bit of a handful?"

"Oh no, much more than that," I admitted. "A handful would be a very meager quantity to relate to Max. More like a truckful. In fact, I'm not sure I contain him at all, sometimes."

"Ah. So it's 'wait till your father gets home,' is it?"

"No, no, his father's dead. Ned died four years ago."

"Oh. I'm sorry."

There was a silence. He looked at me for a long moment and I believe he meant it. His eyes were warm and sincere, and it seemed to me that despite Jess, Teresa, and the boys standing around, something unspoken passed between us. I know I was gazing at him pretty feverishly, but it wasn't just that. Surely his eyes were resting on me equally appreciatively, and with a certain amount of unashamed interest, too?

"Right, let's go then," said Jess, breaking the moment. "The boys are exhausted and I think we've pretty much exhausted this party, too. Rozanna's gone on ahead already, so . . ." She turned to Charlie and gave him a sweet but dangerous smile. "Good-bye. It was lovely to meet you."

"Lovely to meet you, too." He smiled back, seemingly oblivious. Then he turned to me. "Bye, Lucy." He leaned forward and brushed my cheek quickly with his lips. "See you Friday, then."

"Yes!" I gasped. "Super."

"Bye, boys." He gave them a cheery wave. "Teresa." He nodded. Then raising his glass, he turned and walked back into the party.

I stood for a few moments, watching him go. Mesmerized. Paralyzed. When I turned back, the others had gone. I slipped off my shoes and followed them, walking quickly back down the grassy slope, shoes in hand, until I caught up. We went on through the park toward the lake together in uneasy silence.

"Race you back, boys!" Teresa cried suddenly, knowing the air had to be sliced.

The boys yelped and raced off as she ran on ahead of them. That left just Jess and me. She folded her arms and dredged up a great sigh.

"Oh, Lucy. Be careful. Be very, very careful."

"Hmmm?" My face, I could tell, was still flushed, so I didn't look at her but concentrated instead on the boys racing ahead, affecting to misunderstand. My heart was thumping.

"That man. You know what I mean. Jesus, even I felt the heat back there, and I've had a baby. Been impervious to that sort of thing for months."

"Did you?" I stopped. Touched her arm. "It wasn't just me then? Wasn't my imagination? You could sense something, too?"

She laughed dryly. Shook my hand off and walked on. "Oh yeah. I sensed something all right. Something with a few thousand volts attached to it, and both ways, too. Look, Lucy," she struggled. "I don't always want to be the cold water pourer, the voice of your conscience, and I know you've had a really rough time and deserve some happiness, but you *know* what I'm going to say."

I tilted my hot face up to the cool blue vault of the heavens. "I know," I murmured. "He's married. But, Jess, surely, if you're right, if we're both right, and there was something electric going on back there, then ..." I hesitated. "Then surely it follows that there's something wrong? I mean, with the marriage?" I said hopefully.

"What, because a man looks at a pretty girl like that at a party? Do me a favor; it can be the most blissful of domestic setups and lightning can still strike if circumstances allow it. Doesn't mean there's something wrong with the marriage, just that temptation is in the way. A boozy party, a conference abroad . . . that's what's so frightening."

"You're talking about you and Jamie now," I muttered.

"Yes," she sighed. "Maybe I am. And maybe the reason I'm eaten up with jealousy and suspicion is because he has the sort of life where it *can* happen, where lightning *can* strike, and I don't." She narrowed her eyes thoughtfully. "And part of me believes he is faithful, actually. It's just—well, OK, suppose he was at a party, right, like the one we've just been to tonight, and some single girl starts making goo-goo eyes at him like you've just done to Charlie, well, in a way, what's the poor sod supposed to do? He's only a man, for Christ's sake. A pathetic pulse on legs, programmed to act on impulse. So where does that leave me? And where does it leave Charlie's wife? Alone, at home, with the kid, nursing a rotten cold and unaware that some predatory hussy is eyeing up her husband and arranging a date for Monday."

"It's not a date," I muttered. "It's to see about a job."

"Which under normal circumstances you wouldn't even consider," she scoffed.

I struggled to be honest. "Maybe not, and certainly not in London, but, Jess, something about this whole situation makes me want to—need to—take it a step further. I have to—well, just peer around the corner. I can't stop now."

"If you can't stop now, you'll be totally out of control later," she observed sourly. "This is the best time, Lucy, believe me. On this first corner. This is the time to ring him up and say, 'Actually, forget it, mate. Don't come. I'll sort out my own job, thanks very much.'"

We'd arrived at the garden gate now and Rozanna, who'd got back earlier, was opening the barn door for the others.

"The awful thing is, I know you're right. It's just—"

"It's just you're still basking in the afterglow of your titillating conversation back there, longing to go to bed and hug it to yourself. Longing to marvel at the wonder of it all, knowing you haven't felt like this for four years."

"Yes!" I breathed, turning to her. "That's it."

"And you're remembering how it feels to have a devastatingly handsome man look at you like that, kiss your cheek like that."

"Yes. Exactly, Jess."

"And because no one's ever come remotely close to making you feel so alive and excited since Ned died—"

"Yes?"

"You want to know if this feeling is for real. See if you really *can* unfurl your dry old roots and drink again, but of course, you wouldn't do anything silly. Nothing unwholesome. Wouldn't go the whole hog with this guy, nothing naked and horizontal."

"That's it exactly, Jess! I wouldn't. Really I wouldn't."

"Bollocks," she scoffed. "You're a lost cause, Luce; you know that, don't you? Sunk without a snorkel. Because take it from me, my friend, the moment your bum hits that seat in that quaint little country pub, which is where you'll undoubtedly end up just as soon as you've gone through the spurious motions of meeting your future employer, the moment your eyes lock over that bottle of Chablis and that basket of scampi—"

"Coo-eeee!"

A cry rang out through the dark valley. Jess stopped, mid-flow. We swung around together in surprise. As we peered down the hill in the half light, I saw Rose coming up behind us. She was teetering unsteadily through the buttercup meadow in very high heels and waving wildly.

"Christ. That's all we bleeding need," muttered Jess.

Suddenly I felt awful. God, I hadn't even said good-bye to Rose. I'd been so preoccupied with Charlie, I hadn't even thanked her for the party, which had been in my honor, for heaven's sake! I hurried down to meet her in bare feet as she came panting up toward me, one hand clutching a lace hanky to her chest.

"Oh, Rose! I'm so sorry; how awful of me! I didn't come and find you to thank you. And it was such a lovely party, really it was, but the boys were a bit tired, so we thought we'd slip away without breaking it up." I took her arm anxiously as we walked the rest of the way to the barn together.

"Oh, absolutely," she panted, waving away my apology with her hanky. "Quite right, you had to get the boys back as you say, quite right and proper. Although I have to say, young Trisha should have done that for you. I asked her to take them back if needs be; that's why she was there, for pity's sake, not to chat up my nephew, which is what she's doing now!"

I smiled, remembering Jack's eyes glinting in the light of the tummy button stone. "Oh, I don't suppose he minds."

"Well, of course he doesn't! Right up his alleyway, that little minx. But what about you, Lucy?" She looked anxious. "Did you meet anyone nice? Simon Firmly-Williams, for instance?" she added hopefully.

Ah yes, the handsome rectory.

"Well, I certainly *saw* him, Rose. Lavinia pointed him out, and he looked awfully nice, but you know, there were so many people there, and it is quite hard to get around. To have a proper chat at a drinks party . . ."

"Yes, yes," she agreed, "terribly difficult. Maybe I'll have a dinner party next time," she mused. "Much more intimate. Be a bit more select. Then you can meet people properly."

"That would be lovely," I said faintly.

"But meanwhile," she said, clasping her hands together firmly, "what I actually came to say is that you can't *possibly* all squeeze in here tonight, when we have so much room up at the house. Where were you all planning to sleep, for heaven's sake?"

"Jess and I were going to share, and Teresa and Rozanna—"

"No, no, I won't hear of it! Ah, here's Ted." She turned. "He's come to take the bags back. Ted! Come. Quickly now." She beckoned him on impatiently as, mute and resentful, he shuffled obediently up the hill toward us. "Now, Jess." Rose turned to her purposefully. "Why don't you come back?"

"Oh, but, Rose, we're perfectly happy," I objected. "We like being together."

"Don't be silly, all hugger-mugger, Lucy? When there's bags of room up at Netherby? You don't *want* to share double beds, surely?"

She regarded me in horror, as if perhaps I were an unhygienic lesbian or something. Teresa stifled a giggle beside me. I blushed.

"Well, no, but—"

"No, exactly. I thought not. Now, Ted. Kindly go and get Lady Rozanna's bag from upstairs please, she'll show you where, and, Jess, where are your things?"

"My God, she really has looked me up," muttered Rozanna as she filed past me to beat Ted to her belongings.

"And I, of course, will stay here with my son." Teresa smiled firmly. Rose looked at her as if she were something nasty that had crawled out of the woodshed. "Yes, yes, of course. I suppose that does make sense. You brought a friend for Ben, didn't you?" she said, as if that had been Teresa's sole function. "So. You can stay here, and Jess and Rozanna can come back to Netherby and have their own bedrooms. We have got some guests from the party staying, but there's plenty of room. So. That's much better. Right. Everyone got their bags? Come along then, my party. Rozanna, can you manage?"

Rozanna, carrying the tiniest of handbags, shot me a hysterical look as she came out of the barn, whilst Jess, emerging with her canvas sack over her shoulder, shot me one of horror. I shrugged helplessly back. Rose was already making her way down the hill, with Ted carrying Rozanna's case. Jess and Rozanna hesitated.

"Must we?" muttered Jess.

"I think it might be politic," I muttered back.

"Ah. And it's as well to be politic, is it?"

This was Jess's parting shot, together with raised eyebrows, and although I grinned, I have to say I wasn't too distressed to see her go.

Teresa and I stood at the gate as they went down the hill. Teresa giggled suddenly. "She all over Rozanna, that Rose," she observed as Rose turned to wait for Rozanna at the bottom, smiling up effusively. "But my God, she *die* if she had any idea . . ."

"Well, quite," I agreed nervously.

We watched until they got to the lake, then turned and went inside, shooing the boys upstairs to do their teeth. All of a sudden I felt rather relieved to have Teresa to myself.

"And she also," went on Teresa thoughtfully, "seem very keen, I think, for you to meet someone. Some man. Very much the Mrs. Bennet, yes?"

"Oh very much," I agreed.

"Which surprise me, really. When you think, you once married to her so beloved son?"

I shrugged. "I suppose she thinks it's inevitable, Teresa. And because of the boys, she wants to do the choosing." I smiled wryly. "At least, that's what Jess says."

Teresa smiled. "Jess have an awful lot to say on many, many subjects." She glanced at me knowingly. "But you know, sometimes you have to make your own way. Make your own choices. Mistakes even, too."

I hugged her shoulder as we followed the boys upstairs. "And sometimes," I grinned, "I'm glad I have such wise old friends."

Chapter Eleven

TERESA AND I SAT IN THE SUNNY FRONT GARDEN THE following morning, relaxing and enjoying an extremely late breakfast as the boys played in the woods. Suddenly we paused in our chatter for a moment, lowered our coffee cups, and peered. Two heads were beginning to emerge above the long grass beyond the garden, and seconds later Rozanna and Jess appeared, struggling up the hill toward us, dragging their cases and giggling wildly.

"Couldn't you get your batman to bring those for you?" I called.

"No time," gasped Jess. "Had to escape. God, it was like Colditz up there, with Kommandant Rose in full swing."

"She certainly takes a bit of laughing off, doesn't she?" panted Rozanna, flopping down into a spare Lloyd Loom chair, head thrown back, arms hanging limply. "Anyone would think she'd had a sniff at something, she's so fizzed up. So unrelaxing, first thing. Ooh, yes please, proper coffee." She sat up and took the cup I offered her gratefully. "I swear, you could stand your spoon up in the stuff they gave us up there. Thanks, Lucy."

"And lovely croissants, too," said Jess greedily, reaching across for the basket as she dragged up a chair. "God, you should have seen our morning fare. We had to present ourselves at the sea of polished mahogany and wade through mountains of cold, yuk-a-roony kedgeree. Puke."

"And then listen to Lady R. berating poor Lavinia and Pinkie for not snapping up a man apiece last night," said Rozanna.

"Except that the poor woman's clearly blind," put in Jess tartly. "Judging by Pinkie's neck, she went off piste early and snapped up quite a few in the bushes. Mmm . . . this is yummy." She paused to wipe dripping butter off her chin.

"Ah. So, postmatch analysis suggests the party was not entirely to Her Ladyship's liking?" I hazarded nervously.

"Hardly," said Jess darkly. "Having ripped her daughters to shreds, she then had a go at poor old Hector. He really got it in the neck, and all because he hadn't talked to some girl called Sophia Lennox-something, who'd come all the way from Cirencester to see him, and who was in possession of, and I quote, 'the most marvelous seat I've ever seen!'"

"What, ancestral or on a horse?"

"Who knows? Either way, it was all Greek to me, but pure Georgette Heyer. Anyway, clearly Hector had bogged his big chance and is firmly in the doghouse."

"To which he crawled, apologizing profusely, blushing, and stammering?"

"No, he didn't actually. It was really rather surprising." Jess cocked her head thoughtfully and chewed hard. "He told his mother to shut up and keep her bloody nose out of his personal life. Then he stormed out of the room."

"Blimey! That's a turn-up for the books. Completely out of character."

"Well, quite. But then, undaunted," Jess sat up straight, clearly enjoying herself now, "old Rose turned her big guns on those poor, sweet aunts. Oh, they got a thorough going-over. The moment they tottered into that dining room—still, incidentally, in the curtains and jewels they were wearing last night—Rose demanded they delve straight into their handbags and hand over their driving licenses!"

"Oh, for God's sake. I can't believe they did that."

"Certainly not. But there was a terrible row, with Cynthia, quite rightly I thought, demanding that if they did, then Lavinia should be made to surrender her gin bottles, which made her a menace in her Volvo after six o'clock at night, and that Pinkie should hand over her contraceptive pills since—and get this—the threat of getting pregnant might stop her fornicating in the bushes and distracting local motorists. It was all pretty squiffy logic but hugely entertaining. Anyway, Rose banged on a bit more about wanting them off the road and Archie kept his head buried in the *Telegraph* at the other end of the table, and then finally Jack saved the day by suggesting the aunts simply had a warning on their car. 'What, like L plates?' Lady R. demanded, spraying egg through her teeth. 'Exactly,' said Jack. And then dear old Violet widened her pale blue eyes and said, 'Oh, I see. So we could have M for Mad.'"

"Oh God!" I snorted into my coffee.

"Well, Rose was beside herself then. 'You see!' she shrieked, standing up and pointing a quivering finger. 'Even *they* know it! Why doesn't anyone listen to me?' "

"So what happened?"

"A compromise was finally reached, and after breakfast the aunts sped away in a cloud of dust with a sign, made by Jack, slapped to their rear window. It read: BEWARE. IF THEY HAVEN'T KILLED YOU YET, THEY WILL SOON. They were really rather pleased with it actually. Thought it gave fair warning but was suitably macho and punchy."

"Oh, dear," giggled Rozanna, wiping a tear from her eye. "Such a bizarre family. If one didn't know better, one could swear they were terribly aristocratic; they have all the hallmarks. But you know, Lucy, they're really not very grand at all. Frightfully parvenu."

I put my coffee cup down. "How d'you mean?"

"Well, I looked *them* up while I was having a bath—I got the most sumptuous room and en suite in the place, I might add; she clearly wants to be *my* best friend—and I don't know what Ned told you, but they're only first-generation. Quite the arrivistes."

"Ned didn't tell me anything. He wasn't particularly interested."

"Well, Archie's a self-made man like his father before him. Made his fortune marketing frozen pies or something—very definitely 'trade'— and was given a gong by the then prime minister for services rendered to catering, and Rose doesn't even exist. She's actually only entitled to call herself Lady Fellowes by virtue of her marriage to Archie, and not Lady Rose, which she appears to have affected and which would suggest she's the daughter of an earl—which, my dears, she clearly ain't."

"That would explain the rather hectic pink bathrooms and thick carpets upstairs," mused Jess. "I'm no aficionado of these things, but I had a feeling it wasn't quite the ticket."

"Oh, absolutely not," agreed Rozanna. "There are severe lapses of taste dotted all around that house. Look at all that Dralon in the drawing room, and even the house has a façade. It's not really Georgian at all."

"How strange," I pondered. "I'd always heard that she'd . . . well. Rather married beneath her, as she would say."

"All spin," said Rozanna firmly. "She dreamed it up long ago and

has somehow maintained the fiction over the years. Her obsessive snob-
bery lets her down, too, actually. Reeks of social insecurity. The real
McCoy are far more relaxed and wouldn't give a toss if you used the
wrong knife, or threw in the odd 'serviette' or 'pardon.' "

"I wonder who she was before?" I mused, biting into a peach. "I
mean, before she met Archie."

"Word has it," said a low voice in my ear, "that she was a topless lap
dancer in a nightclub."

I swung around in horror. "Jack!" I gasped. "You made that up!"

"Of course I did," he said cheerfully, swinging an elegant denim leg
over the bench beside me and helping himself to a croissant. "But why
let the boring truth stand in the way of a good lie? No, if you really want
to know, according to my aged pa, she was just a rather ordinary tennis-
club type who hung about on shooting weekends awaiting her big
chance. Pretty, but faintly tedious. Until she got her hooks into Archie,
of course, when she became excessively tedious."

"I prefer the lap dancing," giggled Teresa.

"Oh, me, too," agreed Jack. "And that's why rumors start, you
know, Luce, particularly scurrilous ones, because they're far more entertaining. You have to be very, very careful, particularly when you get
into strange men's cars, for instance. People will construe all sorts of
things." His blue eyes twinkled at me as he chewed away.

I stared. Strange men's cars? What the . . . oh, for God's sake! Jess
went pink and hurriedly attended to something crucial deep in her
handbag. Clearly a briefing session had gone on over breakfast.

"I see," I said evenly. "I should be more careful, should I? You mean,
as careful as you've been throughout your colorful career, eh, Jack? Do
tell me, how is the erotic alternative to Mary Poppins shaping up?"

"Now, now, no need to be catty." He grinned. "She's training to be
a nurse back home, I'll have you know, just over here as an au pair to
earn some extra ackers. But since you ask, she's shaping up very nicely,
thank you. I've been helping her perfect her bedside manner, a crucial
part of a nurse's training. As a matter of fact, we've just spent a very
happy half hour with a box of sticky bandages and a blood pressure kit."

"What you do with the blood pressure kit?" Teresa asked curiously.

Jack turned full circle to face her. "I'd be happy to show you anytime," he murmured. "No pain, I promise. We simply strap something

black and stretchy round here." He indicated her upper arm. "Hmm . . . lovely skin . . . and then we do some really rather strenuous exercises. You'd get awfully hot in all those clothes, have to allow me to remove some. And then we have a cozy ten minutes comparing pulses." His eyes widened. "Any pulse will do. Trisha enjoyed that bit very much."

Teresa laughed and licked butter from her fingers. "I see." She grinned and waggled her wedding ring at him.

"Oh, that wouldn't stop Jack," I sneered.

"True." He swung around. "But it would normally stop you."

A silence unfolded and I could feel myself blushing. God, what was this, a bloody conspiracy? At length I found my voice.

"Christ, you've got some gall, Jack Fellowes, and some awesome double standards, too. How dare you lecture me like some . . . some Victorian deacon!"

"Because I'm a lost cause, my love," he said cheerfully, pushing his plate away. "A lecture would do me absolutely no good at all, but it might *just* make an impression on you. Mmm . . ." He wiped his mouth with the back of his hand. "Good tucker. Very good tucker. You do a damn fine breakfast down here, Luce; I'll give you that."

"You mean if nothing else?" I retorted angrily.

"No, I'll give you . . ." He gazed around. "Nice barn as well. Yes, really rather pleasant accommodation. Thoroughly satisfactory setup, all round. Girl done good, eh, Jess?" He grinned at Jess, who averted her eyes guiltily.

"We mustn't bully her too much, Jack," she said uncomfortably. "I laid into her quite enough last night. And we are, don't forget, her friends and guests."

"You could have fooled me," I snapped. "Stop bloody getting at me, you two; you're both the same!"

"Which is strange, don't you think?" hazarded Jack. "That Jess and I should currently see eye to eye when in the past we've differed so dramatically?"

This much was true. For years, whenever Jess and Jack had met, they'd been at each other's throats, bickering and sparring, Jess objecting to Jack's blatantly wayward lifestyle and Jack deriding what he saw as Jess's rampant feminism, which he considered misguided and oppressive. He loved to tease her, too. He turned to her now.

"So how's that Real Man of yours then, Jess—moving smartly on and changing the subject because it looks like Luce is about to go critical on us. Let's press your buttons for a bit, eh? Still trying to keep him on the straight and narrow? Still trying to keep him out of the pub and urge him toward tapestry and Bible studies?"

"Oh, piss off, Jack."

"Strange," he mused, scratching his chin, "when you obviously abhor the hell-raising, Lothario lifestyle that you then up and marry one of our members. Weren't there any teetotal wimps available for selection? No thundering great pansies up for grabs?"

"Oh, Jack, he'd be flattered to be included among *your* number," rejoined Jess smoothly. "He considers himself a mere apprentice to you, a novice at your knee. Depravity in your truly heroic proportions is something he's only ever dreamed of. And anyway," she added sweetly, "Jamie hung up his tankard and running shoes long ago. Three years ago, to be precise. When he married me." She glanced at her watch. "Actually, I must go and ring him. Check how he's getting on with young Henry. See if he's mastered the potty training yet." She shot Jack a triumphant look. He shuddered violently into his coffee cup.

"Why she keep tabs on him so much?" asked Teresa as Jess hurried away into the barn. "Always she say, 'I must ring Jamie. Must check on this, must check on that.'"

"Because she can't quite believe she's snared him." Jack grinned. "Jamie's a good man. He's had his fun and now he's settled down, but she's still wary, still standing at the door brandishing a rolling pin. You're right, Teresa; she should give him a break."

"You think?" drawled Rozanna. She was sitting slightly apart, behind him.

"You don't?" he drawled back, turning to look at her.

She blew a thin line of smoke high over his head. "In my experience, Jack, daahling, she has every right to feel paranoid. I don't believe the spots change that quickly, or that easily."

"Ah, what an old cynic you are." He grinned, reaching out and squeezing her hand. "Such a tonic!"

"Less of the old," she smiled, patting his cheek, "and more of the tonic, since you mention it. With a little gin in it, actually. It's five past twelve for heaven's sake, and although breakfast was lovely, doesn't anyone else feel the need to shape up to something a little more—well, adult? Lucy," she turned to me, "couldn't this supposed hellraiser of a man make himself useful in that department?"

"Of course he could, Rozanna," I agreed staunchly. "What would you like?"

"Well, a gin and tonic would be go down a treat, darling. There's a boy." She patted Jack's arm benignly.

Jack grinned good-naturedly and got up to oblige. He disappeared into the barn, and as he did so, Jess suddenly appeared behind him in the doorway. Her face was drained of blood, as white as a sheet.

"Oh God!" she gasped, clutching the door frame.

"What is it?" I leapt up, knocking the bench over backward.

"It's Henry," she breathed. "He's ill. I must go."

"Oh, Jess, my poor darling." I hurried over to her. "What—has the doctor been? Do they know what it is?"

"Yes!" She nodded fearfully. "They've made a diagnosis."

"And? What is it?"

She turned tragic eyes on me. "Chicken pox!"

"Chicken pox!" Teresa and I exchanged stifled smiles. "Oh, Jess, that's all right. Hardly serious. A bit of calamine lotion, a few quiet days at home. Ben and Max have both had it. Pedro, too, hasn't he, Teresa?"

Teresa nodded, smiling. "Quite normal."

"Yes, but he won't know what to do," Jess hissed. "Don't you see? It's Jamie! He'll be hopeless! Probably tuck him under his arm and take him to the pub, think the change of air will do him good. Lie him on the snooker table for a kip. That is the kind of man we're dealing with here. Oh, gosh, Teresa." She turned anguished eyes on her. "I'm awfully sorry to drag you away, but I wonder, would you mind terribly if we . . ."

"No, no, ees fine." Teresa got quickly to her feet. "I must get back to Carlo, too, make heem some lunch. And get Pedro's homework done, too. So, ees fine."

As they hurried into the house to pack, Rozanna looked horrified. "We're going?" Her eyes widened incredulously. "Just as the sun is finally appearing over the yardarm? Just as we were about to settle back in the buttercup meadow over there, armed with our aperitifs? And all because a baby's got chicken pox, a boy's got some homework, and a grown man can't find his way to the fridge to get himself some lunch? Tell me I'm dreaming."

"Ah no, not dreaming, Rozanna," sighed Jack portentously as he reappeared, armed with drinks. He set them down. "It's the shackles of matrimony for you, I'm afraid." He offered her his arm and she got to her feet. "Come. They'll be at least twenty minutes packing everything in tissue paper and making more stressy phone calls, and Teresa has got to haul Pedro out of the woods yet, so come. Let us go, you and I, while—well, while the morning is spread against the sky. Still blue, you see, and the sun still shining. Let us go, unencumbered as we are by spouses and offspring and a tedious sense of duty, away from the sounds of rattling chains, to sink a strong one, a really hefty one, down in the buttercup field, in peace."

"I'll drink to that," she muttered, clutching her glass. She took his arm gratefully and tottered off beside him in her heels. Their voices drifted back to me.

"Pleasant evening, Rozanna?"

"Lovely, Jack, thank you. Lovely party, and actually, it got better as the night went on. An unexpected visitor dropped into my sumptuous suite to see me last night. . . ."

"Ah. Nice to know the ancient art of corridor creeping still flourishes. Anyone I know?"

"Oh, definitely. A delightful man, and so refreshingly different from the . . ." Her voice faded into the distance. I sat up straight, straining my ears. Who? I wondered, with a sudden qualm. Who on earth had she meant?

I watched them go. Glanced fleetingly inside, then back to the meadow, longing to hear more. I dithered, torn. After a moment, though, I got up with a sigh and headed inside to help. I knew my place.

Chapter Twelve

DAYS PASSED, AND FRIDAY DAWNED BRIGHT, CLEAR, AND full of delicious portent; Charlie was due to arrive at ten o'clock. My preparations, however, began at eight. Having crept out of bed so as not to wake the boys, I took a long, hot soak in a steaming rose-scented bath. I then settled down to a good half hour at my dressing table, surrounded by eye shadows, foundations, blushers, and a myriad of other colorful products I wouldn't normally entertain; however, I'd read in *Vogue* that if subtly applied, they could take years off me and make me look a dewy twenty-six. I was keen to try.

Another half hour was then spent with the hair dryer, as I attempted to coax my hair away from frenzied activity and toward cool, elegant waves, all of which, of course, should have been done *before* achieving the dewy twenty-six, as my makeup, disastrously, began to melt in the heat. Remorselessly did hot air contrive to undo what art had so precariously achieved. By nine-thirty, I was gazing at my reflection in despair. The hair had refused to play ball and gone for a horizontal stance, whilst my face, an attractive orange and shiny from heat and makeup, had recognized favorable conditions and was coaxing out a chin spot even as I watched.

"Bugger!" I shrieked, reaching for a scrunchy. I scraped my hair back with it and ran to the sink, washing it all off with soap and water. "Bugger, bugger, bugger!" I wailed into a towel. "Oh God, what am I going to do. It's twenty to ten already and I look bloody awful!"

Ben put his head round the door. "You don't," he said thoughtfully, picking his nose. "You look nice." He dug deep with his finger. "Better than you did before, anyway. Go like that."

"Like this?" I lowered the towel and peered in the mirror. At least my face looked clean and fresh and the hair, tied back on the nape of my neck, was tamed somewhat. Also, I thought, breathing more calmly,

I did have a bit of a tan and my eyes were clear and green, now that you could *see* them—so, hang on. . . . I added a spot of mascara and a touch of lipstick.

"Better?" I smudged my lips together anxiously.

"Yeah, fine. You look great, Mum, like you normally do. And anyway, what's all the fuss? It's only to see about a job working in a shop, isn't it?"

"Yes, darling, quite right and who cares if I don't get it. And this shirt, d'you think? Or the blue?"

"The blue," said Ben decisively. "And not those horrid tight trousers, either; they make your bum look like an elephant's."

"Really?" I turned around, aghast. I'd been thrilled to bits to squeeze into these.

"Massive. That long skirt you wore yesterday's loads better."

"Oh." I blinked. I'd lost about a stone and a half since Ned died, but actually, I had a feeling Ben was right. Even if I lost four stone I'd still be broad across the beam. I sighed and peeled off the trousers I'd been so proud to peel on, albeit lying on the floor, swearing and wriggling.

"OK, the linen skirt it is," I said, tying it around me, sarong-style, and smoothing down the creases in the mirror. "Now listen." I swung back to him, hands on hips. "Trisha's coming up any minute and she'll either stay here with you this morning or take you up to Granny's."

"Can't we go fishing on the lake?"

"No. I'd rather you didn't go near the water if I'm not here."

"Oh, but Jack said he'd teach us how to get a trout! Please, Mum."

Jack *and* Trisha, I thought nervously. A rather fatal combination, surely?

"Well—let me speak to Trisha. Oh, look, here she is."

"Hi, guys! Hey, you look nice." Trisha strode into the bedroom with a pile of ironed clothes in her arms. She gave me an appreciative glance as she plonked them on the bed.

"Thanks. Um . . . so do you," I added nervously.

It was, admittedly, a warm day, but Trisha was dressed for the Caribbean. Her denim shorts showed at least half her bottom, her top was actually not a top at all but a bikini, and she'd wrapped a bandanna round her head, warrior-style. Her long limbs gleamed.

"Jack and I thought we'd take the boys fishing today," she told me. "Is that OK?"

"Ah, well, actually I was just explaining to Ben that—oh! He's here!" I yelped. I jumped back from the window as a car drew up outside.

"Yep, that's your lift," said Trisha, sticking her head out of the window. "That's Charlie boy, all right. Yoo-hoo! Up here, Charlie!" I winced as she waved extravagantly. "She'll be down in a minute." she yelled, cupping her hands round her mouth. "Just fixin' her face!" I winced again. Trisha turned back.

"It's OK; you've got a mo. Jack's chatting to him outside."

"Jack's here?" I hastened across to the window and shot my head out, grinding my teeth. Bloody man, couldn't keep his nose out of my business for one blasted minute, could he? And what was he saying to Charlie, damn him? "Keep away from Lucy; she hasn't had a man for four years and might throw herself at you?" "She's fatally attracted to married men, seeing as how she lost one herself?"

I snatched my bag from the bed and flew downstairs, intent on damage limitation. As I got to the open door, though, I stopped. Charlie had arrived in a pale blue convertible Bristol and was leaning against it, hands in pockets, chatting to Jack, who had his back to me. Charlie was wearing cream trousers and a rather faded blue shirt rolled up to the elbows. Tall and broad—Jack, beside him, whilst tall, looked almost frail—he threw back his head and laughed at something Jack said. Not about me, I hoped nervously. Then Charlie turned and saw me.

"Hi." He smiled, and it seemed to me that the whole of my front garden lit up like a Hollywood set.

"Hi!" I breathed back. There was a moment's silence as I gazed at him, I hope not too wantonly.

"Hi!" gasped Jack breathlessly, in a direct parody of me.

I turned and regarded him coldly. "Hello, Jack. What are you doing here?"

"My, what a welcome. Well, I was thinking of taking my young nephews for some trout tickling today since you're otherwise engaged. All right by you?"

"I'm not sure that it is, actually. As I've already explained to Trisha, I'm not too keen on Max being near the water when I'm not around. He's only four and he can't swim yet, so—"

"Aw, come on, Luce. I'll keep an eye on him. And anyway, I've promised them. They'll be so disappointed."

This much was true. Already I could hear Ben and Max thundering downstairs behind me, and I knew Jack was right. There'd be disappointed faces, followed by disbelief, followed by uproar if I refused—and all in front of Charlie, when I wanted him to believe I was a model of calm, unflappable motherhood.

"Well, OK. But listen, Jack." I lowered my voice and led him away by the elbow so that Ben, Max, and, I hoped, Charlie couldn't hear. "If you're going with Trisha," I hissed, "I want you to give me your solemn word there won't be any funny business. I mean in front of the boys."

He frowned. Bent his head, deliberately misunderstanding. "Funny business?" he whispered.

"You know what I mean," I said between gritted teeth. "I don't want you to . . . well . . ."

His eyes widened. "Fuck her?" he said loudly.

Charlie's back stiffened. His head turned quickly, then away again.

"Jack!" I flushed dramatically. God, what would Charlie think? "That was totally unnecessary!" I seethed.

"Quite right," agreed Jack, frowning. "No need for bad language. I apologize unreservedly. And I promise to toe the line at all times, particularly in front of your offspring. You were quite right to have a word with me, Lucy, put me straight on a few things. Golly," he rolled his eyes, "just as well you did actually; otherwise who knows what might have happened. I mean, I might have chased old Trisha down that riverbank, pulled down those hot little shorts of hers, and given her a damn good seeing to whilst one boy took pictures and the other one quietly drowned! Phew. That was a close one, Luce; you saved me there. Thanks for the tip." His eyes glittered dangerously.

"Yes, well." I swallowed. "Just see that you—you know, behave responsibly."

"Aye-aye, miss, will do. Will do my very best. Dib dib dib. But when you're back, I mean later on, when the children are all tucked up in bed and it's after the nine o'clock watershed, all right if I give her one then?"

"Oh, for God's sake, Jack, you can do what you damn well like! It makes no difference to me!" I hissed.

He laughed as I stormed off to the car, desperately trying to re-arrange my expression from one of intense irritation, in order to bestow a beatific smile on Charlie. It wasn't hard, actually. He was born for be-atific smiles.

"Sorry about that," I purred as I slipped, I hoped nonchalantly, into the passenger side.

"Problems?"

I sighed. "No, not really. It's just . . . well, I haven't seen him for a while—Jack, I mean—and I'd forgotten how obnoxious he can be. It's all coming flooding back now. Anyway," I beamed, "enough of him; how are you? This is so kind of you to take me to see Kit, especially if it's out of your way."

"Bristol was canceled." He grinned, shifting into gear. "It was a TV project of mine which seems to have gone belly-up and been shelved for the time being, so it's not out of my way at all. If I wasn't doing this I'd only be sitting at home trying to write another wretched ill-fated drama. I'd much rather take you up to Frampton instead."

He smiled and I glowed with pleasure, waving to the boys as we took off down the drive, avoiding Jack's eye. I tried to remember the last time I'd been in a convertible. Years ago, with Ned, on holiday in Greece, one of those Jeep things. Ooh, yes . . . I relaxed back. There was undoubtedly something about the wind in your hair and—oops—up your skirt that took years off a girl.

"Is that what you do then?" I raised my voice above the roar of the engine. "I mean, write for TV?" Oh, cunning, Lucy, cunning. Pretend you don't know.

"When I can. There's so much bloody competition at the mo-ment, though. In the old days I used to just submit a script and they'd say, 'Thanks very much, Charlie; that'll be on air next autumn.'" He grimaced. "Not so these days, I'm afraid. Now there's a fair amount of uming and ahing and muttering about difficult schedules."

"Oh, but didn't you do that marvelous *Light of India* series? That was quite recent, wasn't it?"

He looked surprised, as well he might, for I wasn't supposed to know, was I?

"Lavinia mentioned it," I said quickly, flushing.

"Lavinia?" He looked even more surprised. "Blimey, I didn't think I was flavor of the month with her. Never thought I'd hear her singing my praises. But yes, I did do that, and it might seem recent, but it was actually two years ago, and two years is a long time in TV. Anyway, I'm not complaining. I tick over." He narrowed his eyes thoughtfully into the wind. "What else did the fair Lavinia say? I'd be intrigued to—oops, look out. It's Annie Oakley."

Happily I was saved from having to elucidate on my fictitious conversation with Lavinia, as around the next bend Violet loomed into view. She was on the other side of the fence, in the field, trying to mount a horse. In one hand she had a Tesco carrier bag; in the other, she held a shotgun. She put the plastic bag in her teeth and her foot in the stirrup again, gun under her arm. Charlie glanced at me quizzically.

"Better stop a sec," I muttered.

As he slowed obediently to a halt I stood up in my seat. "Are you all right, Violet?" I shouted.

She swung round to me, pink-faced. "I've just shot Popsy!" she bellowed across the field.

"What?"

"I said, *I've just shot Popsy!*"

I stared at her. "Why?" I yelled back, astounded.

"Because she was mad, of course! Surprised that blasted farmer didn't spot it sooner!"

And with that she hoisted herself up, swung her leg over the saddle, and kicked on hard. As she galloped away into the distance, a cloud of dust shimmered in her wake.

"Popsy?" muttered Charlie, aghast, as I slowly sat down in my seat again.

"Yes."

"What . . . she shot her? Because she was mad?"

"Apparently." I frowned.

"But . . . they're both mad, aren't they?"

I turned. "Sorry?"

"Isn't Popsy her sister?"

"Oh! Oh no, her cow."

He looked hugely relieved. "Oh, her *cow*. God, that's a relief. I knew there were two of them, wasn't sure of their names."

I giggled. "No, hopefully she's not *that* crazy. But you're quite right; they are a bit eccentric."

"You don't have to tell me," he said as we purred off again. "They're well known round these parts. Their latest gambit, apparently, has been to take all the electricity out of their cottage, because they've both become allergic to it. The pair of them fumble around with torches and an ancient Rayburn stove. God knows what it'll be like in the winter."

I sighed. "I know; the whole thing's chaotic. But they love that cottage. Rose wants them to be 'properly looked after,' of course."

"And we all know what that means, don't we?" He grimaced.

On we drove. The noise of the engine didn't necessarily make for smooth conversation, so I contented myself with sneaking sidelong glances at his profile. Lovely straight nose. Square jaw, too. Strong brown hands on the wheel. He caught my eye. Probably my slack jaw, too.

"So what's he like then, this Kit fellow?" I yelled, taking a lump of hair out of my gaping mouth.

"Lovely chap. Bit older than me, I suppose, late forties, but full of energy. Just as well, really. When he bought that house some years ago it was in a terrible state. He did it up himself."

"So it's fully restored now?"

"More or less. It was a hell of a project, and I think he slightly lost interest at the end when his wife ran off with the plumber." He grinned.

"Oh God, how awful! Poor guy."

He shrugged. "Probably just as well. She was undoubtedly that type. Had a very roving eye. It would have happened sooner or later, and probably better for Kit that it was sooner. Gave him some time to get on with his life."

"And has he? Got on with his life?"

He hesitated. "Well, he adored her, so he was some time getting over it, but that's when he started selling the antiques, and it's been a huge success. But if you mean, Get Over It, as in, is there another woman, then no."

"Ah. Children?"

"Two boys—nice boys, actually—almost finishing school. One may even be at university now, not sure." He grinned. Glanced across at me. "You like to know, don't you?"

"Sorry?"

"About people. Get the lowdown."

"Oh." I reddened. "Yes, I suppose I do. I certainly think it helps if you can fill in the background before you meet someone. Find out what makes them tick."

There was a silence. I'd wanted to ask about him, about what made him tick, about his family even, but I felt I couldn't now. Not now I'd been ousted as a nosey parker.

"And you?" he asked, glancing across. "Have you got on with your life since your husband died?"

"Oh. Oh well, for years, no. No, I was pathetic. I mean, not too pathetic; I held down a job and looked after the children and didn't go to pieces in the supermarket or anything, but in private . . . well. It hit me pretty hard. Took a while. I'm much better now, though," I said brightly. "I've—you know, moved on. Moved down here, made a break from the past, from the life I had with him. With Ned. Had to really. I was just hanging on. Clinging to the wreckage, as they say."

He nodded. "One does. Sometimes it's all one can do."

I narrowed my eyes in the wind, tucked back my hair. "You know?"

"Yes, in a slightly different way. Similar, but different. We had another child. A boy, Nicholas, a year older than my daughter, Ellen. He was killed four years ago."

"Oh God, how awful!" My hand flew to my mouth. "How did he— no. Sorry."

"No, no, it's fine. He was walking home from school. Just the little village one across the road from where we live. My wife was with him, saw him across. But he still got knocked over. He was four."

"Oh, how ghastly!" Four. I thought of Max now, Ben, at that age. Divine. Running out of school, socks round their ankles, grubby knees, proudly clutching wet paintings, brand-new book bags with first reading books, ready to show me.

"How appalling," I breathed inadequately. "You must have been devastated. All of you."

"Totally. But one copes. Life goes on and all the other old clichés. Has to. Particularly when there are other children."

"But how *did* you cope?"

"Cope? Well, I threw myself into my work. Tapped away at my computer at all hours. Bought the flat in London in order to do it. To escape." He shot me a wry look. "Grief doesn't do much for one's marriage, as I'm sure you can imagine. In fact, I read somewhere that only one percent of marriages survive the death of a child. That doesn't surprise me at all." He sighed. "No, I bought the flat so we could have some space from each other. Sometimes we couldn't bear to be in the same room, let alone the same house, so—yes. That worked, in a sense." He paused. Considered. "Of course I haven't *coped*, not completely. I've just got by."

"And," I took a very deep breath, "your wife?" There. I'd said it.

"My wife? She found solace with someone else."

"Oh! You mean . . ."

"Oh yes, there are three of us in this marriage, Lucy, as Princess Diana once famously said." He smiled. "But not another man."

I stared, horrified. "Good grief! You mean—"

"Oh no, she's not a lessy, either. No, my rival is God."

"God!"

"Yes." He smiled. "You see, Miranda was saved. Lucky devil. That's how she coped. She saw the light, found salvation. Came home from Waitrose one day, dumped the shopping bags down in the middle of the kitchen floor, and said she'd been reborn."

"Christ. In Waitrose!"

He shrugged. "Apparently. Somewhere between the cheese counter and the bog rolls. Marvelous really."

"Oh. Yes, of course."

"And much better than drugs, or booze, or antidepressants, as all her new, born-again chums kept earnestly telling me. Absolutely bloody marvelous. But awfully difficult to live with, nonetheless."

"What—because she's quite committed?"

"*Quite* committed! Ha!" He gave an explosive laugh. "Just a bit. And not just for herself. She's frightfully keen for me, too. It's her mission, you see, what God put her on this earth to do. To recruit. No, no, Miranda won't be *really* happy until I'm coming out of the water in a white shroud with a heavenly smile on my face, or walking naked across a desert with a burning cross in my hands, and since I'm something of an unbeliever, a sceptic even, we've reached a bit of an impasse. Got a stalemate on our hands. Jesus wants me for a sunbeam, and frankly, I ain't feeling shiny." He stopped at some red lights. Frowned down at the steering wheel. "How bizarre."

"What?"

"Well, I've only known you ten minutes and already I've told you all that. Some of my best friends don't know the extent of Miranda's zeal, how it affects us." He glanced across at me. "Why have I just blurted all that out? We appear to have cut the crap, cut the small talk. I wonder why?"

I stared back and felt my mouth go dry. I held his gaze . . . until we were tooted from behind. The lights had changed. He shifted into gear and we took off again. We were silent for a while.

"I saw her outside your house," I said suddenly, above the roar of the engine.

"Who?"

"Your wife. Or I assume it was. When I was posting my letter. She was coming out of the drive."

He shook his head. "I don't remember."

"Blond? Slim? Blue Jeep?"

He nodded. "Yes, that'd be the wife."

"Didn't look much like a born-again Christian to me."

"That'd be it, too."

We drove the rest of the way in silence. I was lost in heady thought. She was a religious maniac, a zealot. The marriage was unhappy; they made it work for the child. "Quite right, quite right," I muttered feverishly to myself, "admirable actually," and yet . . . to live an empty life like that? To endure such a hollow marriage? And all to keep up appearances. Surely it was better to be honest with each other. To come clean. And wouldn't she be better off in a nunnery or something? With other like-minded souls around her, praying and—I don't know—playing harps together? Threading rosary beads? 'The hills are alive . . . ?' "

"Here we are," he said suddenly.

He swung the car around some towering gateposts and we swept up a gravel drive. A beautiful stone manor house unfurled, Gothic and splendid, with arched mullion windows. On either side of the huge oak door, an enormous stone dragon kept sentinel.

"Oh! It's lovely," I breathed.

"Isn't it just?" he agreed, coming to a halt. "Rather wonderful inside, too. Come and take a peek."

We got out and walked up the drive together, circling a moss-encrusted fountain. Someone I knew would have been salivating all down her Puffa by now.

"Has he met Lavinia?" I asked innocently.

Charlie stopped dead in the drive. His mouth twitched. "Best not to mention that name in this household," he said soberly.

"Oh? Why?"

"Kit came home one night to find her waiting for him in his bed. Naked, naturally, but comatose, too, having drunk his whiskey bottle dry. There were scented candles burning—rather dangerously—everywhere, rose petals strewn all over the bed, and she still had a rose clenched between her teeth. Actually, that was the problem. She'd eaten the rose in her stupor, and as he came into the room she raised herself up on one elbow, smiled seductively, and threw up all down her tits. Terribly sexy. Kit then had a really fun evening dressing a roaring drunk female—and I mean roaring—and cleaning up rose-scented puke."

"Oh God," I giggled. "Poor Lavinia. She does have a terrible time."

"Yes, and she doesn't do herself any favors, either," he said dryly. "Ah, look, it's open. We'll just push on through."

We did just that and entered a lobby, which via another pair of Victorian glass doors led us into a hall about the size of a football pitch. A vast stone fireplace took up most of one wall. Positioned on either side of it, and sitting on a beautiful old Aubusson carpet, were two supremely elegant sofas, lavishly carved, with curled backs, and upholstered in faded gold. A Georgian sofa table stood behind each one, crowded with photographs. On the walls were paintings, drawings, silhouettes, and old plates, whilst up the sweeping staircase a set of Ackermann military prints marched up to a gallery.

"Oh." I was surprised. "It's not a shop at all. It's like a home."

"It *is* a home," agreed Charlie. "Kit lives here, you see. It's just that everything is for sale. Ah, the man himself!"

I glanced up as down the sweeping oak staircase, his hand lightly brushing the banister rail, came a tall, elegant man. His swept-back hair looked faintly prewar, and he had a thin, intelligent-looking face. It broke into a radiant grin when he saw Charlie.

"Charlie! Good to see you. I was expecting you a little earlier, actually, thought you'd forgotten. How've you been?"

"Really well, and sorry we're a bit late." Charlie pumped Kit's outstretched hand enthusiastically.

"Not at all." He glanced at me. "Lucy?"

"That's it."

"Lucy Fellowes." Charlie grinned. "And, Lucy, this is Kit Alexander."

"Delighted." He beamed as we shook hands. "Charlie told me all about you on the phone. Well, a bit about you, don't think he knows that much himself!"

"I've been admiring your house," I said shyly. "It's beautiful. All these lovely things." I gazed around.

"Thank you." He scratched his chin sheepishly. "Yes, they are lovely, although I suppose I notice them less these days. It used to be a bit of an obsession. I was forever shifting things around and trying to get it absolutely right, but now I'm a bit less anal about it. Just sort of live in it, as Charlie's probably told you."

"But that's what's so wonderful. It makes it so uncommercial. And if something sells . . . ?"

He shrugged. "I just replace it. We got through five dining tables recently, and that was a little wearing, I must say. I felt like shouting, 'Stop! That's enough. I've nowhere to eat my bloody supper.' " He grinned. "But most of the time business is slow enough for me to replace at leisure. Go abroad and find unusual things, which is what I like to do."

"Beautiful things," I enthused, stroking one of the camelback chaises reverently.

"Ah yes, terribly lucky with that," he agreed. "Found it in a skip in the backstreets of Montmartre. Some madam had clearly had enough of it. Couldn't believe my luck when I found the matching twin underneath."

"And all those Biedermeier chairs!" I marveled, peering into the next room. "I've never actually seen a complete collection before, just ogled them in catalogs."

"Hence the price," he warned. "Yes, I can't exactly nip out and replace those guys at the drop of a hat, but no one can afford them anyway, so that's fine. They stay put. Come on; come and have a proper look."

He ushered us through the little Biedermeier room and then into the drawing room. It was paneled but painted a cool, discreet gray and decorated unashamedly in the style of a French château. The windows were ornate with heavy silk drapes, and gesso-molded mirrors with cherub sconces reflected back at each other from either end of the room; loveseats and Louis Quinze needlepoint chairs were grouped around delicate tripod tables. Marie Antoinette could have fanned herself by the fire without anyone batting an eyelid.

"How do you keep it like this?" I said, swinging around in wonder. "I mean, if you live in it? If I had the contents of my house up for sale I'd be frantic. It would be a tip!"

"Ah, but then I live alone. And actually, I'm not an untidy chap, so it works. And frankly, if there is the odd coffee cup or magazine lying around, so what? No one seems to mind. And of course I don't have a young family anymore. It certainly wouldn't work with Nintendos and Game Boys all over the place."

"And you sleep here? I mean, in a bedroom upstairs?"

"No." He grimaced. "That would be too invasive. I'm not sure I could cope with people ogling my dressing gown or my tatty slippers, so I have a flat up in the attic. There's a bedroom for me, a kitchen, and two rooms for the boys when they come and stay. That, I can assure you, *is* a tip."

"But in the evening, you don't watch telly in the flat?"

"No, I come down here and put my feet up in this rather pretty sitting room, through here." He led the way into a smaller, cozier room. "It gets the sun in the morning, but at night, with the curtains drawn, it's a very cozy retreat. I light the fire and watch one of Charlie's latest epics, surrounded by beautiful things." He looked at me directly for a moment. "I'm a great believer in being surrounded by beautiful things. I mean, why live up in the garret when I can be down here? And of course when the boys were young it *was* a family home, but turning it into a shop was the only way I could keep it going, really. Keeps me going, too; otherwise I'd stagnate."

"I think it's a marvelous idea," I enthused. "And you sell . . ." I hesitated. "Well, surely not to passing trade?"

He laughed. "No, quite right, I wouldn't survive! Much too pricey. No, it's mostly interior decorators from London or New York who come by appointment. But actually there *is* a little passing trade, generally American tourists, which is why I have to stay open and why, my dear, I'm looking for help. Can't stay here seven days a week, I'd go quietly off my trolley, and Charlie did say you'd be keen to do a couple of days, maybe?"

"Oh I'd love to!" I thrilled. "This is *far* better than I ever imagined. I mean, I just thought . . . well, that you had a shop," I said hastily.

"Tudor Antiques? With a tinkly little bell over the door?" He grinned.

"But," I stroked a delicate little Pembroke table, "nothing has a price tag on?"

"No, because I don't want to live surrounded by tags, so I have an inventory, and if someone is interested in—say, that, for instance," he pointed above the fireplace, "I simply go to the list, look under Sitting Room, and then look up . . ." He paused.

"Early eighteenth-century delft figurine?" I suggested.

"Exactly, or?" He pointed.

"William and Mary balloon-back chair, Hepplewhite, or possibly earlier?"

"Spot on." He grinned. "And I'm sorry to test you like that—you clearly know your onions—it's just I have to be a wee bit careful. I once, out of desperation, employed a girl called Michelle from the village. Remember Michelle, Charlie?"

"Do I," he groaned.

"Michelle swore blind she knew all about antiques cos she had 'a CSE in ashray fart'—turned out to be history of art—and cos her nan had 'loads of them coronation mugs.' Well, naturally we had the utterly predictable problems of her thinking barley twist was a stick of rock and Bernini was an Italian restaurant, but things really came to a head one day when I was in the flat and she was down here on her own. She bellowed up the stairs, 'Oy, Kit! 'Ow much d'you want for the brown chair in the hall?'

" 'Which particular brown chair in the hall, Michelle?' I'd called back, head in hands.

" 'You know, the big brown one. Wiv the hole in it. The one you piss in.'

"Before I could scamper downstairs and assure my American clients that the commode chair my assistant was referring to was not something I personally relieved myself into, they'd naturally taken to their heels and scampered."

"Oh God," I giggled. "A bit of a liability, then."

"Quite. And not something I can see you being. Would it suit you, Lucy? A couple of days a week? So I can escape these four walls and go on my treasure hunts for a bit?"

"Oh yes," I said. "Definitely. Although," I glanced across, "as I mentioned to Charlie . . ."

"Lucy may not be here forever," he put in. "I said you'd understand that."

"Oh, absolutely! It would drive you nuts. But a year or so? Till you sort yourself out?"

"Perfect." I beamed.

"And you'd be able to start right away?"

"Ah. Well. I was wondering. Would September suit? Only the children go back to school then and—"

His face fell a bit. He scratched his chin.

"No, no," I said quickly, "right away is fine. Trisha can fill in for a couple of days a week. The boys will love it, actually."

"Excellent." Kit looked relieved. "And the dog?" He raised inquiring eyebrows at Charlie.

"Ah, yes," said Charlie. "I forgot to mention that. But Lucy loves dogs, used to look after one in London. I'm sure that'll be fine." He smiled.

"Dog?"

"Rococo," explained Kit. "Belonged to my ex-wife, and she left her behind. Together with a stash of unpaid bills. Smart woman. I'll get her. Rococo!" he called.

Instantly an Irish wolfhound bounded in, as if from nowhere but clearly from the garden, since she was covered in mud. Tongue lolling, she bounced across the room and stuck her head straight up my crotch.

"Oooof! Lovely!" I gasped, backing away. I'd seen smaller ponies.

"A bit of a brute," said Kit, tactfully seizing her head away and wrestling it playfully from side to side. "But a complete softy, as you can see."

"Yes. She, um, looks it."

"So." Kit straightened up, smiling. "Next week, then?"

I blinked. "Oh! Yes. Why not?"

We laughed, and he showed us to the door.

"We haven't mentioned money, my dear," he said, scratching his chin awkwardly. "So shall I give you a ring about that, when I've had a think?"

"Fine." I turned at the door. "Oh, and I'd better ask, too—is everything for sale? I mean, I don't want to find I've inadvertently sold the family silver or anything."

He shrugged. "More or less. There are a few bits of Meissen I particularly cherish, but I keep them up in the flat. So . . . no. I mean—yes. It is all for sale. All these possessions, much as I love them, are actually very easy to give up. It's other things one can't afford to lose. Can't replace, either."

He looked beyond me, abstracted for a moment. Then he came to. He smiled and shook my hand warmly as we took our leave of him.

The door shut behind us and Charlie and I walked slowly down the drive to the car.

"He's still sad," I murmured as I got in beside him.

"Hmmm. Well, he lost his boys for a while, too. She got full custody."

"Oh! How awful. Didn't he see them at all?"

"Hardly."

"But now?"

"Now, they're old enough to choose. And they spend a lot of time with him. But you can't ever make up for those lost years. The ones you imagine."

I thought of the son that Charlie had lost, the years that he imagined. Just as I'd often imagined the years the boys had lost, the ones they should have had with their father.

"No," I agreed soberly, "you can't."

We drove home in silence, the wind in our hair, and I was curiously grateful for the roar of the engine, which made conversation, if not impossible, something of an effort.

At length, we purred up the back drive to Netherby and drew up outside the barn. The front door was shut, as were the windows. It looked empty, deserted. Trisha, Jack, and the boys were clearly still out fishing. All around, fields of long grass, ready to be made into hay, rippled gently in the breeze; delicate seed heads shimmered in the midday sun, and from the golden flood of the buttercup meadow came the muffled hums and flutters of bees, butterflies, and dragonflies. Charlie turned off the engine. We didn't look at each other, but in the silence I could almost hear my heart beating. I felt sure he could hear it, too. At length he rubbed the leather steering wheel, nervously, with his fingertip.

"So. Here we are," he said quietly. I detected a faint tremor to his voice. "And now, I suppose, Lucy, we're going to have to address something." He swallowed. "We're going to have to decide . . . what on earth we're going to do."

Chapter Thirteen

"Do?" I echoed stupidly. My heart was racing. I turned to face him.

"Well, clearly something bigger than both of us is going on here, don't you think?" he said softly. "I mean, I for one don't think it's entirely coincidental that we kept tripping over each other in London like that. In fact, if it didn't sound too much like my wife, I'd say it was something of a sign."

I swallowed. I didn't like to say he was right, it wasn't a coincidence, but that, sadly, the only symbolism going on was the Apache Sniffing Tracks kind.

"No. No, you're right," I agreed, contriving to look bewildered. "It was extraordinary, wasn't it?"

"Quite extraordinary. And now, here you are, on my other patch, twenty-five miles from Chelsea, in the heart of Oxfordshire. Don't you find that bizarre?"

"Bizarre," I croaked. Crikey, hadn't we been through all this at the party? Must he persist?

"And so I can't help thinking," he ran a bewildered hand through his hair, "that somehow, something was meant to be, here—if that doesn't sound too corny. And to be honest, even if it *wasn't* meant to be," he shifted in his seat, turned to face me fully for the first time; I could feel my breath coming in inconvenient little spurts, "the fact is, I can't stop thinking about you, Lucy."

"Oh!" My limbs twitched convulsively.

"Ever since I ran into you at that party the other day, I . . . well, I was up all night, actually. Prowling around the house with a glass of whiskey in my hand. Finally I went to bed, but I still couldn't sleep. Couldn't get your face out of my mind." His dark eyes were bright and sparkling, fixed intently on me. I could feel my nostrils flaring back with excitement, my heart pounding. He slipped his arm along the back of my seat.

"I know you feel it, too. I can sense it," he urged. "Please tell me I'm not going completely mad?"

"You're not," I murmured, glancing nervously about. I seemed to be in the grip of an extraordinary dilemma here. On the one hand, the desire to collapse into his strong, brown arms was almost overwhelming, but on the other hand—here? Outside my house? In a convertible car with the windows of Netherby glinting away over there in the sunlight?

"What about a cup of coffee?" I gasped nervously.

He laughed and withdrew his arm. "Excellent idea. And don't look so worried, either. I wasn't going to pounce on you here, with the eyes of Netherby upon us, and neither, I promise, will I pounce on you inside, over the Nescafé. I just wanted to see . . ." he struggled, "well, if you feel even remotely the same way. Have even the faintest idea what I'm talking about."

His brown eyes were like pools of liquid chocolate now. Soft, vulnerable even.

"Oh yes," I breathed. "I do."

God. "I do." Sounded like I'd just *married* him or something. Married. Help! I leapt out of the car and scuttled up the garden path. I was aware of him following, at a more sedate pace.

Christ, what's the matter with you, Lucy? I thought furiously as I scurried around the house opening all the windows, not wanting to be hermetically sealed in, as it were. This is what you wanted, what you've dreamed about for months. God, you even upped sticks and followed him down here, so why are you acting the nervous ninny now? He came through the front door and shut it behind him. I knew why, though. I turned. Swallowed.

"You're married," I said abruptly, accusingly even. I challenged him briefly with my eyes.

He looked back at me steadily. "Quite right, there's absolutely no arguing with that. But you're not going to tell me that comes as a surprise? That you were unaware of that before you accepted a ride in my car?"

I glanced down at my hands. "No. No, I can't say that. I was very aware."

"Lucy." He came toward me, stopped in front of me. "Nothing like this has ever happened to me before; I swear it. I mean, not since I met Miranda. For what it's worth, I've never looked elsewhere. Because of what happened with Nick—well, I never thought there was anything else for me, you see. I suppose you could say I'd got used to unhappiness. Wore it, like a heavy coat, pulling me down most of the time, but these last few days, I've wondered whether it isn't actually time for a little happiness." He picked his words carefully. "You see, I've never really felt entitled to any. Up to now." He frowned. "Does that make any sense at all, or am I talking bollocks?"

I grinned. "Not bollocks. I know what you mean. I haven't felt entitled to much, either."

"And I don't even know," he spread his hands carefully on my slate work surface, staring down as if he might draw inspiration from his fingers, "what form that happiness could take." He looked up. "I'm certainly not suggesting we nip upstairs and have a quick one now, but I do know that I'd like to spend time with you. Walk with you. Eat with you. Talk to you, like we've done today."

"I'd like that very much, too," I breathed.

Oh yes, I thought tremulously. To spend time with him. To look at him properly, study him, and not just in snatched moments. To cook supper together, to have picnics even, to idle along riverbanks, to have days like today. Yes! I went to fill the kettle, happily. Safely. A little spring in my step.

"And equally," he went on, still gazing at his hands, "there's nothing I can do about my marital state. In time, who knows? I think you get the picture about how Miranda and I live, fairly separately, but what I'm saying is—well. It's up to you. This is me, warts, marriage, baggage, and all. It's your decision, Lucy." He looked up.

I turned from the sink with the kettle. "That's a pretty full-on way of putting it."

"It's honest. As honest as I can be, anyway." He thrust his hands deep in his pockets. Frowned down at the floor. "My only other problem is that, having said all that, having been frank and up-front about my marriage and told you how restrained and sensible I'm going to be with you, the fact of the matter is that when I'm with you, Lucy, when I'm *near* you . . . it all goes out the window. Because I do find you so utterly, dangerously, irresistibly," he looked up, "desirable."

I put the kettle down with a clatter. It seemed to me that the barn whirled. Spun like a top, but through it, his dark eyes kindled like fire, burning into my very soul. I gripped the work surface hard. Gazed back. Slowly, his hand crept across and covered mine. I stared down at it. The last time I'd held hands with a man it had been a vicar, when Max was christened. Next to our hands, on the counter, a naked Action Man grinned up at me, arms outstretched, no willy. Was this symbolic? I wondered. And if so, of what?

I glanced up. Fatal. Our eyes collided and in an instant he was around that counter. In another I was in his arms. His lips came down to meet mine. Not slowly and tentatively but urgently, desperately— and then it seemed to me he was everywhere. His hands were in my hair and then all over my back, his lips pressed hard against mine. As we came up for air, his breath roared in my ears. I could hardly catch mine, and yet a second kiss was unfurling fast, the room rocking violently again. Aware that I'd yet to utter a protest, I kept my eyes open as a token of resistance, but his kisses were covering my face now, and I felt weak. Not weak enough not to respond enthusiastically, though, and I seized the back of his head, pulling it down, kissing him madly. I felt his body respond, hard against mine, pressing into me. I shut my eyes, letting desire wash over me, could feel myself slipping into heady oblivion, as a familiar voice said, "God, it must be over a foot long!"

My eyes snapped open. Through the open window I saw Ben, coming up the path, rod in hand, holding up a fish for Jack to inspect.

"Probably more like nine inches," Jack said, "but anglers always lie about length."

"Shit!" I squeaked, and leapt backward. Charlie and I flew apart like deflecting magnets.

"Boys are coming!" I hissed, panic-stricken. Frantically I smoothed down my hair and wiped my mouth. I looked around desperately and lunged for the phone, seizing it. As Jack and the boys came barging through the door, dripping wet, I was laughing theatrically into the receiver.

"Yes. Yes, I will," I trilled. "Lovely, Mum, that would be terrific! OK, super. See you then!" I put it down, turned. "Oh, hi, boys!"

Ben stared. "Who was that?"

"Hmm?"

"On the phone."

"Oh! Maisie, darling."

"But you called her Mum. You never call her that."

"Did I? Gosh, how silly of me!"

"And you're all red in the face. And your bosoms are all heaving. And what's happened to your hair? It's standing up on end."

"Oh, forgot to brush it, I expect."

"Have you been running?" asked Max.

I stared at him. My mouth opened. "Yes." I said finally. "Yes, I have. For the phone. I was upstairs. N-no, downstairs! Anyway, darlings, enough of me. Have you had a good day?"

I crouched down to Max, hiding my confusion in his little face. I didn't want to meet Jack's eye. Had he seen? I couldn't look at Charlie, either, because how composed would he be? Had I rumpled him irreparably? Spread lipstick all around his mouth, wreaked havoc in his hair?

"We caught two really big ones, but Jack said it was kinder to put them back," said Max bitterly. "But Ben was allowed to keep that one, and I caught this wiv a net."

He took his hand from behind his back, and presented me proudly with a jam jar. A huge toad stared back at me, bug-eyed with terror. Eyes possibly as huge with fear as mine.

"Lovely, darling," I breathed. "Lovely toad." I glanced up, finally. "Thank you, Jack."

"Pleasure," he drawled. "I like spending time with them. They're great boys. A credit to you."

I was unsure how to take this compliment. He'd deliberately sounded surprised, as if "a credit to you—*amazingly*," somehow hung unspoken in the air. As if I was already a fallen woman. I straightened up, flushing.

"You know Charlie, don't you?"

"We met at the party," said Jack. "And again outside, today." They shook hands briefly.

"But now, I really must be away." Charlie smiled, looking really remarkably composed, I thought with relief. "Good to see you again, Jack.

And you, too, boys." He crouched down to peer into Max's jar. "That's quite a frog you've got there, young man. He'll take a bit of feeding if you're planning on keeping him. Eat you out of watercress for tuppence."

"Jack says we'll set him free in a pond tomorrow, so we won't be needing much watercress."

"Ah." Charlie straightened up.

I ground my teeth. "Jack says."

"I'll come out with you," I muttered. And somehow, I managed to shut the door behind me, too.

I scuttled after Charlie to his car.

"When will I see you again?" I asked, a trifle desperately perhaps, for a girl who'd been nervous about merely talking to a man in his car, but then you see, the thing was, I wanted him to kiss me again. Like he had in there. Bugger picnics and idling about on riverbanks, I hadn't been kissed like that for years!

"I'll ring you," he promised. "But maybe," he tilted his head back toward the house, "maybe in London." He took my hands and I let him. Held on tight. "There are too many distractions here, and in London, we could walk in the parks, along the Embankment . . ."

"Ooh, yes!" I said greedily. Glorious, glorious London, where I could breathe again—which was strange, when most people fled the city to breathe down here—and, of course, where his flat was.

"Yes, and I could tell everyone I was going to see Maisie and Lucas, my parents," I said excitedly, already formulating my excuse as to why I'd be up there. "Come up for the whole day—a night, even."

It seemed to me that all the birds in the trees, the squirrels on the branches, paused, poleaxed by my brazenness, holding their breath for his response.

He smiled gently. "Great. I'll ring you," he promised again as he got into his car.

Already I could feel myself flushing. A night? You fool! Talk about the sublime to the ridiculous. What are you, a gauche adolescent? Why don't you just run up and get your toothbrush now? Jump in the car with him? Rip off your top and throw up down your naked breasts like Lavinia and have done with it? No, no, restraint was called for here. It was important to calm down, not to act like a girl who hasn't been kissed for four years. I folded my arms, smiled broadly.

"Bye then, Charlie," I said in a loud, public voice. Too loud, perhaps. "Thanks for the lift."

He drove away, waving. I watched him go, hating the moment when I'd have to turn and face Jack again. I prolonged it, standing in the front garden, shading my eyes into the sunshine, watching Charlie's car disappear, letting my heart rate go down a bit. After a while, I bent down and began deadheading the roses. Well, they could all come and find me out here, couldn't they? Why should I go inside to them? As I straightened up to toss the faded petals on the lawn, something caught my eye. Down in the valley, in the distance, a scurrying figure was tottering precariously across the bridge over the lake and up the hill toward me. It was Rose, and for once, I was glad to see her. She was still quite a way in the distance, but I waved and went to greet her at the garden gate. She finally panted up to the top, breathing heavily, clutching her side. When she reached me, she seized the gatepost. Leaned on it, eyes shining.

"Lucy! Oh, I *am* glad I've caught you; I wasn't sure if you'd be in," she panted. "Tell me, have you and the boys had lunch yet?"

"No, not yet. I'm a bit disorganized today. Been, er, job hunting," I added guiltily.

She peered at me. "Yes, well, you should have brushed your hair for an interview, Lucy, but anyway, do please come up and have a bite with us. I've got such exciting news." She beamed. "My dear, *what* d'you think?"

I shook my head and smiled into her shining eyes. "What, Rose?"

"Hector," she paused importantly, "and Sophia Lennox-Fox are— what do you young people call it now—you know, an item!"

I frowned. "Really?"

"Yes!" She clasped her hands. "Isn't that heaven? Apparently he *did* spend time with her at the party, and then he slipped away on Sunday morning—I must say, he was very emotional at breakfast—and followed her up to London. Went all that way to woo her, and then, my dear— get this—apparently spent the entire week with her!" She clapped her hand to her mouth and suppressed a little giggle. "Our Hector!" She lowered her voice. "Hope he knew what to do. Anyway, by all accounts he's been courting and romancing her ever since, and is *completely* smitten, the dear, *dear* boy!"

"Really? Golly." I was surprised. "Well, that's wonderful. But who on earth told you all this?"

"He did!" she squeaked. "At least, he told Pinkie, on the telephone. Started off by just sort of saying he wouldn't be back for a few days because he'd met someone; then I heard her positively shriek with excitement. Of course, I had to grab the phone from her. 'Who is it, Hector darling?' I roared down the phone. 'Tell Mother!' You know how reticent he is. 'You don't really know her,' he muttered back, unconvincingly. 'Don't know her? Must know *of* her, surely?' Then Pinkie hissed in my ear, 'I think it's Sophia Lennox-Fox, Mummy!' and I nearly dropped the receiver."

"And is it?"

"That's exactly what I said, Lucy. 'Is it, Hector? Is it Sophia Lennox-Fox?' Finally he sighed and muttered, 'Oh God, whatever. If you like.' Honestly, Lucy, I could hardly hear him. So I said, 'Well, don't be shy, boy. Bring her down here and we'll all have a glass of champagne!' "

"Oh, Rose," I cautioned, "d'you think? Bit soon, wouldn't you say?"

"Well, quite, and Hector wouldn't have it. Wouldn't even *contem*plate it, but that doesn't stop us having one on his behalf, does it, to toast the happy couple? Because let me tell you, Lucy, this is *it*; I can feel it in my bones. I know that boy like the back of my hand, and I knew full well that one day he'd just shut his eyes and leap. Impulsively. Feetfirst. Just like Ned did with you!"

I blinked. "Er, right."

"So please, *do* come up and have some lunch! I'm dying to talk flowers and catering and mother-of-the-bridegroom outfits with someone, and Lavinia's still a wee bit sensitive because of You Know What. I'm also a bit worried," she fell into a dark and meaningful tone of voice, "that she might be having her own private little hot summer." She raised her eyebrows at me.

I gaped. "Rose! She can't be; she's far too young!"

"Oh, not at all. Tilly Hargreaves got hers at thirty-six, poor girl, and Lavinia shows all the symptoms. Mood swings, hot flushes, and sometimes rather whiffy, too. Anyway, enough of Lavinia. *Do* come up, Lucy; do!"

I looked into her shining eyes. Smiled. "I'd love to. Boys!" I yelled back over my shoulder. It occurred to me that if I played my cards right, I might not even have to go back in the barn at all. Not face the music.

Ben stuck his head round the door. "Yeah?"

"Darling, wash the river off your hands and faces please; we're going up to lunch with Granny."

"Oh, OK." He popped back in; then his head came out again. "Can we see you up there, Mum? We're just gutting this fish. We'll come up with Jack, in a minute, OK?"

"Fine, darling," I said coolly.

Rose linked my arm. "So, now, tell me what you think," she gushed on excitedly. "Obviously the reception will be at her parents' house, which is desperately ugly and will really take some decorating—we'll have to positively drip it with flowers, my dear, nightmare task—but I did wonder . . . d'you think we could host a dance here as well? Or d'you think that would be treading on their toes?"

"Well no, as long as that's what Hector and Sophia want. Don't you think you should ask them first? Ned and I, if you remember, fought rather shy of all that."

"Oh, but that was completely different! You were like a couple of gauche teenagers. And all this," she swung her arm around at her many acres, "was so new to you, Lucy! But this is Sophia Lennox-Fox! *Full* of savoir faire!"

"Ah."

"And this is Hector's big moment, too, don't forget. His house, his inheritance, bringing his blushing bride home, and—oh, my dear, the whole county will be here. I feel I could faint away with happiness!"

"I'm glad." I smiled, meaning it. Finally one of her children had come up trumps for her.

She squeezed my arm delightedly as we strolled down the hill and across the lake, then up the rolling parkland on the other side. As it turned into manicured lawn, we were met by Lavinia, running down the terrace steps and through the rose garden, grinning and waving her arms wildly.

"Isn't it exciting!" she shrieked. "Pinkie told me!"

"Oh, my darling, you are so sweet to take it like this," said Rose, clutching Lavinia's arm anxiously. "I rather thought—"

"My nose would be out of joint because I should have been first? Not at all, Mummy; I'm thrilled to bits. A wedding! Think of all the parties there'll be!"

Think of all the men to trawl, she meant. I took her aside as Rose peeled off, trotting excitedly up the steps to give orders in the kitchen.

"Lavinia." I lowered my voice. "What d'you mean, a wedding? He's only known her about a week, for God's sake. You can't be serious."

"Oh, but you don't know Hector. This is a first, you see, Lucy. The first time he's ever admitted to seeing anyone, any girl at all, and we've always known that when that moment came . . . that would be it. He's all-or-nothing, old Hec. You mark my words, if he's been gassing on the phone to Pinkie, of all people, he's smitten. He's in deep."

"That's what your mother said." I had to admit, Lavinia's words had a ring of truth about them. Besides, she was wrong, I *did* know Hector, up to a point, and I, too, had always had an inkling he'd do this one day. Come up with the goods and surprise everyone. Make his mother proud. Well, good for him, I thought. I just hoped he didn't feel too pressurized; too—oh well, the cat's out of the bag, so I'd better shut my eyes and take a deep breath; it is, after all, what's expected of me.

Behind us, out of the corner of my eye, I could see Jack and the boys coming up the lawn. I stuck to Lavinia like glue and followed her up the terrace steps and round the table, which yet again had been laid outside for lunch. Presumably Archie had been persuaded of the merits of eating outside; certainly he was grinning broadly as he appeared through the French windows. He rubbed his hands gleefully as he sat down beside me.

"Well, my dear, what a to-do! Your ma-in-law is in a perfect twitter, eh?"

I grinned. "It's what she's been waiting for, Archie. She's been thwarted up to now, but this is her big moment."

"It's what she was *born* for, you mean!" he roared. "And grandchildren, too! Your boys are a positive delight to us, Lucy, as you know, but she'd love Hector to have some. The girls, too. Family is so very important, don't you think?" He turned wide, rheumy eyes on me.

"Oh, very," I agreed, wondering, though, whether some families were just a little more important than others.

Ben and Max appeared and scuttled in between me and Pinkie, which left Jack—oh God—opposite.

"So," he eased himself in, "I gather old Hector's set the cat among the pigeons. Spilled some girlie beans. Bad move. But then he's new to this game, doesn't know the ropes. And frankly, I'm surprised. I had an idea the object of his affections was someone entirely different, that's what a little bird told me, but never mind, crossed wires. Sophia Lennox-Fox it is." He glanced around the table. "I don't suppose there's any danger of you lot getting off his back and letting him conduct this love affair in private, is there?" He grinned and reached for a bread roll. "All love affairs need room to breathe, you know, to flourish. Especially sexy new, illicit ones, eh, Lucy?" He winked. I flushed angrily.

"Ah yes, an affair like this," he went on, waggling the bread roll sagely and narrowing his eyes thoughtfully, "needs to be nurtured. It needs to be cherished, to be nourished, and it needs to be conducted in private. It needs to be cosseted and played out in dark, candlelit eateries, then smuggled under a duvet, under the eaves of some delicious little love nest. It certainly doesn't need you lot, with your faces pressed to the window, breathing all over it. Isn't that right, Luce? Give the boy a break, that's what I say!"

"Of course we'll give him a break," said Rose, bustling through the French windows, still smiling and even carrying a bowl of salad, which had Joan's eyes behind her out on stalks. "We'll give him whatever he wants, won't we, darling! If he needs space, he can have the dower house." She beamed at her husband.

Archie blinked. "Steady on, old girl. Within reason, eh? And I do think, my love, that understandably excited though you no doubt are, Jack has a point. Give the lad five minutes' peace, eh? Don't interrogate him, question him rigid the moment he walks through the door. Salad, Lucy? Boys? And don't scare the poor girl away, either. No waggling *Brides* magazine under her nose or mentioning family tiaras; you know what you're like. Get that, would you, Joan?" He turned as the telephone rang.

" 'Scare the poor girl?' Good heavens." Rose's mouth gaped incredulously. "Lucy. Did I ever scare you?" She rounded on me as she sat down.

"Er, well." I scratched my chin. "Intimidate, perhaps, but never actually *scare*, Rose," I added hastily, seeing her face. "And don't forget, Sophia is much better equipped than I was, coming as she does from a similar social background. All that savoir faire under her Gucci belt."

"Well, quite!"

I grinned into my plate as Archie, beside me, got up to take the call Joan had answered.

"Did you feel that, Lucy?" Lavinia asked in surprise. "That you lacked something, amongst us?"

I just loved the way she put that. No guile, either. "No," I answered truthfully, "but I felt others might have done."

"Ah." She frowned, perplexed, as she tried to figure that one out. She gave up. "So!" She clapped her hands prettily. "Pages?" She turned to Ben and Max.

"Pages of what?" asked Ben, bewildered.

"Page boys, darling," she tinkled. "You know, it means you follow the bride up the aisle and take her flowers, that sort of thing. We'll try not to force you into tights."

"What bride?"

"Uncle Hector's bride, of course! Oooh, Mummy, I meant to say," she leaned across the table, "Mimsy Compton-Burrell has just done the most *delicious* flowers for the church. If we wanted to keep it simple, naive, and very un-Londony—and I think we *do*—then we really couldn't do better than her. She does the most heavenly things with cow parsley."

"I agree. I must talk to Angela Lennox-Fox. Not to—you know, foist our opinions on her or anything, because she is, after all, in pole position, but just, you know, to *guide* her."

"Quite right. After all, she's only married three daughters herself," muttered Jack.

"Just to have a word, point her in the right direction. And let's face it, she has got the most frightful taste. The flowers she had at Edward's sixtieth—well, my dear!"

"Ghastly." Lavinia shuddered.

"Which at least means you won't clash at the wedding, Rose," Jack pointed out naughtily. "Since you'll be in the most tasteful ensemble imaginable."

"Oh, heavens, no, we won't clash! She'll be in some ghastly fuchsia pink affair, much too short, particularly with her legs, and with feathers billowing out of her hat, whereas *I'll* be in—"

"Lilac?" suggested Jack, head on one side, index finger pointing campily to the corner of his mouth. "Lilac's very à la mode this year. And with a witty little touch of pale green, perhaps, in the hat?"

"P-oss-ibly," Rose nodded, unaware she was being wound up, "or maybe a very, very pale lemon. I saw a divine lemon suit in Peter Jones recently."

"Oooh, lemon!" Jack shut his eyes ecstatically. "Heaven!" he murmured, clasping his hands.

"Yes, it was heaven, actually," Rose went on excitedly. "It had the most darling little square pearl buttons all the way down the front, and—Archie! Good Lord. Whatever's the matter?"

Archie had appeared back from the house through the French windows. His normally ruddy face was pale; and his lips, thin and compressed.

"That was Hector," he announced. "Ringing from London."

"Oh!" Rose got up happily. "How is the dear boy? Is he coming back soon?"

"Sit down, Rose," he snapped. "No, he rang to tell us about the wedding."

"Oh! So there *is* going to be a wedding!"

"Oh yes, there's going to be a wedding all right. But it's not the one you think."

"What d'you mean?" Suddenly Rose's eyes were huge with fear. She lowered herself into her chair.

"He's not marrying Sophia Lennox-Fox at all. He's marrying someone else."

"Someone else?" she breathed. "Who?"

"He's marrying Rozanna," he said grimly. "Rozanna Carling."

Chapter Fourteen

THE BLOOD LEFT ROSE'S FACE. "ROZANNA? YOU MEAN Lucy's friend—the girl who was here on the weekend?"

"Exactly."

"Oh!" Rose's hand flew to her mouth. "Oh, so not Sophia Lennox-Fox . . ."

"No! Not Sophia sodding Lennox-Fox," snapped Archie impatiently. "Rozanna Carling!"

"So why did Pinkie say . . . ?" Rose turned in a daze to her daughter. "Pinkie, why did you tell us . . . ?"

"Because that's what *he* said," squeaked Pinkie indignantly, coloring up. "That's what he said when I talked to him on the phone. He said Sophia Lennox-Fox!"

"What, with no prompting?" asked Jack.

"Well," she blustered, "I suppose I did rather, you know, press him. But not much. When he said he was with someone, I just sort of teased him, you know, like we do. 'Ooh, Hector,' I said, 'it's Sophia, isn't it?' And finally he just sighed and said, 'Oh God, Pinkie, whatever you want to think.'" She went a bit redder. Looked like she might cry. "I didn't know he was palming me off, did I?" She turned tearful eyes on her father as everyone looked at her. "Daddy, tell them it's not my fault. I didn't know he was going to lie to me!"

"No, no, all right, poppet," said Archie gruffly. "The lad's at fault as usual. Led you up the garden path. And the moral of the story is," he added angrily, "don't corner him. Don't run him to ground unless you want lies, damned lies, and more damned lies!"

"Well. Rozanna!" Rose's voice sounded unnaturally shrill. She was frantically twisting a hanky around her finger. Her face was still pale, but her eyes were suffused with a curious brightness. "I mean, Lady Carling. Yes, and I thought she was delightful, actually. I mean—her father's Lord Belfont, isn't he?" You could see the frantic thought processes at work as she turned to Archie. "And she was awfully pretty, don't you think?" She swung around in her chair to Lavinia. "Lavinia, you thought so, too, didn't you? And," she turned to me, "she's a friend of yours, isn't she, Lucy? You brought her down here." She looked at me eagerly. "I imagine she's absolutely lovely."

I swallowed, feeling faintly sick and wishing I were another form of life. An earthworm would be ideal. "Um, yes," I muttered eventually. "Yes, she is."

"And, Lavinia, you liked her, didn't you darling?" Rose urged.

"I thought she was a complete poppet," gushed Lavinia, clearly not to be done out of her party. "So elegant and sophisticated, and that darling way she does her hair. And to be honest, Mummy, I've never really liked Sophia much anyway. She reminds me of a ferret."

"Smells like one, too," sniffed Pinkie, wiping her nose.

"Well, quite," said their mother staunchly. "Those long yellow teeth, and those ghastly heavy breasts, too. They'd drive me round the bend. You know she had two pounds surgically removed from each one of those, imagine! That's the equivalent of two huge bags of sugar—and she still has to put her hands underneath them if she breaks into a trot. And of course there was that terrible business after Tootsie Pilkington's twenty-first . . . ."

"Oh, with Willie Fergason?" said Lavinia eagerly.

"Exactly. *And* with her mother's new Dyson. Speaking of which, of course, her mother is a prize bitch—quite apart from having no taste and a hideous house. And Rozanna seemed such a *sweet* little thing, really lovely." The color was rapidly returning to Rose's cheeks as she warmed to her theme. "And, Lavinia, did you see the way she knew everyone? And she doesn't even live here! Obviously *extremely* social and well connected, and—*oh!*"

We all jumped as Archie slammed his fist down hard on the table in front of Rose. Silver rattled violently.

"Enough!" he hissed in her face.

Rose blanched. She blinked back in horror. "Archie, whatever—"

"Enough, Rose! Everyone, in fact!" He glared around the table.

"But—but why?" she stammered.

"Because there isn't going to be a wedding. Certainly not to Rozanna Carling!"

"B-but, Archie. I thought you liked her! I thought you knew her; you introduced me to her. Why on earth—"

"Because . . . she is . . . a tart." He enunciated it, in measured tones, through clenched teeth.

Rose stared. "A tart!" She inched back, perceptibly, in her chair.

"What's a tart?" piped up Ben.

"You know, like Pinkie," offered Max helpfully.

"Max!" I swung around, appalled.

"But you said so, Mum. To Teresa. I heard you."

"No, no," I blustered, "not *this* Pinkie, darling." Christ, how many Pinkies could there be? "Pinkie Jameson—the one I was at school with!"

"Ah, *that* Pinkie," muttered Jack dryly.

I glared at him and avoided Pinkie's eye, flushing madly.

"But—but surely you don't mean," Rose was still struggling to get to grips with this preposterous proposition, still glued, in fact, to Archie's uncompromising pale blue eyes, "you surely don't mean a *proper* one? You just mean she's had a few boyfriends. You don't mean—well, like a call girl?"

"That's exactly what I do mean, Rose," said Archie with a terrible clenched calmness. "Rozanna Carling is a high-class courtesan. She is a woman in the mold of Christine Keeler. Very expensive, very select, but a courtesan, nonetheless. A prostitute." There was a silence.

"For money?"

"For money."

Another silence ensued.

"How do you know?" Rose gasped, at length.

Archie ground his teeth savagely. "One . . . just . . . does," he hissed.

Although she wasn't beside me, I felt Rose stiffen. Her lips were bloodless as she gazed into her husband's pale bulging eyes. As he glared back at her, something tacit and unbeknown to the rest of us went on between those eyes. Something that went way back. Suddenly Archie remembered his audience. He went on evenly.

"There are some things, Rose, that happily you have no knowledge of. Things that go on in the world, that happen to other people, away from the safety of Netherby, away from your rose garden, that you simply wouldn't believe." He gave a thin smile.

She stared at him. "Oh, I can believe it all right," she said softly. Her lips were taut. "I can believe it, Archie."

I looked down at my hands. Others regarded their plates with equally false intensity and concentration. Archie straightened up, eyes still on his wife.

"So there will be no wedding," he went on quietly. "And if there is, if Hector persists in seeing this woman, and going through with this ridiculous charade, then there will be no inheritance. He'll get nothing from me. Not this house, this land, nothing. He forfeits everything. This . . . liaison," he spat the word out in disgust, "must end. And if it doesn't, and it may not, then he's finished. He may not bring that woman here; neither may he set foot in this house again. That is my final word on it."

With that he turned and marched back into the house, slamming the French windows behind him. The glass rattled in its frames. There was a shocked silence.

Rose put a trembling hand to her bosom, her face white.

"Oh God, he means it," she whispered. "Oh, my God, my poor Hector. Jack, he means it." She turned imploringly to the only man present. "He'll turn Hector out on the streets! He—he'll be a tosser!"

Jack frowned. "A tosser?"

"Yes, you know," she waved her hanky wildly, "sleeping in doorways, in a cardboard box!" She suppressed a little moan.

"Dosser, Mummy," muttered Pinkie.

"Whatever," she said dismissively. "Either way, it'll be the end of him." She straightened up suddenly with an almighty sniff. "Archie's mind is made up, I can see that. So," she clutched her heart, eyes wide in horror, "so—oh, dear God, that'll be two of my sons gone! First Ned, and now Hector. Oh, where will it all end!"

At this point she was ambushed by tears. Lavinia and Pinkie instantly got up and moved smartly into action like a pincer movement, one at each shoulder, hugging and squeezing hard. This only served to make Rose sob louder. My boys were transfixed, eyes wide, mouths slack, and it occurred to me to wonder if they'd seen enough street theater for one day.

"Ben, Max, help Joan to clear the table, would you please?" I asked them. Neither child moved. "Ben! Max!" The two of them sat defiantly, damned if they were going to miss a moment.

"I'll go and talk to him," Lavinia announced importantly, straightening up from her mother's shoulder and sticking out her navy blue bosom determinedly. "I'll go and see him, make him see reason. Tell him he'll be ruining the family name."

"Yes." Rose brightened perceptibly. Looked up with a sniff. "Yes, darling, do that. Stress the family name. Good idea."

"Er, is it?" inquired Jack. "I mean, d'you think you're the right person, Lavinia? Only, with all due respect, you and Hector have never exactly seen eye to eye, have you?" He cleared his throat nervously. "I mean, you've never exactly—"

"Got on," finished Rose. She nodded firmly. "No, quite right, Jack." She turned to her daughter. "He's right, Lavinia. Hector's always had a thing about you."

"Has he?" She looked astonished.

"Yes, darling, can't bear you."

"Oh!" Lavinia looked startled.

I stared at my plate. God, this *family*. It was all coming out now, wasn't it?

"Well, come on, darling, you know how he calls you Lavvy the Lush. No, Jack, you're absolutely right; she's not the right person to go. *You* go. He'll listen to you. And, Lucy," she turned to me, raising her chin empirically, "you go with him."

"Me?"

"Yes, Hector's always liked you, too. Some drivel about kind eyes. Both of you go, and *talk* to him, my darlings, please! Make him see reason!" She wrung her hanky a bit here, made her famous face, lots of blinking, neck muscles taut. More tears threatened. Jack glanced at me, shrugged. I swallowed nervously.

"You know, Rose, I can't help thinking this may not be the best course of action."

"Oh?" Her chin shot out defiantly in my direction. "Why so?"

"I just wonder if the timing's right. I mean, perhaps the thing to do would be to leave well alone for the moment and let the affair run its course. Let Hector have the time of his life, don't interfere at all, and then perhaps it'll fizzle out naturally, when he realizes it's a non-starter. I'm sure he will realize that, and I suspect Rozanna will, too, but I really don't advise poking our noses in at this stage, when he's six days into his lovers' tryst and when—well, God, when it's all so new to him! I mean, crikey, it's the first time it's happened to dear old Hec; he's bound to be intoxicated, think This Is It. I reckon we should leave well alone."

"Hear, hear," agreed Jack.

"No!" Rose got to her feet, eyes blazing. "No, I insist! Lucy, after all I've done for you—for both of you!" She swept Jack into her icy glare. "I insist you go and talk to him. I know Hector. I know that boy of mine, and I'll tell you something: given half a chance he'll get hitched on some Jamaican beach, barefoot with flowers in his hair, with this—this two-bit *whore*," she screeched, "standing beside him in blasted *broderie anglaise*! They'll have piccaninny bridesmaids and some darky minister marrying them and—OOOoooh!" At this truly terrifying scenario she really did pale. She caught her breath, sat down abruptly, and then suddenly slumped forward. Went headfirst into her Caesar salad, rattling the plate with her forehead.

There was a horrified silence.

"Is she dead?" Ben whispered.

"No, no, darling." Lavinia rallied and swooped to lift her mother's head, wiping lettuce off her cheek. "No, not dead. Pills, Pinkie, quick!" she snapped. "Come on, quickly, in her pocket! No—cardigan pocket you fool."

Pinkie hastily found them and wrestled with the lid.

"Pills?" I breathed, on my feet now.

"For angina. Very mild, but she gets it occasionally. Help me, Pinkie."

We watched as the two sisters helped their mother sit up at the table, simultaneously popping pills in her mouth and chucking water down her throat, getting most of it down her cardigan.

"Slap her—quick, slap her!" commanded Lavinia.

Pinkie hesitated. "Why don't you?"

"Because I'm holding her, you fool!"

Pinkie licked her lips nervously—then smartly obeyed.

"Ouch!" Rose's eyes popped open. She glared fiercely at Pinkie.

"Right, now, swallow!" commanded Lavinia.

Her mother seemed to know the ropes and gulped obediently at the glass of water held at her mouth. We watched, rapt.

"Better?" barked Lavinia.

"Much, darling. Thank you," Rose muttered bleakly. Some color did indeed appear to be returning to her cheeks, but then it could have been Pinkie's handiwork.

"Come on then," ordered Lavinia. "Upstairs for a little rest. Up to beddy-byes for a bit of shut-eye. It's all been much too much for you, hasn't it, hmmm?" Adopting a tone normally reserved for the mentally subnormal, she hauled her mother to her feet. "Upsa-daisy!" Jack got to his feet, too, but Lavinia shook her head firmly. "No, Jack, we're fine. Quite used to this. We'll manage. Quite normal. I'll tell you what you could do, though. Get hold of David, ask him to pop over."

"Right." Jack got to his feet and made to go in, to ring David Mortimer, Archie's oldest friend and the family doctor.

"Yes, get David," Rose muttered as she was maneuvered off by her minders. Suddenly her head swung around like a machine gun. "And you'll go?" She gazed at us both. "To see Hector?" I glanced at Jack, his foot inside the French windows. Blimey, the control! Even when she was dying.

"Yes, we'll go," agreed Jack.

"Tomorrow?" she pleaded. "Please say you'll go tomorrow, Jack?"

"We'll go tomorrow," he soothed.

She inclined her head graciously. Gave him a shaky smile. Even blew a little kiss, before being led away.

When they were out of earshot, I stood up.

"Oh, terrific. Marvelous. Tomorrow, eh? Because you were too weak to say no. We will *not* go tomorrow, Jack; she is not running my life to that extent. We'll think about it, and go when we choose! Next week, perhaps, or even the week after, but only when the time is right. Only when I've spoken to Rozanna, warned her that we might be bowling up on her doorstop, and for her to be prepared. God, why should we tear up the motorway ruining Hector and Rozanna's fun the second it starts. Oooh, this family. Drives me insane! Come on, boys."

"Right, fine." Jack held up his hands. "Christ, I don't want to bloody well do it, either, I just want to get it over with!"

"And you were too wet to say no to her," I snapped. "This is what happens when one's beholden to people." I eyed him beadily.

"I am not beholden to her."

"You live in her house, just as we do. The difference is, though, that I refuse to feel pressurized because of it. I refuse to feel indebted!"

"You're quite right," he said evenly. "I do live in her house, temporarily, but the real difference is that in six weeks' time I shall be out of here, out of her jurisdiction, so I feel no pressure. What I do feel though, intrinsically and emotionally, is obviously slightly different from you, Lucy. You see, I really rather like Hector, ridiculously naive as he is, and I'd like to help him. I'd like to make sure a wedge isn't driven between him and his family. Now it may be that he doesn't need my help, but I'd like to try. He is, after all, my cousin, and Rose is my aunt, and your mother-in-law, who actually I feel rather sorry for, right now. You see, whatever you might think of this family, Lucy, however much you deride them, we seem to be affiliated to them. I don't actually regard myself as the sycophantic recipient of their charity, but the fact that you clearly do, and it bothers you, is your problem. Let me know when you do feel the time is right, Lucy. No pressure."

He put his hands in his pockets and walked calmly into the house through the French windows. I stared at his departing back, fists clenched at my sides.

"Ooooh . . . bloody man!" I seethed after him, hoping he could hear. I unballed my fist and stuck it out to Max. "Come on. We're going home."

"What, is everyone just having salad for lunch then?"

"Yes, just salad!" I snapped.

And with that we set off down the terrace steps and stomped down through the rose garden.

"Why are you so cross?" panted Ben, trotting to catch up with me.

"Because he thinks he's effing well right all the time, that's why!"

Max and Ben looked at each other in delight. "Stre-ssy," murmured Ben.

Yes, stressy, and furious, too, or, correction, infuriated actually. Principally because, I slowed down a bit here, I had a nasty feeling Jack *might* effing well be right, damn him. I watched the boys run on. He'd shamed me back there, with his talk of duty and family, and he'd also been right about Rose. There had been something terribly vulnerable about her, which had moved me, too, albeit momentarily. Something awfully touching about the way she was so desperate for everything to be all right. Sophia was off the marital agenda, but—so what! Rozanna must surely be lovely. She'd been determined to like her, until of course the beans had been spilled, and then—well, who in God's name would want their son to marry a call girl? How delighted would I be if Ben or Max pitched up with one on the doorstep?

Which brought me to Rozanna. What the hell was she up to? I wondered. What planet was she on? Clearly something had happened when she'd stayed the night at Netherby—acquiring not only the most sumptuous room but Hector, the mysterious corridor creeper, with it—and obviously a little benevolence had gone on on her part, as she'd treated him to a heavenly time, but Christ, she wouldn't be *marrying* him! The whole thing was a nonsense! A figment of Hector's imagination. There was no need to go all the way up to London, for heaven's sake. No, no, I'd just give her a ring. Find out what the devil was going on. I strode determinedly up the path to the barn, ready to give her a piece of my mind.

As I flung open the front door with a flourish, a chaotic scene met my eyes. The fish had obviously been gutted by the boys on the kitchen floor in a bowl of water, and the toad jar had been kicked over. There were bloody knives and pools of rank water everywhere, and the place stank to high heaven. Oh, terrific. Thanks, Jack.

"Aaaarrgh! *Bloody* man!" I yelled, picking up the fish by its tail and flinging it squeamishly into the sink. "Clean this place up *now*, boys. I am not amused. And I am not a skivvy!"

"I've lost my toad," moaned Max, looking desperately about. "I was going to call him Nigel."

"Never mind bleeding Nigel; I just want—"

"Oh, there he is!" cried Ben as we saw him hop under the dresser. The pair of them skidded through the bloody water in hot pursuit.

"I said never mind the wretched—Christ! Now you've knocked the bowl of water over!" At that moment of complete pandemonium, the telephone rang. I snatched it up with irritable emphasis.

"What!" I shrieked furiously.

"Oh! Um, Lucy?" It was Charlie.

My heart leapt right out of my mouth. All around the room, in fact. Probably hand in hand with the toad.

"Charlie!"

"Gosh, Lucy. Didn't sound like you."

"No! No, no, sorry, it wouldn't. I was . . ." I put a hand to my forehead. Shut my eyes. "Oh well, never mind. How are you?" Suddenly I felt all the anger and the tension of the last couple of hours seep out of me. It drained clean away, right through the rugs, through the polished wooden floor, right down to the earth, the rubble, and the substructure below.

"Fine. Really fine. And so much better for seeing you this morning. I feel . . . well, I just feel rejuvenated, Lucy. Can't stop thinking about you."

"Oh!" I clutched the receiver with two hands. "Yes, me, too."

"And, Lucy," he lowered his voice, "I know we said we'd take this thing really gently and sensibly and that it's literally only about two hours since I saw you, but guess what?"

"What?" I breathed, looking guiltily at the boys, who were flat on their tummies now, diving under the dresser with sticks.

"The most tantalizing thing. I suddenly have the most amazing excuse to go to London tomorrow. The BBC have just rung to say there's a possibility they're going to make a new *Townbirds* series, which they'd like to talk to me about. I'd be busy for much of the morning, but I'd be free after that. Lucy . . . is there *any* chance of you getting away? Tell me if it's impossible, my love, but I would just adore it. I'm desperate to see you."

My knees buckled and I sat down hard on a convenient sofa.

"Not impossible," I croaked. "Not impossible at all. In fact, really rather possible." My head whirled. "Oh, Charlie, I'm desperate to see you, too!" I whispered.

"Oh, Lucy, that's brilliant. Listen, my meeting's at nine, so I should be able to get away by eleven and be at the flat from about twelve onward. I have to be back here by teatime, but we should have a couple of hours . . . OK?"

The words "a couple of hours" seemed to possess a resonance of illicit naughtiness. I shut my eyes and tried not to think of all the things that could happen in a couple of hours. "OK," I murmured.

"I must go, my love; I hear a car. Miranda's just got back from the shops. I'll see you tomorrow then, my darling. Oh, and by the way—Twenty-two Langton Villas!"

The phone went dead and I threw myself headlong onto the sofa, pressing my mouth ardently to a kilim cushion. "Twenty-two Langton Villas, twenty-two Langton Villas," I whispered passionately to the fringe. "Oh, my darling, I'm desperate, too."

"Desperate for what?"

I glanced up. Ben was standing over me, frowning.

"Oh!" I smiled radiantly up at him and sat up. Crossed my legs. "The loo. I think Max is in there."

"No, he's not. He's found his toad and he's cleaning it up. What are you doing to that cushion?"

"Hmm?" I glanced down. The cushion appeared to be up my T-shirt. "Oh." I pulled it out. "Feeling it. And smelling it, too. Mmm . . ." I sniffed. "Divine. Imagine all those lovely ethnic hands, making it."

"But who were you talking to?" he persisted.

"Oh, just someone I used to work with," I said breezily. "Why, darling?"

"Because you were pulling your tummy in and flicking back your hair and doing that silly shrieky laugh. 'Ah, ha ha *haaa*!' " he mimicked, strutting round the room. Max joined in and they pranced around together, chests and bottoms thrust out, nostrils flared. "Ah, ha ha *haaa*!" they shrieked in unison.

"Thank you, boys," I said, straightening my hair. "That will do. Oh, shit! Tomorrow!"

"Shit!" they squeaked, looking at each other in delight. "*Really* bad Mother," said Max, in awe.

That's nothing, I thought grimly as I scurried to use the phone. What they didn't know, and what I hoped to keep firmly from them, was just how bad I was about to be.

As I dialed Netherby, I realized, in my fever, that I hadn't quite worked out what I was going to say. Oh God, please don't let Rose answer. I hesitated, about to put it down, to formulate a plan, when Jack picked it up.

"Oh, Jack. Good, it's you."

"Lucy." He sounded disconcerted. I had, after all, called him a bloody man not two minutes ago.

"Um, listen, Jack." I ran an uncertain hand through my hair. "Er, I was thinking. You know, you're probably absolutely right."

"Oh? What about?"

"About wanting to go up to London tomorrow. To see Hector. "I mean—you know, the sooner we get it all over with, the sooner it's finished sort of thing." God, did that sound callous? "I mean, heavens," I added quickly, "we are a family, aren't we? A unit! Terribly important to stick together, don't you think? After all, blood is thicker than water, and all that."

"Well, not your blood."

"No, no, but Ned's blood." I glanced guiltily at the sky and crossed my fingers. Sorry, Ned. "Just as important. Oh! Oh, and the boys," I cried, suddenly remembering. "The boys' blood, too."

"Yes, all right, I think that's enough blood," he said dryly. "We'll be swimming in it soon." He paused. "You've changed your tune."

"I know, but—well. You know. I've had time to think."

"What, two minutes? I've just walked in."

"Yes." I ground my teeth and shut my eyes. "Yes—two minutes. Because that was literally all it took, Jack, to see that you were absolutely right. As usual. As per bleeding usual you were completely and utterly spot on, and your way is undoubtedly the way forward, OK? So now that we've established that, got that bit of humble pie out of the way, why don't we make a plan and stick to it, as they say in the army. Get this show on the road. I'm sure Trisha won't mind having the boys, so I'll pick you up at the house at ten o'clock tomorrow, OK?"

"Couldn't be more thrilled," he said with weary indifference. "Really. Couldn't be more thrilled. Whatever you say, Lucy. Just, whatever you say."

Chapter Fifteen

WHEN THE BOYS AND I ROARED UP THE DRIVE TO Netherby the following morning—late, naturally—Ben and Max already had their hands on the door handles, keen, it seemed, to get away from me and tumble into Trisha's more relaxed hands. She'd got my message and was ostensibly waiting for them at the back of the house, although what she was actually doing, I noticed, as I screeched to a halt on the gravel, was flirting outrageously with Jack. He was balancing on the little wall around the fountain, arms outstretched, and she was shrieking with laughter, goading him on, rushing up to whisper something in his ear as he jumped off, something too risqué and unpalatable to say out loud, no doubt. I pursed my lips, tartly.

"Stinks in here," muttered Ben as Jack opened the passenger door for him. "And watch your p's and q's, Jack. She's really, *really* hyper this morning."

"I am not hyper, Ben," I hissed, getting out and running round to help Max out of the back. "It's just you're so hopeless at getting out of bed, and now you're making me late!"

"There's no rush," said Jack easily, lowering himself into the vacated front seat. "I mean, they don't even know we're coming, do they? Blimey, Ben, you're right; there is a terrible pong in this car. What is it? Something died?" He looked around and sniffed. "A rat?"

"It's Chanel Number 19, actually," I snapped, getting back in and sniffing my wrist anxiously. Damn, I'd wondered if it was stale when I'd opened it. I hadn't used it for five years and the top was loose. Had I overdone it? "And no," I said, letting out the hand brake and reversing at speed, "they don't know we're coming, because when I rang the answer machine was on and I didn't think it prudent to leave a message in case the drawbridge went up. No, the point is, Jack, I've got other things to do in London today besides seeing Hector and Rozanna, and I don't want to be late, OK?"

I ran a harassed hand through my hair and turned back to wave to the boys. As I did, I saw Trisha blow Jack a kiss. She looked lovely. Tanned, slim, and, what was it now . . . ? Oh yes, young, that was it. I glanced in the rearview mirror. I, on the other hand, looked like a Rembrandt self-portrait. Bugger—my mascara had smudged already. I licked a finger and ran it under my eyes.

"What things?" Jack clutched his seat in mock alarm as we shot off down the drive. "Christ, you are in a hurry, aren't you? What things, and why are you all made up?"

He peered at me. I flushed and declined to answer.

"Ah, right." He nodded. "Don't tell me. Plan A is for you to go in all hot and vampy and steal Hector right from under Rozanna's nose, is that it?"

"I do not look hot and vampy!" I tugged desperately at my, admittedly, rather short skirt. Nothing was more annoying than making oneself look faintly sexy for someone in particular to find someone else vicariously enjoying it.

"Nothing wrong with hot and vampy," he mused, eyeing my legs appreciatively. "Depends what it's all in aid of. Or who, more to the point. What other things?"

"Hmmm?" I sniffed my wrist again. Definitely stale.

"You said you had to do. In London."

"Oh. I'm, um, going to see Maisie and Lucas. You know, my parents." I felt my color rise.

He regarded me quizzically. "Yes, I know your parents." He glanced ostentatiously at my skirt again. Raised his eyebrows. "Right. I'll meet you there later on then, shall I? I, too," he gave a secret smile and folded his arms, "have things to do this afternoon."

"No, actually, Jack, don't meet me there," I said quickly. "I'll pick you up when I've seen them. They live miles away, you know, right over in Westbourne Grove, and you don't want to trek all the way over there."

"It's not miles. And anyway, I'd like to see them. Haven't seen them for ages."

"I'll pick you up, Jack, OK?" I said between clenched teeth. I flashed him a glare and nearly went up a lorry's backside. God, he was really annoying me now, and I wasn't sure I liked being forced into using my parents as an excuse, either. Although I phoned regularly, I should pop in on them. I hadn't seen them for ages. I felt suffused with guilt and irritation.

"Where will you be?" I snapped.

"Hmm?" He gazed down at my legs again, smiling.

"I said, where will you be!"

"Ah yes, let me see. Where *will* I be?" He narrowed his eyes reflectively out of the window. "Chelsea, I believe," he concluded with a nod. "Yes, Chelsea. If you insist, you can pick me up from there."

"Chelsea?" I shot him a panicky look. "Whereabouts?"

"Cheyne Walk. Just off, actually. Why?"

"Oh. No reason." God, that was a relief. Cheyne Walk. Bit close for comfort, but at least it was right down by the river. "What are you doing there?" I asked lightly.

"Oh, this and that." He winked. "Passing the time. Concluding a little unfinished business."

"Ah. I see." I smiled knowingly. "You don't change, do you, Jack? Trisha know about this unfinished business?"

He frowned in mock alarm. "Now why on earth would Trisha want to know?"

"I can't imagine."

"No, me, neither. Now, Lucy, please don't quiz me anymore. I tend to crack under pressure, and anyway, I'm not used to getting up at this unearthly hour. I'm a poet, not a Eurobond dealer. I need my shut-eye."

"Go ahead; you get your beauty sleep. Have a power nap. You're going to need all the power you can get if you're going to expend all that energy later on."

"Well, quite."

He leaned back on the headrest with an equable smile, folded his hands across his chest, and shut his eyes. A few minutes later, the car reverberated to the sound of his faint rhythmic breathing. I glanced across, envying him his totally relaxed disposition. Personally I needed to be horizontal in a darkened room, preferably with an eye patch and a bottle of Benylin to hand, before I could even contemplate winding down. I sighed and turned to Classic FM for comfort. As we purred up the motorway to the soothing melodies, I tried deliberately to relax, breathing all the way up from the diaphragm as I'd read one should in the *Daily Mail* and, oh yes, thinking about something pleasant, too.

Charlie, obviously. Mmm . . . Charlie. I breathed deeply and turned up Ravel's *Bolero*, letting it wash over me, humming along to the *rum*, pu-pu-pu *pums*, which were getting really rather climactic. No wonder Torville had let Dean drag her about the ice like that. I gripped the wheel, going with the music, and as it rose to an almighty final crescendo felt my vital organs convulse with a palpable frisson, as no doubt Torville's had, too. The windscreen seemed to be steaming up. I rubbed it with my hand and wondered, nervously, if I wasn't a bit old for all this. I drove on.

As I wove off the main A40 and down the North End Road, through the backstreets of Fulham, along the Broadway, and into the narrow roads I knew so well, I really did relax. I purred into wider avenues, gazing up at the tall, creamy buildings; pale and moody, they rose into a misty blue sky, window boxes tumbling with tasteful pink geraniums, black front doors and wrought-iron railings gleaming in the hazy eastern light. Home. I turned into the bustling King's Road, crowded as ever, kicking with vitality, even at this hour; little cafés and wine bars spilled onto the street, and people clutching baguettes kissed each other hello as they met on the pavement. I felt a rush of love for the place. People. A variety of people. Some in saris, some in turbans, some in high heels, some buying yams, some buying chilies—that's what I missed. The conviviality, the chance meetings, the friendships with people one was thrown together with, the wonderful spontaneity of dear old noisy, womblike London. Not for me the formal, calculating way Lavinia saw her friends—a dinner party in a diary two months hence and then a twenty-mile journey to sit around a vast table with sixteen clones of herself—no. Spaghetti in the kitchen with my neighbors. A cappuccino with Jess on a hot pavement. That was my style, if I had one.

As I drew into my old road, I thought, too, how lovely it would be to see Charlie here. Back on familiar territory, in home clothes, mufti, as it were, where I felt most comfortable. As I glanced up at number 24, flicking my old, just about valid parking permit into the window, I realized, with an almighty pang, that stupidly, I hadn't even considered how I would react to being back home. How overwhelmingly nostalgic I would feel. How jealous of whoever was in my top-floor flat right now, walking about in my kitchen, putting the kettle on in my window. To my horror, a heavy weight descended on my heart and tears welled. I swallowed hard and willed myself to buck up, blinking desperately. Suddenly I saw a face appear at Rozanna's ground-floor window. It was Hector. A light went on, the curtain closed, and I remembered, with a jolt, why we were here.

I glanced across at Jack, still sleeping soundly. Wiped my eyes. Oh God, we hadn't even *talked* about what we were going to say, let alone how we were going to approach this. I leaned across and shook him awake.

"Jack—wake up! Listen, we're here, and we haven't really got a plan at all, have we? What are we going to say?"

"Hmmm?" Jack opened his eyes. He yawned and stretched. "Oh, I'd say we pretty much play it by ear, wouldn't you?" He scratched his head sleepily.

"Yes, but—"

"Look, Lucy. All we can do is watch and listen, really. We can't force anything out of him, and we can't drag him home by the scruff of his neck. He's thirty-six, for God's sake."

I stared up at the house. Thirty-six. Christ, yes, thirty-six! What were we *doing* here, anyway? Hector was practically middle-aged, not a child. It was purely because he behaved like one that one forgot. I got out of the car and followed Jack nervously up the steps. My steps. The ones I'd dragged shopping up countless times, carried pushchairs and sleeping children up. I knew them intimately. Every line, every crack, every indentation.

I no longer had a key, so we had to press the buzzer. As we stood on the step, Jack smiled at me.

"How does it feel to be back?" he asked gently.

I shrugged nonchalantly. Pulled a face. "OK. A bit weird, actually," I lied. But it didn't. It felt safe. Like home.

"Oh!" Rozanna squawked through the intercom after we'd announced ourselves. "It's you. Well, you'd better come in."

We pushed the heavy black door and waded through the familiar sea of circulars that accumulated on the doormat no matter how often one picked them up, and then on down the long corridor.

Rozanna was waiting. She was standing at the entrance to her flat, arms folded in her blue silk dressing gown, leaning against the door frame. She smiled ruefully.

"Well, I don't know why I'm surprised," she drawled. "I suppose we should have expected this. Hey, Hec," she threw over her shoulder. "It's the Seventh Cavalry. They've come to rescue you at last."

"Idiot," I said, kissing her as she let us in. "We're not rescuing anyone. Just came to see you, that's all."

"Hees mother," wheedled Jack, twiddling an imaginary Mexican moustache, "she say she pay twenty thousand Amereecan dollars for the gringo's release." He grinned at a surprised Hector, who was reading in the window seat at the far end of the room. "Hi there, Hec." He turned back to Rozanna. "What you say to that, beetch?"

Rozanna grinned back. "I say you tell her no! I say you take hees leetle finger back in a box and tell her, for twenty thousand dollars, ees all she's getting!"

"And that's the only extremity you're prepared to relinquish?" Jack enquired, lowering his voice. "Nothing," he waggled his eyebrows, "nothing larger?"

She giggled. "No, I'm rather partial to the rest, aren't I, Hec?"

Hector swung his legs round off the seat and stood up indignantly. "Bloody cheek. She sent you up here, didn't she? Well, I'm not going back, you know." He blinked hard, fists clenched by his sides.

He reminded me of a child, defiantly declaring he wasn't going back to boarding school at the end of the holidays. On closer inspection, though, I did a double take. I'd hardly recognized him, reclining on that window seat, and now I realized why. He was dressed, not in his usual uniform of Viyella checked shirt and cords but in a bright pink shirt and black jeans, for heaven's sake.

" 'Course you're not going back, Hector," I soothed. "We just wanted to talk to you, that's all. See—"

"How the land lies," interrupted Rozanna. "Have a nose. Take notes, report back, that kind of thing. Well, go on then; get on with it."

"Yes, that's it," agreed Jack cheerfully, removing a laundry basket from a chair before flopping down into it. "But please, let it be noted, that we're 'nosing,' as you put it, under duress. As Luce and I were bound to agree earlier, we still have to suck up to old Ma Fellowes, because we still live there, don't we?" He shot me a look. "Unlike you, you bastard." He grinned at Hector. "You made it over the wire, lucky sod. I take it the forged passport worked, then? And the civvies I made for you from my old underpants?"

"I'm not going back," repeated Hector, ignoring Jack's banter, "and that's final. You can tell her that from me. I love Rozanna, and I'm not giving her up. I'm going to marry her, and that's the end of it, OK?"

His face was flushed with emotion, and I couldn't help thinking it was probably the longest speech he'd ever made.

"Good for you, old boy," said Jack quietly. "That's all we need to know. All we need to hear, in fact. No doubt about your feelings, we'll report back immediately." He plucked a bra from the laundry basket beside him and put it on his head, aping earphones. "Mayday, Mayday, ship's going down," he reported into his clenched fist. "No use sending lifeboats, captain's going down with it. Hmm? What? First mate? Hang on; I'll ask. Rozanna?" He turned quickly, smiling but regarding her carefully. "You going down, too?"

She wrapped her blue robe around her with a smile. Plucked the bra off his head.

"Ah yes, I see," she said lightly, but it was the lightness of metal. "You think Hector is the innocent here, don't you? And that obviously his feelings will be pure and true, because it's the first time he's fallen head over heels in love, poor darling. But dear old Rozanna, well. I mean, she's knocked about a bit, hasn't she? She's a tart, for crying out loud; how can she possibly have feelings about anyone? All that bonking must have numbed her emotions, petrified them rigid. *Paid* bonking, too. And all those men! Heavens."

There was a silence as she went to stand beside Hector. "Except that actually, Jack, despite all those men, I've never met one like Hector." She paused. "Oh, I've met some charming ones, don't get me wrong, and I've had a very nice time, been treated quite splendidly, in fact; otherwise I wouldn't have done it. And I never had to do it, either. I could always turn a guy down if I didn't fancy him, walk out of his luxury suite at Claridge's saying, 'No thanks, mate, simply not interested,' as was often the case. But you know," she puckered her brow, "interestingly, out of all the ones I did fancy, all the ones I did spend the night with—city businessmen, captains of industry, diplomats, pop stars—I never, ever wished I could take one home. Never met one I'd like to keep. But then," she turned fondly to Hector, "like I said, I never met one like this before." Their eyes seemed to collide. Ignite, almost. "A decent, kind, sincere, straightforward man, who isn't afraid of his emotions, who tells me what he's thinking the moment he thinks it. A good person." She turned back. "Prior to that, I'd only ever met men who couldn't get over themselves. Men like Archie."

I blanched. Glanced quickly at Hector. Rozanna smiled wryly.

"Oh, it's OK; he knows. In fact, he knows everything about me now." She slipped her arm through his. "How could he possibly not? I've told him everything. Told him how I slipped into this game in the first place, how—"

"Told him about Tommy?" interposed Jack quietly.

She flinched.

"Tommy?" I demanded, glancing first to Jack, then back at her. "Tommy who?"

"Tommy Parker," she said quietly, not taking her eyes off Jack. "My fiancé. Or ex-fiancé. Who ditched me—not quite at the altar but near as, dammit—five years ago. Tommy, who I'd known forever, since I was a child. And who I believed I'd love forever, too. Tommy I loved more than life itself. Like you loved Ned."

"Oh, Rozanna." I stepped forward. "I had no idea. You never said—"

"No, I didn't," she said softly, shaking her head. "I never said. But yes, Jack, in answer to your question, Hector does know. He also knows how I picked myself up from that, grief-stricken, shattered, demoralized, and vowed I'd never love again. How I hated men, loathed them, loathed the way the so-called sexual revolution had enabled them to sleep with whoever they wanted, for as long as they wanted—with no strings attached. With impunity. I loathed the power they seemed to wield. Hated the concept that apparently, it was OK, because we women were empowered, too. Wondered if there weren't any small, lone female voices who didn't want that power, preferred the way Mother Nature had intended it to be for us, preferred, after five years of sharing a man's bed, to have a wedding ring and babies to show for it instead." She gave a wry smile. "All very warped and bitter, a psychologist would no doubt tell you, and all, doubtless, because I'd been scorned. Oh yes, I told Hec everything. I told him how, almost out of revenge, I started sleeping with men—and then never seeing them again. Never returning their calls. Tossing them aside. How I, in turn, enjoyed that power. How it snowballed. How an aristocratic friend of mine introduced me to men who, as he coyly put it, didn't want any commitment, and how suddenly I found myself turning from a jilted twenty-two-year-old deb with some serious hang-ups into a highly desirable high-class whore."

She ran her hand through her mane of long blond hair. Sighed ruefully. "And for what it's worth, I haven't actually slept with that many, either. Like I said, I'm fussy. More than twenty, but less than thirty. Not a patch on you of course, Jack," she shot him a sharp look, "but probably on a par with your average girl about town. The difference being, of course, that unlike your average girl about town, I didn't just take dinner off them. I took their money, too. Possibly some of their dignity as well, who knows. I certainly never felt they took any of mine." She paused, looked past us reflectively. "Yes, Hector knows all that. How could he not? It's a fundamental truth about me. There's no getting away from it."

Hector put his arm protectively around her. "She's had a tough time," he said simply. "But that's all going to stop now. It's all going to change, isn't it, Rosie?" He looked down at her.

I caught my breath. God, there was such a stunning naïveté about him. It was as if his attitude was: Oh well, that was that. An unfortunate chapter in Rozanna's life, but now we move on. Forget it. And yet . . . I looked at his open, generous face, thought how tall he looked next to Rozanna, who was tiny, actually, but then I'd only ever seen her in very high heels, swathed in cashmere and silk, playing out her costume drama. How small and vulnerable she looked now, her face bare of makeup, and quite young, too, in her late twenties perhaps, and I'd always thought she was much older than me. I licked my lips nervously. It seemed so unfair to say it, but—

"Rozanna, his family. Hector's family. They're obviously very upset."

"Of course," she agreed, "and so would I be if I were them. And that's why I've told Hector to ask me in a year's time. I've told him to forget it for at least as long as that. To ask me then."

"Oh! Good idea," I breathed.

"Seems sensible," Jack nodded.

She smiled wryly. "Because you think it'll all be over by then, don't you? Blow out in a couple of months, probably. 'Oh, *she'll* want it all right, old Rozanna, you bet she will, because, my God, it's her only lifeline, isn't it? She'll grasp at anything, anything that means she can have a half-normal life—a home, a family, some respectability (so long as no one finds out, nudge nudge)—but he'll come to his senses, eventually. Oh yes, he'll wise up. Realize that his family and most of Oxfordshire will ostracize him, see his inheritance going down the pan, and come to in double-quick time.' It won't last a minute, that's what you'll all think. No." She held up her hand to halt my protest. "That's what *everyone* will think. Not just you. And with good reason."

"You'll all shake your heads," broke in Hector quietly, "and think, 'Poor, stupid Hector. What a fool he's made of himself. First time over the hurdles of course, so he's bound to think he's fallen in love. Christ, we all felt like that, but we were more like eighteen!' " He smiled. "But actually, it's not so. Contrary to popular belief, I'm neither gay nor a virgin," he eyed us, quite beadily for Hector, "and whilst I haven't exactly been sexually promiscuous, I've had my fair share. I've just never understood what all the fuss was about. Until now. But then . . . I'd never experienced this. The two together. Sex and true love. Bingo." His eyes widened. "And I do know this to be true love. You see, it's the only time in my life, I've ever felt . . ." He paused, searched for the word. "Complete."

He smiled down at Rozanna. "And I'm not waiting a year, whatever she thinks. I'm going to ask her every day. Every morning when I wake up with her, see her face on the pillow beside me, watch her blue eyes open. And you mark my words." He glanced up. "One fine day, she's going to say yes."

There was a silence. Jack and I regarded them, standing there before us. Hector seemed to have grown in stature overnight, tall and protective, whilst Rozanna looked smaller, softer. It seemed to me that they were almost standing before us as they might in church. That it might already have happened.

Jack cleared his throat. "Well, Hector." He strode forward and stuck out his hand. "If that's the lie of the land, then all I can say is good for you, mate. More power to your elbow!" He pumped Hector's hand enthusiastically.

I hugged Rozanna. "Congratulations," I whispered. "Lucky you." And I meant it.

She held me, then stood back and touched my shoulders, blue eyes shining. "I know. Lucky, lucky me!"

After that, it seemed only natural to sit down and have breakfast with them, share the tray of *pain au chocolat* they'd had warming in the oven, and listen, in slack-jawed wonder, as Hector told us exactly what his father could do with his Oxfordshire pile and the coffers that went with it. Actually, it transpired Archie couldn't completely swipe the carpet from under Hector's feet, because of a trust fund that kicked in eventually, which his father couldn't touch. But trust fund or not, we heard that Hector intended to be independent of his family, to make his own way, and that for the first time in his life he was going to get a job.

"As what?" I asked in awe, spraying crumbs around and I hoped not looking too incredulous.

"As an artist," said Rozanna proudly. She hastened to the window seat and picked up the book Hector had dropped as we came in. As she came back, I saw that it wasn't a book at all, but a sketch pad. She plonked it down in front of us.

I turned the pages. "But these are amazing," I breathed, gazing in admiration. "I had no idea . . . Oh!" I stopped as I turned the last page and found myself staring at a brilliant sketch of Rozanna, stark naked and reclining on a rug by the fireplace. He must have been working on it in the window, literally the moment we arrived, hence the light going on, the curtain closing. Just before Rozanna whipped on her dressing gown to meet us.

Ridiculously, I felt myself blushing. Such a recent intimate moment, and yet what knocked me out was how proud and unashamed they were to share it with us. I stared. My God, it was good, though. He'd caught her perfectly.

"Bloody good," said Jack, taking it from me and flicking back through the pages. "Bloody good. Self-taught?" He glanced up.

"Pretty much, although recently I've been going to life classes in Oxford."

"Rather daring?" I suggested.

He grinned. "What, you mean sneaking out of that house to paint pictures rather than shoot pheasants?"

"Precisely," I giggled.

Jack shut the book. Sighed. "They're excellent, but, Hector, I have to warn you. Far be it from me to be the voice of doom, but speaking as one who tries to make a living in a similarly esot-Theo fashion, there ain't no money in this creative malarkey, you know. I mean, unless you really strike lucky, you're going to be struggling away in your garret, eking out the pennies, and you—"

"I might have to teach," Hector interrupted, nodding. "I know, and I've thought about that. I think I'd like it. I couldn't do anything as advanced as university level like you, obviously, but after a year or so at teacher training . . . maybe a local primary school? Something like that?"

"Close your mouth, Lucy," Jack grinned.

I snapped it shut. They all laughed, but—I'm sorry. The idea of Hector teaching at the local primary school, and coming home to Rozanna, who'd just put the children to bed and was making a nice rice pudding before darning his socks . . . well.

An hour or so later, after Jack and I had drunk more coffee, finally said our good-byes, hugged them both at the flat door, and given them our warmest wishes, we headed off down the corridor and I shook my head in disbelief.

"Startling enough for you?" murmured Jack as he opened the heavy front door for me.

"Totally. Totally and utterly mind-blowing. Lovely, too," I replied.

"Oh, I agree. But not without its problems." We stood for a moment, side by side on the checkered steps, gazing thoughtfully into the misty blue morning.

"Too big, d'you think? The problems?"

"No-o," he said slowly. "No, nothing insurmountable. And they've certainly got the determination. And the love." He smiled. "And you know what they say. Love conquers all."

I sighed. "It is rather romantic, isn't it?"

"In the purest sense of the word."

Another silence unfolded. I gazed at an elderly couple, sitting on a bench together in the gravel square I knew so well, feeding the pigeons. Felt a lump come to my throat.

"So . . . what do we do now?"

He shrugged. "What *can* we do? Nothing. Aside from wish them well, and report back accordingly."

"Rose will kill us," I said nervously.

He grinned. "All right, Lucy, I'll take the first bullet."

"Well, it wouldn't surprise me. I bet she keeps a small silver pistol under her pillow for just such an eventuality."

"We'll see." He glanced at his watch. "Coffee? Or even—God no, wine. Definitely wine. It's nearly twelve o'clock. We've been hours in there."

I gazed at him in horror. "No, it can't be." I grabbed his wrist, stared. "Oh God, it is!" I squeaked. "It's quarter to twelve!"

"Is that a problem?"

"It's just I said I'd *be* somewhere at eleven!"

He frowned. "Only Maisie and Lucas's, surely?"

"Yes," I gulped, hastening down the steps. "Yes, only Maisie and Lucas; they'll understand."

I glanced up at him as I hovered on the pavement, wishing he'd go. I had a parking place, and Charlie was only round the corner. I could walk. Run, even. I didn't want to have to go through the rigmarole of pretending to drive off to my parents', didn't want to repark.

"If you're going via the King's Road, I'll cadge a lift," he said, walking toward my car.

I stared. "No. No, I'm not going via the King's Road."

"Ah. Tower of London, perhaps? Madame Tussaud's? The scenic route?"

"Of course not," I blustered. "It's just—well, I thought I'd pop in on Teresa. For a moment. Since I'm here. See you later, Jack."

"Ah. Sorry, my mistake, I thought you were late. But there we are. Well, we'll both go up, shall we? I'd like to say hello while I'm here."

Somehow, against my will, and to my complete and utter horror, I found myself being herded, almost manhandled, back through the front door and up four flights of steps. It was the work of a moment. We reached the top and stood panting, bang opposite my old front door.

"This is Teresa's flat, isn't it?" Jack was grinning hugely.

"Yes," I gasped, staring dumbly at the familiar green door. "Yes, it is."

"So?" He raised his eyebrows. "How about knocky-knocky?"

How about fucky-offy? I thought, teeth gritted, but I obediently raised my knuckles and tapped. Very, very lightly.

"Not there," I muttered, turning smartly away.

"Ah, I think," Jack caught my arm, "to be fair, only a very small mouse would have heard that, don't you? Shall I try?"

He raised his fist and hammered violently, making me jump. The door reverberated. Jack beamed delightedly.

A few moments later the door flew open. Teresa stood there in a panic.

"Ah! My God!" She clutched her throat. "I thought the police at very least—Drugs Squad maybe—but it you!" She leaned forward and embraced me. "And Jack." She hugged him, too. "But you no tell me you coming," she scolded as she shooed us inside. "In, in!"

"It was a spur-of-the-moment thing, Teresa, very last-minute, and—and the silly thing is, I really can't stay."

"Can't stay? I no have that. Quick, coffee!" She pushed me toward the kitchen, but Jack saluted her in the doorway.

"Lovely to see you, Teresa, but I'm away. I'll be at 69 Upper Cheyne Street, Luce, when you're ready. Have fun." He gave me a strange look, nodded at Teresa, and then left. The door closed behind him.

"Teresa . . ."

"Oh, this kitchen, so messy! Here, you sit down," she dragged up a stool, "and I unpack while we talk. Shopping bags everywhere, see, because I been to Safeways—but I make you coffee while I unpack. And somewhere," she dived into one of the carrier bags on the floor, "somewhere I got those biscuits, those tiny chocolate ones we like, and—"

"No, no, Teresa, I can't!" I hissed, backing away, whispering in case he was still outside. "I mean, I'd love to, but—"

"But?" She straightened up, biscuits in one hand, Nescafé in the other.

"Well . . . I'm seeing Charlie!"

"Charlie?"

"Yes, Charlie! You know, you met him at the party. Lovely, gorgeous, hunky Charlie."

She frowned. "Married?"

"Well, yes, OK, if you must," I blustered. "But you were the one who said go for it, remember?"

She narrowed her dark eyes thoughtfully. "I say no such thing. I say, sometimes, we have to make our own mistakes, yes?"

"Well, OK, similar," I conceded. "But, Teresa, actually, it's all fine. You see, the thing is, his wife is a religious fanatic—isn't that wonderful? I mean, terribly sad and all that, but impossible to live with—chants her way round Tesco's, wears yashmaks, bangs her forehead on the floor, that kind of thing."

Teresa blinked. "Muslim?"

"Er, no, Christian, I think, but *very* devout. Incense swinging from the rearview mirror, that type of thing, poor guy doesn't stand a chance. Oh, Teresa, I'm desperate," I pleaded, "mad about him, and I must go; he's waiting for me. I'll ring you, OK?"

She regarded me, hands clasped beseechingly at the door, and grinned. "OK," she said. "OK, if you mad about him, you go. But you be careful."

"Of course I'll be careful!"

She made to open the door, but I was already outside. "And you going out for lunch? He take you somewhere nice?" She looked me up and down as I hovered in the hallway, longing to fly. "You look nice."

"Er, no. No, probably not . . . out for lunch. Exactly."

"Ah." She leaned on the door. "He not taken you out, yet?"

"Um, not as such. You see, we thought we'd—you know. Get to know each other first."

"Ah, I see. So first he shag you, and *then* you eat, huh?" She shook her head. "So different, the courtship rituals in this country."

I gulped. Golly. Put like that.

She grinned suddenly. "I tease you. Go. Don't be crestfallen. Go to your lover. You know, in these past few days, I see so many transformations. First I see Rozanna, then I see Hector, and now . . . I see you. And you look . . . well. Go now." She gave me a little push. "But you take care!"

"Oh, I will; I will!"

I kissed her gratefully, then spun around, tripping down those stairs as fast as my legs would carry me. My feet clattered on the stones as I ran outside, echoing in the empty street.

Chapter Sixteen

Outside in the street, I paused for a moment, looking feverishly in both directions, just to make sure Jack really had gone. Then I started running, very fast, due south. Down to the end of my road I scampered, then left, along a bit, and up the second turning on the right. Oh, I knew precisely where Langton Villas was, had trudged up and down it many a time, and usually with that wretched dog of Theo and Ray's under my arm. I must have literally gone past Charlie's nose, all hot and bothered and looking like a berk, just as—well, I was pretty hot and bothered now, wasn't I? I slowed down abruptly. Good grief, Lucy, so what if you're a few minutes late? The man can wait, can't he? D'you really want to appear on his doorstep in a complete lather, keen as mustard, with a shiny face and gushing pits? And apart from anything else, I thought, slowing to a necessary limp, I'd break my ankle in these ridiculous kitten-heeled mules if I wasn't careful. Such seduction paraphernalia was not made for Olympic sprinting.

I stopped in front of number 22, then teetered up the mountain of stone steps, my heart hammering away in my esophagus. I scanned the doorbells nervously. MR. CHARLES FLETCHER was on the ground floor, apparently, and not, I noticed with relief, MR. AND MRS. CHARLES FLETCHER. A good sign, surely? A sign that the split was imminent, already a fait accompli, and had, in fact, been on the cards long before my arrival on the scene?

I pressed the bell and prepared, for the fortunate Mr. Charles Fletcher, my most dazzling smile. As the door opened and he appeared, I bestowed it on him and, happily, got an even more dazzling one in return. It came streaming off his face, out of his brown eyes, his wide, generous mouth, and for a moment, I just bathed. He looked heavenly, naturally, in slightly faded black jeans and a white T-shirt, with an open checked flannel shirt over the top.

"Hi."

"Hi."

With these brief words did we salute each other. He, too, gazed appreciatively, taking in, I hope, the freshly washed blond hair, the tanned legs encased in a slightly too-short skirt, which I longed to tug down but just about resisted, and my favorite Portobello Road bargain, an ex–naval officer's jacket with loopy gold braid on the cuffs. At length, he remembered his manners.

"Come in; come in." He ran a hasty hand through his hair. "I had a nasty feeling you weren't coming actually; you're late. I started doing a bit of room pacing," he admitted with a grin as he ushered me down the passage.

"I know; I'm sorry," I said, trying not to beam with pleasure at his words. He'd been pacing, *pacing*. I felt unaccountably nervous all of a sudden. "I, um, had to pop in on some friends first. Well, not friends exactly, my brother-in-law and my ex-neighbor. Well, obviously, they *are* friends, but I mean—you know." I was wittering uncontrollably, seemed unable to stop. "They've, um, got themselves entangled in what some would maintain was an unsuitable liaison." Unsuitable liaison? Now I was sounding like a policeman. I'd be saying "heretofore" and "notwithstanding" next. "And I was asked to intervene."

"But they maintain it's suitable?" said Charlie easily, seeming not to notice my nerves.

"Oh yes, they're mad about each other, and at the end of the day, that's all that matters, isn't it? I mean, if both parties love each other, what's the problem?"

"Well, quite." He turned and faced me in the hall.

I swallowed. Really wished I hadn't brought up the *l* word quite so soon in the proceedings. There followed a rather steamy little moment as our eyes feasted greedily, the delights of being mad about each other no doubt occurring to us both. I suddenly had a feeling he might grab me right here and now in the hallway, scoop me up into a passionate embrace on the communal stairs, but instead, he glanced down, almost shyly. He reached out and polished a convenient doorknob with a feverish finger.

"Lucy, you know, you really are . . . so very lovely."

I gulped as tears unaccountably welled up inside. It had been so long, you see, since anyone had said anything like that to me. I was aware I'd had my emotions on hold for years, shutting them up in a dark cupboard where I felt they belonged, never letting them see the light of day, until now. Until this man, this tall, almost bearlike man—so different in stature from Ned's slight, wiry frame, with his chocolate brown eyes, which shone with such unabashed admiration and honesty— unlocked the cupboard door, opened it a crack. I had a horrid feeling everything might tumble out in an almighty muddle, though, in disorderly confusion, rather like my underwear drawer. I must hold myself in check, I thought desperately. I must not rush in boisterously, waving my emotions, like said underwear, I must be cool and dignified. Except that surely, I thought, gazing up at him now, rather as a cat contemplates a saucer of cream, surely those tanned arms would be around me soon? Surely I'd be smelling the fresh, laundered cotton of his shirt, leaning back against the Osborne and Little wallpaper? Surely an embrace, a kiss of some sort, was more or less due? After all, I'd been here nearly a whole minute.

"Would you like something to eat?" he asked tentatively.

"Oh!" I was momentarily nonplussed, but then I thought of Teresa. See, Teresa? *See?*

"You mean, out?" I hazarded doubtfully. I mean full marks for chivalry and all that, but I couldn't help feeling that Out was a retrograde step. What, back into the extremely public world I'd just scampered in from? Away from this dark, cozy brown hall and whatever sumptuous king-size delights lay behind one of those white paneled doors? Added to which, I had to be back in a few hours to relieve Trisha . . .

"No no, I just meant here, in the kitchen." He led the way. "I threw a few things together earlier, just a bit of salad and cheese, but if you're not hungry—"

"Oh! Oh no, lovely. Yes, good idea."

Golly, we had time for a bit of bread and cheese, surely—I tried not to glance at my watch—and here, in his flat. So intimate, so familiar. I followed him into the kitchen, resisting my impulse to bound. It was an airy black-and-white double-O-seven affair, with lots of stainless steel, but we didn't stop to admire; we bowled right on through, and out the other side, in fact, into the garden. French windows issued onto a tiny paved area, surrounded by raised beds full of leafy green foliage and cherry trees, and there, on the terrace, a wrought-iron table with two chairs was laid for lunch.

"Oh, how lovely!" I exclaimed.

Yes, and how extremely civilized, I decided as he pulled my chair out for me. The table even had a red gingham cloth on it. There was a basket of French bread, some rather strange-looking cheese, and a bowl of salad; he wasn't rushing me, wasn't treating me like some two-bit floozy he'd picked up at a party; he was doing this properly; he'd made an effort. I felt a rush of warmth for him. As I sat down, I smiled up and simultaneously felt my skirt ride up to somewhere around my pants. I saw him glance down and blushed. Oh God, why had I worn it? I quickly flicked the tablecloth over my lap. It must look like such a come-on, as if I was desperate.

"Remember how desperate you were for it in that shop?" He grinned, sitting down opposite me.

My jaw dropped, and I was about to protest that I jolly well wasn't desperate when suddenly I realized he was nodding towards the cheese. An oozing, evil-looking affair, with such a colossal whiff it was making me clench my nostrils already, was spreading over a plate.

"Oh, yes!" I tinkled a merry laugh, straining hard to read the label, which was upside down. "Of course. Espouse, isn't it?"

"No no, Epoisses," he said, helping me to a great soggy dollop. As it plopped onto my plate, the ammonia shot up my nose.

"Ah. Right." I flushed, realizing that *espouse* meant something entirely different, something I hadn't meant to mention at all. The awful thing was, though, the more I thought about it, or her, or spouses in general, and trying not to mention them, or her, the more horribly compulsive it became.

"And, and how, how is your . . ." I realized to my horror that I was veering unaccountably, disastrously, toward the word *wife*. "Your daughter?" I finished, realizing this was not great, either, but miles better than the former.

"Ellen?" He looked up from his cheese ladling, surprised. "She's fine, thanks. Came up with me this morning, actually. She had a ballet exam in London, along with her cousin Sarah. She's staying with her cousins for a while, over in Chiswick. Well, just for a couple of days.

They're all great mates, and with Ellen being an only, it's quite fun for her."

"Oh. Yes, how nice."

"And your boys?" He colored. It was unavoidable, though, wasn't it? I'd asked, so it seemed rude not to ask back, but were our offspring by other partners really quite the ticket, here? Couldn't we get back to that nice, intimate eye holding and hand brushing of just a moment ago?

"They're fine, too," I said shortly, and strove to change the subject.

"Mmm . . ." I shut my eyes and popped a dollop of cheese in my mouth, thinking it really couldn't be that bad. It was much worse. I held my breath. "Delicious!" I moaned. Oh God, it was putrid. Was I going to be sick? I rolled the revolting lump of phlegm around in my mouth in agony. Suddenly I lunged for my glass, took a big gulp, and miraculously, the cheese went down with it.

He grinned. "Quite cheeky, isn't it?"

"I'll say!" I heaved.

"Have some salad."

"Thanks."

I helped myself to a huge mound of greenery to cover its cheekiness and tucked in heartily, beaming up the while, chomping away like a happy rabbit to prove how delicious it was, when—oh Christ. Vinegar. In the dressing! The only other one of my all-time greatest hates—and I swear, I'm not a fussy eater—but vinegar . . . I put my fork down miserably and stared at the mountain on my plate, vowing that if this man and I ever did share a special spiritual harmony, I'd come clean about salad dressings and cheeses, but right now, when he'd made such an effort . . . Oh, hell. I looked up and realized he was watching me.

"You can't eat," he breathed, really rather excitedly.

"N-no!" I admitted, spotting a convenient loophole and swimming toward it. I even summoned up a bit of heavy breathing, which wasn't difficult. "No, I can't. Can't even . . . swallow."

For some reason, this news excited him even more. He pushed his plate away. "I'm not sure I can, either." Then, "Sod it," he declared impulsively.

I waited, paralyzed with excitement, transfixed in my wrought-iron chair. What would "sod it" bring?

"Seems such a waste," I ventured, but firmly pushed my own plate away, too, sending it sailing joyously off. We gazed at each other, enjoying our own, far more delicious, private feast, swimming in a sea of mutual attraction.

"It's no good," he whispered, in tones I'd previously only ever encountered in pulp fiction. "I can't resist you any longer. I've done my best to be cautious and chivalrous, but—oh, my God, Lucy . . ."

In an instant he was on his feet, and so was I—almost, except my loopy cuff braiding had got caught on the arm of my spindly chair, so I was sort of half up—and stuck.

"Oh, my darling!" He rushed to embrace me but found himself hugging a hunchback, fighting the arm of a chair. My face was in his stomach, somewhere.

"Hang on!" I gasped. "Just got to—there!" I freed myself and shot up to almost chin level and, ignoring his startled eyes, was in his arms. His lips met mine, our eyes shut, our heads swam, and we slipped into an endless kiss. It was such a relief after all that cheese and vinegar, and oh my, it was passionate. His hands gripped me close but explored me, too, and my goodness he was dexterous. There was nothing slow and calculated about this; this man was hot, aflame, and all the while raining desperate kisses over my face, my mouth, my throat. I felt the excitement surge through me, coming up like a torrent, as if with a deafening crack of melting ice, the spring floods had burst down through the parched old valleys, taking with them everything in their path.

Welded together by various vital organs, we started to inch our way inside, moaning with excitement, unable to prise our lips apart, but moving, with a tacit consensus, toward the kitchen, and the relative comfort and privacy of Indoors. Movement was difficult, though, with his hands still frisking me the while, first cupping my face, then exploring my back, then—hello—up to grasp my neck again, and of course we couldn't really see, so . . .

"Ooops!" A flowerpot took a bit of battering. Fell over and smashed to smithereens, in fact. Then: "Ouch—bugger!" from Charlie, as he tripped over the sharp terracotta pieces.

But finally we were inside and inching slowly through the kitchen, still locked in a mighty embrace, except now my jacket was leaving my shoulders—I wriggled eagerly—and being dumped unceremoniously on the kitchen floor. His hands slipped quickly up my shirt as we made for what I presumed was the bedroom in this ground-floor flat, except that the kisses were getting more and more intense and we seemed in danger of never actually *leaving* the kitchen. In fact, we seemed to be heading irrevocably for the kitchen table. Now attractive though that might be at a later date, I was keen, in the first instance, to be more comfortably installed, so I led him decisively by the lips, and the shirt collar, down the passage.

At the first door we came to, I felt behind me, turned a handle, and leaned determinedly against it. It flew open with our combined weight, and we landed horizontally, but rather uncomfortably, in the cupboard under the stairs.

"Oh God, sorry!" I gasped from beneath him.

"Fine, no, it's fine," he panted back, wrestling with my shirt.

My eyes froze open. What, fine as in—This Will Do? I wasn't convinced myself, but there seemed to be precious little I could do about it. His weight was colossal, and as I spat out a bit of feather duster and maneuvered a vacuum cleaner nozzle out of my back, I reasoned that actually, it was quite spacious, and certainly dark enough to hide any cellulite or stretch marks. He was all over me now, anyway, clearly convinced I'd found the perfect spot, and d'you know, as heady pleasure overtook me, I was beginning to think I had, too. I did shut my eyes tight, though, when I spotted a box of nails by my right ear. I didn't want to catch sight of any heavy-duty screws at a seminal moment.

As storming hands and a rare old breeze roared around my midriff and farther north, too, there came a sudden, shrill ringing in my ears. We froze, mid-caress. Stared at each other in horror.

"What was that!" I gasped inanely, knowing full well.

"The doorbell," he panted back.

We stared at each other, horrified, in the gloom.

"They'll go away," he reasoned, "eventually."

We waited, paralyzed with fear, ridiculously half-dressed, and then it came again. A shrill, persistent summons, accompanied, this time, by a sharp rap on the glass pane.

"Bloody hell," muttered Charlie.

The rapping came again. He hesitated. Then, "Hang on; I'll have a peek."

Charlie stuck his head around the cupboard door and I couldn't resist doing the same below him. We peered down the hallway like a couple of cartoon characters, one head above the other. In the top, glazed section of the front door, a woman's head and shoulders were framed, sideways on. A blond woman, with long hair. My heart began to hammer. Oh God.

Charlie shot back in. "It's my sister."

"Oh!" I clutched my heart. "Oh, thank God for that! I thought it was your wife!"

"No, no, it's Helen. What the hell's she doing here?"

I stared. How the dickens would I know?

"Listen," he reasoned, "it's probably nothing, but I'll have to go and see. Then I'll get rid of her. She's probably picking up something Ellen left behind. Wait here and I'll be back in a tick."

He quickly did up some shirt buttons and smoothed his hair down, while I did up a few of my own.

"OK?" he asked. "Back soon, my angel—stay right there!"

"Is there a light?" I squeaked, as he made to shut the door behind him.

"Oh yes. Here." He flicked it on and left me in the 100-watt glare of what transpired to be a very dingy, unattractive cupboard. As I crouched there, in amongst the buckets, the firelighters, the shoe polish, the hoovers, and the squeegee mop, horror and shame rose within me. God, what was I *doing* here? Shirt up around my armpits, in a *broom* cupboard, for heaven's sake, like some cheap floozie? And suppose that had been his wife. How awful could that little scenario have been? Oh no, I thought determinedly, frantically smoothing down my hair, no, we wouldn't be staying here, and I'd tell Charlie so the moment he got back. We'd be off to the double bedroom *tout de suite*, off to the comfort of the duck down duvet, thank you very much! Or was that even worse? I wondered, with sudden horror. Even more slutty? I mean, in her bed-room? Except that, of course it wasn't her bedroom, was it? This was very much his bachelor flat, his pied-à-terre. I gulped. The connota-tions of that weren't too great, either, because actually, he wasn't a bachelor. I willed myself not to think about that, either, knowing that the moment he was back and I was in his arms I'd be so overcome with passion, none of that would matter. I frowned hard in the overhead glare, wondering if that was a good thing or a bad thing—that passion could overcome scruples? Actually, I didn't want to think about that, either. If only he'd bleeding well hurry up!

I put my ear to the door, wondering what the hell was going on out there. Suddenly I realized I could hear voices, more than two, and that they were coming this way. I shrank back in horror and quickly flicked the light off, thinking that if she was the thrifty, domestic type, she might see the light under the door and open it to turn it off. God, how humiliating, to be found in here by his sister! The voices seemed to be fading again now, and I waited, rigid with fear, until the door opened softly. I blinked in the gloom. Charlie put his finger to his lips.

"She's gone," he whispered, "but Ellen's not very well. She was sick after her ballet exam, so Helen brought her back here. I've settled her in front of a video in the sitting room, but, my darling, I fear our magical afternoon is turning to dust and ashes. I really don't think we can— well, prostrate ourselves, either here or in the bedroom, with an eight-year-old girl in attendance."

"Of course we can't," I said, horrified. "No, no, I must go. I must leave at once!"

I felt awful, tawdry, terrible. Golly, his *daughter*, lying next door on a sofa, feeling sick. How would I feel if it were Ben or Max?

"Do I have to go past the door?" I said, frantically tucking in my shirt. "I mean, the sitting-room door? On the way out?"

"You do, but it's shut. She won't see you. Come." He made to lead me by the hand, then turned and kissed me very thoroughly on the mouth. "But, Lucy," he whispered urgently, "we have unfinished business here, my darling. I'll see you very, very soon."

I nodded, gulped. Unfinished business. The very words Jack had used to describe his liaison just south of here. So I'd joined the gang, eh? No time to consider the implications of that, either. Right now I had to concentrate on tiptoeing down that hallway, shoes in hand, past the sitting room where I could just hear the television, to the front door. As I turned to say good-bye on the steps, I spotted, with horror, my jacket, lying on the kitchen floor, right at the end of the passage.

"Oh! Damn, my jacket. Shall I—"

"I'll go." He squeezed my hand and nipped off. He popped into the kitchen, around the table, and scooped it up neatly. He was on his way back with it dangling from a finger, grinning broadly, when the sitting-room door opened.

"Dad, where's the remote control? I can't—oh!" She stopped. Saw me, and stared. A small blond girl with little round glasses, wearing jeans and a T-shirt, her hair still up in a tight ballerina bun. She blinked at me behind her spectacles, then turned to her father.

"Ah! Ellen darling, this—this is Laura. Laura works with me at the BBC. She's just popped round to collect some papers, haven't you, Laura?"

"Yes! Yes, I have," I agreed as she regarded me. She glanced at the shoes in my hand. "Hello!" I quaked cheerily.

"Why haven't you got your shoes on?"

"Oh! Blisters. It's tearing all over those . . . those wretched fields," I gabbled nervously, clutching wildly at somewhere as far away from Langton Villas and her father as possible.

"Fields?" She frowned. "What—at the BBC?"

"Oh well, I do—you know, out-of-studio productions. On location. Animal shows, that kind of thing."

"Oh, cool. What, like *Pet Rescue?*"

"Mmm. Sort of."

"I love that program. There was a really, *really* lovely hamster on the other day, with only one leg, that *badly* needed a home, but Mum said no. Do they mostly end up with good homes, though?"

I glanced at Charlie, who was inspecting the wallpaper carefully.

"We . . . try to place them as best we can," I croaked. "You know, depending on suitability." I nodded.

She nodded, too. "Ah, right. So . . . you wouldn't let a pony go to someone who lived in London, for instance?"

"Noo," I agreed, swallowing. "I wouldn't, on the whole, do that."

"Or a Labrador to someone in a high-rise flat?"

"Mmm, no. No, quite right." Chatty little boffinlike child, this.

"Come on now, Ellen," broke in her father, and not before time in my view, "back to the sofa. You're looking a bit peaky and you'll catch a chill."

"But just suppose—hang on, Dad," she brushed him off impatiently, "just suppose, OK, that I didn't live in the right place for, say, a snake, right, but you still thought I was the best, most *loving* person, to give it a home?"

"Well." I gazed into the wide blue eyes that posed this moral dilemma. "Well." I licked my lips. "Obviously, I'd have to think very carefully." She waited. "Very carefully indeed." Still she waited. "And—and I think that if a child was passionate about snakes . . ."

"But only had a bathtub to keep it in," she warned.

"But only had a bathtub to keep it in," I agreed, aware that Charlie's eyes were on me, huge with wonder, "then I really think," her glasses flashed ominously, "well, I really think I'd still be inclined to let it go to the child who had the most suitable home," I finished desperately.

She regarded me coolly through her spectacles for a moment. Smiled.

"Good. I think that's the right answer. Passion is all very well," she warned, "but it can pass."

"Oh! Quite right!" I gasped.

"You know, you *think* you're in love with something, or someone, and then—*bam!* Suddenly you're not. I mean, look at me and S Club 7. I think they're the pits now. And if it's an animal, it's much worse. You end up with something that you just don't love anymore. And that's not very nice, is it?"

"It most certainly isn't," I agreed humbly.

We all considered this sobering thought, me ogling the doormat; Charlie, still transfixed by the wallpaper.

"So," Charlie eventually broke the silence. "I'm glad we've got that sorted out. Now, back to the sofa, young lady, before you catch your death."

And this time, happily, she obeyed.

When she'd disappeared and the door had closed behind her, I leaned, weakly, against the door frame. Slipped on my shoes. Felt all in, actually. Charlie took my face in his hands.

"I had no idea you knew so much about snakes," he murmured.

"Tip of the iceberg," I muttered. "Trust me. There's plenty more where that came from."

"I can't wait," he whispered. "I'll ring you, my precious." He bent down to kiss me. "À *bientôt.*"

And with that, I turned and tripped down the steps into the street, where actually, I was very pleased to be.

I hurried along, not stopping until I reached the relative safety of my own road. Well, you know, my old own road. I bent my head against a chilly breeze and folded my arms, trying to gauge my feelings. I was obviously disappointed to have had our afternoon curtailed in such an abrupt manner but, annoyingly, rather ashamed, too. Guilty, even. And it wasn't even as if we'd done anything much to feel guilty about, I reasoned, with mounting irritation. Just a grapple in a broom cupboard, for heaven's sake. But it was as if, before the fun had even started, before we'd even begun to live dangerously, all the gremlins were closing in around us. Threatening to spoil things for us, forcing us to think about the implications our affair would have for others. So unfair. I kicked miserably at an old Coke can. I mean, sure, six months into an affair, you might kind of feel you deserved all that, but on the first date—blimey.

I pulled my jacket around me, glad of its warmth. The sun had gone in and the first few huge spots of rain were plopping down. I wished I had my jeans on and not this stupid skirt.

As I reached my house, I stared up. Behind that ground-floor curtain would be Rozanna and Hector, shaping up to lunch after a nice nudie sketching session. Upstairs would be Ray and Theo, playing cribbage perhaps, enjoying a prelunch sherry and listening to *The World at One*. Upstairs again would be Teresa, draining a pan of spaghetti in the sink for Carlo, who, Italian-style, insisted on putting his feet under his own table every lunchtime and sharing a bottle of wine with his wife. I hesitated. Should I join them? I could, easily. But on the other hand, what would I say? "Oh, hi, Teresa, I'm back. Yes, you see, my lover and I were disturbed by his eight-year-old daughter, oh, and his sister, too," who, now I came to think of it—I narrowed my eyes reflectively at the wet pavement—I was sure I recognized, just from that brief glimpse through the door. I'd seen her before, somewhere, but couldn't for the life of me think where. Oh well. I shivered. Consulted my watch. I couldn't possibly pick Jack up yet; it was much too early and he'd be sure to know I'd had a disastrous afternoon. I wasn't convinced I could cope with his smirking. Instead, on an impulse, I turned on my kitten heels, walked smartly up to the end of the road, then headed left down the King's Road, to buy a pair of jeans.

Chapter Seventeen

WHEN I ARRIVED AT JACK'S LOCATION A LITTLE WHILE later, it's fair to say I wasn't in the best of humors. I drove down a quiet, leafy backstreet just off Cheyne Walk, gazing up at a row of tiny mews houses of all different shapes, sizes, and colors, stopping outside the requisite one, a rather dear little pale blue affair. At the top of some smart well-scrubbed steps, a gleaming white front door with a large, shiny brass knocker in the shape of a lion's head rose up; on either side of the door, a square Versailles planter frothed over with a delightful abundance of ivy and petunias, and in the window boxes lacy lobelia blossomed. All of this, for some reason, made me even more cross. I stared up in grudging admiration at this exquisite doll's house, small, but on three floors, and no doubt absolute heaven inside, all chintzy and feminine, and with a sweet little manicured garden at the back, which, I was sure, if you stood on a chair and craned your neck, would offer a splendid view of the river. It was the sort of house I would cheerfully have killed for, but then again, I thought with a sigh, how many people would kill for a beautifully converted barn in idyllic Oxfordshire? Or any sort of house at all? A cottage, a council house, a shack, a box, a—yes, all right, we get the point, Lucy.

All the same, I thought, glancing back enviously as I purred past, trying to find a parking space, it was typical of Jack to have a floozie in such an exclusive location. For all his irritating, libertine ways, you had to hand it to the man, he had some style, even if I couldn't park in this wretched, stylish road, full of wretched, stylish—

"Arrggh!" I finally gave up and screeched backward until I was bang outside the house again. I sounded the horn impatiently and glared up. No response. Damn. Where was he? I opened the window and peeped the horn again, rather more urgently this time. Two seconds later, an upstairs sash window flew up. A pretty, auburn-haired girl with dark, glittering eyes stuck her head out.

" 'Ello?" she cooed.

"Oh, hello, is Jack there, by any chance?" I yelled.

"Jacques? Yes, he here, hang on. Ja-acques!" she called in a heavy French accent. She popped back in.

And that was another thing, I seethed as I waited, tapping the steering wheel impatiently. They were always bloody foreign. Buxom Brazilian beauties, pneumatic Australian au pairs, and now this dusky French maiden. He seemed to conjure them up like a magician from a hat, all in national dress—or undress presumably—like a stream of silky hankies. What was wrong with a homegrown, indigenous one, for heaven's sake? Too parochial? Too pedestrian? Too unimaginative in bed? Oh come *on*, Jack!

A moment later she was back at the window, and with "Jacques" beside her. At least they were dressed.

"Oh, hi!" He looked surprised. Leaned out on the windowsill in his shirtsleeves. "You're early. I wasn't expecting you until a bit later."

"Something came up," I said coolly. "Not too inconvenient, I hope," I muttered through clenched teeth.

"Sorry?"

"I said, I hope it isn't inconvenient!"

"No, no." He grinned. "It's fine. We'd pretty much finished here, hadn't we, Pascale?"

He turned to his French pal, who giggled wildly behind her hand. "I don't zink so!"

"Oh, come now, Pascale." He grinned. "Can't go on all day. Well, I know you can. This is Pascale De Maupessant, by the way," he called, turning back to me. "Lucy Fellowes."

"A pleasure." She beamed, prettily. "Won't you come in?"

"I can't park," I yelled. "Jack, I'm sorry to be a bore, but could we— you know . . ."

"Give me five minutes," he called down. "Just one or two things I need to clarify with Pascale."

He winked broadly at me before shutting the window again. Their figures moved away from the glass, and out of sight. I imagined them, though, moving back toward the bed, her reaching up to his shoulders, pouting prettily and trying to cajole him duvet-ward, covering him with kisses, whilst he, kissing her back, reached for his jacket, his wallet, fumbled for his shoes, simultaneously murmuring that of course he'd see her soon, very soon, the very next time he was in London, in fact, but the old tartar outside was clearly in a filthy mood and mustn't be kept waiting *too* long, otherwise . . . mmmmm . . . mmmmmm . . . OK, just one last . . . kiss . . . at which point he'd drop his jacket and wallet, take her firmly in his arms, and kiss her, very comprehensively, on the mouth.

I leaned back on my headrest with a deep sigh. A sour and angry feeling flooded through me. In an effort to dispel it, I rummaged in the glove compartment and found an old Polo mint. I crunched hard, but the bitter taste of uncontrollable jealousy prevailed. God, where was I going so wrong? It should have been me having the gaudy afternoon, not him. I hadn't chauffeured him up here to get his rocks off while I had an unsatisfactory grapple in a broom cupboard, for heaven's sake! I ground the mint to a pulp and by the time he emerged through the front door was ready to blow.

He sauntered casually down the steps, jacket nonchalantly slung over one shoulder, looking, I had to admit, rather attractively rumpled and postcoital, as he glanced up to the top floor and blew Pascale a beguiling kiss. She blew an equally coquettish one back.

"Oh, for pity's sake!" I reached across and flung open the passenger door with an impatient flourish. "Get in, can't you. This isn't the bloody balcony scene."

"Ahh . . ." he sighed happily, settling himself down beside me and ignoring my evident irritation. "Lovely girl, that, absolutely lovely. You haven't met her before then, Lucy?"

"I don't believe I've had that pleasure," I snapped, shifting into gear.

"Have you not? Ah well, you must. You must meet her properly; you'd love her. She's one of the De Maupessant clan. There are five of them, you know—five sisters."

"And which number are you on?" I said snidely, glancing behind me for traffic.

"Oh, Pascale's the youngest."

"Naturally. Number five."

"Otherwise known as Bright Eyes." He kept a smile at bay and waited, poised to reel me in, but I knew better.

"Which I presume," I said lightly, "has nothing whatever to do with her eyes, but everything to do with her going like a rabbit?"

He grinned. "Ah, by golly. You have to get up pretty early in the morning to get one past you, eh, Luce? But actually, you're quite wrong. It has everything to do with her lovely eyes."

"Really," I said dryly. "Well, if you swivel your head back, you'll see she's still waving, Jack. Can't seem to keep her lovely eyes off you."

He turned and beamed back extravagantly. Gave another dinky wave.

"Pretty house," I said grudgingly as we pulled away and out of the road.

"Isn't it? And such an encouraging number, too."

I glanced back. Sixty-nine. "Oh, for heaven's sake, Jack."

"Sorry," he said. "Too adolescent, even for me, I agree, and actually," he frowned, "enough of me and my exploits for five minutes. I mustn't hog the limelight so persistently. How about you, little Luce? I trust you've had a pleasant afternoon? Enjoyed your jaunt up to Town? If you don't mind me saying so, you look a bit down in the mouth. Like the cat who didn't quite get the cream, am I wrong?"

I glanced at him quickly. How on earth did he— But his eyes were wide and innocent. I swallowed. Just a lucky guess, no doubt.

"Not at all," I said lightly. "I had a lovely time with Teresa."

"Ah. So, you didn't get to see your parents, then?"

I licked my lips. Damn. I'd forgotten about that little lie. How awful.

"No, I—well, you know. I don't often get to see Teresa. And we had so much to catch up on. We just sort of curled up on her sofa and gossiped. Lost track of time."

"Really?" He frowned. "How extraordinary. I popped out for a bottle of wine at one point. Could have sworn I saw her in her shop."

I gripped the wheel and concentrated hard on the road. "Ah yes, that's right. She had to go back to work. I sat with her—while she served. Behind the counter."

"Ah." He nodded. "In that case you must have been in the loo."

"What?"

"When I popped in. Well, I couldn't very well walk straight past, could I?"

I flushed and stared straight ahead. "Are you spying on me, Jack?"

"Good heavens, no," he said in mock horror. "Why on earth would I want to do that?"

"I have no idea," I said, between clenched teeth. "But I think you should know that I don't take kindly to having my private life scrutinized. I'm a grown woman, you are not my keeper, and what I do in my own time is my own affair, got it?" I flashed him what I hoped was a fierce look. He didn't actually look too terrified.

"Got it, miss." He grinned, tugging his forelock and settling back in his seat. "Message received and understood. Entirely laudable, too. Of course you should have a personal life."

"Of course I bloody should!" I blustered. "God, it's about time. And talk about the pot calling the kettle black—look at you, you old roué!"

"Touché," he agreed. "The only difference being, of course, that this old pot may be as black as sin, but it hasn't got any innocent dependents looking to it for any sort of moral guidance. Any sort of shining example. Ahh . . . I must say it's nice to be back in this comfortable old wagon again. I've been looking forward to this return trip, principally because if it's all right by you, I intend to spend it in precisely the same way I spent the outgoing one. It's been an exhausting afternoon, one way or another."

And so saying, he rested his head back, shut his eyes, and laced his fingers across his chest, so that by the time I'd puzzled over his words and made sense of what he'd said, he was fast asleep.

Bloody cheek! I seethed, eyes popping with sudden realization. Innocent dependents—how dare he! He'd just stuck that in to make me feel guilty. Christ—four wretched lonely, blameless years and I finally dip my toe into the outside, heterosexual world that he'd been rutting around in for years, and here he was trying to ruin it for me! Dragging my children into it! I'd like to wake him up and give him a piece of my mind. Although actually, I conceded, a few moments later, as the memory of the ghastly tiptoeing-past-the-daughter episode reared its unattractive head, maybe I wouldn't wake him. Perhaps it was as well he slept. I wasn't sure I wanted him to know just how many innocent dependents there were, knocking around.

WHEN WE FINALLY MADE IT BACK TO NETHERBY A COUPLE of hours later, Joan was in the front drive, trying to pull a rug out of the boot of a very twisted and mangled red Escort.

"Oh God—it's the aunts' car!" I gasped, getting out in horror.

"They're fine," Joan assured us as we hastened toward her anxiously. "Escaped with a few cuts and bruises, but the car's a write-off, as you can see. Wrapped it round an oak tree in the park, and not before time if you ask me. Anyway, they're both in there now," she jerked her head toward the house, "convalescing. And with everyone gathered in the morning room. Waiting for you, most likely," she intoned darkly.

"Ah. I wondered if we'd have a reception committee," murmured Jack as we walked up the mountain of steps together.

"I wouldn't mind seeing the boys first," I said.

"Wouldn't mind a pee, personally."

But as we crept through the front hall and past the morning-room door, we were halted by Archie's commanding tones.

"In here!" he called.

We stopped mid-creep, glanced warily at each other. Then dutifully, tracked left.

Sure enough, Archie, Rose, Lavinia, Pinkie, and the aunts were all assembled. Also in the room, but standing slightly apart from the group, over by the French windows, was Sir David Mortimer. David was the family doctor and a very old friend of Archie's; a small, dapper man with a quick, bright smile. I'd noticed, since my marriage to Ned, that he tended to be present at most important family gatherings. I'm not sure in what capacity his presence was deemed necessary—perhaps to be on hand if Lavinia passed out insensible, or Rose had another attack of angina—but he was a calm, sensible man, and actually, at a potentially explosive meeting of this kind, his presence was welcome.

Archie was pretending to read the obituary column in the *Telegraph*, Rose was sitting opposite him on the other sofa, bolt upright, twisting her rings and not even attempting to occupy herself, and Lavinia and Pinkie were at a little table, playing Scrabble with Cynthia, who had a huge Elastoplast on her head. Violet was squeezed in beside Rose and was trying to talk to her, muttering insistently about a race meeting she wanted to go to.

"You see, I haven't got a car now, so—"

"Yes, I *will* take you, Violet; I said I would," Rose snapped, brushing her away like a fly. "Now shush, Jack and Lucy are back. Darlings!" She got to her feet, eyes bright with anxiety. "How was it?"

"Ah, you're back." Archie gave a stage-managed jolt as if we'd surprised him, but of course he'd called us in. He folded his newspaper and set it aside with a flourish. He, too, stood up, beside Rose, back to the fireplace, hands clasped behind him, bushy brows furrowed. He rocked back and forth on his heels.

"Well?" he barked. "What did he have to say for himself?"

Jack held up his hands in defeat as I quaked in behind him. "Look, don't shoot the messenger, Archie, OK? It ain't our fault." Then more gently, "But no, I'm afraid it's no go. I'm sorry, but he's adamant. His mind's made up, and he wants to marry her. I must say they appear to be blissfully happy and very much in love, and with the best will in the world, Archie, I think there's damn all anyone can do about it."

There was a silence at this. Rose put a trembling hand up to her throat and fingered her pearls. Her face was pale.

"That's what he said? Those were his words, not hers? That he wants to marry her?"

"I'm afraid so, Rose." Jack perched on the arm of the sofa she'd just vacated. "But for what it's worth, Rozanna is acutely aware of the hurt she's causing, and also that Hector is something of an innocent, so she's asked him to wait a year. Not to ask her until then."

"Oh!" Rose brightened.

Archie's eyebrows shot up. "Ah-ha. Promising."

"No, not really, because Hector's response to that was that he wasn't having any of it. He wants her now, and he's determined he's going to ask her every day until she says yes."

"Oh," breathed Pinkie. "How romantic!"

"Shut up, you stupid girl!" Rose rounded on her furiously. "There's nothing remotely romantic about a scheming manipulative whore who's got her claws into my only boy!" Her voice cracked slightly at this and a hanky came out of her sleeve. She clasped it to her mouth, sank into a chair, and gave a little moan.

"Steady, Rose," said David quietly from the window, back still turned, gazing out at the view.

"Well, it's true!" she sobbed.

"Maybe so, but David's right, no point getting hysterical," said Archie tersely. "You'll only upset yourself. If Jack says it's no go, then it's no go. Hector's clearly made his mind up—which, I must say, is a first—and he's a bigger fool than I thought he was. I said it yesterday, but I'll say it again, and you can all bear witness. He'll get nothing from me, and he'll never set foot in this house again, not on that woman's arm. I don't want to hear his name mentioned in my presence, either, and I don't want you," he turned to his wife, "getting on that phone and begging pathetically into it, got it?" His fists, by his side, were clenching and unclenching as he glared at her. "He's made his bed, and as far as I'm concerned, he can bloody well lie in it." With that he turned and left the room.

There was a silence. "He doesn't mean it," piped up Pinkie, at length, in an unnaturally shrill voice. "I know Daddy. He says that now, but he's upset. I can talk him round; I always can. He doesn't mean we'll never see Hector again. After all, this is the twenty-first century! So what if she's a tart? So what? Golly, we've all been around, haven't we?" She glanced defiantly at Jack.

"It's *where* she's been that's the trouble," muttered Lavinia, gazing at her feet.

"I don't see why." Pinkie was indignant. "I mean yes, OK, she does it for money, but that's the only difference. I mean—"

"We're playing for money?" Cynthia glanced up, startled, from her Scrabble letters. "You didn't tell me that."

"No, no, we're not playing for money," soothed Lavinia.

"I wouldn't have let you have *dyke* if I'd known. It's only in the dictionary under 'derogatory,' you know."

"Hector's girlfriend's a dyke?" inquired Violet, from the sofa.

"No, dear, she's a whore."

"What?" Violet cupped her ear.

"*She's a whore!*" yelled Cynthia. "You know, like Lucy's mother." She nodded across at me.

I gasped. "Um, well actually, can I just say, my mother is *not* a whore. You've said that before, but I think you've got her muddled up with someone else."

Cynthia laid her hand on mine. "I admire your loyalty, my dear, truly, but I think you'll find financial transactions did take place. I remember old Roddy McLean emerging from her rooms in Cadogan Square looking quite startled and shell-shocked, poor man. I'm sure *he* had no idea what he was getting himself into and—"

"Stop it!" Rose's voice rang out shrilly. She got to her feet, trembling. "Stop it!" She breathed. "Oh, my God, this *family!* Doesn't anyone have an iota of sensibility? Doesn't anyone have any idea what I might be going through, how I might be feeling?"

"Are you not feeling well?" Violet peered anxiously. "You do look awfully pale."

"Of course I'm not feeling well! I've just heard that my only boy, my—"

"Because if you're *really* not well," Violet raised her voice importantly, "I shall ask Marcia Wainwright to take me to the races tomorrow. I have to go, you know, I bred that horse. And he's the favorite. It's very important I see him run."

Rose fought for composure. "Violet," she hissed, "I've said I'll take you to the races tomorrow, and I will, but we're not discussing horses at the moment. We're talking about my son!"

"I'll have to introduce you to the trainer," said Violet doubtfully.

Rose gaped. "Is that a problem?" she demanded, exasperated.

"Well . . ." Violet paused. Frowned at her, perplexed. "Who are you?"

Rose stared at her. "*Arrrgh!!*" she shrieked suddenly, and lunged for the poker by the fire. She sprang toward her, brandishing it wildly.

"Mummy, no!" Lavinia and I rushed forward in unison.

"Rose, you're upset," I soothed, restraining her, taking her arm. "Lavinia, don't you think your mother should lie down?"

"Of course I'm fucking well upset!" Rose shrieked, dropping the poker with a clatter and rounding on me suddenly.

"Mummy!" gasped Lavinia, horrified.

Rose shook me roughly away. "Of course. And you're the cause of it!" Her eyes glittered with rage.

I stepped back, stunned. "Me?"

"You brought that girl into this house, to my lovely party," she trembled, "in my lovely rose garden, knowing who she was. Knowing *what* she was. You let me introduce her to all my friends; you let me make a fool of myself by telling them all she was the daughter of Lord Belfont—"

"Well, she is the daughter of Lor—"

"Yes, but she's a great deal more than that, isn't she, Lucy?" she demanded, shaking with anger. "And you kept very quiet about that, didn't you? And then you introduced her, most specifically, to my darling boy. To Hector! Not content with taking one son from me, you wanted to take another!"

"Now, Rose." Sir David moved forward. "I really think that's unreasonable. I don't imagine Lucy—"

"Quiet, David!" she ordered. He pursed his lips. Frowned at his shoes.

"And then," she went on in a quavering voice, "then you let me invite her to stay in my house for the night, where God knows what atrocities went on, under *my roof*! Oh yes, heaven only knows what foul practices were played out that night, what promises in return for favors she extracted from him. And now he's lost to me forever." She gave a strangled sob. "And you engineered all of that. I'll never forgive you for that, Lucy, never!"

Her pale blue eyes were huge as they fixed on me; her face, bloodless and quivering with emotion. She gave me one last, defiant stare, then turned and ran from the room.

Chapter Eighteen

I WOKE UP THE FOLLOWING MORNING AND IMMEDIATELY felt sick. The full force of Rose's invective came flooding back and I sat bolt upright in bed, wishing to God I still smoked, so I could at least fumble around on the bedside table for some Marlboro Lights and suck the life out of one of them. Instead, I put my face in my hands and groaned.

"Ooooh, nooo . . ." I parted my fingers and stared bug-eyed at the floral duvet. How awful. She must hate me! Well, clearly she hated me, and blamed me, too, for everything. For the whole dreadful debacle, and in a way—I flushed with horror and raised my face from my hands—in a way, she was right. I *had* known about Rozanna, but then again—I agonized, narrowing my eyes at my bedroom wall—then again, Rozanna was a friend. Was I supposed to jettison her, refuse to know her, just because my circumstances had changed?

Should I have disowned her, down here in conservative, rural Oxfordshire, even though I'd socialized with her in London? In vibrant, cosmopolitan London, where anything went and where she lived in the same house, for heaven's sake, so it would have been rude not to? And had introducing her to Hector been wrong, too? Hector was a grown man, for pity's sake. I couldn't be held responsible for his actions, surely? I slid my legs miserably out of bed and hobbled off to the shower like some rough beast crawling out of its cave.

As I peeled off my rather damp T-shirt—golly, anyone would think I was the one having the menopause—I glanced at the clock. Nine o'clock. What? I peered incredulously. No! Crikey, it was. I must have overslept. And the boys must have had their breakfast already and gone out to play, because apart from the throbbing of my head, it was awfully quiet. I turned the shower on full blast and lifted my face up to the torrent, hoping to wash away the guilt and the pain but knowing full well

224 · Catherine Alliott

that much of the pain stemmed from a monumental hangover, due to a grotesque overindulgence last night.

After Rose's walkout, everyone had been terribly sweet, rushing to ply me with drinks, making me sit down and patting my hand, telling me how she was just upset and *could* fly off the handle like that, but that it didn't mean anything, really it didn't. I have to say, I'd felt genuinely shaky and gulped down all the gin and sympathy they could offer. David had been very kind, bustling off to see Rose first and giving her a sleeping pill but then coming back and sitting beside me, explaining that Rose was terribly overwrought and, actually, had secretly hoped for a much better outcome from our mission to London. She'd been full of optimism, even though everyone had told her to expect the worst, and her diatribe was just disappointment talking.

"Shrieking, more like," I'd muttered, sinking into my gin.

"I know, I know, but don't hold it against her," he'd advised. "It's all hot air. She doesn't think things through, you see, Lucy. Says things before she's even considered them."

"You think?"

"I'm sure." He'd smiled, seeking to reassure me.

I shivered now in the shower, even though it was warm, remembering Rose's glacial blue eyes glaring at me. And how on earth were we supposed to carry on, I wondered, in such close proximity to each other? What sort of *modus vivendi* were we supposed to adopt, now I knew she despised me? I'd voiced this sentiment to Lavinia last night, who'd pooh-poohed it, saying it was all a storm in a teacup and would soon be forgotten, but I'd seen the worry on her face, too. Sensed the tension in her voice as she'd tried to convince me.

So stupid, I thought, with awful dawning realization as I scrubbed away furiously, to get myself into this situation in the first place. Hadn't it occurred to me I might fall out with my in-laws? Blimey, Ned hadn't got on with them, and he was their son: whatever had made me think I'd be able to handle them? Jess had warned me, everyone had warned me, and—oh God, now that was the bloody *telephone*!

I rushed out, swearing and dripping, to answer it.

"Hello?" I gasped, grabbing a towel en route and wrapping it around me.

"Lucy? Hi, it's Kit, here."

"Kit?" I went blank for a second. Sat down damply on the bed. Then I jumped up with a start. "Oh! Oh God—Kit!"

"I just wondered, only I was sort of expecting you at about quarter to and it's five past now. But if it's a problem," he hesitated, "well, maybe we should make it a bit later or something. If it's too much of a rush for you. Say half-nine?"

Suddenly I felt horribly hot. Christ—my job!

"N-no! I'll be there. It's not a problem at all, Kit; it's just, well, one of the children . . ." I glanced guiltily at the Calpol bottle by the bed, "one of the children was sick this morning. I'm just sort of sorting it out. There's a bit of a mess, and of course I should have rung, but—well, I'm on my way."

"Oh, that's great," he said with evident relief. "I thought for an awful moment you'd changed your mind. And it wouldn't matter, normally; it's just that I need to go to Cheltenham today. There's an auction I want to get to, but I don't have to be there till lunchtime, so . . ."

"Kit, I am *so* sorry. Of course I haven't changed my mind. Give me five minutes to sort myself out and I swear to God I'll be there. I promise!"

I put the phone down, horrified. Christ! My first day at work—how could I have forgotten? I clutched my head. My first normal day, at a normal job, in the normal, outside world and—"*Max!!! Ben!!!*" I shrieked, rushing wildly to the door. "*Where the hell are you?*"

I charged downstairs like a maniac and tripped over a dumper truck Max had kindly left on the bottom step, landing smack on my forehead on the wooden floor. I lay there for a moment, seeing stars—real stars—gasping with pain. After a moment I got up and, abandoning the towel, limped, yelping and wincing in agony, holding on to furniture, toward the ironing basket, over by the washing machine.

"Clean pants," I moaned, crouching down and riffling through it, my head hurting like hell. "Please let there be pants." Then: "*Max!! Ben!!*" I yelled over my shoulder.

Oohhh . . . no, that hurt. I paused and clutched my head. Don't shout, Lucy; don't shout. Pants, I prayed, tipping the basket upside down, oh, pants, please be here, but actually, I knew they wouldn't be, because I'd spotted them all in the dirty washing yesterday and meant to do something about it.

I panicked. Could I recycle some? I wondered. Or was that too re-volting on my first day? Shake them out a bit or—hang on. I seized a pair of Ben's. They were—I peered at the label—aged nine to ten, and he was quite a big boy, so . . . I stood up and put my feet into them. Got them up, actually, past my knees and up to my thighs. J-u-s-t about squeezed them *over* my thighs, but—crikey. I wriggled hard. Young boys were very slim-hipped. And unless I really squished my bottom in, with my hands, at the back, like this, there was no way they were going to—"*Aargh!!*"

I nearly fell over with fright. Coming up the garden path toward the plate-glass door, with a boy on each hand, was Jack. I froze, naked but for the vicelike grip of my World Cup knickers. Horrified, I grabbed a Royal Horticultural tea towel, whipped it round me, and with my top half covered in herbs and spices and my bottom by a grinning David Beckham, I fled—well, minced actually, totally impeded by the minus-cule pants—upstairs.

"What the hell are you doing here?" I hollered, ripping them off be-hind the safety of my bedroom door. "You don't just walk into my house like that. Who the hell d'you think you are?"

"Sorry," he said mildly, from the bottom of the stairs, "but I found these two down by the lake. One's a bit wet."

It took a moment to sink in.

"Oh!" I threw on a dressing gown and flew downstairs. "Oh God—Max. Darling, did you fall in?" I rushed to him, sinking to my knees to hold him. "Oh God, you're sopping! You are *not* to go down there alone!"

"It was only up to my waist, Mum, and I didn't really fall. I saw a trout, and was just sort of reaching for it, but Jack grabbed me from be-hind and made me come out. Mum, can we fish today?"

"No. No, absolutely not, I've got to go to *work* today! I completely forgot, should be there already. I need Trisha; I need her *now!*" I stood up, tore at my hair. "Max, go and change. Ben, pass me the phone. The *phone*—quick. So I can ring Trisha!"

He narrowed his eyes. "Why were you wearing my pants?"

"What? Oh, because I'd run out. I thought they might fit, but they didn't, OK? Now pass me the phone!"

He threw it at me. "God, you're weird. What would you do if I wore yours?"

"Despair," I muttered. "Even more than I do already. Have you and Max had breakfast?"

"No."

"Well, why not!" I shrieked, rounding on him. "Quick!" I reached up to a cupboard and threw a packet of Frosties at him. "I've got to *go*, Ben, understand? Now quick—eat!"

I was aware that I was panicking and that Jack was watching me. I took a deep breath. Turned to him and smiled.

"Thank you so much for bringing the boys back," I purred, hoping to convey the right amount of gratitude and dismissal. "It was so kind of you."

He inclined his head. "Pleasure. Listen, I'm fishing myself today, so if you're stuck for someone to look after them—"

"No. No, thank you, Jack, but I'm not stuck. I'd like Trisha to have some quiet time with them. They haven't looked at a book since they left London, haven't played board games or anything like that, so thank you, but no."

I was indebted to enough people round here, I thought, frantically punching out Netherby's number, without adding *him* to the list.

"Oh, hi, Pinkie, is Trisha there?"

While I talked to Trisha, I turned my back rather pointedly on Jack, hopefully indicating that whilst I was grateful to him for hauling my child out of the river, his presence was no longer required. When I'd finished talking and turned back, I saw with relief, and a little guilt, that he'd gone.

"Oh, great," muttered Ben, as he brushed past me and stormed upstairs. "Quiet time. Books with Trisha, instead of fishing with Jack. Really great, Mum, thanks."

I stared at his back as he stomped upstairs.

"Yes! Because you know full well, Ben, that I absolutely forbade you to go down to that lake on your own, and you went. With Max! And apart from anything else, a few quiet hours won't hurt you. Life is not all beer and skittles, you know," I shrieked. "Someday you'll find that out!"

"Oh, really? Seems like it is for you. Seems like you're just jaunting off again, leaving us with the nanny. Just like you did yesterday, and the day before that. So much for family life. And you smell like a brewery, Mum, too. Really pukey." He slammed his door.

Did I? Horrified, I cupped my hands over my mouth and nose and breathed. Oh God, I did. How awful. And I still wasn't bloody dressed!

Twenty minutes later I was driving fast down the A41, wet hair, long denim skirt, sandals, no pants. A few more minutes saw me negotiating the lanes like a demon, and at half past nine, precisely forty-five minutes late, I performed an emergency stop outside Frampton Manor, gravel flying.

I flew inside to find Kit, trying not to pace around the hall but clearly agitated and ready to leave, even down to the jingling of his car keys in his hand, jacket on.

"Sorry!" I gasped, steadying myself and clutching the back of a chair. "So sorry, Kit; you go—go. Everything will be fine, I promise. I've got your mobile number if I need you—now go!"

He grinned. "It's OK; I'm not that desperate. Get your breath back and I'll just quickly show you a couple of things." He moved across to a desk in the corner. I scurried after him.

"Fax is here, and answerphone, too, should you need it, and if anyone buys—which I have to tell you is highly unlikely—for God's sake don't forget to put the check details on the back. Oh, and give them a receipt. There's a book of them over there." He pointed.

I nodded, panting, clutching my side. "Right. And ten percent for trade?"

"Absolutely, or anyone else who claims to be for that matter, since they all do these days, but I have to tell you, sales are unlikely. Most of your time will be spent taking telephone inquiries and sending photographs of stock, a pile of which are in here." He pulled out a drawer. "They're all numbered."

"Right. Brilliant."

"So. That's all fairly straightforward. It's Rococo that's the problem."

Rococo? I blinked. Oh God, Rococo. At the mention of her name, a coffee table levitated, and from under it Rococo emerged, shaking it off her back. She gazed mournfully at me and wagged her tail slowly, droopy-eyed. I have to say, she didn't seem quite so keen to stick her nose up my skirt and suggest hot sex as she had on our first meeting.

"Not well?" I queried.

Kit shrugged. "Just not herself. I took her to the vet yesterday and he said she's a bit below par. It may be that we have to adjust her insulin."

"Insulin?"

"Oh yes, didn't I tell you? She's diabetic. Has to be injected twice a day."

"Oh! By me?"

"No, no, I've done it this morning and I'll do it again tonight, but what I would like you to do, and what the vet suggested, is to test her urine. It's quite simple. You just syringe some up with this pipette, three times a day, drop a bit on here," he showed me a piece of litmus paper in a tray, "and record what color it goes. D'you think you could handle that?" He looked at me anxiously.

"Of course," I said, looking down at the pipette rather nervously. "Has she been, you know, done yet, or—"

"First thing this morning, yes, and I haven't let her out since because I wanted her to store up some more, if you see what I mean. If you take her out after I've gone, she's bound to go. All right?"

"Fine," I said faintly. Then, realizing he was looking to me for reassurance, I squared my shoulders. "Fine," I asserted. "Now, Kit, you go. I'm conscious you've been waiting for me and you'll be late, so just go. Rococo and I will be fine."

"Great." He relaxed and smiled with relief, and I thought how attractive his slim, intelligent face was when he smiled. It quite lit up. "Thanks, Lucy; this is such a lifeline to me. I've been rather tied to the wretched place. It's wonderful to leave it with someone I trust."

I smiled up into his flecked hazel-green eyes, the color of birds' eggs, and thought how refreshing it was to be thought well of, for a change. To be considered trustworthy and responsible. Yes, this was just what I needed.

"Right," I said briskly, folding my arms and following him smartly to the door. "Now don't you worry. You whiz off to Cheltenham and get bidding. What have you got your eye on today, by the way?"

"Oh, the most wonderful console table. Napoleonic, and in fabulous condition if the photo's to be trusted. Look." Eyes shining, he whipped a catalog out from inside his jacket. It fell open on a color photograph.

"Oh," I drooled. "What heaven. D'you know, we had one of those at Christie's once; it was stunning. Went for a fortune, of course, but, actually," I peered at the estimate, "this reserve isn't bad—"

"Exactly," he said excitedly, rolling the catalog up again and stuffing it in his pocket. "So maybe it's a fake, or maybe half the world will be there and it'll go sky-high, or maybe, just maybe, I'll be the only one to spot it's the genuine article, and return home the proud owner of a cut-price seventeenth-century console table!"

"How exciting," I said, and meant it. I remembered the thrill of the auction room, the buzz that went round Christie's when something dramatic happened, when the press were all there, when an Old Master or an Impressionist painting was sold.

"I wish I was coming with you."

He turned at the door. Regarded me for a moment. "D'you know, so do I." There was a silence. "Anyway," he collected himself, "I must be away. Have fun, Lucy, and don't work too hard. See you at about six."

What a nice man, I thought as I shut the door behind him. I moved to the window and watched him drive off out of the gates, making sure I couldn't be seen. A *very* nice man. And with such a sad past, too, like so many of us.

I sighed and walked back through the huge empty house, sauntering through the paneled rooms downstairs, familiarizing myself with it again. My fingers trailed thoughtfully over the exquisite furniture in the drawing room. So many treasures here, lovingly collected over the years, really quality antiques. He had the most fantastic eye. I bent down to look more closely at a Georgian needlework table with intricate marquetry on its legs. It was no wonder, either, I thought, straightening up, that he got hardly any passing trade. Some of these things were practically museum pieces, and presumably with prices to match. I couldn't imagine anyone "popping in" without having a coronary.

I wandered upstairs, prowling around the bedrooms with their four-posters, canopies, and washstands, relishing the peace and quiet of this vast old house, where only the sound of ticking clocks prevailed. It made a welcome change, particularly after the melodrama at Netherby yesterday. As I completed my tour and sat down at the desk in the front hall, Rococo at my feet, thumping her tail on the floor, I realized what a relief it was to have time to collect my thoughts in this sanctuary. No children, no Felloweses. Except . . . I doodled on the pristine pad in front of me . . . except that, sadly, my thoughts were full of foreboding.

I abandoned the doodle and glanced up, staring into the mirror on the opposite wall. Being an ancient piece of glass, it was pitted and blackened, so my reflection was muted, but there was no mistaking the worry in my eyes, the dark circles under them due to lack of sleep, and the lines around my mouth. I willed myself not to think about Rose and her accusations last night, about the cleft stick I'd forced myself into here. As I swallowed hard, my hand moved toward the phone, and almost on an uncontrollable impulse I found myself tapping out some familiar numbers. No one answered for ages. Then, just as I was about to put it down . . .

"Hello?"

"Hi, it's Lucy." My voice cracked.

"Lucy! Well, hello, stranger! We were beginning to wonder if we'd ever see you again. Thought you'd been spirited away by aliens."

"Lucas, I'm so sorry." Suddenly I knew I was on the verge of tears. "I've been meaning to ring you and get you down here; it's just—well, everything's been so hectic recently."

I felt so ashamed. I'd spoken to them, of course, periodically, since I'd been here, but usually fleetingly. Always rushed off my feet and needing to cut short their chatter before charging off to do something else.

He laughed. "I'm joking love; now don't you worry. Your mum and I said you'd be settling in and that's always a difficult time."

"How is Maisie?" I asked anxiously.

He hesitated. "Not so good actually, kiddo. Her arthritis, you know. It's been playing up again. But she'll get there. No question about that, it's just the pain."

My heart gave a palsied leap. "She's in pain?"

"Oh no, not always," he said hurriedly. "Just when it's bad, you know. Sometimes in the evenings. Now, Luce, you're not to worry."

"Come this weekend," I said desperately. "Come and see us, Lucas. The boys would love it."

"Ah, but it's the journey, you see, love. One position for that length of time, she couldn't do it."

"Oh!" My hand trembled on the receiver. "Lucas, God, she *is* bad. Why didn't you tell me?"

"I didn't want to worry you. You've got enough on your plate at the moment, new house and all that, new schools for the boys."

"But shouldn't you have some help? A nurse, or—"

"We've got a nurse, now," he said quietly. "Lives in, at the moment. Up in the top flat, the spare rooms."

"Oh! When? You didn't tell me."

"Only since a couple of days ago. And only for a bit, too. It's moving your mum around, you see. With my bad back, I can't always lift her; it's just an extra pair of hands we need. And it's just for a bit," he repeated hastily. "Just till she's over this bad patch."

"I'll come tomorrow," I said, my mouth dry, hand gripping the receiver. "I'll bring the boys; I—"

"She'd hate that, love," he interrupted. "Please don't. She'd hate for you all to see her like this. Come in a week or two, when she's over the worst. When the drugs have really kicked in, which the doctor says they will. You know Maisie; that's how she'd want it. When she's up and about again, and not lying in bed like an invalid."

I couldn't speak. My eyes filled with tears. I knew he was right, though. Maisie—vibrant, lively, exotic Maisie, in her ethnic clothes and headbands and beads, with Max on her back, lampshades on her head, lying pale and drawn in bed. It would shock the boys, and she'd hate that.

"I'll come," I said firmly. "I'll come on my own."

"No, Lucy," he said, equally firmly. "Leave it a week or two, eh? We've managed so far, and we're coping well. Right now I don't want anything she doesn't want."

I wondered, numbly, what he meant by that. She was so proud, we both knew that, but . . .

"OK," I whispered. "But, Lucas, you'll let me know? Every day? You'll keep me informed, tell me the truth? I don't want any fobbing off."

" 'Course I will, my duck!" he chortled, more brightly. "But I promise you, it's nothing serious. Now listen, you give our love to those two young scallywags. Tell them to behave themselves, and we'll see them soon. Tell them we love them, too, eh?"

I couldn't speak for a minute. "Course I will," I managed finally. "Love to Maisie."

I put the phone down. Then I put my head in my arms and wept.

Maisie. My lovely Maisie. In pain. And I'd been up there, only yesterday, in London, could have gone to see her. But instead . . . I squeezed my eyes tight, remembering. Ashamed. And now I was being warned off, by Lucas. For the right reasons, I knew, but he wouldn't have been able to do that if I'd just pitched up at the door. And I knew, too, why I'd rung them. Knew, subconsciously, that I'd wondered if I could go home. Forever. Scoop up my boys and head off to that safe place that was always there, to a mum and a dad who always had their arms open, where I could curl up in the fetal position, stick my thumb in my mouth, and say, "Nasty Rose has been horrid to me. Make the big bad world go away." Give a tug on the umbilical cord and let Lucas and Maisie reel me in. But there comes a time when we can no longer do that. When they need help as much as we do, more so. When the top floor is occupied by a stranger, with no room for me and the boys. A subtle moment in time, when the tables turn and when the children become the protectors, not the protected. It seemed to me that that highly significant moment had happened very recently . . . and I'd missed it.

I thought with horror of a world without Lucas and Maisie. Tears of fear filled my eyes. I blinked them away, knowing it was unthinkable and couldn't happen and that that way madness lay.

Instead, I seized the pad in front of me and found a pencil. I quickly scribbled down how much money I had left from selling the flat in London. Then I wrote down, quite conservatively, how much I spent on groceries a week. Then I estimated how much the rental would be on a small two-bedroom flat in, say, Clapham, or Wandsworth. Then I wondered about state schools in Clapham.

I sucked my pencil and stared into the mirror again. I saw a teeming classroom of thirty children; Max, in the back row, ruling the roost, flicking a rubber, catapulting it toward the blackboard, the class hooting with laughter, egging him on. I smiled. Then my mind roved to another classroom, this time with Ben in it, not at the back but at the front, a missile, sailing though the air, hitting him smack on the ear. As he turned, crimson-faced, the whole class roared with laughter. I saw him later on, at the edge of a heaving playground, hating football, not joining in, scuffing his shoes in a corner, a book in his pocket. My clever, sensitive Ben ... I quickly wrote down two sets of private London school fees. My eyes boggled, and I scribbled it all out again, horrified.

I paused for a moment, then ripped the sheet out, crumpled it up, and started again. I smoothed the new page out carefully with my hand. This time, though, I thought, back at their *old* state school, in Chelsea. The one they knew, the one that Ben had just about survived, and with a flat—well, it would have to be close by, wouldn't it, or they wouldn't get in. Wouldn't be in the catchment area. So, how much would that cost? I wondered. And would Battersea count? I wrote down an optimistic figure. I could get a mortgage, of course, and I still had the capital from the old flat to put toward it, except—no, I didn't, I realized with a jolt. A lot of it had gone to paying debts, and I no longer had a full-time job to qualify for a mortgage, just two days a week here, so ... I got up quickly from the desk. Screwed the piece of paper into a ball and threw it in the bin.

I paced about the room. Right. So I was snookered, wasn't I? She had me cornered, Rose, I mean, and there was precious little I could do about it. I'd sold myself, quite comprehensively, down the river, and now I was peering over the rapids. I came to a halt at the mirror. Saw my frightened face. Oh, don't be so wet, Lucy; of course that's not so! Because it doesn't have to be London, does it? Flipping expensive London or even crippling fashionable Oxfordshire. How about somewhere a bit more reasonable? A bit more remote, a bit more far-flung? How about—well, Norfolk, say? Or Wales? Suffolk perhaps. Suffolk's awfully pretty, with those lovely pink houses, and terribly cheap. Suffolk? My mind boggled. But I didn't *know* anyone in Suffolk. What, and start again? *Again* again? Having started here, so very recently? My heart was pounding as I walked to the window. Outside, it had started to rain.

"Buck up, Lucy," I muttered, pressing my hot cheek to the splattered glass. "It's not that bad. You're having a grotty day, that's all. And actually, it's no good chopping and changing locations; it would be so unsettling for the boys. Things will work out with Rose; you'll see. After all, it could be worse, couldn't it? Could it?" I wondered bleakly, plucking an old Barbour off the back of the door and clicking my tongue to

Rococo. She leapt to her feet. Of course it could! You've got the boys, you've got a job, you've got a roof over your head, and right now you've got a diabetic dog who needs her urine tested in the pouring rain. So get out there, girl. Get testing.

"Come on, Rococo," I muttered, striding purposefully out of the front door and pulling on the Barbour. "Let's go. Let's get this show on the road. Get it over with."

She perked up instantly and followed me joyfully as I led her to a patch of grass under a convenient tree. I patted its fat trunk.

"This is a nice big smelly one, Rococo. Lovely tree. How about it, eh?"

She gazed at me quizzically, head on one side, wagging slowly.

"Atta-girl. Here, sniff." I sniffed the bark. Shut my eyes. "Mmmmm!"

She regarded me a moment, then suddenly turned her back and bounded off down the garden.

"Oh! No—wait!"

I dashed after her, but she was out of sight. By the time I reached her, she was in the depths of the shrubbery, at the bottom of the garden, grinning widely, tongue lolling. Damn. Had she had a quick one while I wasn't watching? Why hadn't I put her on a lead? I sniffed the rhododendrons anxiously, looking for a telltale wet patch, but it was raining hard now, so it was impossible to tell.

"Oh, Rococo, have you? Where . . . here? Over here?" I scanned the wet leaves for a puddle, crouching down, sniffing, and wondering what on earth I was *doing*, sniffing ruddy *leaves*? Well, Rococo clearly thought I was playing. She sprang gleefully onto my hunched back, nearly knocking me over. I gasped, just about saved myself from nose-diving the wet ground, then shook her off angrily.

"Down, girl. Down!"

But Rococo was enjoying herself and had her front paws up on my shoulders now, dancing cheek to cheek.

"Down, damn you!" I shoved her off.

I was cross, and she didn't like that. Didn't like my tone of voice. She glared at me. Christ, she was big, I thought nervously.

"Yes, yes, lovely game, darling," I soothed, "but the thing is . . ." Suddenly I had an idea. Over by the stables, in the yard, I spotted a tap.

"Quick, Rococo—come!"

Joyfully she bounded after me. I hastened across the garden, into the yard, and turned the tap on full blast. Rococo backed away, astonished at the torrent splashing on the cobbles. I turned it down, right down, to a tiny trickle. She gazed at it for a moment, head on one side, ears cocked. Then lo and behold, she turned, sauntered languorously across to a patch of grass, lowered her hindquarters, and . . . ahhh . . . I beamed.

Oh God, the syringe! I was so delighted and transfixed—and it was inside! I'd forgotten to bring it out. I looked around wildly. A flowerpot, perfect. I ran across to a tottering pagoda, seized the top one—happily no hole in the bottom—ran back, and shoved it underneath. Yesss. Oh, joy. I crouched down, beaming. Oh, deep, deep joy. The obliging Rococo was filling it to the top (overfilling it actually; this girl could fill a swimming pool) and then, relieved, was straightening up and wandering off to inspect the stables. Perfect. Now all I had to do was take it up to the house and—hang on. I froze as I reached for it. Golly. Was that a car? On the gravel?

I picked up the pot and, carrying it carefully, crept around the side of the house, realizing, with a pang of horror, that I'd left the front door open. Oh God, what if it was a customer? I peered. It was! There was a car in the drive. With no one in it. I wondered, briefly, if I should make for the back door and intercept whoever it was in the hall, breeze in with a musical, "Hello, can I help you?" But suppose the back door was locked? Damn. I had no choice. I took a deep breath, strolled nonchalantly round the front, and as I did so realized that actually, I recognized the car. I stopped. Glanced to the porch, where—oh! Oh, the relief. Instead of a clutch of indignant Japanese tourists wondering where the hell the patron was or a matching pair of Americans in Burberry macs, there stood a familiar figure.

Leaning against the porch, in a way I'd come to know and love, one foot propped up against the wall, smiling that lovely sexy, tigerish smile that made his face crease up and his eyes slant, was Charlie.

"Charlie! How did you—"

"Know you were here?" He grinned. Unpropped himself and sauntered over to meet me, hands in pockets. "Well, I was all present and correct at your initial interview, if you remember. Had a pretty good idea I'd find you here today, although I must say, I was surprised to find the door open. Thought maybe you'd done a bunk already."

"No. No, I had to pop out for a moment, but—oh, I'm so pleased it's you. Oh, Charlie, it's *so* lovely to see you!"

I couldn't help it. I knew it wasn't cool, but it was. So lovely. It seemed to me that in that one moment, all the horrors of yesterday—Rose, Netherby, and all my angst about the future, the boys, money, schools—just melted away. It didn't matter. None of it mattered. It had all been put into perspective by this one man. This one lovely man, who sought me out wherever I was, at a moment's notice, and who'd come to find me now, in my darkest hour. As long as I had his love, which I clearly did, I could—well, I could move mountains. I smiled, basking contentedly in his warm, appreciative gaze. His eyes seemed to smolder with desire.

"Poor Lucy, I can't seem to leave you alone, can I?" he whispered.

"Which is fine by me," I whispered back. I put the pot down and in a moment was in his arms, lost in an endless embrace, as one sweet kiss unfolded after another.

When we finally parted, he glanced down. "What's that?"

"Oh," I murmured, still gazing up, mesmerized by his deep, chocolaty eyes. "Just a urine sample."

"Oh." He looked surprised.

I smiled. "I'll get rid of it. Come on; come in. I'm sure you're allowed in. You are, after all, a friend of Kit's and I am, after all, supposed to be working. I'm slightly nervous about being caught snogging in the garden!"

I picked up the brimming pot and he followed me. "That's very impressive," he said, eyeing it nervously.

"What? Oh, yes. Went on forever. Can't wait to wash my hands, actually."

"Um" He looked uncomfortable. "Cystitis?"

"Oh no, diabetes."

"Golly! Poor you." He looked startled.

"Yes, such a pain. Has to be done three times a day."

"Right." He swallowed. "And always . . . alfresco?"

"Sorry?"

"D'you always do it outside? In a flowerpot?" He gestured toward it nervously.

"Well, she'd make a terrible mess *inside*, Charlie!" I laughed.

"She?"

"Rococo. The dog."

"Ah!"

I frowned. "What did you—"

"No, no! Nothing," he interposed, beaming. Looked strangely relieved, actually. "Excellent. No, excellent news." He strode on and flung the door open for me with a flourish. "Now. Shall we?"

Chapter Nineteen

"So."

"So."

"An empty house." He rolled his eyes dramatically.

I giggled. "An empty shop, Charlie, and not so fast. I am not ending up in a broom cupboard again!"

"Quite righ." He grinned. "And humble apologies for my loutish behavior yesterday. Desire definitely got the better of me, I'm afraid—all your fault for being so captivatingly attractive and inflaming me like that—but I do promise to be a model of self-restraint today. Scout's honor. In fact, I shall be a perfect gentleman starting with—damn!" He banged his forehead with the heel of his hand. "Left them in the car."

"What?"

But he'd already beetled outside, to return a moment later, beaming from ear to ear and bearing a huge bunch of lilies and a bag of Danish pastries.

"For you."

"Oooh, my favorites," I said greedily, peering into the bag. "Yum. And I'll put these in water." I seized the lilies joyfully. "I really can't remember the last time someone bought me flowers."

"Rubbish, I don't believe that for one minute," he said, settling down in one of Kit's squashy sofas and spreading his arms along the back. "In fact, I'm more inclined to believe you've got a whole host of admirers you keep very quiet about. Anyway, a small token of my affection, and part of my new resolution to treat you with the utmost respect and not leap on you and kiss the life out of you the moment I see you, which frankly is what I feel like doing right now. See how I'm resisting manfully, though? See?" He waggled his hands.

"Angelic," I agreed, shaking the pastries onto a pretty Chinese plate, "and quite right, too. There's more to getting to know each other than just falling into bed, you know, Charlie," I said sternly, turning round to put the kettle on.

"Except, of course, that we haven't even done that yet," he sighed wistfully. "Fallen into bed, I mean, so please don't talk about it, or I shall become inflamed all over again and have to sit on my hands, which is a shame because I really want one of those cakes. Unless, of course, you'd secretly like me to leap the coffee table and ravish you over the Georgian chaise, in which case I'll happily forgo the Danish."

I giggled and sat demurely opposite him, determined this would not dissolve into a tussle.

"For your information, the chaise is reserved for a rich brigadier down the road, who's having a good old dither but could walk in at any minute and claim it. I'm not convinced being draped stark naked across it would improve my sales patter."

He groaned. "You see? You're at it again! Talking dirty is not designed to make me behave myself, Lucy." He got to his feet and thrust his hands deep in his pockets, jingling his change. "In fact, I shall *have* to come round to your sofa now and make you see reason, and it's all your fault."

"Sit!" I commanded, spraying crumbs everywhere. "No, Charlie, I absolutely forbid it. I insist we keep this table between us; in fact . . . you stay there while I make the coffee." I jumped up, thus neatly avoiding him as the kettle boiled. "I'm at *work*, for heaven's sake, and you can jolly well behave. I want to talk to you, find out more about you, that kind of thing."

"Ah me," he sighed, and obediently flopped down into his sofa again, raising his eyes to the ceiling. "I shall just have to think hard about the Euro or something, or maybe the Chancellor of the Exchequer himself. Something terribly dry, whilst my eyes, of course, feast on your delicious derriere as you pour out the coffee." He waggled his eyebrows up and down.

I glanced back. "My son says this skirt is too tight for me. Says I should stick to frocks. I think he means maternity smocks."

"That, my dear Lucy, would be an entirely retrograde step, in my opinion," he drooled. "I'm a great admirer of the Baroque and think your posterior quite perfect. Who on earth wants to cuddle up to a stick insect with bones you can play the zimmer frame on?"

Who indeed, I thought, stirring the coffee, and yet his wife, whom he must have loved enough to marry, was just like that. Well, at least, that was the impression I'd got in the briefest of glimpses outside their farmhouse. Tall, blond, and very skinny, lucky thing. I sighed and took the coffee on a tray to the table, setting it between us. I sat down and reached for a pastry.

"Mmmm." I groaned, biting into one and shutting my eyes as the icing dripped down my chin. "Delicious." As I licked the sugar from my fingers, though, I hastily averted my eyes from his, which, as he watched me, were glazing over ominously again.

"So," I said briskly, brushing crumbs off my lap and sitting up straight. "What exactly *should* you be doing today, Charlie, instead of pestering overweight women in antique shops and plying them with calories and flowers?"

"Oh God," he sighed, leaning his head back resignedly, "all sorts of things. I should, for instance, be settling down to write a script for a new sitcom, the thrust of which—two mixed-race divorcées with zillions of children living happily ever after in a cramped flat—would stretch the credulity of a two-year-old and require the viewer to suspend his belief from a crane. Yes, even now, I should be busily peopling it with characters that would seem wooden even to the cast of *Camberwick Green*, tapping away at my computer with alacrity, tongue hanging out."

"Is that what they asked you to do yesterday then?" I brushed some sugar off my skirt. "At the BBC?"

"Yes, indeed. That, my dear Lucy, is my brief. My mission, as outlined by the good people of Broadcasting House, should I wish to accept it. And of course," he sighed, "I do accept it. Naturally I do. I am, after all, (a) a coward, (b) short of money, and (c) secretly thinking that if I don't accept it, they'll never ask me to do anything again, seeing as how I'm a bit past it and, like all dogs, have probably had my day. But I'm afraid the actual sitting down and writing of it is going to prove a bit more tricky."

"But hang on." I frowned, put my cake down. "I thought they were going to talk to you about a new series of *The Townbirds?*"

"Me, too, Lucy, me, too. Sadly, though, it turned out to be something of a ruse to get me up there, and *Happy Ethnic Minorities* was shoved under my unsuspecting nose before I could say, 'How's about another series?' "

"But d'you have to write what they want? Can't you just make it up? Do your own thing?"

"Of course I could, and I'd have a lovely time doing it, but it would never be commissioned. They'd smile politely, even discuss it indulgently, but then wonder—brows puckered, heads cocked thoughtfully—if there wasn't something just a teensy bit eighties about it? A bit dated and reactionary?" He took a resigned swig of his coffee. "Oh no, these days anything with a plausible plotline which takes a while to develop and combines humor, pathos, and characters one can empathize with is *right* out the window. That is not what the public wants. What the public wants, apparently, is sex, violence, and face slapping. Not necessarily in that order, but they certainly want all of them—and constantly. I, on the other hand, write about middle-class people going about their ordinary, middle-class lives. I'm becoming a relic, Lucy. A dinosaur." He rubbed his face wearily with the palm of his hand.

"Nonsense," I said, thinking I'd never seen such an attractive relic, sitting opposite me as he was in his battered old khaki linen jacket, dark trousers, and pale blue shirt, with that fatal wistful smile playing about his lips, encircling my heart, and those mesmerizing brown eyes gazing dreamily in my direction. I was also thinking that I was really doing awfully well keeping him at arm's length and resisting him.

"Well, anyway, I love all the stuff you do," I said staunchly. "What was it Rozanna said you wrote . . . oh yes, *Family Values*. I loved that!"

He grimaced. "*Family Values* was twelve years ago."

"Was it?" I blinked. Wondered, briefly, how old he was. "Oh well, something more recent then, um—"

"*Girl Power?*"

"That was it! God, did you write that? That was brilliant!"

"Again, eight years ago." He sighed. "They're just running repeats, that's all."

"Oh. Oh well, better than nothing, surely?" I said encouragingly.

He smiled. Didn't answer.

"And um," I said quickly, "what does your wife think of all your programs?" Oh, very smooth, Lucy, yes. Moving smartly on from a subject he clearly found depressing and subtly introducing the wife to discover more.

"She doesn't really watch that sort of thing. Not serious enough." He scratched his head ruefully.

"Ah no. No, of course not." I nodded sagely. "More *Songs of Praise* and Thora Hirdy–type things, I suppose?"

"Well." He hesitated. "I'm not sure she'd go that far . . ."

Golly, perhaps she didn't watch TV at all, I thought with a jolt. Regarded it as the evil eye in the corner, the demonic lantern. I, on the other hand, couldn't imagine life without the telly, curled up in my dressing gown, glass of wine, box of Celebrations . . .

"OK, so," I struggled to think what she might like to do of an evening, "she what—goes to prayer meetings and things? Bible reading, that kind of thing?"

He looked uncomfortable. "Sometimes," he admitted.

"Or is she more into, I don't know," I went on boldly, waving my hands about casually, "putrefacation of the flesh?"

"Sorry?" He looked startled, but then he wouldn't have any idea I was so knowledgeable, would he? Wouldn't know I'd read up quite a bit recently on religious zealots. The library at Netherby had yielded an absolutely fascinating book—admittedly on sixteenth-century zealots—but I was sure it was pretty much the same thing, without the hair shirts and the birch whipping, of course.

"Putrefacation?" he blinked. "Don't you mean mortification?"

"That's the one."

"Um, well, no. Not really. Although I suppose there's a bit of self-denial. You know, fasting. At Lent."

"God, it must be ghastly for you, Charlie. How on earth do you cope?"

"Well, with difficulty. But you know," he said, looking strained, "if it helps her, Lucy . . ."

"Oh, quite!" I agreed. Gosh, I didn't want to sound like a cow. "Oh *God*; yes, if it helps her I'm all for it. But . . . wouldn't she be more comfortable with—you know—like-minded people?"

He gave a shout of laughter. "What—you mean in a nunnery?"

I flushed. "Well no, of *course* not," I said, secretly thinking, Well, yes, absolutely, because in my dreams . . . Well, let's face it, in my dreams, I'd created an entire screenplay. Had his wife packed off long ago, to exactly that. A convent. Oh yes, Charlie and Ellen had driven her to the convent gates one morning, to be met by the Mother Superior, arms open, ready to embrace her new charge. In she'd drifted, Wifey, I mean, all kitted out in her new habit, eagerly clutching a crucifix, a beatific smile on her face, turning to say good-bye to her husband and child—except, no. No, wait, perhaps Ellen wouldn't be there; that might be too harrowing. Just Charlie then, who'd wave her off with a tear in his eye, but knowing full well that it was for the best and that she'd finally be happy. Then he'd beetle back to his car, rev up the engine like nobody's business, and roar over to my place.

Naturally I'd be waiting for him, looking terribly sexy and unreligious and, oh, *thin*, having lost two stone—and wearing size 8 jeans and a skimpy cardigan with nothing on underneath. He'd take me in his arms, stride manfully upstairs, treat me to a fantastically sexy afternoon, and then we'd all live happily ever after. One big, happy family. Me, Charlie, the boys, and—oh yes, Ellen. God, yes, the rather scholarly-looking child with the animal fixation. I wasn't entirely sure she'd be Ben's cup of tea, but golly, we'd all learn to love her, and maybe when she was older some contact lenses would help. And perhaps we could get her a gerbil or something. Or were they smelly? And would I have to muck it out, deal with its—you know—gerbil business? Blimey. I boggled at the carpet. How on earth had I got onto gerbil business when I hadn't even slept with the man?

I glanced up guiltily. My eyes snagged on his like barbed wire. He'd been watching me intently.

"What were you thinking?" he breathed.

"I . . ." I flushed again. "Well, I . . ."

I stopped. His eyes were heavy with something that looked like love but could just as easily have been lust. As he feasted on me, refusing to let me off the hook, the room seemed full of the scent of lilies and the smell of danger. He held out his hands. I impulsively stretched out mine—and he took them, covered as they were in sugar. He raised them and licked each finger, one by one, slowly, sensually. I had no idea that sort of thing happened in real life. I almost passed out.

"Lock the door," he whispered, holding my eyes.

"No, Charlie," I croaked feebly, "I can't possibly. I work here. What if Kit—"

"Kit won't. He's in Cheltenham, won't be back for hours. OK, *I'll* lock the door."

He got up, went across, and turned the key. Then he turned the *Open* sign around to *Closed* and came back to me, with the naughtiest of smiles.

"Charlie," I protested desperately, "this is absolutely *not* what I had in mind. I mean, on my first day at work, in my new job, my new employer, and—*mmmmmm!!!*"

Suddenly the breath was being squeezed out of me and he was on his knees before me, kissing my mouth, my throat, back up to my mouth to quell my protests. I tried to resist, but oh, hell, it was so delicious, I appeared to be joining in. The next moment I found myself being scooped off the sofa as, with a silken tackle worthy of a Harlequin Blue, he slipped his hands under my thighs and hoisted me up into his arms.

"No!" I squealed in horror. "No, you can't possibly carry me. I weigh a ton!"

I was more concerned about my colossal weight than anything else, and—shit! The fact that I had no pants on! This terrifying detail momentarily paralyzed me. I went rigid in his arms, horribly aware that a struggle at this point could prove deeply embarrassing. Galvanized by my lack of resistance, he strode on, and before I knew it I was being carried upstairs, up the grand sweeping staircase, across the landing, and into a bedroom, as he kicked open the first door we came to. It was the blue room, with the peacock silk wallpaper and the vast four-poster bed.

"But . . . this is the Tudor Suite!" I squeaked. "Mary Queen of somewhere-or-other was the last person to sleep in this!"

"So it hasn't seen much action since," he murmured, stopping my mouth with another flow of kisses. " 'Bout time it did. Let's treat it to a little Renaissance period, shall we?"

And the problem was that although my head resisted on absolutely every single level, my heart, my blood, my arteries, in fact my whole body, shimmered and collaborated with this powerful man, this force of nature, who physically and emotionally was overpowering me and making himself all I'd ever wanted.

The room whirled as he deposited me on the bed and lay down on top of me; everything whirled, in fact, my senses, the tapestries, the Old Masters on the walls, the plush violet canopy overhead, spinning round like a Catherine wheel, blurring madly as he enveloped me in his arms, closer than my own blood and just as heated. Articles of clothing were tugged and investigated as an attack was launched on my top half—thankfully, under the circumstances—but I'd chosen to wear a sort of crossover top, with ties that poked through holes at the sides and knotted at the back, an arrangement with which Charlie clearly was not *au fait*. He struggled gamely with it, albeit with a few muffled "Buggers" and "Christs" and, "What have you got *on* here, Lucy?," and was just about getting to grips with it when somebody snored.

We froze, mid-caress. Stared at each other.

"What was that?" I gasped.

"I don't know!"

I pulled away. "Listen."

We did. And it came again. A deep, sonorous, long-drawn-out snore, which was surely much too proximate.

"There's someone in the bed!" I shrieked, sitting up in horror, pulling my top around me.

Charlie sat up, too. We glanced about frantically. It was a huge bed, to be sure, and we'd only, in our haste, occupied one small corner of it, but still, there were no ominous lumps to be seen. No Queen Mary, flat on her back in her wimple, hands clasped in prayer, kipping deadly after all these years. And then it came again.

"Hrrroooumph . . . ."

I leapt off the bed.

"It's coming from underneath!" Charlie hissed, scrambling off, too.

"Christ! Who is it?" I tied my top frantically around me and backed away in terror.

Charlie bent down, cautiously lifting up the bed skirt. He peered. There was a horrible hush. Then: "Blasted dog!" he roared.

"Oh! Oh God, Rococo!" I gasped with relief. "Is that all? I thought—"

"Rococo! *Out!*" Charlie yelled. "Come on—*Out!*"

I waited for her to appear.

"She's not waking up," Charlie reported, peering under again.

"And she's right in the middle. Seems dead to the world. D'you have any real objections to having her there, or—"

"Yes, I bloody do!" I spluttered. "I'm not convinced we should be up here at all, Charlie, let alone with a sleeping dog under the— mmmm . . . mmmm . . . well, maybe just a little kiss and . . . mmmm . . ."

Already he was stopping my mouth, keeping my objections at bay, sensing I might balk. But balking didn't seem to be in the cards, because already I could feel appetite getting the better of discretion: could hear Aphrodite whispering in my ear, telling me to button it, to let sleeping dogs lie.

He lay me down on the bed again and golly, where were we? Oh yes, exactly . . . mmmm . . . lovely, except—God. Bugger. There it was *again*. Only louder, this time, and the thing was, I couldn't really concentrate, because it didn't even sound like a proper snore. It was too harsh, too sort of disjointed.

"Hang on." I sat up, pushed him off.

"What?" he murmured, sitting up and nibbling my ear.

"Charlie, why didn't she wake up? I mean, you called her, and she just didn't move, did she? Suppose she's ill?"

"Don't be silly," he told me, lifting up my hair and attending to the back of my neck. "She's not ill, just asleep."

"No, but she has been ill, you see. Recently, Kit said so, and—listen."

He sighed but obediently paused for a moment, abandoning his ministrations.

It came again. Long, drawn out, and actually, now, with a slight whimper at the end.

"That's not a snore; that's a death rattle," I said. "Oh, Charlie, she's dying!"

I leapt off the bed and peered underneath, where Rococo was indeed flat out, eyes worryingly half-open, the whites showing.

"Jesus! She's probably in the final throes! Charlie, get her out!"

Swearing, Charlie dutifully rolled off the bed, reached underneath, and grabbed Rococo by her back legs. I crawled under, too, and grabbed the front, and together we slid her out across the wooden floor. I regarded the huge hairy beast anxiously. Her breath was coming in tiny sharp gasps; her mouth was wide open, her tummy going up and down quickly, almost in spasms.

"Oh God, Charlie, I know what this is," I said, trembling suddenly. "It's a diabetic coma. My uncle was diabetic, and this is exactly what happens. They just sort of collapse suddenly; it's a reaction to the insulin."

"Really?" He scratched his head. "So, what do we do?"

"Sugar! We need sugar," I said urgently. "Quick, Charlie, run! And bring a bowl of water to mix it in!"

"Righto," he said wearily, straightening up. He frowned down at Rococo, scratched his head again; then off he shuffled. I kept watch anxiously, and a few minutes later he was back with the wherewithal.

"Right. Now, we mix it all up," I demonstrated, sloshing sugar and water about, "and pour some in her mouth, like this."

I watched in despair as it all dribbled out again, onto the floor.

"No no, that's hopeless! She has to be sitting up or we'll never get it down her. Charlie, you sit back against the bed, that's it, and then open your legs, and sit her . . ."

Between us we dragged her up until she was propped between Charlie's legs, her back to his chest, hairy, palpitating tummy to the fore, face lolling against his cheek.

"Hold her; cuddle her to you like a child—that's it." He gripped her round the middle.

"Now," I instructed. "I'll open her mouth and try to pour. . . . Grip her, Charlie; grip her! She's—oh, bugger! It's going all over *you*, you're not holding her tightly enough!"

"I'm trying!" gasped Charlie. "But she's huge, Lucy. God, she weighs a ton—more than you, I should think."

"Oh, thanks! And you need to massage her throat, while I pour." I tried again, but still Rococo lolled in Charlie's arms, mouth open, eyes staring.

"She's dying!" I cried. "Oh, Charlie, do something," I wailed, wringing my hands. "Breathe into her or something, you know!"

"What?" He looked aghast.

"You know, the kiss of life!"

"Yes, I know *what* it is, but I'm not bloody doing it!"

"Oh, Charlie, please, she'll die if you don't, and it'll be all my fault!" Tears sprang.

Charlie stared at me for a moment. "Oh, *shit!*" He bent his head and put his mouth to the dog's, breathing hard.

"Anything?" I asked anxiously when he came up for air.

"Well, I don't bloody know," he choked, grimacing and spitting on the floor. He retched. "Feel her pulse!"

I seized Rococo's paw and felt just above it. "Here?"

"I very much doubt it, Lucy," he growled, wiping his mouth in disgust. "Try her chest. Yuk! I think I'm going to be sick. Christ, I'm not doing that again, not for you, not for anyone!"

"Here, I've got her heart—it's beating! She's still alive, Charlie; she's still alive!"

"Well, Halle—bleeding—lujah."

"Hold her more upright, Charlie—that's it; that's great. She obviously likes that, yes—she likes you! Look, she's smiling, opening her eyes!"

"Terrific."

"Just hold on to her, Charlie; she's coming round."

"You know," he gasped, wincing under her weight, "if you'd asked me this morning, I'd have said it was an odds-on certainty that by this time today I'd be lying beside a beautiful blonde with the most fabulous figure, a glass of Merlot in my hand. Instead of which, I'm sitting here in the appropriately named doggy position, with a bitch called Rococo, who I've damn nearly had sex with."

"Rubbish," I scoffed. "You saved her life."

"Yes, but lifesaving isn't quite what I had in mind for this afternoon. I've had more physical contact with her than I've ever had with you. Certainly more foreplay and—oh, Jesus Christ, she's passing out again!" Rococo's head flopped dangerously.

"The vet," I said, standing up decisively. "This is no good; we must get her to the vet."

"Yes, God, *yes!*" he groaned. "Staggeringly good idea, best you've had all day. Why didn't you say that before I had to snog her?"

"And you can take her," I went on determinedly, "because I can't leave the shop. I'll ring and say you're coming. Come on, Charlie; let's get her in the car."

Between us we lugged, dragged, and carried Rococo down the

stairs—eyes rolling, tongue hanging, paws flailing—and out, into the drive, to the car, which, luckily, was a convertible. We hauled her into the backseat, mouth foaming all over the pale beige leather interior. Charlie winced.

"Drive fast," I urged. "And when you get to the surgery, beep your horn loudly and someone will come and help you."

"How d'you know?" he wailed. "How d'you know I won't be left with a dead horse-dog in the back of my car!"

"Of course you won't," I soothed, "because I'll ring and *ask* them to come out. Now don't worry, Charlie; just go—*go!*"

Something of the urgency in my voice galvanized him, and he got resignedly into the driver's seat. He buzzed down the window.

"It must be love," he said bitterly. "There is literally nobody, no other woman on the face of this earth, I would do this for."

"I think it's love, too," I whispered, leaning in and kissing him warmly on the mouth. "And I think you're a lovely, lovely man. Now go: go!"

With a deep sigh, he pulled off, and I dashed back inside to call the vet. I also called Kit, on his mobile, and gave him the bad news, but not too melodramatically, and I told him not to worry and rush back, because Charlie was quite happy to stay with Rococo at the vet's and I was quite capable of holding the fort here.

"But she's all right?" he asked anxiously. "I mean, you think she'll recover?"

"I'm positive she will," I said, crossing my fingers hard. "And, Kit, Charlie was amazing. He saved her life, I'm sure."

He didn't stop to ask what the devil Charlie was doing at his shop in the first place, but I think he probably guessed, and I made a mental note to smooth down the bedspread in the Tudor Room before his return.

An hour or so later, Charlie rang me. Rococo was coming round and was "comfortable" now, apparently. She had indeed had a reaction to the insulin, and they were going to rejig it. Apparently her rather nervous disposition had been a contributing factor to her flaking out like that, too.

"*Her* nervous disposition," Charlie said bitterly. "I tell you, my nerves are shot to bits. I can't take any more of this coitus interruptus,

Lucy; I'm too old for all this. It's got to be a good old-fashioned dirty weekend in a cozy country hotel, with no sick children, no dogs, no broom cupboards, and no Tudor queens. Just you, me, and a locked door, in a delicious little eyrie somewhere, with a bathroom en suite and no distractions, so I can ravish you to my heart's content. What d'you say?"

I giggled but hesitated. "A whole weekend might be a bit tricky, Charlie. The boys, you know."

"But a night?" he persisted.

"A night," I agreed, "would be very acceptable." I imagined a cozy old pub, by a millstream perhaps, a drink in the bar, huge log-fire burning, holding hands together in the inglenook, then a table for two in the tiny candlelit restaurant, faces glowing, senses heightened, then later on, full of wine and love, off up the rickety staircase to a cozy feather bed, beams over our head, owls calling quaintly in the dark outside, wrapped in each other's arms, away from the world and its prying eyes. . . .

"Ooh, yes," I breathed. "In fact, it would be more than acceptable. It would be downright perfect."

"Right," he warned dangerously. "You're on. I'll book it this very minute. I know just the place. Oh, Lucy, my love, I long for you; I want to explore and ravish you. I seem to be cursed with the most terrible potency. I shall go pop if I don't get to grips with your delicious personage soon!"

I giggled and bade him desist from popping, then put down the phone, my heart exulting, pounding with joy. It did occur to me to wonder, though, if at some stage he'd like to explore my intellect and relish my mind, as well as my body. But no matter. Our delicious tryst was on, and there was plenty of time for all that getting to know each other stuff later, wasn't there? Humming away happily I tidied up Kit's desk, lined up the receipts with the pads and pencils, and told myself I was just being picky.

Chapter Twenty

Kit didn't get back until quite late. Having called in at the vet's and agreed that Rococo should stay there overnight, he finally walked through the door at about seven o'clock. I'd dithered about staying on. I was only supposed to stay until six but decided, under the circumstances, that I'd better wait to hand over the keys and give him a debrief on the day, rather than just abandon ship and leave him to find an empty house.

"You were right," he said, flopping wearily into a sofa. He looked tired and disheveled. "It was a reaction to the insulin. Too much, they think, and too often, but they're going to test her over the next couple of days and let me know. Thank God you were here, Lucy. I can't imagine what would have happened with Michelle at the helm. This is exactly what I mean, why I need someone responsible."

I cringed, recalling my fairly irresponsible exploits upstairs. I scuffed my toe on the woodblock floor.

"Er, well, you do know Charlie popped round, I suppose?" I muttered. "I hope you don't mind, Kit." I glanced up fearfully.

"Mind? Good grief, why would I mind? Of course I don't. It seems he might have saved Rococo's life, and anyway, I'm delighted if your friends pop in, makes it much less boring for you. I mean, it's not as if you're a teenager, sneaking your scruffy boyfriend in for a quick one on my sofa! I had my suspicions about Michelle, I can tell you."

I cringed a bit more and stared at the floor. Crikey. But then of course, Kit wouldn't suspect a thing, would he? Charlie was married, and I was a responsible widow, a mother of two. So what the hell was I up to, then? Not for the first time, a wave of shame washed over me, but before it threatened to engulf me, Kit interrupted my thoughts.

"No takers, then?"

"Sorry?" I came to.

"I mean, were there any punters at all, or was it a totally disastrous day all round?"

"Er, well, no, not totally disastrous. Two elderly women came in this afternoon."

"Really?" He sat up a bit. Seemed inordinately excited by this.

"Yes, but . . . they didn't buy," I added hastily. "But then a couple did come in, just now, before you got back, and were quite interested in the walnut lowboy."

"Excellent!" His eyes shone.

"Yes, thought it was absolutely stunning, and went away to think about it." I lied a bit here. They'd actually given it a cursory glance and asked for directions to the M4, but Kit seemed so thrilled, I over-egged it.

"And any calls?"

"Yep, two. Both from Americans. One, a decorator in London who said you'd know what it was about. Said he'd got a slight problem vis-à-vis the provenance of some silver you sold him recently." What he'd actually said was that if it was Georgian, he was a Chinaman.

"Stupid prat. Doesn't recognize a Georgian hallmark when it smacks him in the face. And the other?"

"She was calling from New York. Said she'd be popping over some-time next month to have a look at your pair of seventeenth-century chandeliers. I told her she'd better make it snappy, because I had an Argentinian polo-playing client who was very interested in shipping them out, pronto."

"*Did* you, Lucy? Good for you! Excellent—thinking on your feet! This calls for a celebration drink. You'll join me, won't you?"

It did? I was astonished as he bustled happily over to the sideboard where the decanters were kept. Golly, I thought, I'd sold precisely nothing, had a paltry two clients in for two seconds, nearly killed his dog, almost bonked his friend in the Tudor Suite, and here he was busy with the tonic and lemon. But who was I to demur? I glanced at my watch. It was almost the boys' bedtime and I felt I hadn't seen them properly for a few days, but it did seem rude not to. He handed me a whopping great gin, which I must say I supped at rather eagerly, and then settled himself down beside me on the sofa, loosening his tie.

"Ahhh . . . that's better. God, bloody long day. And the console went for an astronomical sum."

"Ah. I was going to ask."

"Yes, well, don't. Total waste of time." He rubbed the side of his face wearily. "But no matter. Someone told me about a gem of a house clearance sale going on in Paris next week—the Marquis de Saint Germain's pad—so I shall whiz across for that and, once again, leave the reins in your capable hands." He leaned his head back on the sofa and sighed. "This is working out *so* marvelously, Lucy, I'm so glad you're here. You weren't bored, I hope?" He turned his head anxiously.

I sipped my drink nervously. "Er, no. Not at all."

Not today, heavens no, hadn't had time, what with a diabetic dog and a red-hot lover, but without them? For two long days a week? On a regular basis? Staring at the highly polished floor, the gleaming furniture, and listening to the tick of the longcase clocks, waiting for a chance passerby? And this had clearly been an exceptionally *good* day.

I snuck a sidelong glance at the thin, sensitive face beside me and wondered if he didn't perchance want me to run the London shop instead? The one he had in Ebury Street, which Charlie had told me all about and where, according to Charlie, people came from all over the world to view Kit's wares. I hadn't realized he had a second string to his bow, but apparently, this was the jewel, the showpiece, where all the real treasures went, having begun life here, in what was effectively his warehouse. Well, golly, I could do wonders with that, I thought. I could be extremely front-of-house and charming, could even set up home in the dear little pied-à-terre that was by all accounts above it: move the boys in, ditch Oxfordshire, and go back to London *tout de suite*. Maybe I could stand in for him on one or two of his trips abroad, too? A couple of days in New York would suit me down to the ground—quick flit round Bloomingdales, then back to Ebury Street, except that was what Kit himself was planning to do, it transpired, as we chatted. With my help. Spend a few days a week in his smart London showroom before motoring back to his country manor at weekends. Unless of course he was traveling, in which case, he informed me, he could be found at the George V in Paris or the Hilton in New York. I listened enviously. A good life, a balanced life, a cosmopolitan, interesting life, and one with a fair smattering of luxury thrown in for good measure, the life of a suave, charming, erudite man, so why on earth, I wondered, had his wife left him for the *plumber*?

I shook my head in disbelief as I drove home later that night, having actually shared more than just the one gin with him, and having had quite a giggle, too. As we'd talked long and hard, we'd realized we knew pretty much the same people in the antiques world—an eclectic, often hysterically effete bunch, particularly in New York—and had shrieked and roared away at their idiosyncrasies. And she'd swapped all that, I boggled, for S-bends and ball cocks? Well, I'd like to meet the guy. Like to meet the plumber who could top all that, but then again, Charlie had said she'd been totally uninterested in the antiques world— a gym bunny, he'd described her as, with sensationally streaky highlights, a year-round tan, and a passion for wine bars—and since it clearly *was* Kit's world, and not just his job, I could see how the marriage might have come unstuck.

It certainly helped to have a smattering of interest in a spouse's work, I mused as I negotiated the dark country lanes home. Ned had always enjoyed coming to private views, even if he knew nothing about the collection, and had loved the drama of an auction, soaking up the atmosphere, seeing it as a piece of theater, with curtain up and then, with the final bang of the gavel, curtain down. I, in turn, had spent many happy hours with him viewing rushes, and not necessarily understanding the minutiae but enjoying watching him run footage again and again, chewing it over, deciding when to cut into a tricky piece, knowing it could make or break a film, patiently waiting until he was completely happy with it. There had been a meeting of minds, even though our worlds were far apart.

I breathed deeply as I swung through Netherby's gates. It still gave me almost physical pain to recall those days. A dull ache in the pit of my stomach, because I knew. I knew we'd had it, you see. We'd had that elusive special harmony that everyone looks for and so few find. Or, perhaps, pretend to find, marry, and make do. Rub along and make the best of it, smile wryly and say, "Oh well, you know, we get along. But it's like any marriage, has its ups and downs . . ."

But our marriage wasn't like that. We'd experienced the real thing. And I knew I was out there looking for it again because human nature will; it can't do without. But when I stopped to think, like now, in the car, coming up to the house Ned grew up in, it frightened the life out of me. Because the person I hoped to find it with again was just as unavailable, in his way, as Ned. I'm not saying Charlie might just as well have been dead, but he was married. And OK, who knows, he might leave his wife, but—the car lurched suddenly in my hands—*might leave his wife?* And child? Is that nice, Lucy? Is that what you want? A chill ran down my spine. God, I horrified myself sometimes. But only occasionally. Mostly, you see, I put my head in the sand and didn't think about her. Or when I did, I draped her in a nun's habit and had her taking Holy Orders. Her choice, her decision. Nothing to do with me.

As I drew up outside the barn I gazed up at the night sky, picking a star, as so often, during the day, I'd pick a cloud.

"Well, what would you do?" I whispered to it hoarsely. "What would you do, if it had been me that had gone, Ned? If it had been the other way round?"

I often wondered. And I think the answer would be, the same as me, eventually. Go looking for someone else. But I also think he would have been more circumspect, more considered. He would have been grief-stricken, naturally, as I had been, and then he would have gone through the obligatory motions of railing at the stupidity of someone's inability to drive a simple *car* for heaven's sake—oh yes, there'd been a lot of that, a lot of anger—and then, a period of calm. A quiet time, of looking after the boys, putting one foot in front of the other, getting through the days, and being alone. But then surely, Ned, I got out of the car and stared at the sky, surely you'd have put a tentative toe in the water? Just as I had, now? You wouldn't be on your own forever, however deep and strong our love? I found I couldn't quite look the star in the face, though. Found myself wondering if Ned's toe might have dipped into clearer, less murky, less married waters. If he might not have found someone infinitely more suitable.

"Like Kit Alexander," I could almost hear my inner self shriek in exasperation as I shut the door. Yes, OK, how much more convenient would that be, I thought with a sigh. Not that he'd necessarily be falling over himself to take me on, but I knew, too, there'd been a spark of interest back there. Knew, in the offering of that second gin, there'd been a suggestion that he was enjoying my company and would like to prolong the party. As little as that but as *much* as that, too, and at our age, in our circumstances, and with our baggage, it was enough. One does get to read the signs. And wouldn't that be just so neat? A clever, interesting man, mad about antiques, mad about me, with two big boys for my two little boys to admire and look up to (but not actually need their nappies changing; hell no, a bag of dirty laundry would be the most I'd get from them). Yes, and we could all gather round the huge oak table in Frampton's kitchen, Ben and Max listening wide-eyed as Kit's good-humored boys told tales of their gap years in Africa, or Peru, both quietly relieved to see their dear old dad settled with a lovely, like-minded girl. A big, happy family. And something that Ned would approve of, I was sure. Oh, Ned would have no problem with Kit, but Charlie? I cringed, ducking under the glittering, reproachful gaze of the heavens, and made toward the barn.

As I walked up to the door, I glanced up. The boys' bedroom was in darkness, so hopefully they were fast asleep. Trisha had forgotten to draw the curtains, I noticed. I peered through the glass as I put my key in the door. The lighting was very subdued, just a couple of low table lamps, and I couldn't see her. Must be in the loo or upstairs. It occurred to me that of course, I should have rung, warned her I was going to be late, but actually, Trisha was jolly sensible. Sensible enough just to put them to bed and wait. When I walked in, I heard movement. She was sitting on the sofa with her back to me, except that when she stood up and turned around, it wasn't Trisha at all; it was Rose.

"Oh! Rose, what on earth—"

"Sorry to startle you, Lucy." She smiled.

"No—no, it's fine. Are the boys—?"

"Up at the house. We popped them into bed in the spare room."

"Oh! I thought Trisha was going to baby-sit down here?"

"I'm afraid I can't spare her constantly, Lucy. Joan needed some help in the kitchen. I've got a big dinner party tomorrow, so Trish is working for me this evening."

"Oh. Right." I flushed, embarrassed, and walked across to the counter. Yes, how presumptuous of me to assume she'd work for me all the time, but actually, that's what I'd been led to believe. And I wasn't sure I liked the boys not being here when I got back, sleeping up at Netherby, but then again, that was my fault, too, I supposed, for not ringing and checking arrangements. So stupid, Lucy.

"I should have rung Trisha," I admitted. "If I'd known she couldn't stay on, I'd have come back earlier. I just stopped to have a drink with my new boss."

"Or two?"

"Sorry?" I startled.

She looked at her watch. "Well, it's after nine. I can't believe he expects you to stay that late. It clearly turned into a drinks party!"

"Well, it was just rather an unusual—a busy day. And he didn't get back until very late, so—yes, we did have a couple."

Christ, why on earth did I have to explain my whereabouts to her? Or count my drinks? I put my bag and car keys down carefully on the work surface.

"Um, Rose, how did you get in here?"

"Oh, I have a key of course," she said, matter-of-factly.

Of course. And it appeared she'd made herself a cup of coffee, read a couple of my magazines that were lying open on the table, opened a packet of peanuts, and found a bowl for them, none of which I'd mind if it were Jess or Teresa, say, and they'd rung first to check, but Rose, just fishing a key out of her bag, settling herself down in *my* home . . .

"And, my dear, the reason I'm here is to apologize profusely." She smiled graciously. "I acted abominably the other night; it was quite shameful of me to accuse you like that. I wanted to ask—well, to beg, really—for you to forgive my ridiculous outburst. Do let's let bygones be bygones and start again, eh?" Her blue eyes widened anxiously, appealing to me, as she twisted her rings nervously. I'd never seen Rose nervous.

"Of course," I said, perching on a stool at the counter. God, I'd almost forgotten. Only yesterday, but it seemed so long ago. So much had happened.

"I can't think what came over me. Of course I was upset. But what it had to do with you I can't imagine."

"Well, in a way you were right," I said slowly, wondering where this huge capitulation was leading. "I did introduce Rozanna to Hector. But as I said last night, Hector's a grown man."

"Well, *quite*," she agreed staunchly. "My sentiments entirely. A silly grown man, with his brains in his trousers, and what he does is his own affair. I pray to God he'll see sense and come back to the fold of course, but what I don't want, Lucy, under any circumstances, is for it to get in the way of our relationship. We have such a close friendship now, don't we, and I don't want it to come under any sort of threat."

I found myself taken aback once more. Close friendship? Did we? I'd never considered us bosom pals, but then again, Rose was so cold, maybe this was her idea of mateyness, as matey as she could get, anyway. In any event, I decided firmly, it was a relief. She was quite right; we couldn't have carried on with such an atmosphere hanging over us. Some air clearing was in order. I smiled.

"I quite agree. It would be awful to live cheek by jowl and be under any sort of strain."

"Precisely," she agreed. "And even worse would be if you felt so uncomfortable, you decided you couldn't live here. I was up all last night worrying about it, but you wouldn't think that, would you, Lucy?"

Ah. So that was it. I regarded her, perched on the arm of one of the squashy terracotta sofas she'd installed, surrounded by the tasteful kelim cushions she'd ordered through a smart catalog, in the glow of a soft table light she'd chosen from Peter Jones. I knew in my heart I'd been bought, that Jess had been right, and I knew, too, that this was a key question and I had to answer it carefully.

"No, I'm not thinking of moving out of here, Rose."

"Oh, I'm so pleased!" She beamed.

"But," I hesitated, "I can't, either, give you a rock-solid guarantee that I'll be here forever."

"Well no, obviously not forever!" She laughed nervously. "Not when you're eighty-six and I'm a hundred and something, of course not!"

"No, I'm not talking about as far off as that. What I'm saying is, I don't know what shape my life will take. I don't know where I'll eventually work, for instance."

"Oh, but your job at the manor! Splendid, and ideal, all those antiques."

"Yes, splendid for the minute, but it's not a career."

"Oh, but surely with two small boys to bring up and financial security under your belt, any sort of work is—well, just a bit of posturing. I know you young girls feel you have to do something these days, but let's face it; you don't actually need a career!"

"Need, no, but might want," I said firmly. "I always had one and never considered it posturing, and anyway, who knows, there might be other factors to consider. I might meet someone. Someone I might even want to marry," I added brutally.

Her eyes clouded at this, and her chin shot out, almost as a defensive reflex. She collected herself.

"Well yes, of course you might. You're young, no one expects you to be a widow forever, but this place is plenty big enough for a family, and you know, you could always add on at the back."

I caught my breath at this. How much she'd already thought through.

"Yes, I suppose I could, and who knows, it might not happen. I may stay single. And maybe I won't be able to get back onto the career ladder, either, and get a proper job, because I've left it too late. In which case I may well stay here and bring up my boys, and jolly lucky I'd consider myself to be, and jolly grateful to you, too, for letting me have this lifeline. What I'm saying, though, is," I struggled to be honest, "well, I simply don't know. I can't predict the future. Can't make any promises."

She nodded. Glanced down at her lap. "Of course not," she said shortly. "But for the boys, you know, there's such stability here. And they're starting a new school in September; you surely wouldn't want to hoik them out again?"

"I have no intention of hoiking them out," I said patiently. "But if I did, I think you'd find it would be fine. Children are very adaptable."

"And of course, the extended family here," she swept on, ignoring me and trying another tack, "is marvelous for them. Not having a father, but to have his family, his parents, their grandparents, right next door—"

"Is wonderful for them, sure. But don't forget, they had all that in London. With my parents." I looked her in the eye. "Who they now don't see so much of."

"Of course," she said tersely, "but then the boys are Felloweses, aren't they? That is their family name, a very old family name. And roots are so important, don't you think, Lucy?"

I nodded. Probably best not to speak. Probably best to hold my tongue. Not to say, "Oh, as opposed to my family name? My Polish/Irish immigrant roots?" Not for the first time I experienced a nasty taste in my mouth.

"And look what they've got here, too. So much space, acres to run in, lakes to fish, the swimming pool—they're having the time of their lives!"

I nodded again and didn't mention that they'd had the time of their lives in London, friends in the square to skateboard with, parks to cycle in, dinosaurs to gape at in the National History Museum, less time in cars, a five-minute walk to school. Instead I picked my words carefully.

"Rose, I'm delighted you came across, and it was sweet of you to feel you had to apologize. There was no real need, I promise; I wouldn't have taken offense. But if you're looking for a guarantee that we'll stay here long-term . . . I can't give you one. I'm grateful, so grateful, as I've said before, but I truly don't know which way my life will go. If I was privy to the denouement of that little plot, I'd be delighted to share it, but I'm not, so . . . I suppose what I'm saying is, I can't make promises."

Her eyes glittered dangerously for a moment. Then she raised her chin. Smiled. "Of course you can't, and who can. Golly, even those of us with the most settled of lives can't tell what's around the corner." She lapsed into reflective silence as at that moment, headlights shone in, glaring through the huge plate-glass windows, illuminating the barn and causing us both to shield our eyes. The lights dipped, and a moment later a car came to a halt outside, the engine still running.

Rose got to her feet. "That'll be Archie. I told him I was popping down here; he probably thought it was too dark for me to walk back."

I slid off the stool and walked her to the door, struggling with my emotions, hoping I hadn't been too harsh. "Rose, we *do* love it here," I began, "the boys and I. Don't get me wrong, it is idyllic, it's just—"

"I know." She stopped me with an unexpected peck on the cheek. "You just don't know yourself, that's all." She gave a wan smile. "And who does?"

I watched her get in the car, carefully tucking in her feet and closing the door behind her, but as they turned around and purred back past me, I realized it wasn't Archie driving at all but David Mortimer.

Well, of course. I smiled. I couldn't actually see Archie consulting his watch in the library, setting his whiskey aside, and heaving himself out of his chair to collect his wife, worried about her walking home in the dark, but I could see him giving a nod to the man in the armchair opposite, "Would you be so kind, dear boy?"

Yes, as ever, I thought, locking the door behind me, they had a loyal dependent at their beck and call. Unpaid, of course, but probably in receipt of favors any elderly bachelor would covet. A day's shooting here, a Sunday lunch there, unlimited access to the drinks cupboard. And he sang for his supper, too, was always good-humored and charming. But he was a dependent, nonetheless. Around to do their bidding.

Chapter Twenty-one

WHEN I WENT UP TO NETHERBY THE FOLLOWING MORNING to collect the boys, I discovered they weren't there. Nobody seemed to be there, in fact, but I finally ran Archie and Pinkie down, in the pale blue breakfast room. The white linen cloth was covered in crumbs and most of the breakfast things had been cleared away, but they were still lingering over cold toast and marmalade, bathed in sunlight and buried in the *Telegraph* and the *Mail*, respectively. Archie looked up, surprised, when I asked.

"Ben and Max?" He leaned back in his chair and rustled his paper. "No, my dear, they've gone into Oxford with Rose. Left about an hour ago. There was some talk of a puppet show, or something, I think, at the Bloomsbury. That was it, wasn't it, Pinkie?"

He glanced at his daughter, but Pinkie was absorbed in Nigel Dempster, mouth open, lips moving slightly as she read.

"Think that was it," muttered Archie, going back to his own paper. "Didn't she mention it?"

"No! No, she didn't."

"Ah."

"So, did she say what time she'd be back?"

"Hmmm?" He frowned abstractedly from the depths of *Court and Social*, then glanced over at his daughter, who was audible now. "To yourself, please, Pinkie!" he snapped. "Bloody expensive schools and you end up with retards."

I cleared my throat. "Any idea what time she'll be back, Archie?"

"Didn't say, my dear," he muttered, then glanced up. "Could well take them out to lunch, though, I suppose? Loves their company, eh?" His pale blue eyes widened.

Yes, I thought hovering, and so did I. I sucked a piece of my hair nervously as he went back to his paper. And I didn't seem to be seeing much of them these days. They were always either up here or out with some member of the Fellowes family, but then again, that was probably my fault, I reasoned guiltily. I had been rather preoccupied of late.

Archie glanced up again. "Sorry, Lucy, was there something else?"

"Oh no. No, nothing else." I turned to go.

In other words, "Why are you lingering, woman, when a chap's trying to have a quiet breakfast?" Not, "Pour yourself a cup of coffee, Luce, and pull up a chair." And Pinkie hadn't even deigned to raise her head to say good morning. It hadn't escaped my notice of late that without the boys in tow, my presence lost a lot of its attraction at Netherby. I turned on my heel. And nice of Rose, too, I thought, as I stalked angrily down the oak-paneled passage, to take the boys without asking me. I mean yes, sure, a puppet show with Granny was terrific and I was determined not to overreact, but I'd only seen her last night. She might have mentioned it.

I headed off toward the back of the house, my footsteps muffled by Persian runners, then crossed through the main hall, shoes squeaking suddenly on the black and white limestone flags. The French windows were already thrown open to the terrace at the back to accommodate the anticipated heat of yet another glorious day. The frazzled thyme and sage squeezed between the yellowing York stone didn't look up to bracing itself for yet more baking, but down below, the rose garden bloomed more confidently. Beyond the roses, the shimmering expanse of pale green park stretched down to the lake, which was visible only as a phosphorescent glow, and then rose up again and away into the distance. Swapping this sudden burst of light for the door under the stairs, I followed the gloomy back corridor, pushed through the green baize door, and headed for the stable yard.

As I made for the back door, I passed the kitchen. The smell of bacon grease hung in the air, together with the usual steamy fog that seemed to accompany anything Joan cooked. I was about to walk on when I was halted by a sob. I paused, stepped backward, and peered in. Joan's broad back was obscuring my view and the steam didn't help, but she was standing behind someone seated at the kitchen table. The sob came again. I hesitated, then went in. Trisha was sitting with her elbows on the table, forehead propped up in her hands, whilst Joan, a plump arm around her, patted her shoulder awkwardly. Trisha swung a tearstained face round at my approach.

"Sorry." I hesitated. "It's just, well, I heard—"

"No, no, it's OK," sniffed Trisha, wiping her nose with the back of her hand. "Come in, Lucy. I was going to come and talk to you anyway."

"What is it? What's wrong?" I hastened over and sat beside her. Joan, relieved to be able to abandon her post, hurried away to the boiling vat of water on the stove, which had clearly been bubbling away for some time.

"Boy trouble," Joan muttered darkly, snatching a tea towel from a rail to drag the cauldron off the heat. "And with the worst possible candidate if you ask me." She picked up the heavy pan and staggered with it to the sink, pausing to rest it on the edge. She turned. "I told her, right from the start, Lucy: it ain't no good hankering over someone like Jack Fellowes. He'll never settle, and that's the end of it. I'm not sayin' he's a bad lot, but I've never seen him more than five minutes with a girl and that's a fact. I told you, right from the start, didn't I?" She jerked her head accusingly at Trisha before pouring half a hundred-weight of potatoes, together with the boiling water, into a vast colander in the sink. Clouds of steam obscured her.

I covered Trisha's hand with mine and squeezed it. "Oh, Trisha, Joan's right, I'm afraid." I sighed. "Jack is just too fickle. God, I wish I'd warned you, too, but I had no idea you were in so deep."

This prompted a fresh outburst of tears and her head dropped like a stone into her arms.

"I am, I am in deep, and I can't help it. I . . . just love him so much!" Her muffled voice came up from the scrubbed pine table. "And, Lucy," she raised a tearstained face, "he had no idea! Absolutely no idea! Thought it was just a bit of fun, thought hanging around with me was great, until I mentioned yesterday that it might be nice to get away from this place, 'cos I've got a bit of holiday coming up, just a weekend, but I thought, you know, we could go away. Stay in a nice pub or something, but he was like, 'Oh, my God, a relationship!' I tell you, you've never seen anyone retreat so fast in your life."

I grimaced. "Yes, well, I can imagine one might not see him for the dust on the soles of his trainers. God, he makes me cross sometimes. It's just so typical of him, isn't it, Joan?"

"As I say, he ain't a bad lot," Joan muttered carefully, intent on shaking the colander full of hot potatoes in the sink. "But he can't settle, that's his problem."

"And the thing is," Trisha sniffed, "I'm sure there's someone else. The other day he went to London—you know, with you, Lucy—and when he came back, he was really, oh, I don't know, distant. Distracted. Hardly spoke to me. I'm sure he was with some tart up there," she finished vehemently.

I swallowed, recalling the svelte, beautiful, and hardly tarty Pascale as they'd snuggled and cooed out of her bedroom window.

"Ye-es, well, possibly," I conceded, not wanting to twist the knife. "One never quite knows with Jack, although he could just have been distracted by work or something," I said encouragingly. "That poetry book of his is coming out soon; he might be worried about reviews or something." Joan snorted derisively from the sink.

"But even if there is someone else," I hastened on, "it's absolutely no reflection on you, Trisha. He's just that kind of man. Can't keep his hormones to himself, and actually, the sooner you realize that, the better. He is what I believe used to be called a bounder." I grinned and squeezed her shoulder, trying to buck her up.

She gave a weak smile in return. "He's also the nicest, kindest, most generous, funniest man I've ever met in my life," she said in a low voice. "And I can't help loving him. I can't help it, Lucy!" Her head dropped onto the table again as she was ambushed by tears.

I sighed and looked to Joan, ready to raise my eyebrows, to share a how-many-times-have-we-been-here-before moment, but Joan's back was resolutely to us; she was slicing her potatoes like a demon, the blade of her knife glinting.

"Listen, Trisha," I tried again. "I know it seems like the end of the world at the moment, but I promise you, in a couple of weeks you'll look at him and wonder what you ever—"

"I won't; I know I won't!" she bellowed into the wood, her nose an inch from the table. "And what's worse is I have to see him every bloody day, look at him every bloody day, and hear his voice every bloody day! And I just don't know how I'm going to bear that."

With another strangled sob she jumped up and, blinded by tears, knocked her chair over backward and fled from the room. I heard her run down the corridor; then the back door slammed.

I reached down slowly and picked up the chair, setting it upright. Joan didn't comment. Trisha had been crying so hard, the table was wet, and as I reached for a tea towel to wipe it with, I felt my blood rising. I screwed up the cloth and flung it down, furious.

"Where is he, Joan?"

"In the library, as usual. Writing those wretched poems of his, no doubt."

"Right. I'll give him something to write about."

I got up and marched out, heading off back down the tiled passageway, pushing smartly through the green baize door, back to the formal side of the house. As I crossed through the front hall again, I could feel fury mounting with every step; my pace quickened as I rejoined the oak passageway down to the library.

I paused there a moment in the quiet paneled gloom, breathing heavily. The door was closed. I raised my hand to knock, then, dammit, turned the handle and strode in.

The book-lined room was unnaturally bright, but then I was used to seeing it in the evening, when Archie presided over a log fire, the green velvet drapes drawn. Shafts of dusty sunlight streamed in now through the tall windows and fell on the shelves, flitting about the leather spines. It was a large room, and with the sun in my eyes it took me a moment to see Jack at the far end, sitting facing me, behind the huge mahogany desk in the bay window, his back to the view. Despite the bright light, his head was bowed under a green glass desk light, intent on—not a pile of papers but a paperback, with a lurid red-and-black cover, propped up in front of him. He put it down, guiltily almost, as he heard the door open, looked momentarily annoyed. Then his face cleared.

"Oh, Lucy, hi." He quickly shut the book and put it in a drawer.

"Don't you 'Oh, Lucy, hi,' me," I snapped, striding across to him. "What have you done to that poor girl?"

He looked bewildered as I rested the palms of my hands on his desk and leaned toward him. He sat back in the wing chair. "Which poor girl?"

"Trisha, of course! My God, you've only gone and broken her heart and you can't even remember which girl it is! Christ, what's wrong with you, Jack? What kind of emotional delinquent are you?" I searched his face. His blue eyes looked back blankly at me. "Haven't you got any sense of decency? Any sense of responsibility? Any—I don't know—any heart, for crying out loud? Don't you know when a girl is falling in love with you? Can't you read the signs, or is it that you *can* read them but couldn't care less? Just carry on humping her regardless, prior to dumping her when she shows any hint of commitment?"

He regarded me across the desk. Slowly he put the top on his pen, replaced it on the blotter in front of him. "Actually, it wasn't like that at all," he said carefully. "In the first place, I had no idea she was 'in love with me,' as you so romantically put it, until she sprang this weekend break on me, and in the second place, I didn't encourage her, unless you count passing time with her and the boys. I'm sorry if she's upset, genuinely, but—"

"Oh, spare me that 'genuine' bollocks," I spat. "You couldn't give a monkey's! Couldn't care less whether she's topped herself or gone back to Australia, and if Not Encouraging Her includes making love to her on the riverbank, whispering sweet nothings in her shell-like, and generally letting her believe she's the most wonderful woman on God's earth, then you're on dodgy ground, Jack. Don't forget, I've known you a long time, I've seen you in action, and I know the routine. This isn't the first girl I've had sobbing on my shoulder over you, I'm sure it won't be the last, and to be honest, I'm getting just a little bit fed up with it. You're not a teenager, for heaven's sake; you're not even a young blade about town, as in: 'Gosh, what a lad, the guy can't help himself, so virile, couldn't possibly settle down, wouldn't last a moment—no!' You're not in any of those categories anymore; you're just a sad aging Lothario, a serial shagger who chases his female students around the lecture theater and can't keep a grip on his trousers for ten minutes!"

I could feel myself shaking with rage. I was also vaguely aware that quite a lot of pent-up anger that might have been better directed at my mother-in-law, sitting smugly between my two sons in a darkened theater, was winging Jack's way.

"I see," he said quietly, seemingly unmoved. "So what does that make you?"

"What?"

"Well, if I'm a sad aging Lothario, what does that make you, Lucy?"

"We are not talking about me," I said between clenched teeth.

"We're talking about you, and your irresponsible behavior, which has resulted in a young girl sobbing her heart out at the scullery table!" I pointed a finger down the hallway. "She's down there, Jack, or was, with Joan and me, but she's probably prostrate on her bed now, soaking her pillow. And do you care? No!"

"Well, I do, but then again," he paused, "she's not married, is she?"

"What?" I narrowed my eyes incredulously at him, panting slightly with the exertion of so much yelling.

"I said, she's not married."

I stared. "Oh, that's pathetic, Jack," I said at length. "Truly, childishly, ridiculously pathetic. And cheap, too."

"Is it?" He got up and came round to my side of the desk. He seemed very tall all of a sudden, and a little too close, actually. I took a step back. "Cheap, is it? To suggest that before you come marching in here talking about duty and responsibility you take a look at your own glass house? Pathetic to suggest that before you start lobbing stones in my direction, you consider the effects of your own actions, do a little reinforced double-glazing to ensure against far more shattering consequences?"

"Oh, you're so clever, Jack," I spat, "with your English tutorial metaphors, but I know what you're talking about, so let's call a spade a spade, shall we? Yes, he's married. OK? Happy? But the marriage is not mine, and it is not my duty to maintain it."

Even as I said it I knew I was shot to bits.

"You don't believe that for one minute," he scoffed. "That's just cowardly cant. That's not you talking at all, Lucy; that's someone small, weak, and deceitful, looking for someone else to hide behind. That's unworthy of you, not like you at all."

"Oh, really?" I flushed, furious I'd let myself be cornered. "So what is like me, then, Jack? You don't know me nearly as well as you imagine, but I know you, and if you're trying to tell me you've never fallen for a married woman you're a hypocrite and a liar."

He paused. "Only once. And it was unrequited."

"Rubbish," I scoffed. "You've been nipping in and out of marital beds and making a perfect nuisance of yourself for years. Shinning down drainpipes as the husband's key goes in the front door—oh, you've been there all right, and what you don't like is that now *I'm* there, too. You don't like the fact that I'm finally getting out and having a good time. You want me in widow's weeds forever!"

I turned and walked angrily to the door. When I looked back, his face had paled. His hands were clenched at his sides.

"That's a despicable thing to say," he said in a low voice, "and you know it."

"Oh, do I?" I retorted, opening the door. "I'm not sure I know anything about you anymore, Jack."

I slammed the door behind me and stalked off down the corridor, a mixture of fury and guilt rising within me like a surging torrent. I gulped it down hard as I crossed the checkered hall and made for the open doors onto the terrace. Pinkie had transferred herself out here, installed in a steamer chair, still gripped by the *Daily Mail*—she'd made it to the horoscopes—a cup of coffee beside her. She glanced up as I strode past, shading her eyes with her hand, but I ignored her and ran on down the steps to the gravel below. I felt horribly hot as I skirted the fountain and made for the rose garden, back toward the barn.

My parting shot had been below the belt, I knew that. In the bad old days, no one had tried harder than Jack to help me get over my grief. No one, except perhaps Jess, had spent more evenings in my tiny, miserable flat—the worst times, those evenings when the boys had gone to bed—just being there, sitting with me at my kitchen table, as I let rip, sobbing into old photograph albums while he mopped the photos dry with kitchen towel. I remembered the endless bowls of spaghetti carbonara—the only thing he could cook—that I'd toyed listlessly with before my eyes would fill up again and I'd set down my fork and dissolve. I remembered his patience, his kindness, his perseverance, his total lack of compassion fatigue which had overcome other pilgrims who'd visited me on the top floor. He'd helped me through some dark days, there was no disputing that, and I'd been wrong to . . . well. I swallowed, shoved a piece of hair in my mouth and chewed hard.

But then again, I'd been provoked, I thought quickly, anger rising self-righteously to balance the guilt on the grocer's scales of my mind. I'd lashed out like that because—I quickly replayed our conversation in my head—because of all that sanctimonious moralizing! He'd preached to me back there like some wise old paternalistic sage, and yet everyone knew he conducted his life like a randy old mongrel, sniffing out every bitch in heat in the county. That was what I objected to, I decided angrily as I picked up speed, threading my way along the grass path through the rose garden; that was what had goaded me—his hypocrisy. How dare he adopt the high moral ground with me?

Pink and indignant now, I considered the magnitude of his gall. Jack Fellowes, of all people—what a nerve! Double standards, I seethed, making for the bridge over the lake, double bloody standards and, yes, actually, some jealousy, too. Jealousy at someone else having fun for a change, someone else having a good time. Not that I was, I thought bitterly, spitting hair out of my mouth as my footsteps echoed on the wooden bridge. Not in the sense that he thought, anyway. Not in the sense of being awash with hot sex, no, just hot guilt. All the shame and the finger-pointing and none of the fun. Ter-rific.

I marched up the hill in the heat, the sun burning down on my forehead now, panting hard as I reached the gate. As I went up the little brick path to the barn, I slammed the door theatrically behind me. The huge glass pane rattled ominously and I clutched my head in horror, waiting for it to shatter. Happily it didn't. God, I was like a petulant child, I thought guiltily, lowering my hands. That was the sort of thing Max would do. Max. Hadn't seen him for ages. I touched my temples again. It came to me with an awful dawning realization that I had the beginnings of a monumental headache. I stood still, fearfully, on the doormat. All that shouting, all that stomping around in the heat—it could even be the onset of a migraine, something I hadn't had for years.

Walking slowly to the sofa, I sat down, holding myself like a native carrying a vase on her head, knowing any sudden movement would be fatal. This had to be handled with care. I waited. Yes, there it was again, thumping away ominously behind my eyes, like an approaching marching army. Three or four years ago I'd been plagued by pains like these, and I knew that nothing more than a handful of Nurofen Plus and a darkened room would do.

I got up carefully and made slowly for the stairs and held on to the banisters as I went. Bloody man, I thought, groping my way into the bathroom at the top and peering in the cabinet for the bottle. I hadn't had to resort to this for years, and that I did now was all his fault. I felt along the walls into my bedroom and sat down on the bed, armed with the painkillers. One at a time, I carefully slipped them down with sips of water, trying not to gag, trying not to throw my head back too far. As I took the last swallow, the telephone rang on the bedside table. I held my head, horrified, protecting it against its shrill summons, until it occurred to me that it wasn't going to stop unless I picked it up.

"Hello?" I whispered, then held the receiver about a foot away from my ear.

"Lucy?" I just about heard it.

I brought the receiver back tentatively. "Oh, Charlie, hi."

"Sound a bit faint, my love; you're whispering. Can't you talk?"

"No, no, I can; the boys aren't here; it's just . . ." I shut my eyes. Put the palm of my hand over one of them. It seemed to be leaping out of its socket. "Thumping headache, I'm afraid. Hurts like hell."

"Oh dear, poor you. Aspirin?"

I grimaced. "Something a little stronger than that, but yes, I've resorted to it."

"Excellent. Now listen, my love," he hastened on, "I'll be brief, because she's only popped to the shops, but something rather marvelous has happened. My darling, it looks remarkably as if our cunning plan could bear fruit if you could possibly get away on Saturday night. An old schoolfriend of Miranda's is coming to stay and I know she'd like me out of the way, so, under the guise of 'working in London' I've taken you at your word and booked *the* most idyllic bide-a-wee retreat imaginable. It's in a tiny village somewhere near Bicester—not too local, you understand—complete with romantic four-poster bed, roaring log fire as stipulated in the brief, not that we'll need it in this heat, the requisite number of olde oake beams, horse brasses galore, and the most stunning view of the Cotswold hills imaginable. What do you say, my darling?"

Saturday night. My heart pounded. My head, too. Quite a cacophony going on, one way or another. My eyes were still tightly shut. I tried to think. Saturday was only a few days away, and the subterfuge and machinations involved in getting away for the night made me feel quite sick.

"Lucy?"

"Yes, yes, I'm thinking, Charlie. It's just I've got to come up with some sort of excuse. The boys, you know."

"Jess?"

"Sorry?"

"Your friend in London?"

"Oh yes, Jess. Yes, I could, I suppose . . ."

"Well, Lucy, only if you want to." He sounded peeved. "I mean, it took quite a while to dig it out of the *Michelin* and everything, but if you don't wan—"

"No, no, of *course* I want to." I sat up, realizing I was hunched on the bed like a cowed little dwarf. God, *bloody* man. *Bloody* Jack, spoiling it all for me, making my head split, making me think too hard, making me reconsider everything, but I would *not* let him ruin it. "Of course I'm coming, Charlie," I said firmly. "And Jess is the perfect excuse. I haven't seen her baby for ages, and he is my godson."

"Good." He sounded relieved. "For a moment there—oh, Lucy, I can't wait."

"Neither can I," I breathed, the infantry in my head for one blissful moment retreating slightly, as a rush of love—or perhaps Nurofen—kicked in. "Oh, Charlie, I know this is right," I said, holding the mouth-piece with two hands, "don't you? No matter what anyone says!"

"Anyone?" he repeated sharply. "Who's anyone?"

"Oh no, just Jack. Ned's cousin. He's—no one, really. It's just—well, I was with him a moment ago and he was peddling some holier-than-thou twaddle. I've had a bit of a row with him actually."

"About us?" He sounded nervous.

"No, no, not directly," I assured him. "We weren't talking ostensibly about anyone in particular." I crossed my fingers here. "No names, he was just sounding off about people who have," I faltered in the face of the word *affairs*, "our sort of relationship," I finished lamely. I wanted to go now, actually. Wanted to put down the phone. We'd arranged our date, we were meeting on Saturday, and all I wanted to do was draw the curtains and lie on my cool white bedcover nursing my head. No more pressure, please.

"He doesn't understand," Charlie said soberly. "He has no idea. If he did, my God, he wouldn't be so quick to judge. This sort of love, the sort that we have, is blind to all obstacles."

I sat up a bit, took my hand off my eye. Was it? "Yes, you're right. You're right, Charlie. It is, isn't it?"

"Of course it is. My God, when I think of you, Lucy, well, I just go off the scale. I long for you. I want to eat you."

Eat me. Golly. I went a bit hot. Took my cardigan off. "I long for you, too, Charlie," I assured him, feeling a bit more gung-ho, "and I can't wait for Saturday. Can't wait to walk into that pub, see you standing, smiling at the bar, take our drinks over to the cozy, inglenook fireplace—"

"Could do, or take them upstairs."

"Then a meal in the restaurant—"

"Yes, or apparently they do room service."

"And then up the creaky stairs to that delicious, sumptuous feather bed."

"Don't," he groaned. "Oh, don't, Lucy. Now I shall have to have a cold shower! I—oh!"

"What?"

He paused. "She's back," he said in a low voice. "I hear the car. Till Saturday then, my darling. The Hare and Hounds, Little Burchester, seven o'clock. Don't fail me, will you, my angel?"

"Not for one moment," I assured him.

The line went dead as he hurriedly put down the phone. I shut my eyes, and lay down carefully on my side, still with the purring receiver clamped to my chest. No, not for one moment.

Chapter Twenty-two

SATURDAY DAWNED BRIGHT AND PROMISING. PROMISING because, as I drew back my bedroom curtains and leaned out into the sweet morning air, resting my arms on the honeysuckle-encrusted ledge, its heady scent mingling with that of the roses from the garden below, I realized, with relief, that my head had cleared. The pounding and sizzling that had kept up its relentless double act for two whole days (as I knew it would) had finally abated, and the dull, monotonous thump in the temples, interspersed with—just to keep me on my toes— a shooting, white-hot pain, like a guided missile behind the eyes, was no more.

I tentatively looked toward the sun, apprehensive, waiting to flinch, to cry out. But nothing. The demons had gone, and as I gazed into the hazy blue distance it occurred to me, with some surprise, that effectively, I'd missed forty-eight hours. I noticed, for example, that the sweeping expanse of parkland that rose up to Netherby had scorched almost yellow in the heat and looked like a tropical savanna, whereas the last time I'd looked, it had still been a cool green. The flowers, too, in my little garden below, all jostling for position in the beds, were wilting terribly now and had clearly been gasping for a drink for some time.

Oh, I'd carried on of course, these past two days, hadn't taken to my bed or anything wet, but it had been in something of a blur. I'd even limped into work on the first day, pathetically grateful for the peace and quiet I'd previously derided, but spent much of the time with my head on the desk. The following day I'd trudged painfully and slowly around a jam-packed Sainsbury's in Oxford, feeling my way along the shelves and even, at one point, leaning against the loo rolls with my eyes shut, before collapsing in a darkened room on my return. The children, understandably, steered well clear and amused themselves elsewhere. It had, and I'm not looking for sympathy here, been an excruciatingly painful episode, but now, this morning, on this most momentous of mornings, and after ten hours of dreamy, paracetamol-induced sleep, I knew the worst was over. My eyes, wide and optimistic, marveled, for instance, at the shiny yellow buttercup heads in the meadow beyond, which yesterday had looked like an oppressive shield, a blazing carrion designed to make me cry out in pain, and the shimmering lake, which previously had had me swishing the curtain shut as it flashed menacingly in the sun, seemed now only tranquil and calm.

A broad grin spread uncontrollably across my face, and my tummy leapt with excitement as I hung out of the ledge in my pajama top. Tonight, then, was most surely the night, and considering the ease with which the potentially difficult logistics of the evening ahead had fallen into place, the omens were good. Trisha, last night, sniffing on the other end of the phone and blowing her nose loudly, had readily agreed to baby-sit, on the basis that she certainly hadn't got anything better to do on a Saturday night, had she, and anyway, she'd rather be down here than up there. She didn't want to be in the same house as *him*.

I'd felt rather guilty about taking advantage of her misery, but— golly, it passed. All the same, I decided, narrowing my eyes thoughtfully to the windows of Netherby, glinting away in the sunlight, I'd better just nip up and confirm the arrangements with her. I didn't want anything scuppering my plans at the last minute.

I hurriedly threw off my top and grabbed some shorts and a T-shirt from a drawer. My plan was to take the boys out for the day before delivering them back here to Trisha, where she could oversee pizza, crisps, ice cream, and all manner of tooth-rotting comestibles in front of a new video, all bought in Sainsbury's yesterday. I wasn't too proud to buy my way into my children's good humor, and anyway, I was keen to get into Ben's good books and silence any of that mutinous "we see less of you now than when you worked in London" malarkey. I, meanwhile, would whiz upstairs to begin my devotions, anointing my body with all the expensive lotions and potions I'd grabbed, eyes half-shut, from the Body Beautiful shelves yesterday. I'd actually planned to then pour the body beautiful into something tight and sexy snapped up in Oxford yesterday, but feeling about as sexy as a stale sardine as I'd groped my way blindly down the High Street, I'd decided, on the threshold of Monsoon, that the combination of throbbing disco music, fiercely intent shoppers, and overwhelming heat might just finish me off. It had also occurred to me, on the way home, that vamp dressing might not be quite the ticket for the Hare and Hounds, and so I was even now pulling out of my bottom drawer my black jeans and a cream antique lace camisole top, over which I planned to throw my favorite beaded cardigan, all the way from my darling sister in Italy. There. I laid it all on the bed and stepped back. Oh, and some black suede boots. I dragged them out from under the bed. Perfect.

The boys were still asleep, so I left a quick note to tell Ben where I was and scuttled up to Netherby. As I bowled through the back door into the boot room, sailing through generations of riding boots, Wellingtons, bowler hats, brown felts, and Panamas, I could feel excitement mounting. I skipped down the back corridor to the kitchen and wondered if Charlie was feeling the same way. I couldn't actually imagine him hurtling into Oxford intent on being at the cutting edge of fashion for tonight's rendezvous, but all the same, I had a sneaky suspicion he might be glancing at the hands of the clock occasionally, urging them on as I was. I clattered through the kitchen door with a cheery "Morning all!" expecting to find Joan and Trisha finishing their breakfast chores—only to find Rose, alone, standing facing me behind the huge oak table, unrolling bundles of silver from gray felt cloth.

"Oh!" I stopped, startled. "Rose, I—"

"Didn't expect to find me in this part of the house?" she finished smoothly. "Oh, I do venture out here occasionally, if only to check everyone's doing their best, which, judging by the terrible state of the silver," she held a fork up to the light and peered critically at it, "they're not. Can I help?"

"Oh, well, no, not really. I was just looking for Trisha. She's going to baby-sit for me tonight, and I wanted to check that she was still OK."

Rose frowned at me through the fork prongs. "Then it's just as well you came up, Lucy, because I'm afraid she is most definitely not 'OK,' as you put it. I have a luncheon party for twenty-two tomorrow, and both Joan and Trisha will be spending their evening polishing all this silver, ready for Sunday. Fancy putting it away like this. Just look at this fork, caked in old egg! Can you believe it?"

I gazed at her in horror, all my dreams turning to dust and ashes in the face of her frosty geniality.

"Is that a problem?" She raised her eyebrows. "What were your plans for tonight?" She put down the fork and cast a thin smile in my direction. "I hear, on the grapevine, that there might be a man on the horizon."

I regarded her with even more horror. Christ, what did she know? "N-no," I stuttered, "no man, as such, but—well, I promised to go and spend a night with Jess in London. Her . . . little boy hasn't been well."

"Oh, really? Not still the chicken pox? Surely he's over that by now?"

"Yes—no. I mean, he is, but . . . he developed complications." I could feel a huge guilty blush unfolding from the soles of my feet. "High temperatures, all night. That sort of thing."

"How extraordinary; chicken pox is usually so straightforward." She eyed me steadily. "But of course you must go, if she needs you. The boys can stay up here."

A mixture of relief and uncertainty filled me. "Or . . . I might be able to get another baby-sitter," I said quickly.

"What, at such short notice? And you don't know anyone, do you?"

No, I didn't know anyone. Except the Felloweses. Hadn't got a local pal to speak of, no one I could call up and say, "Hi, listen, I'm in a bit of a corner; could I possibly borrow your nanny?"

"Well, Lavinia, perhaps."

"But why on earth should Lavinia traipse down to your barn when she could be in her own home up here!" She widened her eyes incredulously. "Don't be silly, Lucy."

I gazed into her steady, confident blue eyes. She was right. Of course she was right. I was being silly. And hypersensitive, too.

"You're right," I said timidly. "I'm sure they'll be fine up here. I mean—of course they will. They love it here. I'll go back to the barn and tell them."

"Oh, I don't think you'll find them there," she said, slotting spoons and forks back in felt pockets and rolling them up efficiently into a neat bundle. "I saw them pottering around in the greenhouse with Archie a moment ago."

I started. "Really? But—"

"It's already nine o'clock, Lucy," she said patiently. "They quite often pop up and have breakfast here while you're having a lie-in, you know. Now, if you'll excuse me, I must get on. I must find Joan to sort out this ghastly silver situation. Joan!" She swept past me and disappeared down the corridor.

I stared after her. The boys were already up here? But their bedroom doors had been shut, so I'd thought—had assumed—but I hadn't looked, had I? Hadn't opened them. I flushed. How *awful*. And they came up here for breakfast on a regular basis? I frowned. No. Well, yesterday, perhaps, and maybe the day before, too, when my head had been holding me prisoner, and OK, maybe a few other times, because actually, I'd noticed them scampering off early occasionally, but that had pleased me. I'd thought that was the fun of being in the country, the freedom to run out to play whenever you wanted. And I certainly hadn't been lying in bed, I thought angrily. I licked my lips. Well, except this morning, when admittedly I had overslept a bit.

I turned and walked slowly down the passage I'd just bowled along so buoyantly, back through the rows of coats and hats, out across the stable yard, and down the little brick path toward the walled garden. Feeling crushed, I pulled the head off a dead poppy as I passed. I knew I'd been cleverly insulted back there. I also knew that she had the ability, the arrogance of her class, to suck the confidence out of me, like a leech. I breathed deeply and squared my shoulders, wondering at myself. Wondering at how quickly my moods could be transformed, how easily my emotional power to be happy was so often exhausted.

I stopped and shaded my eyes into the distance. Yes, sure enough, there they were, Ben and Max, in the long Victorian greenhouse that leaned against the huge crumbling kitchen-garden wall, picking tomatoes with Archie. Well, how lovely, I decided staunchly. Picking fruit with Grandpa. What could be nicer? Except that Rose, far from rushing off to find Joan, was also present. Why? What had she scampered down so quickly to say? I went on apprehensively, feeling like the outsider, peering in from behind the cucumber frames. Rose took a brimming colander from Ben as I approached and without so much as an "Oh, look, here's Mummy!" declared, with her back to me, "Splendid, Ben. A splendid bounty. I'll take this up to the kitchens right away. They can make a salad out of it for lunch."

Rose always referred to "the kitchens" as if it were some vast engine room with a fleet of chefs, instead of which Joan, heavy and rheumatic and with only part-time help, struggled to get by in what was, by today's standards a totally unmodernized kitchen without even a microwave for help. It was inadequate for a house this size, particularly in view of the amount of entertaining Rose insisted on, and I wondered how strapped for cash they really were. Rose spent money like water—just look at my barn—but it couldn't be a bottomless pit, could it, with just the home farm for regular income. Money seemed to be on Rose's mind, too.

"This greenhouse is a disgrace," she was saying. "I can't imagine what people will think when I open the gardens next month. Look at all the broken panes! And the frames just crumble to the touch." She flicked an immaculate nail at the flaking paint. "I've had a quote, Archie, and it's nearly two thousand pounds, but it must be done."

"Buy an awful lot of tomatoes for two thousand pounds," muttered Archie, crouched at the bottom of a vine.

"What?" she barked.

"Nothing, my love." He straightened up. "Quite right. We must get it fixed."

"And you can get that bloody dog 'fixed' while you're at it," she said angrily, brushing past me and stepping over Archie's faithful, smelly Labrador, lying in the doorway, her huge belly swollen. "She's quite obviously in pup again—no doubt by one of the village dogs—and we shall have to cart all the puppies off to the RSPCA again. What will they think? Why you can't get her spayed I don't know."

"Certainly not," he growled. "Spayed bitches get fat and aggressive. I should know."

"What?"

"Nothing, darling. Quite right. I'll look into it."

"Well, see that you do, Archie!"

And with that she turned and stalked off back up the brick path. We stared after her.

"Granny's in a bad mood," muttered Ben.

"No doubt about that, old man," agreed Archie. "Can't think what's bitten her. Been like this for days now." He gazed after her, thoughtfully.

It occurred to me, though, as I watched her stalk off, that this was more like the Rose I knew, the Rose I remembered when I'd been married to Ned. This coldness was far more familiar; in fact, I felt, with a gathering sense of dread, that she'd simply reverted to type, at least as far as her dealings with me were concerned. The show of geniality these past few weeks had been just that. A show.

"Anyway." Archie turned back, "Come on, boys; they're dripping off the vines here. Let's see if we can't pick another big bowlful, eh?"

"No Ted today?" I inquired, giving him a hand and dropping huge overripe tomatoes into the bowl, thankful she'd gone.

"Not every day," he admitted. "Just three mornings a week now. Got a bit pricey, you know."

"Ah." So I was right. We worked on in silence. At length I stopped, straightened up.

"Listen, boys." I turned to them brightly. "If Grandpa can spare you from the greenhouse, I thought we might drive into Oxford today, take a boat down the river. Would you like that?"

"Oh, cool!" Max jumped into my arms and even Ben, who I noticed hadn't even acknowledged me this morning when I'd ruffled his hair, glanced round with a smile.

"Can we go for the whole day?" he asked suspiciously.

"Sure, why not? I need to be back at about five, though. You know I'm going up to Jess's tonight, don't you?" I said anxiously.

"Yeah, you said," he admitted grudgingly but not too grumpily.

"Go on then, boys," said Archie, passing Ben the bowl. "Take those up to Joan for me, then get out in the sunshine with your ma."

"I'll make some egg sandwiches," I promised, squeezing Ben's shoulder as we stepped out of the boiling-hot glasshouse into relatively cool air. We strolled back across the lawn to the terrace. "And we can pack some peaches, and some biscuits."

"And sweets?" added Max hopefully.

"And sweets," I agreed, "and put it all in a rucksack."

"With gallons of ginger beer?" inquired Ben. "Sounds to me like you're trying to be a bit of an Enid Blyton mother." He eyed me craftily.

"Does rather, doesn't it?" I said evenly. "So. Why don't you take those tomatoes round to Joan, and I'll see what Lavinia's getting all excited about."

Up on the terrace, Lavinia was flapping and waving her arms at us like someone guiding in a 747. Behind her, by the open French windows, sat Jack, in a Panama hat, apparently reading the same paperback he'd been engrossed in yesterday. Call that a job? I thought wryly. All right for some.

"What is it, Lavinia?" I called, not wanting to get too close to Jack after yesterday. The boys scampered off to the kitchen.

"Oh, *there* you are. I've been looking for you everywhere!" She scampered down the steps all pink and breathless, and looking like something out of the Lower Fourth. "You haven't forgotten, have you?" she said anxiously.

"Forgotten what?"

"It's the second Sunday in the month tomorrow. You're supposed to be doing the flowers for the church today."

I gazed at her. My mouth opened. Oh God, I had comp*letely* forgotten. "Oh, gosh, Lavinia, I'd totally forgotten. Could I possibly do them tomorrow?" And then remembering I was supposed to be cosily ensconced in a sumptuous four-poster sipping my morning tea, added quickly, "I mean, at lunchtime or something?"

She laughed. "Don't be silly; they've got to be ready for eight-thirty in the morning! For Holy Communion. No, no, they have to be done today."

"Do they? Oh God, it's just—well, I've promised to take the boys out today."

"Do them tonight then; that's fine. It only takes about three hours."

"Three hours!"

"Well, by the time you've picked them all and sorted out the foliage, and got them to the church and chucked the old ones away and cleaned out the vases and arranged them—yes, it does. Takes a while."

"Damn." I bit my lip, aware that Jack was watching me under his hat. "No, well, I certainly can't do it tonight; I'm going out. Oh, look, Lavinia, I couldn't do it next week, could I? Would you be an angel and step in for me?"

"Well, normally I would, of course, but I'm off out for lunch today!" She beamed and did a twirl, and it occurred to me that the reason she looked so strikingly 1950s schoolgirl was the stripy blue-and-white summer dress. All she needed was the ankle socks to go with it. She smoothed it down. "Like it?"

"Love it," I lied.

"Roddy's taking me to Brown's," she said proudly.

"Roddy?"

"Roddy Taylor. Met him at the Rochester-Clarkes' the other night. Sweet, actually."

"Ah. Bit of a rectory?"

She giggled. "Sadly not. In fact, desperately Mock Tudor, and on the edge of a golf course, but," her face softened, "he's terribly nice. Seems rather fond of me, too, actually," she said with some surprise. "Said he'd been wanting to ask me out for ages but hadn't got the nerve." She went a bit pink. "He's an accountant."

"Oh, Lavinia, that's great." I was genuinely pleased for her. I had a sudden vision of her waving her hubby off to work at the door of her suburban house, pinny on, feather duster in hand, beaming away. Could be the making of her. "Right," I said resignedly. "Well, of course you can't do it, so that's that then. I'll do the flowers; of course I will. It's just—oh dear. The boys are going to be so disappointed."

"About what?" Ben appeared at my elbow.

I licked my lips. "Darling, I've made the most ghastly boo-boo. I completely forgot, I promised to do the flowers for the church today."

He stared. "What, so we're not going?"

"Well, Ben, how can I? I promised you see, so—"

"Yeah, and you promised us, too!"

"I know, Ben, but it's not so bad; you could help me. We'll pick the flowers here, together. I'm sure Granny won't mind, and then we can have a picnic in the buttercup field like we did when we first came, and then take the flowers up to the church. You can help me arrange them."

"Oh, great, a poxy flower-arranging day instead of a boat on the river. No thanks!" he said angrily.

With that he turned and ran back toward the barn, the lights on his trainers flashing as he went.

"Oh, Lucy, I'm so sorry," said Lavinia, touching my arm, as I turned to watch him go.

I shook my head. "No, it's fine. Don't worry. It's my fault. And it's just—well. I don't think he's all that happy at the moment." I bit my lip anxiously as I watched him dash across the bridge, forge on up the hill, throw open the garden gate, charge up the path, and dart inside. A moment later his curtains drew upstairs, and I knew he was sitting on his bed in the dark, a Walkman clamped to his head. It occurred to me that not so long ago a voice behind me might have said, "Look, don't worry, Luce, I'll take them. I'll take them on the boat." Ridiculously, I even waited a moment, wondering if he'd say it. Not that I'd have taken him up on it of course, heavens no, too invidious for words, but— nonetheless . . . Silence. Still gazing resolutely toward the barn, I cleared my throat.

"And anyway, the thing is," I declared to Lavinia, or anyone else who was interested, "children do have to accept disappointment occasionally. It's all part of growing up. They have to realize that adults have certain commitments and that they must fit in with their plans. Particularly when it's something like this," I added piously. "Particularly when it's the church."

I couldn't resist glancing round to see how this little homily had gone down, but the steamer chair was empty. Jack had departed, leaving his hat on the seat but taking his book with him.

I took a deep breath and swallowed. Ah, right. Well. No matter. I raised my chin. I didn't need an audience to tell me that I was right. That some things simply had to come first. I held my head high and swept off down the lawn, full of the righteousness of my commitment that would keep me from entertaining my children and forgetting, conveniently, the gaudiness of the other commitment, which prevented me from being in church, later on.

Chapter Twenty-three

In the event, Max and I picked the flowers. Ben stuck to his guns, and to his bedroom, and didn't appear, but his brother and I were given a cool nod by Granny and told that yes, we could gather from her garden, as long as we picked carefully and sensibly and didn't decimate an entire plant. But on no account, she eyed me sternly as I quaked before her, was I to go anywhere near the hotbed. I flushed, as a creaking four-poster immediately sprang to mind. I scuttled away from my audience with her in panic. What did she mean? Did she have an inkling?

"What's the hotbed?" I muttered to Lavinia as she quickly showed us where to pick before going on her date.

"Oh, it's over there behind the shrubbery. Everything in it is red or orange. You know, flaming azaleas, red asters, that type of thing."

"Oh!"

That was a relief, and my guilty conscience sank below the water-line again, but the creaking-bed image was replaced by one of damnation and hellfire. I cringed. How like Rose to have a little piece of hell behind the shrubbery, I thought nervously, all ready for lost souls like me to blunder into, whirling through the deepening circles of red-hot pokers to the inferno below.

"Keep away from there then, Max," I warned him in a low voice. "Just the herbaceous border and the walled garden for us. No, darling, nice long stalks like this." I showed him as he pulled a rose off by its head.

Lavinia scuttled away to meet her man but promised that her friend Mimsy would be at the church to show us the ropes. She'd rung her and she wasn't doing anything.

"Oh, thanks, Lavinia," I breathed. "That'll be a great help."

I wandered off to the potting shed to get a trug, a plastic sheet to put everything on, and some secateurs. When I got back, I concentrated on the herbaceous border to the left of the lawn, trying not to pick too many bright colors, and trying to keep it tasteful, with plenty of white and, oh, a bit of foliage, I thought, grabbing a handful, remembering Lavinia's instruction. I picked some long, feathery ferns, too, heaps of them, and then, straightening up, wondered idly how Max was getting on. I gazed around. Probably picking a coat of many colors in the kitchen garden, fistfuls of marigolds and nasturtiums, but never mind, I thought indulgently. I could find him a separate vase, tuck it away in the vestry somewhere. I shaded my eyes against the sun, anxious now. God, I couldn't see him anywhere. Well, he wasn't in the hotbed, that was a relief, I could see that from here, but was that him . . .? I strained my eyes up to the house. Yes, that *was* him, coming out of the French windows, carrying armfuls of . . . oh, dear God . . . oh, Jesus. No!

I dropped my secateurs and ran toward him. He was struggling across the terrace, puffing and panting, and dragging ten, maybe fifteen even, of Rose's two-foot-tall majestic rare amaryllis plants.

"Max!" I gasped, leaping up the crumbling steps. "Max, what have you done!"

"I found them growing in the conservatory." He beamed proudly. "I picked all of them, Mum, except one which I thought was a bit manky. They're wicked, aren't they? And there's loads more lying on the floor inside."

"Oh, Max," I groaned, clutching my head and gazing horror-struck at the carnage; at the beautiful rosy trumpet flowers on truncated stalks as thick as leeks, lying in state on the York stone. "Oh, darling, not inside the house, just the garden!"

"But Granny didn't say that," he insisted. "She never said that! And anyway, I thought you'd like them." Tears welled.

"Oh, I do; I do," I said, meeting David Mortimer's horrified eye as he came out of the study onto the terrace to see what was going on.

"But so did Granny," he finished grimly, eyeing the huge plants, snapped off in their prime. "Nurtured them for the best part of three years. Pride and joy, as it were."

"Oh, David, she'll go insane," I whispered fearfully.

"Just a bit." He took off his Panama and scratched his head. "What made you pick them, Max?"

"Mummy's doing the flowers, and I thought they'd look nice in the church," he said defiantly.

"There's no disputing that."

"Oh God, David, what are we going to do!" I wailed, wringing my hands.

"Come clean, I suppose." He put his hat back on. Gave the crown a smart tap. "All we can do."

"We?" I yelped hopefully.

He grinned. "Well, she'd flay you alive, that's for sure, and I don't necessarily fancy my chances, either, but on balance, I think they'll be better than yours. Come on, young Max."

He was right. Interesting, though, that he should know. That he should be aware I was persona non grata.

"But . . . you think Max should go?" I glanced anxiously at my son, who, far from quaking in his boots as Ben would have done, was sticking his chin out and still declaring defiantly, "But they're lovely, Mum. Look at them; they'll be perfect."

"I think one representative from your family might be a good idea, don't you?" said David with a wry smile. And so saying, he gripped Max's shoulder, turned him firmly around, and marched him off, back through the French windows and to the morning room.

I gulped and watched them go. Thank goodness for David, I thought, lowering my bottom gingerly onto a wrought-iron chair. He was a good sort, no doubt about that. A good man to have in a crisis. I gazed, horrified, at the carnage at my feet. Suddenly I jumped up and hopped through the French windows into the study. I didn't, actually, want to be too close to those plants, too associated with them, when Rose came out to inspect. Instead I slipped behind the heavy green curtains and chewed my nail, not exactly hiding, you understand, but, well . . . skulking.

I chewed my nail for ages, feeling about fourteen, and waited for David to come back. Finally I heard footsteps. I peeped around, but— oh, hell, no, wrong direction—it was Jack. Striding across the gravel, past the fountain, toward the stable yard where the cars were kept. I ducked back and, when I was sure he'd gone past, peered round again. His back was to me now, and he looked all set to go somewhere. A leather bag was packed, a linen jacket slung through the handles. Heading back to London, perhaps, to see his publishers? Or Pascale, maybe? Or was he leaving Netherby entirely? That would be a relief, not to have him breathing down my neck, watching my every move, but ridiculously—I felt something like regret wash over me, too. I bit my lip as I watched his tall, erect figure, russet curls gleaming, stride confidently toward a car in the yard. As I leaned against the glass, wondering why on earth I should feel unsettled, the French windows flew open with my weight. Jack turned, just in time to see me stumble out. I hopped back in again, behind the curtain, and huddled in the silk lining, blushing furiously. Oh God, oh *God*. Of *course* I should step out now, explain why I was sneaking around in curtains, but . . .

When I finally did emerge, he'd gone. I stepped onto the terrace and gazed at the empty space in the yard where his car had been, feeling foolish. A moment later, David appeared with Max, the latter looking perhaps a little less defiant; the former, relieved.

"Not too bad," he said, loosening his tie. "I mean, hysterical, naturally, ranted and raved and tore hair for a bit and all that, but seeing as it was Max, well . . ." He grinned and settled into a chair with evident relief. "It seems your boys can do no wrong."

"Oh, thank God." I ran a hand through my hair. "Whilst I, of course, can do no right," I added soberly, perching opposite him. "Still, I'd be pretty livid if someone smashed all my Asiatic Pheasant plates. It was good of her to take it on the chin, if she has. D'you think I should go and speak to her now?"

"Er, no," he said nervously. "Perhaps not. Leave it a bit."

"Ah, right." I swallowed. "Well, thanks so much, David, for bailing us out. You didn't have to."

Not for the first time it occurred to me to wonder what David saw in this family. It had always baffled Ned, who couldn't understand why he'd latched onto them. But then again, with no family of his own, perhaps he relished these little dramas. The ups and downs of family life.

He grinned and stretched out his legs. "Pleasure. It's not the first bit of 'bailing' I've done for the Felloweses today, either."

"Oh?"

"I was accosted by Violet in the village, on my way over here. She ran up to me outside the post office in a terrible state. Hair standing on end, black bra flashing, cow shit on trousers, the usual fashion statement . . ."

I giggled. "Of course."

"And told me in breathless tones that she was being pestered by all the men in the neighborhood. All the men in the local garages, apparently, can't stop bothering her, won't leave her alone. Keep ringing her up."

"Men in garages? Ringing Violet? But why?"

"Well, I rang one local dealer and asked him what the story was, and he said the fact was, she'd ordered and paid for a car and he was simply trying to deliver it. Then I rang the rest, and they all had the same story. It seems that Violet, having pranged the Escort, has ordered a staggering total of eight identical Toyota Roadsters—that's a rather groovy jeep model, incidentally, usually driven by budding pop stars and hairdressers—from as many different garages."

"Good God! But has she paid for them?"

"Oh yes. Evidently all the checks had cleared and all the cars were sitting on forecourts, waiting to be driven away. I spent much of the morning retrieving at least seven of the checks. The dealers were all very understanding. Charming, in fact."

"But how on earth did she get the money?"

"Oh, the aunts are rolling in it. Never dipped into their trust funds set up by Archie's father, you see. They've got that Scrooge mentality. Unlike the rest of the gang," he added darkly. "At the rate Pinkie and Lavinia are going, they'll have to be very careful." He winked. "Might even end up having to get jobs. As for Rose, rocketing through Archie's share." He broke off, jingled some change in his pockets, and looked genuinely worried. "Well. I shouldn't wonder if the banks aren't going to close in on her soon, and of course Archie has no idea. She holds the purse strings and he's hopeless with money." He frowned down at his trousers.

"But . . . how d'you know all this?"

"Hmm?" He glanced up. "Oh dear, have I been frightfully indiscreet?"

"No, no, I just wondered."

"Well, Jack's mother's a trustee. Old friend of mine, too, as it happens. And Jack wouldn't gossip, of course not, not like him, but—well, he was quietly voicing a few concerns to me the other day over a whiskey and soda. Concerns that had come via his ma."

Jack's mother. Of course. Archie's sister. I waited. Would have liked a bit more but had a feeling David wasn't a gossip, either. Had a feeling he felt he'd said too much already. I stood up. Smiled. "Well, David, thank you again. I really don't know what we'd have done without you this morning. What d'you say, Max?" I gripped him by the shoulders.

"Thank you," he muttered sulkily, kicking at the stones.

"Pleasure. But don't waste them now, will you, those huge great triffids. Now you've got them, may as well put them in the church."

"Oh, d'you think?" I gazed down doubtfully.

"Why not? At least that way Rose will get something out of it. Imagine, the whole village will think she's kindly donated three dozen amaryllis, grown especially for the church. I'm sure that's the spin she'll put on it, whilst quietly gnashing her teeth and forcing a smile in the front pew. Oh, I think the eleven o'clock service tomorrow is a must, don't you? Not to be missed! Come on; I'll give you a hand." And so saying, he bent down and scooped up an armful. Grinning hugely, he made his way purposefully toward the courtyard, to put them in the back of my car. I gazed after him for a moment, then—oh, what the hell. I grabbed another armful and followed suit.

Half an hour later I was hurtling down to the church in a car that looked like a hearse, it was so jam-packed with flowers. I'd been unsuccessful in my attempts to get the boys to accompany me, but in view of my shot nerves and increasingly skippy excitement about this evening, it was probably just as well. As I mentally scurried through my itinerary, I reached for my mobile to ring Jess. It had suddenly occurred to me that it would be just like Rose to flaming well ring and check I was there. Catch me out.

"Jess? Hi, it's me."

"Lucy! How's things?"

"Fine, and listen, Jess, I've been meaning to ring and ask about Henry, but—"

"Oh, he's fine, *so* much better," she gushed. "Yes, no, completely over it, thanks. He's lovely at the moment, actually. It's such a sweet age."

"Oh! Good." Not a hideously demanding two-year-old, then. Blimey, she sounded chipper. "And, um, Jamie?" I asked tentatively. Still away? I wondered. Still a bastard? It had to be gone through, though, this ritual. She had to get some ranting off her chest.

"Divine," she purred very uncharacteristically.

"What?" I frowned into the phone. "Not a two-timing love rat, then?"

"No, no, completely yummy actually. We're madly in love."

"Jess!"

"I know," she giggled. "Spooky, isn't it?"

"But . . . how come?"

"Oh God, long story, and embarrassing actually, because I don't come out of it too well, but—oh hell, all right. Since it's you."

"Too right, since it's me! What?"

"Well, I overheard him talking on the phone the other day. He was upstairs and didn't know I'd come in, but he was talking to Phil—you know, his mate from work—and pouring his heart out in a most un-Jamie-like way. I'd just come back from Tesco's and I could hear all this impassioned stuff going on upstairs, so I quietly put the bags on the doormat, crept up, and listened outside the door. Well, it was absurd, Lucy, totally ludicrous. He was banging on and on about how he thought I was having an affair, because I was so cold and funny toward him—can you imagine? The prat! Where would I find the time, or—more to the point—the inclination!"

"And the *reason* you were all cold and funny," I sighed, "was because you thought *he* was the one having an affair. You're the prat, Jess."

"I know," she agreed. "I told you I didn't come out of it well. But his fault, too, a bit. Just think, all that time we'd been circling each other like suspicious sharks, checking each other's pockets for stray telephone numbers, searching each other's wallets for restaurant bills, and if I hadn't heard him on the phone it would never have come out. We don't communicate, you see; that's our problem. Don't say what's on our minds. Too proud, I suppose, but—oh boy, are we making up for lost time now! Honestly, Lucy, it's so good. I can actually remember why I married the guy, why I fell in love with him in the first place!"

"Of course you can," I said staunchly, "because he's a complete and utter honey. I've always said so."

"You have," she agreed humbly. "And I didn't listen."

"Oh, Jess, how wonderful. So . . . everything's worked out." I meant it; it *was* wonderful. So why did I feel a pang of jealousy? Surely my life was wonderful, too? Of course it was. I had my Charlie! I suddenly remembered why I'd called and told her the wheeze. Where I would be. Where I was *supposed* to be, i.e., with her.

"What—so you want me to lie?" she asked coldly.

"No! Not lie, Jess; no one's going to ask you, for heaven's sake. I'm just covering my back here. Just in case. But no one's actually going to come round banging on your door demanding to see me."

"This isn't like you, Luce. Sneaking around. Being deceitful."

"Isn't like . . . oh, for God's sake, Jess, don't go all pi on me! I told you, it's not going to happen. It's just—well, you know, if the boys need me. I thought, if they rang, you could say I'd just popped out or something. I didn't want Ben ringing for some reason and you saying you had no idea where I was, that's all." I felt hot, sweaty. Awful suddenly. Why had I rung her? Ben was unlikely to ring; why had I bothered? All she was going to do was throw cold water on my lovely plans.

"Never mind, Jess," I said hurriedly. "I can see it puts you in a difficult position." I drew up outside the church. "Forget it."

"Of course I won't forget it. Of course I wouldn't let Ben be scared and upset and wonder where you are. If he rings, I'll say you've popped out, but listen, Luce . . ."

I listened. But held the phone quite a long way from my ear. Didn't actually hear too much. When she'd finished, I brought it back. "OK?" She was reasoning. "You do see that, don't you?"

"Of course I do," I agreed.

"So just be careful."

"Of course I bloody will!" I seethed. God, what was I, a six-year-old?

"Well, I know you, and—oh. Must go; that's the front door. Jamie's popped back for some lunch and—well . . ." she giggled. "You know. Speak to you soon, Luce, OK? Lots of love."

I nodded miserably. "Lots of love."

I snapped the mobile shut. Stared at it. God, who needs friends? I thought bitterly. Who needs them?

I hunched my shoulders and walked up the narrow gravel path to the church door. Inside, that evocative smell of damp stone, waxed wood, and candles prevailed, and the inevitable sadness I always feel when I enter a church descended. I waited for the heavy studded door to gently close behind me and took a deep breath. Up near the altar, Mimsy Compton-Burrell was already busy, carefully collecting vases of nearly dead flowers in greenish water and bustling across with them to a side room.

"Sorry I'm late," I called, pulling myself together and hastening down the aisle. I followed her into the little whitewashed vestry with its high latticed window and long table, laden with vases and green foam. "This is just so sweet of you to come and give me a hand. I'd have been absolutely hopeless on my own."

She grinned at me from behind the table and pushed her heavy blond fringe out of her eyes. "You wouldn't; you'd be fine. But it's not a problem, I wasn't doing anything today, so good grief." She stopped short. "Whatever have you got there!"

"Oh." I grimaced and dumped them on the floor. "Rose's entire collection of amaryllis plants."

"Well, I can see that, but . . . heavens. Bit extreme, surely!" She gazed down, astounded. "How come?"

"Max picked them," I sighed. "Thought he was being helpful. Doing his bit for God."

"Oh!" Her hand flew to her mouth. "Rose must have gone bananas! She'd grown them from bulb, hadn't she?"

"Don't," I groaned, shaking my head wearily. "I have no idea. And being a complete wimp, I didn't even witness her going 'bananas,' either. I left that to David Mortimer, who thought it might be prudent to let him and Max do the explaining. Pathetic, actually. I should have faced her. I don't know what's happened to my moral fiber recently," I said miserably. "It's seriously frayed." I picked up a few of the wretched plants and spread them out on the table.

"Nonsense," she said staunchly. "You were quite right not to get involved. You know what Rose is like where little boys are concerned, particularly yours. No, much better to let young Max do the talking. It was the same when Ned and Hector were young; they could do no wrong, and Lavinia and Pinkie might just as well have not existed as far as Rose was concerned, except to help Joan lay the table. Where is Lavinia, by the way? She sounded awfully breathless on the phone."

"Hot date," I said wryly, watching admiringly as she dealt deftly with the towering plants, arranged them in concentric circles in a crystal vase.

"Oh!" She stopped. "Who with? Not that ghastly Rochester-Clarke buffoon?"

"No, someone called Roddy Taylor?"

"Oh, Roddy Taylor! Oh God, I was about to scoff, but actually he's rather sweet. Rochester-Clarke's ghastly. I made the mistake of going out with him once—well, a few times actually, must have been desperate—and he kept taking me to all these really swanky restaurants. It was in the old London days when I was perpetually poor and hungry. I didn't fancy him, but in the end I felt so guilty about taking his scoff, I thought I ought to—well, you know."

"Oh God," I giggled. "I remember that feeling. *Awful*! So did you?"

"Well, I invited him round to the flat one evening and I think we both tacitly understood there might be some action. I even offered to cook him supper—*madness*. Anyway, he appeared, complete with an overnight bag, which I thought was a bit rich, and inside it was a pair of pajamas, a toothbrush, slippers, a packet of All-Bran, and—I kid you not—a disposable loo-seat cover."

"No!" I shrieked. "For a night of passion?"

"Well, of course it never happened. I simply couldn't face it." She narrowed her eyes thoughtfully. "I think it was the combination of the All-Bran *and* the loo-seat cover that did it. As if one would inexorably lead to the other. I think I imagined myself hosing down the entire bathroom by the time he'd finished exploding in there. Not a sexy thought."

We shrieked with horror, then hastily covered our mouths. It sounded wrong, somehow, laughing like drains in a church, but lovely, too. The familiar, cozy, companionable sound of women's laughter. I glanced at her as she expertly lined up the crystal vases, deftly aiming long stems at the back, short at the front, a droopy one here, an erect one there, making it look so easy and effortless. But then by all accounts she ran a flourishing business doing exactly this, for society weddings. Her blond hair flopped into her merry green eyes as she worked. It was good to see her again. I should see more of her. Meet her friends. Bet she had loads, I thought enviously.

"So what do you do down here for entertainment then, Lucy?" she said, almost reading my thoughts. "I heard you were working up at Kit Alexander's place, but that's not going to offer much in the way of a social life, is it? I should think you're bored out of your skull, after London; aren't you?"

"Well, not yet," I said carefully. "After all, I haven't been here long, but I can see that it might . . . well. Be on the quiet side."

"Quiet side! Listen," she said, pausing to wave a flower under my nose. "Take it from one who knows her patch; there's absolutely zilch going on down here. Unless you're into frightfully formal dinner parties where the ladies leave the table before the port, or bridge fours, or whist drives, it's hopeless. Your only hope is the local disco in Portaberry."

"Good?"

"If you like spotty boys under seventeen, it's excellent. I tell you, Lucy, you'll never meet a man down here. You'll have to dash back to London periodically, to ferret."

"Oh, but I already have," I said happily, unable to resist. "I mean, met somebody. And he's absolutely gorgeous, but I must admit, I did meet him in London first."

"Really?" Her eyes widened. She abandoned her arrangement for a moment and gazed at me admiringly. "Quick *work*. I'm impressed. And when I know you better and we're sharing a bottle of wine I'll probe a little more," she teased. "But for the moment, please tell me it's not Kit Alexander?"

I stared. "No, it's not," I said slowly. "But actually, for one very brief moment, I did kind of flirt with the idea of him. In a very abstract way, of course. I thought he was terribly nice, and terrifically eligible, too. What's wrong with him?"

"Oh, nothing," she said hastily, picking up her ferns again. "You're quite right; he is lovely. And as you've already gathered, a complete sweetie. It's just . . ." She hesitated. "Well, he has a little personal problem, which I'm afraid, being a mate of Julia's, I was always privy to. I can't divulge."

"Julia?"

"His wife. Or ex, I suppose."

"Oh. Right!" I put my flowers down, rapt. "God, I was wondering about her. What d'you mean, you can't divulge? What was she like? Did she really leave him for the plumber?"

"Oh yes, she really did, but only after years of trying not to. You see," she wrestled with her conscience, "well, I probably shouldn't say. But then again, Julia took so much flak when she ran off—everyone thought she was a complete hussy—and it was so unfair, because she wasn't the one with the problem. The thing is . . . Kit's impotent."

"Oh!" I gazed. Then frowned. "Oh, hang on, I can never remember. Does that mean he can't have children, or he can't get it up?"

"Delicately put, but the latter, which of course does preclude the former. Having said that, though, they did manage two boys in the early years."

"Oh dear. But in the later years . . . no sex?"

"No sex, exactly, though not for want of trying. On both parts. Poor Julia moved hell and high water to become a sex kitten and steam Kit up, and it wasn't really her scene. At heart, she's a strident, horsey sort of girl and likes nothing better than mucking out stables in jeans and wellies, but when she realized that did nothing for him—turned him right off, apparently—she went to the gym instead. She got all toned up, acquired an all-over tan, had her nails done, and if you rang her she was always out, not on her horse but riffling through the negligee rails in John Lewis. Oh God, did she dress up for him. Baby doll, vamp, Miss Whip Lash—you name it, she wore it, and then she'd shimmy out of the en suite bathroom, with Kit, in an agony of anticipation on the bed, dancing and high kicking for him, all ready for Kit to unleash the rod of iron that lay rigid in his underpants when—oh. Oh dear." She held up a crooked little finger.

"Oh Lord." I suppressed a giggle. "How depressing. So it never actually happened?"

"Well yes, it did, very occasionally, but always at the most inopportune moments. Julia used to joke that she'd be quietly ambling round Sainsbury's and suddenly get Kit on her mobile, yelling, 'I've got one! Darling, quick, I've got one!' And she'd abandon her trolley and dash out hissing, 'Strap it to my riding crop; I'll be right there!'" She sighed. "Oh no, no one could say Julia didn't try, and actually, they both went to terrific lengths to save that marriage. Ten out of ten for creativity." She narrowed her eyes into the distance. "Yes, naked croquet was a big theme, as I remember, at one time. Although Julia didn't go in for it much. Bit chilly, in the buff, she said, on a cold and frosty lawn, particularly when Frampton's overlooked by half the village. Kit insisted, though, that the stance, and the swing of the mallet, did wonders for his libido."

"I'm not surprised. If that didn't work, nothing would! God, it's no wonder she opted for some boring straight sex with a blue-collar worker then."

"Well, quite. He arrived one day in his overalls, did masterful things with a ball cock, and she never looked back. And as you say, can't really blame her." She sighed. "So no, not a great bet, our Kit, although a more likable chap you couldn't wish to meet." She grinned. "And of course, some women would go weak at the knees at the idea of no sex. What— *ever? Promise?* But not our Julia. She was quite physical." She glanced at me slyly. "So go on, then. Not Kit, happily, so who is it?"

I flushed and grabbed a handy amaryllis for support. Hesitated as I twirled it in my hands. Under normal circumstances, yes, of course I'd tell her, she was so nice and jolly, but for obvious reasons . . . I bit my lip.

She nudged me. "Don't worry; I can see it's all still beautifully new and precious and not available for scrutiny yet. I'm just being nosy as usual. I get it from my mother. She's the one who had her binoculars trained on Frampton's croquet lawn. Oh—hello." She paused as a car horn tooted urgently from outside. "That'll be for me." She stepped around the table and, with her hands full of greenery, kicked the vestry door wide open so we could see into the church. Outside, a car door slammed. There were voices, another cheery toot, and then running footsteps.

"At last." Mimsy looked at her watch. "She's been to a party," she explained, "and I knew I'd be here giving you a hand, so I asked one of the mums to drop her off."

"Drop who off?" I asked as the church door flew open and a sharp gust of wind blew in.

"Oh, didn't I say? My daughter. Hello, darling!"

The church door slammed shut behind her, and the accompanying wind blew all the service sheets and papers on the back pews up into the air, like a flurry of confetti. A moment later, a child's running footsteps echoed noisily on the flags as, hurtling down the aisle, pigtails flying and dragging her fleece, came Ellen.

Chapter Twenty-four

"HI, DARLING, HOW WAS IT?" MIMSY SMILED AS ELLEN ran into the vestry.

"Really cool, actually." She skidded to a halt on the other side of the trestle table, grabbing it to steady herself. "I thought it was going to be babyish, all sort of pass the parcel and stuff, but it wasn't. We had a totally brilliant conjurer who had rabbits *and* white mice, and then Polly's dad did a barbecue with a pig on a spit. Oh, and we got wicked party bags, too; look!" She pulled a huge gob stopper out of a plastic bag and popped it into her mouth with a grin. Then she looked at me and popped it out again, into her hand. "Oh, hi!" she said, surprised, blinking behind her spectacles.

"Hi," I breathed back, wanting to vomit. I'd seriously considered leaping the table and beating her to the door, actually, when I'd seen her clattering down the aisle. I could have passed her quite neatly, a moment ago, sprinted away into the distance, but there was no escape now. She'd recognized me, and here I was, trapped in the vestry with her and—oh, my God. I turned horrified eyes on Mimsy, or should I say *Miranda*? I stared. Couldn't help it. Boggled, actually. Was this really her, then? The wife? The apprentice nun? The sanctimonious religious fanatic, with the floppy blond hair, the merry green eyes and infectious giggle? Where was the hair shirt, for heaven's sake? The incense burner? God—this girl had a turquoise vest and Capri pants on, looked more like Kate Winslet than a bride of Christ!

"You two know each other?" Mimsy said, surprised.

I gazed, stupefied. Opened my mouth but couldn't speak.

"Yes, we met in London, with Daddy. She works with him, don't you? You're a researcher or something, aren't you?" Ellen's beady blue eyes peered up at me.

"That's right," I breathed, finally finding my tongue but hardly daring to use it. Sweaty hands were clenched by my sides. "But . . . I, I hadn't made the connection," I faltered, bafflement briefly getting the better of fear. "Lavinia said you were Compton-Burrell, and Ellen's father is—"

"Fletcher, yes, that's right, and that's my married name, but I hardly ever use it. Compton-Burrell's always been my professional name and let me tell you, it gets me far more bookings at smart weddings than Fletcher ever would." She grinned. "They like the Mimsy bit, too, frightfully U and nursery, you see, particularly since they're all called things like Spanker and Crumpet. Charlie can't bear it, though, thinks it's too twee for words, so he's always called me Miranda. But how extraordinary that you know each other! He didn't say."

"Well, he probably didn't make the connection, either," I mumbled, prickly with sweat now, a panic attack imminent. I looked longingly at the door.

"Yes, but I still don't quite understand. You met Ellen in London?"

"Yes, at Dad's flat," piped up her daughter.

"At your house, in Chelsea, that's right," I gabbled quickly. Less of the "Dad's flat," please. "It was . . . a research meeting. The BBC organized it, you see." I inched gingerly round the side of the table and glanced warily at the child, who was studying me rather too closely and blocking my way to the door.

"Research! Golly, Charlie is getting highfalutin. I remember the days when he just sat down at the kitchen table and scribbled out a script. What sort of research material did he need?"

"Oh, Mum, it's totally cool; she does animal stuff, don't you?" Ellen beamed up at me eagerly. "Works on a sort of *Pet Rescue*–type thing!"

Mimsy's eyes widened, as well they might. "Really! Gosh, I had no idea. Lavinia said antiques and you're working at Kit's, so I assumed . . . "

"It's a sideline," I broke in breathlessly.

"What, the antiques? Or researching for the BBC?"

I stared at her. My mouth dried. "The antiques. I mean . . . the research. Both. Both are—well, they're both about the same, really. You see, I could never decide which I preferred, so I sort of troubleshoot, between the two."

"Troubleshoot!" She laid down an amaryllis in wonder. "Heavens, how glamorous. But I wouldn't have thought that was possible. Antiques and animals don't seem to mix, do they?"

Fear was filling every vein now; every crevice of my body was popping and fizzing with it.

"Oh, you'd be surprised," I croaked. "Some things make the strangest bedfellows." I almost fell over with fright as that came out. *Bed*fellows! Had I really said that? How *aw*ful, but Mimsy had moved on, captivated by my scintillating career.

"But how fascinating. So how does that work, then? One week you do one and the next week the other? Sounds awfully peripatetic. Or are they somehow connected?"

I waited. Yes. Yes, perhaps they were connected. And perhaps, if I waited long enough, she'd tell me how. She seemed to have all the answers. Because if I tried and failed, failed miserably, to explain exactly how I boomeranged back and forth between Broadcasting House and the auction rooms, and if she suspected, in reality, that I was simply bonking her husband, what might she do to me? Might she bash me over the head, for instance, with that handy crystal vase? Finish the job off with a blow to the cranium with that Gothic candlestick? Make a sacrifice of me, and offer me up to the Almighty on a bed of amaryllis?

"What, you mean, are animals and antiques connected?" I faltered, seizing a handful of greenery and busily arranging it.

"Yes. I just can't imagine—"

"Oh! *Antiques Roadshow*!" I dropped the leaves.

"Sorry?"

"Well, you know, antique animals," I gabbled with relief, trying not to sound as if I'd just thought of it. "Ha! Sorry, I thought you realized. Yes, you see, what happens is, if, for instance, Hugh Scully, or one of the other presenters on the show, comes across a Chinese lion from the Ming Dynasty or . . . or, I don't know, a Tibetan lead horse from the fourteenth century, then they come to me for advice."

"Do they really? Gosh, and I always thought they knew their onions on that program. You mean they're just regurgitating what you tell them?"

"Well, some of them," I said uneasily, burying my face in the greenery. "Not all of them, of course. Some of them are very clued up. It's just the odd one or two, the glamour ones, who don't know their Canalettos from their Sèvres—and that's where I come in."

"But—so hang on. How does Charlie fit into all this? Antiques sound a bit stuffy for him, and he never writes animals into his scripts. Says the actors curse him for it, hate working with them."

"Yes." I felt faint. "Yes, I can imagine. They might. Not relish it." I licked my lips. Swallowed. "Well, Charlie comes into it because," I was interested to hear how my voice would go on, marveled at its brazenness. "Because, well—"

"I know!" Ellen suddenly seized my arm. "It's prehistoric animals, isn't it? Really antique ones!"

I gazed at her. It wasn't, but the trouble was, I didn't have a better idea.

Mimsy laughed. "Oh Ellen, don't be silly!"

"No," I hastened, "not so silly, actually. But the thing is, I can't really say anything at the moment. Can't divulge." What a handy little phrase that was. Why hadn't I thought of it earlier? I tapped my nose conspiratorially. It was dripping wet. "It's all a bit, you know, hush-hush. Early stages, you see."

"Oh, cool! You mean Dad's writing one of those *Jurassic Park*–type scripts? With dinosaurs? Oh, Mum, that's real Hollywood stuff; we'll be rich!"

"But how extraordinary." Mimsy's brow puckered. "He never mentioned it."

"Well, as I said, it is a bit—you know. Under wraps."

"Which ones?" persisted Ellen.

"Sorry?"

"Which dinosaurs?"

I regarded this boffin-child before me. I was grateful to her, naturally, for getting me out of a tight spot, but now I wished she'd die. I was tempted to grab the candlestick and do it myself, actually. I was also beginning to realize why Charlie felt the urge to escape this probing pair with their persistent questions, these inquisitors, who wanted the lowdown on one's every waking moment. My mind fled back to an outing with Ben and Max to the National History Museum. I wished I'd paid more attention.

"Oh, just the usual ones," I said airily, "for this project, anyway. Just, um, tyrannosaurus rex, stratosphere rex—"

"Stratosphere! Don't you mean stegosaurus?" said Ellen incredulously.

"Possibly," I conceded, tight-lipped.

"And you're the expert? I mean you identify them?"

"Well—"

"How d'you do that, then?" Her spectacles flashed.

"Bones," I hissed finally, through gritted teeth, spotting a handy tomb, no doubt full of them. "We have bones, of course. How else d'you think we do it?" I demanded witheringly, and perhaps a trifle vehemently, in front of her mother.

There was an exhausted silence as they took all this on board. I'd floored them, finally, with a baffling litany of career moves, and they were grappling now with the implications. Visions of me on my hands and knees, fitting dinosaur bones together like a jigsaw puzzle, perhaps in my leisure moments at the *Antiques Roadshow*, perhaps during a coffee break in the *Pet Rescue* studio, perhaps at Kit's or out on location with the BBC—all scenarios were doubtless springing, bewilderingly, to mind. Ah, the left fibula . . . this must be a triceratops. . . . Oh, sorry, Hugh, you'd like me to value an eighteenth-century porcelain dog?

"Gosh, Lucy, what a fascinating career you've had," said Mimsy at length, with evident feeling.

"Yes, I suppose I have," I conceded, equally exhausted. "So. Two big vases either side of the altar, d'you think?" I grabbed one and made to take it away, my heart pounding. I'd had a lucky escape.

"Lucy?" echoed Ellen, suddenly. "I thought Dad called you Laura?"

I froze, the vase in my hands. A terrible hush fell over the church. A ghastly, sickening silence, punctuated only by the crows, cawing in the ancient yews outside, swooping around the gravestones, calling to one another as they soared into the sailor blue sky. Finally, Mimsy spoke. I couldn't look at her. Could only stare at the cut-glass pattern glinting before me. But I had a feeling her face was pale.

"Ellen, wait for me in the side room, would you?" she said quietly. "There are some coloring pencils and books in there, left over from Sunday school. I won't be long."

Her daughter went without a word, perhaps sensing in her mother's voice something serious, perhaps even recognizing the situation for what it was. I hoped not. I put the vase back down on the table and stared at the thick, erect stems before me. I seemed to be seeing stars, as well as flowers. There was a silence as Ellen's footsteps shuffled away. A door banged; then a voice seemed to come, as if from on high.

"Are you having an affair with my husband?"

I breathed in sharply and inadvertently rattled the vase on the table. For a moment I couldn't look at her, but then I knew I had to. I forced my eyes up. Her face was indeed very pale, and I saw faint lines fretted around the eyes and mouth; the green eyes no longer sparkled with fun and vitality but were flat, defeated, vulnerable. I saw the face of a sad, middle-aged woman, who'd already had her share of grief and who was now enduring more, heaped on her, by me.

"I . . . well. No, I . . . I'm not," I whispered. "I mean . . . not quite. But we . . . were going to."

"Going to?"

"Yes, we . . . we haven't actually got round to it yet," I muttered miserably. Oh, how awful. Like getting round to having a dinner party. Only the entertainment I was contemplating was infidelity with her husband.

"I see. You mean . . . the intent was there."

I hung my head, eyes slithering away from hers in shame. I felt despicable, dirty, cowardly. "I . . . was going to meet him tonight," I admitted, swallowing. "After I'd done the flowers here."

"After church," she said flatly. "Off to a hotel. How fitting. And he'd told me he had a meeting up in London."

"I'm so sorry!" I gasped desperately, looking up. "I had no idea he was your husband."

"And that would have made a difference? If you'd known?"

I shook my head in shame, eyes slinking away again. "I don't know. I mean . . . yes, now, but I don't know then. But it does make a difference, now. I mean, you're so nice, and so totally not what I expected, and . . . I almost felt I had an excuse," I blurted out, "because he'd said you were so—oh God, I'm so sorry!" To my utter horror and shame, I burst into tears. I covered my face with my hands and wept. In an instant she was round the table, and to compound the shame, swooped to put her arms around me.

"Not that that should have anything to do with it," I sobbed into her shoulder, quite unable to stop myself now, "whether you're nice or not. I shouldn't have done it anyway and—oh God, this is even worse!" I gulped between hiccups, desperately pulling away and wiping my face with my sleeve. "It should be you in tears, not me! You should be the one having the breakdown. I can't even get that right, had to be a self-ish cow about that, too!"

"Oh, don't worry." She smiled sardonically, still squeezing my shoulder. "Even if you weren't hogging the limelight, I wouldn't be having a breakdown. I've had too many in the past over this kind of thing. Haven't got the energy."

"You mean," I glanced up quickly, fighting for control, "this has happened before?"

"Oh yes, quite a few times," she sighed.

"A few!" I was aghast. My eyes dried dramatically, and I stepped back, horrified. So appalled was I, in fact, that I had to lower my bottom onto the little wooden pew against the whitewashed wall. It felt cold. She sat down beside me.

"Well, let's say more than twice," she said hurriedly. Kindly, even.

"But I thought I was the only one!" God, how naive it sounded. How familiar, out there in the open. "He said—said he'd never felt like this before, never strayed. Always been a model husband and—"

"Ah yes, he's quite good at that line. Or so I've been told."

"You've been *told*?" I said incredulously. "By who?"

"Oh well, let's see now." She frowned. "First there was Jenny, who ran a garden center somewhere near Cirencester—she left mud everywhere, all over his clothes; I had to wash them constantly—and then there was Patrouska, ridiculous name, nightmare woman, too. She was an actress in one of his plays in London. Kept ringing up in the interval, wanting to tell me my husband was a genius, daahling—silly tart. And then of course there was Eleanor. . . ."

"Eleanor?" I echoed faintly.

"One of my best friends. Well, a new best friend, actually, moved down here quite recently. She kept suggesting we all go on foursome boating holidays together, barges down the river, that sort of thing, and no doubt I'd be stuck with her wally husband Malcolm, with the freckly bald patch. Happily we resisted that temptation."

"Good God," I said humbly. "I had no idea." I thought back to Charlie's protestations of love, of deep, true, and meaningful love, all, if I'm honest though, couched in rather physical terms of endearment.

"So," I said tentatively, sneaking a look, "so, in fact, you're not really very surprised?"

She sighed. "Surprised, no. But always disappointed. You see, when he's not seeing anyone—and I usually know if there *is* someone on the scene—I always think, Oh good, he's better. But then it happens again."

"Better?"

"Yes." She gave a sad smile. "He's only been like this these last four years, you see. Before that, we couldn't have been closer. We were so happy, he wouldn't have dreamed of straying."

I struggled. "Four years? But why—"

"That's when Nick died."

"Oh."

"And this is his way of trying to forget. To distract himself."

I frowned. "You think?"

"Oh, I know. He's desperate, Lucy. It's his way of coping."

"Because your son died, because—"

"Because he knocked him over."

I stared, horrified. "No!"

She nodded. "He was coming out of the driveway. Too fast, in his car. Zipping round the corner, just as I was walking round with Nick. I'd picked him up from school, literally from just across the road, and had hold of his hand when Charlie's red Mercedes came swinging round the gatepost. Nick was on the wrong side. Knocked him flying in the air."

"Oh God!" I clutched my mouth, froze. Slowly I lowered my hand. "How *awful!* He never said—"

"No, of course not, how could he? He can't accept it himself. Can't bear what he's done, so when he meets new people who don't know, he tells a slightly different story. People like you."

"But surely everyone around here knows!"

"Of course, but it's not mentioned, because Charlie feels so terrible about it. And how do you get over something like that, Lucy? It's bad enough for me, losing a child, but far worse for him. He has to look at me every day. Look at himself in the mirror. He can't forgive himself, so he tries to lose himself. Tries to reinvent himself. Jenny lived in Cirencester, far enough away not to know, Patrouska in London; you and Eleanor were both new to the area . . . perfect. Then lots of frantic sex to make it all go away."

"He's not well," I said soberly.

She shook her head. "No, that's too strong. And too easy. As I said, it's his way of coping. We all have to find a way."

I looked at her. "And you found God?"

She smiled. "Is that what he told you? That there were three of us in the marriage?" She pushed her fringe out of her eyes. "Yes, that's what he told Eleanor, too. And in the beginning, yes, it was true. I *was* desperate and Charlie and I couldn't begin to look at each other, so I did turn to God. And I was infatuated to start with, fanatical, on fire, evangelical, sure, whatever you like. But like any new love, new passion, it can't go on like that, at that rate, forever. That frenetic pace has to settle down, find some balance. So now . . . well, now I've got it more in perspective. I still have a very strong faith; it's still my rock, but now it's part of my life, not my whole life. And yes, I do come here a lot. But I come here to feel calm, to find peace, like a lot of people do." She smiled. "So sadly, I'm not the mad, breast-beating zealot that Charlie would like me to be. Not the convenient excuse he needs. Maybe I was once, four years ago. I don't know. I was quite mad then. Mad with grief. I know that."

I nodded slowly. "Four years ago, I was mad, too."

She nodded. "I know. I knew that. So you see, you do know how it is. You know how I've tried to cope and how Charlie's tried to cope. We do crazy things. Grief does crazy things. I don't know you very well, Lucy, but I'd hazard a guess you're not the type to sleep around with married men."

I swallowed. "Now you're giving *me* an excuse," I muttered. "Letting me off the hook."

She shrugged. "Maybe, but let's see. By rights you should be living in London, now, with Ned. A big house, perhaps near the river, long garden, two small boys, and maybe another baby, maybe a little girl. Perhaps a weekend cottage in the country, dinner parties with friends, holidays in Cornwall. But then your life was shattered, just as mine was. Who's to say what that does to us? When we're forced to take a completely different route, one we don't recognize, and who's to say, as we're groping blindly in the dark, which side lane we might inadvertently slip down, when we're at our most vulnerable, at our lowest ebb?"

"But I thought I *was* better," I said. "Thought it had taken me four years to get to Charlie. I thought he was my salvation, my compensation, even, for all those ghastly years. I couldn't see it was still the wrong lane."

"Because you wanted to be better. You'd made up your mind you were going to be. I've done that so many times. Seen so many things as a miracle cure. It's only now I'm realizing it has to come from within. That no outside influence, no other person, can cure you."

We sat silently together, side by side, on that low wooden pew, in that tiny vaulted whitewashed room. A single shaft of sunlight streamed through the high mullion window and fell on discarded stems on the trestle table; pools of water glistened in the light. I thought how marvelous she was, how strong and brave, and I wondered if it would have been different if I'd known earlier, at that first meeting with her, here, with Lavinia, in church. Would I have shied away from Charlie then, if I'd known? I hoped so. But then, I thought suddenly, at the time I'd thought his wife was someone else. I'd thought . . .

"Oh!" I said aloud. "How odd. The reason I didn't think it was you, originally, was because when I described someone to Charlie, someone I'd seen coming out of your house—blond, slim, pretty—he said, 'Yes, that'd be the wife.' I remember he put his arm around her shoulders, walked her to a blue Jeep. Discussed a shopping list."

She nodded. "Probably Helen, my sister-in-law. She's been a tower of strength to us. Always coming down, even though she lives in London. Wonderful with Ellen, always having her to stay, with the cousins. Integrating her."

"Your sister-in-law! Charlie's sister?"

"Exactly. And same blue Jeep." She grinned. "Although I'll have you know I bought mine first."

"Yes, of course. Because I saw her again when she dropped Ellen off at the flat in London. I knew I recognized her, through the door, but couldn't think where from. Saw the car behind her, too."

She nodded. "That would be it, then."

We fell silent again. Both lost in thought. I remembered that day at his flat. Shivered.

"I'll ring him," I murmured, getting to my feet.

She stopped me, reaching up and touching my arm. "Please don't. Please go to him, go and meet him as planned. Tell him gently. Or even." She hesitated. "Even, carry on."

I stared down at her. "What!"

"I just don't want him to be hurt," she said quickly. "To suffer any-more. And somehow, knowing it's you, and that I like you . . . well, I'd rather it was you than someone else."

"You can't mean that!"

"I . . ." She licked her lips. Struggled. "Look. Just don't write him off altogether, that's all. He's a good man, a kind, loving, funny man, and that's why you fell for him in the first place. Why I fell for him, too. Please remember that, and if you feel like doing anything for me, please try to help him. He's still in anguish."

I felt humbled by her strength. Her compassion. "Oh, Mimsy, I . . . I couldn't," I mumbled. "I mean, I just don't feel the same way about him. Knowing—well, knowing about you."

"No, I can see that," she conceded. "But he's not a bad man, Lucy, remember that. We were so happy together, years ago, and one day, I know he'll come back to me. And I so badly want him back in one piece. Be gentle with him, won't you?"

She fixed me with her sea green eyes, unblinking, clear, and true.

I gazed at her. Nodded. "Of course I will," I whispered. "Of course."

And I might also tell him, I thought, as I crept out of that vestry and off down the long flagstone aisle to the door, how lucky he is to have you.

Chapter Twenty-five

I ARRIVED AT THE HARE AND HOUNDS SOME TIME LATER and drove into the car park with a heavy heart. Charlie's blue convertible was already there, tucked away in a shady corner, sheltering under the boughs of some trees. I got out and shut my car door, locked it slowly, and then stood still for a moment, staring down, gathering myself. Eventually, I turned and crunched across the gravel car park toward the stable door at the side of the pretty, whitewashed pub. As I pushed on through, absently noticing the abundance of pots and tubs about the porch, frothing over with pink and white summer bedding, I dropped down a step to the cool slate floor within. Inside, it was softly lit and muted, but as I glanced around in the gloom I saw him immediately.

The pub wasn't crowded, just one or two men lounging around the bar and a few couples, bent over little round tables on the periphery. He was sitting by the far wall, over by the huge brick fireplace, both arms stretched along the back of an old oak settle, head back, and laughing with a couple of old men who sat opposite him on an identical seat. Their gnarled faces looked for all the world as if they'd been carved from the oak itself, as if they were permanent fixtures. I could see he was in his element already, buoyed up, excited, entertaining the locals with tall stories as they guffawed into their beers. My heart lurched as he swept a hand back through his dark hair, brown eyes dancing. I swallowed hard. Charlie. My Charlie. But it was not to be. He saw me and raised a hand.

"Lucy! Hi, darling—over here!"

"Hi."

I made myself walk over. His eyes were alive with excitement and he looked more attractive than I'd ever seen him. The beer, and the fact that we were twenty miles from Netherby in the depths of Gloucestershire, away from prying eyes and keen ears, had emboldened him. These old boys were not likely to know our circumstances. He encircled my waist with his arm. Squeezed.

"My girlfriend." He beamed. "Lucy Fellowes. I didn't catch your names. . . ."

Ron and Dud introduced themselves with toothless grins and nods over their pints. "Pleased to make your acquaintance," one of them leered, looking straight at my chest.

I gave a tight smile back. Charlie had obviously been here some time, judging by the glinting eyes and flushed cheeks all round, but now he was getting up, skillfully distancing himself from them, and leading me over to another table.

"I'll get you a drink," he promised, parking me on another bench. "Helped to pass the time," he muttered in my ear, winking at the old boys by the fire. "Bye, guys, take it easy now!" he called over.

"Oh, we will, but not as easy as you're gonna take it, I'll warrant!" one of them quipped, nodding at me. The other one cackled hard. Nearly fell off his bench.

I cringed but wondered, if things had been different, if I might have cackled back? Winked and nodded knowingly, raised my glass to them, toasted my night of passion ahead, enjoying my child-free evening in the bar with these delightful fellows, thinking only what a relief it was not to have to put the pair of them to bed, brush their rotten old teeth, and tuck them up with a bedtime story. As it was, I stared hard at the beer mats on the table, my cheeks flushed, until Charlie came back from the bar with the drinks.

"Straight out of Central Casting, don't you think?" he said, squeezing in on the bench next to me. "Couldn't resist them, I'm afraid. You'll probably meet them in my next play, heavily disguised as a couple of old winos on a park bench. All grist to a writer's mill of course, but you'll be pleased to hear they won't be joining us for supper." He grinned and sucked at his slopping pint. "I'm not that committed to my art."

I smiled back, unable to speak, and sank into my lager. Charlie didn't seem to notice, high on adrenaline.

"Oh, and incidentally, I've been up to check out the room, and I promise you, you are not going to be disappointed. Just what the doctor ordered. A long low-ceilinged attic affair with beams you're guaranteed to bonk your head on at every step. The only answer, I've decided, is to spend the entire evening horizontal, sunk in the heavenly plumped-up feather bed, only to emerge, dazed—but not by the beams—at, ooh, shall we say, midday tomorrow? What d'you say we have a couple of sharpeners down here first and then have supper in our room? I've had a chat with the barmaid and I'm pretty sure I can swing it."

I swallowed. Gripped the stem of my glass hard. The Kronenbourg flag swam in and out of my vision, like a mirage. "Charlie, I don't think I can stay for supper."

He paused, a frothing pint at his lips. "What?"

"I said, I don't think I can stay."

He frowned, lowered the glass. "What d'you mean you can't stay? If you can't stay for supper, how the hell can you stay the—" He swiveled on the bench to look at me properly, brown eyes bewildered. "Lucy, what's happened? Is it the children? Tell me, quick."

"No, it's not the children." I licked my lips. Glanced quickly round the room, then back to him. "Charlie, I met your wife this afternoon. Miranda. Or Mimsy, as I know her. Because actually, you see, we've met before. We're on the church flower rota together. It's just, I never made the connection."

I forced myself to look up. His eyes looked blank for a moment; then the dawn slowly came up. The sparkle disappeared from them as he looked away, down at the table.

"I see," he said quietly, carefully. "And now that you've made that connection, suddenly this whole shooting match is off, is that it? Suddenly I'm about as attractive as one of those desiccated old boys over there. I'm out the window." He took a quick slug of his beer.

"Charlie, look." I struggled. "In the first place, she's nothing like I imagined. Nothing like you described. Icons and genuflecting and religious freak shows—well, it's just not true!"

"It used to be," he said obstinately. "In the beginning. Couldn't get into the bedroom for crucifixes."

"Yes," I nodded, "and she admitted as much, but not anymore. And you're clinging on to how she was, because it suits you, because it furthers your cause. But . . . well, she's come a long way since then, Charlie; you know she has. She's lovely and talented and beautiful and . . . well, just gently buoyed up by her belief, not overpowered by it at all, and—"

"And in the second place," he interrupted, in a deathly quiet voice, "she told you what really happened, is that it? Told you about Nick."

I took a deep breath. Let it out slowly. "She had to, Charlie. It's part of the bigger picture. I had to know. And I'm . . . so sorry." My hand closed over his on the table.

He stared down at our hands for a moment. "Sorry for me, for what I did to my son, or sorry that you can't be with me? Can't love me. Even though we haven't even begun?" He looked up and found my eyes, beseechingly. "Haven't even given it a chance?"

"Both," I said softly. "So sorry for what happened, for your terrible, terrible loss—God, any words sound trite—but," I struggled to explain. "Look, Charlie, I can't be part of your healing process. It sounds brutal, but I can't be with you for that reason. I just can't do that!"

He paused to take this in. "I see." He traced a pattern in spilt beer on the table with a slow finger. "And, I suppose, that's what she told you, is it? That this is how I forget. How I lose myself. How 'coupling' with another woman is the only thing that takes away the pain. Is that what she said?"

"Well, she—"

"Lucy, it's not like that with you!" he said desperately, turning right round to face me. "I know you won't believe me now, now you've talked to her, but I do feel differently about you. Yes, of course there have been other women, but none that I've felt like this about, none that have really got under my skin like you have, none that I've really loved!"

I looked into his eyes. They were wide and vulnerable. Honest, too. I made myself take my hand away. "Charlie, I can't," I said in a low voice. "Not now I've met her. Not now she knows, don't you see?" I pleaded. "It changes everything!"

There was a silence. He seemed miles away, sunk in the pattern of beer on the table but somewhere else, too. Somewhere distant. More terrible. After a while, I spoke.

"Did you know that she was aware? I mean, of all your affairs?"

"I suspected," he muttered, coming back from far away. "But nothing was said. Nothing's ever said, in our house. At all." He ran desperate hands through his hair. "Oh, Lucy, you have no idea what it's like. It's almost worse that she *lets* me, doesn't confront me, doesn't put her foot down, almost—well, almost passively encourages me, by her damned silence!"

"She doesn't want to stop what helps you."

"Because she's so frigging good, and kind!" He banged his fist on the table. A few people glanced around in surprise. "I can't *bear* her kindness sometimes, and the fact that she's actually forgiven me, for what I've done to Nick, is almost too much to endure." He turned agonized eyes on me. "Christ—would you forgive someone who killed your precious four-year-old? Your precious Max? Wouldn't you rant and rave, blame, sob, recriminate, have ghastly screaming bloody hell moments? Moments of 'Why didn't you look where you were sodding well going?' Well, wouldn't you?" he demanded. "No!" He sank back, defeated. "Not Miranda. Uh-uh. Nothing. Not once. Not even in the beginning. No guilt whatsoever, Lucy, has ever been laid at my door, and believe me, that makes it far, far worse." He shook his head.

I felt out of my depth here. I wasn't qualified for this. I knew they should see someone, someone objective, who could get them to talk, sort this scramble of emotions out, help untie this knot of guilt and blame that was strangling them, but it felt like such a cop-out to say so. Such a trite bit of buck passing.

"How can she forgive me, Lucy?" he cried, again.

"Because she has to. It's the only way forward; otherwise she'd go mad. And she'd lose you, too. If she blamed you, you'd part, the two of you, and that would be too much for her to bear. She's lost her son already, don't you see? She doesn't want to lose the rest of her family. She loves you!"

"She has lost me," he said bitterly. "I can't get back now. She's become too good, and I became too bad. She scurries off to Bible classes, and I scurry off to the flat for a night of lust. We're drifted too far apart, with poor Ellen stuck in between. There's no going back."

"Of course there is," I insisted. "There's always middle ground. Meet her there, Charlie; talk to her; communicate; tell her what you've just told me. Talk about her piety, how the contrast makes you feel blacker and dirtier than ever and how it just makes you worse—tell her! Talk about her faith; talk about the other women in your life—I bet you never have."

He shook his head. "We wouldn't know where to begin," he said sadly. "It's been going on too long. There's too much crap to sift through. Wouldn't know where to start."

"But you have to sift through it, for Ellen's sake."

He sighed. It was a sigh that seemed to come from the depths of his soul. "Ellen." His face buckled with sorrow. He was unable to speak for a moment. Telltale muscles in the side of his face fought for control. At length, he spoke. "She'd like another child," he observed, matter-of-factly. "I know that. Two, maybe."

"You see?" I twisted round properly to face him. Took both his hands in mine. Shook them. "Why not! Come on, Charlie—four years has gone by; now's the time!"

"I'm scared, Lucy. What happened to Nick, what I did to Nick . . . I don't know." He took his hands away from mine, weary now. I saw the resignation in his eyes, the shadows beneath them. "How can I create another one? How *dare* I? And that's why—why being with other women helps, I suppose. I'm not getting her pregnant, you see. Not impregnating her." He gave a strange secret smile into his beer.

Again I floundered. Felt I'd hit quicksand. I didn't know what to say.

He looked up abruptly. "And there was nothing wrong with our sex life, incidentally. We used to have terrific sex, Miranda and I. Had a fantastic marriage, too; everyone said so. Everyone said how lucky we were. I was mad about her, loved her so much."

"Of course you did," I urged, "and I did, too, Charlie, I loved like that, and I'd give anything to have it back. To have Ned back. And the thing is, you *can* have it back. If I were you, God—I *know* I'd make it work!"

"Yes, but that's easy to say when you haven't killed anyone."

I stared at him. Took a very deep breath. "How d'you know?"

"What?"

"I said, how d'you know?"

He looked at me blankly.

"Charlie, what I'm about to say, I have only ever told one person. One living soul. Because . . . it doesn't help anyone. Least of all, me. But it might help you. You see, as far as I'm concerned, I killed my husband, Ned."

He frowned. Tucked his chin in, sharply. "What?"

I licked my lips, wondering if I could go on. If I could finish what I'd started. Make my mouth form the words.

"But—hang on; I thought you said he died in a car crash? While you were in labor, or something?"

I nodded. "He did, and I was. But at the time he died, he was on his mobile phone. He was talking to me. I'd rung him, you see, as I lay there, doubled up in pain on my hospital bed, minutes away from giving birth, alone with my contractions, and furious that I *was* alone, that he wasn't with me. Hating him for not being there, as he'd been for Ben. Knowing he was in some dark editing suite, trying to get away but somehow not quite getting out of that door. So I lunged for my phone, and I rang him. Got him in the car as he was leaving Soho. *Shrieked* at him as he tore along, 'What are you playing at, Ned! Get over here *now*! I'm having your bloody child, for God's sake!' " My eyes filled up with tears as I remembered. I looked up at the ceiling to contain them.

"And that's when he crashed? You heard it happen?"

"Yes. No," I said, blinking hard, slowly bringing my eyes back down. "I mean—I was in such a state at the time, I didn't really register anything. Just a hell of a noise, and then the line going dead. I didn't think, Oh Christ, that's my husband crashing and burning. I just thought, Oh damn, the bloody line's gone dead. I even tried to ring again. And it didn't even click when my parents came to tell me what had happened, that the lorry driver had said he was on the phone. It was only much later, in retrospect. Hours, days later even, that I realized. That I put the pieces together. But . . . don't you see, Charlie? I did kill him. If he hadn't been distracted, if he'd had two hands on the wheel, if he hadn't been talking to me, trying to pacify me, hysterical, irrational me, he'd have seen that lorry coming. He'd have rounded that bend perfectly. He'd still be here!"

Charlie looked at me for a long moment. Finally he shook his head. "You don't know that. You can't possibly torture yourself with that."

"I don't," I hissed, leaning forward. "Too much, at least, or too often, which is precisely my point. Oh, sure, in my darkest moments there have been times, definitely, when I've beaten myself up over it, but not continually. And not to the detriment of my family. And only once, in a very grim and drunken moment, have I ever admitted it to one other friend, because, Charlie, there is no point! It's like pressing the self-destruct button, not to mention being totally destructive to those around you, to your loved ones. And, Charlie, you *do* love Miranda and Ellen—and don't tell me you don't—so stop messing around and go back to them! *Make* it work. Don't hide in other women's beds; be a family man again, make more babies—it is *not your fault!*" I stared at him, wishing my eyes could pierce holes, bore through his skull, embed my words in his head. "You didn't see him, for heaven's sake! You didn't see Nick coming round that corner; otherwise you wouldn't have come out so fast, would you? Don't you see? Accidents do happen, tragic ones, and there's nothing we can do about it. Bad things happen to good people all the time, but it doesn't make them bad people all of a sudden. It doesn't make *you* a bad person!"

Charlie didn't answer. Our eyes were still locked, and for a second or two neither of us flinched. Then he looked away.

"OK, if nothing else," I whispered, "do it for Nick. Do it for him. Because I tell you, Charlie, there are still mornings when I wake up and feel like grabbing a bottle of something and going back to bed, still. But I don't. I get up, and I make the breakfast, and I carry on; and the reason I do that is not for me, and not for the boys, but for Ned. I make myself believe he's watching me. Watching me bring his sons up."

Another silence prevailed. At length he spoke.

"I meant what I said about you being different, Lucy. I know you think I'm just a terrible old philanderer, a desperate old roué, but I felt—still feel—very deeply about you. Even though we've never—well. You know."

I smiled. "I know."

"And the terrible thing is," he sighed, "I think I know why." He looked up quickly. "Why I fell for you in the first place. You remind me of Miranda. When I saw you, with Max, in London, in and out of shops, on buses, blond, smiling, pretty, a small boy in tow. Miranda and Nick, holding hands, coming out of school. Miranda and Nick, off to the corner shop for the paper and some sweets. You move like her, too, speak like her."

I thought back. Realized I'd spotted that resemblance, that Lavinia had mentioned it, too.

"I'm not as nice," I observed. "Not nearly."

He smiled ruefully. "She never used to be so nice," he said, almost defensively. "Used to be really naughty. Really, really hot stuff." His eyes glinted as he remembered, as if lit from behind. "And God, we had some times. Before the children were born. After the children were born, even. Wonderful, wonderful times."

"And they'll come back, Charlie," I urged. "Really they will, because she's still there, that girl you fell for, that girl you loved. You just need to look a bit harder, that's all. And she's still hot stuff. She's just been put on the back burner, by you. I think you'll find she's still simmering gently, though."

"Ready to burn?" He looked up at me through his lashes. "Like I was convinced you were? Light the blue touch paper and stand well back?" He grinned, and a hint of the old Charlie came back. I was glad. I smiled.

"Precisely."

His smile faded first, though, as if he didn't quite have the energy any longer. Didn't have the strength. He looked away, and we lapsed into silence again. I felt him retreat back into his past, slip back down his road in life. It was the same sort of road I'd been on, one filled with loss, and pain, and grief, but I knew he'd been further down it than me. At length I stood up. I swung my bag over my shoulder and bent down to kiss his cheek. He reached out and squeezed my hand tight, but he didn't speak. Didn't look up at me, either. I think maybe he couldn't.

"Bye, Charlie," I whispered.

He nodded, and I stared down at the top of his head, at the swirls of dark waves, with only a few strands of gray here and there, and at his broad shoulders in his blue-and-white gingham shirt, the sleeves rolled up to his elbows. I looked for a long moment.

And then I walked away.

Chapter Twenty-six

I DROVE AWAY, SPENT, EXHAUSTED, AND FULL OF OUR collective sadness. The injustice of it all enraged me; it almost seemed too much for two people individually to bear. Who was Mimsy's God, Who let such things happen in milliseconds and then shatter lives forever? A child thrown in the air, a husband through a windscreen, and forever after all that guilt and unhappiness rippling out into the lives of those left behind. It didn't make sense, any more now than it had when Ned had died. And naturally I'd walked all around God then, considered Him from every angle, questioned Him closely, asked Him exactly how much had been down to Him pointing the finger and how much to my own finger, punching out that mobile number. I knew, from bitter experience, that no answers were forthcoming. I also knew that this way madness lay, together with sleepless nights and horrified wide-eyed sobs in the bathroom mirror, hating, loathing myself. Oh, I'd been there many times in London, but I'd taught myself, too, to fold up that guilt and put it away carefully, to turn the key. And I did that now, with a practiced firmness I was almost proud of, so that as I drove along the country lanes, through the snowy banks of cow parsley billowing from either side, I didn't think of Ned or my revelation back there in the pub. My mind flooded only with Charlie.

Charlie, who had undoubtedly been to hell and back, but now that he was back, four years on, could surely face up to it, start again, start a new life with Miranda? I knew how terrible the pain had been, but I also felt there was new tissue there and that it might not tear as easily as the old. I hoped so, for both their sakes. I was aware, too, of how easy it was to make that decision, to start afresh, and how hard it was to carry it through. To wake up—on a good day—and say, "Right, move on! Four years is enough, no more moping, a move to the country is what you need, Lucy, a change of scenery, and—oh yes, a man! And—oh

318

look, there's one, an attractive one, walking right down your street. He'll do, perfect!"

Had it been like that? I wondered, looking back. That random? That arbitrary? And had what Jess had said, about deliberately picking a married one, one that ultimately Would Not Do, now have a ring of truth? Because now that he wasn't available for selection, was I distraught? Beside myself with grief over the loss of the man I'd loved— and lusted after, I added guiltily—and had now lost? If so, where were the tears? Why the dry eyes? Or was there in fact a sense of relief stealing over my soul at the narrow escape I'd had? At being safely back on my own again?

I sighed and glanced ruefully in the rearview mirror. Swept a weary hand through my hair. Not a tear, it was true, but pale and drawn nonetheless, and looking older, too. Careworn. I rubbed the side of my face with the palm of my hand. And had I loved him? Could I have, if I felt so implausibly calm about the whole thing now? Or had I just been going through the motions to get back on track, to no longer be considered derailed, but not in a wholehearted way and not with someone single, because that would have been too scary, too much of a move toward a proper relationship, another husband even, when, let's face it—and Charlie's words came back to me—look what I'd done to the last one. How *dare* I, he'd said. So how dare I, have another? I gripped the wheel and realized tears were welling, finally, but not for my lost love, for myself. I knew I was opening cupboards I much preferred to keep closed. "Shut it, Lucy," I muttered. "Just shut it!"

I couldn't, though, and my mind sped on. I wondered, for instance, was Charlie braver than me? After all, he really did confront his guilt, daily, because he knew he was to blame, and I didn't because— well, because perhaps Ned had simultaneously been lighting a cigarette? Perhaps the lorry driver had? Perhaps the sun had been low in Ned's eyes and, after all, he often drove and spoke on the mobile at the same time . . . but then again I really had yelled down that phone, had screamed blue murder. Sworn at him, accused him of deliberately absconding from the birth of his second child, of letting his squeamishness get the better of him. "No. Not *down* that route, Lucy!" I cried aloud, furiously banging the wheel. The tears were taking their chance now and pouring down my cheeks. "We don't *do* that, we don't *go* that way, remember?"

I nodded dumbly, mouth taut. I took deep breaths and wiped my face with the back of my hand.

There. Now. Now I was in control. I drove on and tried to clear my head. Tried to think of absolutely nothing at all. After a while, I glanced at my watch. Nine o'clock. My interview with Charlie had been brief, and I'd been driving fast down these lanes, so before long I'd be home, and it wasn't even dusk. I didn't want to go back to the barn. Didn't want to drive past Netherby, where no doubt, on a balmy summer's evening, the Felloweses would all be having supper on the terrace, amazed to see my car sweep in, drive past when—hang on, wasn't she supposed to be in London for the night? What on earth could have happened to bring her back so soon?

No, I decided. I couldn't go back yet, couldn't face the interrogation, not until it was quite dark and I could slip in quietly. So, how about if I *did* drive to London? I'd be there in an hour and a half, could see Jess. I thought of Jess, happy and at peace with her man—finally. I knew I'd have to spill the Charlie beans and then brace myself for the "I told you so" scolding that would follow. I wasn't sure I was up to Jess tonight. Teresa, then? Dear, soft Teresa, happily ensconced with Carlo, cooking him something scrumptious in the kitchen, with Hector and Rozanna, curled up cozily on a sofa on the floor below, when—oops, hello, a car draws up outside, and it's poor old Lucy again. Better bring her in from the cold, rally round, give her a drink, pat her hand, and— yes, yes, *do* go and get Theo and Ray, too. The more happy loving couples we can surround her with, the better.

I swallowed, horrified at myself but unable to dispel the sour taste of jealousy in my mouth. Jealous, Lucy? Of your friends? That's a pretty unattractive emotion. No, I decided, opening the window and breathing deeply to keep calm, no, I wasn't. I just couldn't cope with them tonight. Not when I'd just lost my lover. I blanched. My *lover*. Even I was struck by how shallow and tawdry that sounded. A mistress, in the back of a car, down a shady lane. Childhood memories of being at my grandmother's in Ireland, with Maisie and Lucas, driving past a steamy car in Granny's lane, a flash of white legs, high up, wide apart, me fascinated, and Lucas muttering, "Bob Tyler again, with someone else's wife, no doubt." I flushed. And how delighted would they be, I wondered, if I barged in sobbing, "Oh God, I've just split up with a married man; I'm so depressed!" No. No, I couldn't do that, couldn't go there. So, where could I go? I wondered with that familiar rising childish panic I was so prone to recently. Where?

As I drove along, feeling increasingly sorry for myself, I realized I was driving through Frampton. I slowed down, leaning my head out of the window to cool my burning cheeks, and nearly swerved off the road as I approached the manor house gates. For a moment I thought I'd spotted . . . yes. Yes, it was. It was Kit. Kit, in his front garden. Tall, lean, and in a bright blue shirt, strolling amongst his box hedges and lavender parterres, pulling a stray leaf here, a dandelion there. Kit, a friend, surely, albeit a new one, but would he want to be bothered? I raised my hand, tentatively, and at the same moment he saw me. His hand shot up in the air, and he waved back. I grinned with relief and slowed to a stop as he strode toward the gates, smiling broadly. He had a glass tumbler in his hand, clinking with ice and lemon, and as he approached he raised it quizzically to his lips, eyebrows cocked.

Oh *yes*, I thought with a rush of relief, yes, please. Dear, kind Kit; dear, kind, *safe* Kit, more to the point, particularly after what Mimsy had told me. *What* a good idea. I nodded back enthusiastically, and he came down to swing open the old iron gates for me.

Perfect, I thought, crunching up the gravel drive. Just exactly what the doctor ordered. A large gin and tonic on his sunny terrace, chatting happily of Hepplewhites and Chesterfields, the sun sinking low behind his apple orchard, the dragonflies humming and dancing in the gathering gloom, oh, that would do the trick, for sure. And maybe we'd even talk of Charlie, too? He was, after all, a close friend, and I would like to know more. Would like to indulge in a little melancholy postmatch analysis. Try to expunge the sadness. I jumped lightly out of my Jeep and slammed the door, smiling.

"Well, *what* a pleasant surprise," he called, striding down the drive toward me. He swooped to plant a chaste kiss on my cheek. "I was just thinking, What a glorious evening, and no one to share it with. No one to escort round my garden, glass in hand, admiring my borders and my wildflower meadow, and now here you are! Perfect. What'll you take for it, my dear? You are stopping for a tincture, I hope?"

"Certainly I'm stopping, and I'll take exactly what you're having. A large gin and tonic by the looks of it, and definitely followed by a stroll around your magical garden. Feeling a bit Lord of All I Survey with no one to survey it with?" I teased.

"Precisely." He grinned. "It's absolutely no good having all this to show off about and no one to show off to. That's half the fun."

"I can imagine."

He chuckled and ushered me inside to collect a drink.

For a while we stood chatting in the dark hall, leaning on the low-boy that housed the bottles, and then, fully equipped, clutching drinks and—oh, a bowl of olives, Kit decided, dashing back on an impulse—we sauntered around the back of the house to the terrace. It issued onto the glorious wild garden, where the musky scent of nicotianas mingled with poppies and cowslips, and beyond that the apple orchard, with its ancient gnarled trees. Under their branches, golden farmland rolled away into the distance, haystacks piled high, all ready for an early harvest.

I sighed with relief, settling down on a bench in the shade of a huge canvas umbrella. I felt quite weak after the emotions of the pub. Quite shaky. I swallowed hard and concentrated instead on the fabulous scenery.

"You know, you're right, Kit; this is an enchanting garden. Far more enchanting than Netherby, which for all its grandeur seems—I don't know—tucked up. Very tamed, controlled. All that manicured park-land and immaculate rose beds with neat edges—it's all a bit repressed, somehow, don't you think?"

"I do, but then it's much easier to keep it like that. This is the hard bit," he said, sitting beside me and surveying the casually haphazard scene before us, the mown paths cutting swathes through the long grass, poppies and oxeye daisies nodding beside old roses, stocks, and del-phiniums. "Tarting something up to look neat and tidy is easy, but it takes ages to achieve the natural, wild look, as any woman applying her makeup will tell you. And speaking of wild women . . ."

Rococo padded up the terrace steps from the garden below and put her huge head in her master's lap; brown eyes doleful, tail slowly wagging.

"Fully recovered?" I asked, reaching across to stroke her.

"Completely. And all thanks to you and Charlie. I don't know what would have happened if the pair of you hadn't been so quick-witted."

I sighed, remembering that strange, funny day. Charlie, so desperate to get me into bed, and me, well, not exactly dragging my heels, either. I remembered him scooping me up in his arms in this very house, passion gathering and dancing in every vein. A deep melancholy rose within me.

"Ah," said Kit softly, seeing my rueful face. "Have I mentioned the wrong person?"

"No, not at all," I said quickly. "As a matter of fact—well, I'd like to talk about him." I glanced across tentatively. "You knew . . . I take it?"

"About you and Charlie? Well, I didn't know for sure, but I suspected, certainly, and in the past my suspicions about Charlie have been pretty well founded." He lit a cigarette and regarded me kindly over it. "If you follow my meaning."

I nodded. "It's all right; I know. I mean, I know about his other women." I paused. Licked my lips. "Lots of . . . other women?"

He hesitated. Blew a line of smoke thoughtfully above my head. "Well, I wouldn't say lots, but a few. Although no one ever quite of your caliber, Lucy."

I smiled. "You're very gallant, Kit, but it's OK; you don't have to be tactful. It's all over now, so you can tell me what a shit he really was."

"He wasn't a shit," he said slowly. "Just a guy with big problems to sort out."

"I know." I flushed dramatically. "And I hate myself for saying that. I don't know why I did, except maybe to protect myself, I suppose," I finished miserably. "To maintain some sort of false pride." I dredged up a deep sigh. "I *do* know about his problems, Kit, horrific ones; it's just that—oh, I don't know. I suppose I've had a bellyful of my own, and tonight you find me feeling—not shattered and devastated that my so-called 'love affair' is over but actually, really rather pissed off and sorry for myself."

He smiled. "Well, I don't know the details, but I suspect the reason for that is that you never really loved him."

"Didn't have the chance," I said gloomily, picking at my nails. "Just the odd grope now and then. But no, you're right; I think I just persuaded myself I did. I think I was infatuated with him, and that can't last. As Mimsy said about her faith, passion like that runs its course very quickly."

"You've met Mimsy, then?"

"Oh yes." I gave a wry smile. "Church flower rota."

"Ah." He grinned. "Naturally. Yes, strong woman, that," he reflected. "Very strong woman indeed. Part of the problem, of course, because her strength belittled Charlie. He could never quite match up, so he exaggerated her religious fervor to extract pity in the pub. Couldn't help himself. Let it be known that she was building shrines in the back garden—complete tosh of course, but in a small community like this such stories get about. And people want to believe gossip because they lead such boring, mediocre lives and, hell, it's fun to have a real-live soap opera going on on your doorstep." He massaged his chin ruefully. "God, I should know. Stories abounded about me and Julia; I know that for a fact. Outrageous stories. About our sex life, of all things, and desperately humiliating, it was, too. Particularly since none of it was true. But it helped her, you see. Gave her an excuse to go. Gave her departure some credence. Everyone thought she had a legitimate reason to leave me."

I stared at him. I was dimly aware that my mouth was open.

"And let's face it," he went on, "no one really knows the truth about a marriage, do they? No one knows the real nuts and bolts, except the two sharing the double bill. Everything else is just rumor and speculation, however close to the truth the rumormongers claim to be."

I swallowed. "Well, quite," I said slowly. "Quite. No one else really *does* know." I was thoughtful for a moment.

"Another drink, Lucy?" He stood up with a smile.

I gazed up at him for a moment. His eyes reminded me of a bird's egg. Speckled, with little flecks of hazel and green. I came to. "Please," I said, handing him my glass.

"Was that about right?"

"Hmmm?" I frowned. Still elsewhere.

"I mean, strengthwise. I don't like to make them too strong."

I blinked. "Oh! Oh yes, perfect. Same again would be lovely. Thanks, Kit."

"Oh, and while I'm gone," he reached across to another chair and threw a glossy catalog at me, "try this for size. Gregorio de Conquesca's private collection. It's up for grabs in Venice next Thursday, and my God, it's going to be special, Lucy. Talk about a complete one-off. Some of the furniture—nearly all of it seventeenth-century, incidentally—hasn't moved from the family palazzo since it was shipped in by Conquesca's forebearers four hundred years ago. Take a look; it's awesome."

"Oh. Thanks." I took it, still miles away. Good grief, he was right. No one really *did* know about a marriage, except those involved. All sorts of distorted stories could get about. I flicked distractedly through the pages, but eventually a Jacobean pitcher and bowl got the better of my abstraction.

"Oooh," I groaned, "just look at this pitcher! *Beautiful* condition, and look at all this early Meissen," I marveled. I flicked on. "And these Limoges enamels, masses of them!"

"Exactly," he called from inside. "And some of it's never even been seen before. Never seen the light of day. There's going to be the most almighty scrum of course, dealers from all over the world will be going, but it'll be great fun, with plenty of jolly lunches and jaunts across the Lagoon to the Lido. Come with me if you like."

I glanced up quickly from the book. Come with him? What, to Venice? I blinked. Golly, well . . . but why not? This was the sort of opportunity I'd dreamed of, wasn't it? Venice. But . . . why had he asked me? On what basis? As a colleague? As a friend? Or even . . . no, don't be silly, Lucy. As a colleague, of course!

"Damn. Bloody freezer's on the blink," he called. "Not a lot of ice, I'm afraid."

"Don't worry," I called back distractedly. I shut the book carefully. Popped it back on the chair and slid the chair under the table out of sight. I'd change the subject when he got back. Give it some thought.

"Beautiful roses." I smiled, nodding down the garden, as he reappeared a few moments later.

"Aren't they just," he agreed, ducking under the umbrella to hand me my drink. As I took it, I could have sworn he'd undone another button. On his shirt. Quite a lot of chest was showing. But maybe not. I looked away quickly. Maybe I just hadn't noticed before. He smiled and settled down beside me.

"Thanks." I sipped. "Delicious."

"Pleasure. Ahh . . ." He sighed happily and settled back on the bench, stretching an arm along the back. His long legs were straight out in front of him, crossed at the ankles. "Ah yes, the roses," he said, narrowing his eyes into the distance. "It's been a good year for them." He turned his head and looked at me very directly for a moment. "In fact, it's been a very good year all round."

I met his eyes, surprised. Then I flushed and looked away. I was aware of his hand, on the back of the bench, a millimeter from my hair. It seemed very important, all of a sudden, to carry on staring intently at the rosebushes. The garden seemed terrifyingly still. And was it my imagination, or was that hand actually *touching* the back of my hair? Or had I inadvertently moved my head? I went rigid, hardly dared to breathe. Slowly I raised my glass to my lips. Sipped it.

"Tell me, Lucy," he murmured at length. "Do you play croquet?"

A mouthful of gin and ice shot straight out of my mouth. I choked violently.

"Golly, poor you!" He got up and patted my back in consternation.

"Sorry," I croaked, coughing noisily, trying to catch my breath. "Went down the wrong way."

"Clearly." He hovered over me anxiously for a moment. Then he sat down again. Waited for me to recover. "Better?"

"Yes, fine now, thanks!" I gasped. "Absolutely fine."

"No, I was just wondering," he went on, undeterred, "only there's quite a decent lawn hidden behind that box hedge, and I've got a lovely old set of hoops and mallets in the summerhouse. Belonged to my grandfather, in fact. What d'you say we have a little round before the sun completely disappears? We could take our drinks with us."

I wiped my mouth and put my drink down carefully on the table.

"Actually, d'you know, Kit, I've just realized I really ought to be getting back. Only, the thing is, Rose is baby-sitting, so I shouldn't be late and I did have a drink in the pub with Charlie, so this one's really going to tip me over the limit. I don't know why I didn't think of it before, and I feel awful now you've poured it, but—well." I stood up, quickly. "Sorry, stupid of me, but I lost all track of time!"

"Not to worry," he said easily, getting to his feet. "Of course, you're driving, and I should have thought. We'll do it some other time. The croquet, I mean."

"Y-yes, lovely." I faltered, blushing furiously. "I—I'd love to have a . . . a game. With you."

"Excellent!" He rubbed his hands delightedly, and I reached for my bag on the floor, hiding my crimson face in it. I clutched it protectively to my bosom and scurried around the side of the house, pretending all the while I was searching for my car keys, keeping my face well hidden. He didn't seem to notice and strolled leisurely beside me, hands deep in pockets, pointing out the glorious fig tree on the sunny south wall, the wonderful sunset, seeing me to my car.

He opened the door for me and leaned against it as I got in. "Bye then, Lucy, see you next week."

"Will do!" I chortled back. I couldn't look at him and busied myself with putting on my seat belt, turning the ignition, shifting into gear.

I took off almost before his weight had left the door—he didn't quite fall over—and gave a cheery backward wave. Then I swept through the gates, bumped down onto the tarmac with a jolt, and sped away.

Oh, how awful. My hand flew to my mouth. How *awful*! Had he really thought—had he seriously imagined I'd be interested in a little . . . no. No, of course not. He wouldn't think that. He *couldn't* think that, because after all, I'd only just split up with Charlie! He surely couldn't imagine I could transfer my affections so quickly? Or could he? Had he imagined he'd catch me on the rebound, perhaps? A desperate thirty-something woman, so determined to get back into mainstream monogamy that any gin in a storm, any guy in a mansion, would do? Jumping from one man to the next, my heart not even skipping a beat? Good grief, it was unthinkable. And insulting, too!

I gripped the wheel and bombed through the dusky countryside, desperate to get away, to distance myself from the whole embarrassing episode. But then after a while I slowed. A rogue thought had entered my head. Suppose I'd been wrong back there? Suppose I'd jumped to conclusions? Been irrational, small-minded, just like the gossips in the pub, made a mountain out of . . . I slumped miserably in my seat. Yes, yes, of course I had. I'd overreacted. A large gin, an offer of a business trip, an auction in Venice—how marvelous. And I'd instantly assumed he was after my body. I felt hot. Ashamed. Oh, poor Kit. Poor, dear, kind Kit, just being a good host, just dreaming up some entertainment on a summer's evening, a drink, a game of croquet . . .

Croquet. Lordy! My heart gave a palsied leap and I took a hairpin bend with an astonishing lack of care, almost colliding with a tractor. I righted myself on the road and groaned. Oh no, not my job. Please, God, don't let that element of my life go pear-shaped. I needed that job, desperately, but I certainly couldn't handle a predatory employer chasing me around stark naked, a mallet swinging between his legs and heaven knows what else. Really I couldn't.

Well, I'd have to make it plain, I thought, roaring up to the lodge and swinging through Netherby's gates defiantly. I didn't want to lose my job—didn't see why I should, either. Golly, I had rights—but I'd have to clarify my position. Have to—Jesus Christ, what was that? My foot came off the accelerator for a moment and the car swerved violently up the verge. I got it back on the drive and gazed straight ahead. Away, in the distance, but not that far, just behind Netherby in fact, and lighting up the night sky, was a huge blazing orange glow. Somewhere down by the lake, the trees seemed to be crackling, seemed to be—almost alive. I picked up speed and turned the bend transfixed. As I drove along, faster and faster, my eyes hooked on the horizon, a terrible knowledge began to squeeze my heart, tight, like an ice-cold hand. The bright orange ball was like a sun, except it wasn't the sun; it was—oh, dear God. My hand shot to my mouth as the flames blazed high into the night sky. Oh, dear God—the barn. The barn was on fire.

Chapter Twenty-seven

I ROARED UP THE HILL AND SKIDDED TO A HALT, WHEELS
screeching on the tarmac. Flames were licking out of the top windows,
and part of the roof was blazing, the timber frame crackling and burning
like a matchbox, the whole building a vivid ball of orange flames. For a
moment I was transfixed with horror. Oh, thank God the boys weren't
inside, I thought, leaping suddenly from my car. Thank God they were
up at the house!

"*Archie!*" I screamed.

Archie, David, Pinkie, Lavinia, and the aunts in their dressing
gowns were standing in a huddled group on the lawn, staring up. I ran
toward them.

"Oh Jesus, Archie—what happened!" Even as I spoke I had to put
an arm over my eyes, the heat knocking me back.

"Lucy!" He swung around, white-faced, fear blazing in his pale, bul-
bous eyes. He seized my arm. His breath was short and he stretched his
lips across his teeth in a strange grimace. "Lucy, you're not to—they'll
be all right!"

He held my arm in a vicelike grip as if to stop me in my tracks, stop
me hurling myself at the flaming building.

"They'll be all right? Who'll be all right? Shit!" I stared at him in
horror, terror rising fast as I saw it in his own eyes. "Oh Christ, the boys!
But they're not in there, Archie! They're not in there; they're up at the
house!"

He didn't answer for a moment, just held on tight, fingertips digging into my flesh. Then he gripped my other arm in the same way,
brought his white, quivering face down to mine. "Jack's in there," he
breathed in measured tones. "He's in there, and he's getting them out.
It'll be all right, Lucy; he's getting them out!"

I gazed at him, appalled. Then, "*Nooo!!!*" I screamed, pulling away.
"No, they can't be! Oh God—Ben, Max!!!"

I struggled to escape, fighting him off with my whole body, bucking away, as he held on tight. *"Ben!!"* I screamed. I swung my head around, all that I could move in his tight grasp, as at that moment a figure appeared. It was Jack, running from the blazing house, a child in pajamas in his arms.

"Ben!" I finally wrenched free of Archie as he let me go, and hurled myself toward them. "Ben! Are you all right!"

"He's fine!" yelled back Jack, black-faced, as Ben collapsed, coughing and spluttering in my arms. "He's just full of smoke, that's all. Take him away, Lucy, back there, up on the bank!"

"But Max," I shrieked, dragging Ben away from the heat, "where's Max!"

"Keep her out!" roared Jack, pointing a finger at Archie and then back at me. His eyes were glittering in his black face, but this time David lunged forward to grab me. He held my arms, pinning me from behind, as Jack went running back in. But there was no need. I was paralyzed with fear now. Frozen with shock.

"Oh, dear God," I prayed, shutting my eyes tight and bending my head to little Ben as he clung on around my waist. "Oh, dear God, help him. *Help* him. Is he in bed, Ben?" I trembled. "Where *is* Max? Is he asleep or—"

"No, no, he's not in bed; he's at the bottom of the stairs! I tried to drag him out with me, but he was too scared, and too scared to come with Jack. But Jack'll get him out now, won't he? Won't he!"

David had loosened his grip and was beside us now, encircling us, a tight arm round both of our shoulders. "Of course he will," he said calmly. "Stay right where you are, both of you; he'll be fine. Jack'll see to it. He got Ben; he'll get Max; it's all under control."

"It is *not* under control," I gasped. "My baby's still in there. He's in that fire and—*oh, thank God!*"

I lurched forward as Jack suddenly reappeared, this time with Max in his arms, blinking, eyes streaming. I ran up and snatched him to me, sobbing.

"Oh, darling, my poor darling—are you all right!"

Max nodded, eyes huge.

"He's fine," croaked Jack, "but find something to wrap him in."

"Yes! Oh God, in the car, a rug, but, Jack, where are you going!"

"One more," he said grimly, turning back.

"But who?"

"Rose is still in there," said David quietly, beside me.

I swung around to him. Then looked back at the barn in disbelief. "*Rose!* But why? And why were the boys in there, and—oh Jesus Christ, David . . ." I ran desperate hands through my hair as Jack, bent double, head low, disappeared back in. "Where's the bloody Fire Brigade?"

"Coming!" sobbed Lavinia, running up and clutching my arm. "Daddy rang, ages ago, and they should be here by now, but—oh God, Lucy, they're taking forever, and she'll die up there, won't she? She'll die!"

She clung onto me, trembling. We were being beaten back all the time now, pulling the boys with us, wrapping Max in a rug, the heat seeming almost to take the skin off our faces as we gazed, petrified, at the top floor. I held Max tight, Lavinia had Ben, the aunts clutched each other, and Pinkie stood alone, sobbing hysterically, eyes wide and helpless, arms limp at her sides, staring up at the house. Archie was behind her, white-faced.

"Get her out, lad; get her out!" he hissed as we watched the flames shoot ever higher.

My mind spun like a top as the seconds ticked by. Oh God—Jack and Rose. Jack, burned to death in there, overcome by fumes . . . I felt sick to my stomach, my head ached with an agonising white heat, and smoke and vomit were rising in my throat. I thought I might physically throw up. Oh, please, God, don't let them die, I prayed. Don't let them die!

Suddenly, glass shattered. Pinkie screamed and hid her face in her hands as a black face appeared at an upstairs window. A north window, at the side, which the fire was working its way toward but hadn't quite engulfed. We all ran round.

"Staircase has gone—catch this!" yelled Jack. "And hold it out— taut!"

We rushed forward, shielding our faces, as he threw down a blanket. David and Archie grabbed a corner each. I seized another and Lavinia elbowed Pinkie out of the way to secure the fourth. "Don't be silly, girl; you'll drop it!"

"Now—don't let go!" Jack ordered. As we stood beneath him, bracing ourselves and squinting against the intense heat, it seemed to me I was burning already. He was poised up at the window, a small, limp body in his arms. Rose.

"Now—catch her!"

He let her go, and down she came, fast, spiraling through the air like a tiny rag doll. I've never held on to anything so tight in my life, and as she hit the blanket only a hint of her body touched the ground. Archie ran forward and scooped her up, cradling her in his arms, dragging her away from the flames. Her head lolled and I saw her eyes, wide with shock, her mouth wide open, the inside of her mouth very pink against her black face.

"Jack!" I swung back up to the window as, at that moment, we heard sirens, wailing in the distance. "Oh, thank God. Archie—David, grab the blanket again. Jack, jump! Damn you, Jack—where are you!" I screamed.

A moment later he reappeared.

"Jump, Jack! We'll catch you!" yelled Archie.

"Don't be bloody ridiculous; I'd break my neck!"

"Well, how are you going to—"

But he'd disappeared back into the furnace, leaving my words hanging in the air.

"He'll find a way," said a quiet voice beside me.

"Oh, David, will he?" I gasped. "How will he? There's no staircase!"

David put an arm up to his eyes and, seizing the blanket, threw it over his head. Bent double, he ran toward the front door, as far as he could, to look inside.

"He's coming!" he yelled, inching backward. "He's coming over the gallery, on a rope! He's here!"

As the fire engines and ambulance came roaring into view, Jack's figure stumbled out of the front door, arms over his head, coughing and staggering. David threw the blanket around him, pulling him away. Finally they made it to the bank and sank down on the grass. I flew to his side.

"Jack—are you all right?"

He couldn't speak, didn't want to speak. Raised a slow hand to show he was fine. Then he sat, hunched, with his head between his knees, his shoulders heaving with exhaustion. I sank beside him, letting him get his breath back.

"Boys?" he croaked finally, looking up and glancing around, blinking, his face blackened.

"Absolutely fine," I breathed, "thanks to you."

"Rose?"

We both looked across. Her family were gathered around her, as she lay still on the grass. The ambulance came to a halt, lights flashing beside us.

"Not sure," said David quietly as he left us and went across to join them.

We watched as the back door of the ambulance flew open and two men jumped out, swiftly followed by a stretcher. Rose's tiny body was lifted onto it, a red blanket tucked up around her neck—but not over her head, I thought thankfully. She was carried inside. Archie and the girls followed, the aunts, too, all somberly climbing in. The ambulance man looked doubtful.

"I'm not sure you can all—"

"Don't be silly, man," snapped Archie. "We'll do as we please. My family have all inhaled smoke, and these two elderly women need to be seen to."

The driver demurred with a shrug and the doors slammed. Before he got in the front, though, he ran across to us.

"Rest of you all right?" he shouted. "Was anyone else inside?"

"My boys!" I said, standing up and pushing them forward.

He took a quick look, peered in their eyes and then down their throats. "Well, they look OK, but there's another ambulance coming. It should be here soon, but we're short-staffed tonight. Make sure they get in it, though, when it comes, all right? They should be checked over."

I nodded and he disappeared off. A second later the doors of the ambulance slammed shut and it roared off down the drive, siren wailing into the night.

Meanwhile, hoses unwound and gushed into life as the Fire Brigade, running back and forth and shouting orders, took their water from the lake and shot great jets at the flames. Jack and I watched from the bank, a wide-eyed child in each of our arms.

"A lost cause," said Jack eventually. "A timber-framed barn—no way. No bloody way. God knows what happened in there."

"God knows," I echoed numbly. "Ben, what—"

"No, not now," said Jack quickly. He got to his feet and hauled me up with him. "Come on, this sodding ambulance won't appear for hours, and we'll only be lying on trolleys in hospital corridors waiting to be checked for carbon monoxide poisoning, which even if we've got they can't do a great deal about. We've got David anyway. He can look at the boys. We'll go up to the house."

"But shouldn't we wait? Shouldn't we be with the Fire Brigade and—"

"Watch your house burn?" he interrupted gently. "You don't want to do that. And neither do Ben and Max. Come on."

He was right. Of course he was right. Sitting there uselessly, helplessly, watching our possessions burn, like staring at some sort of freak show. But I didn't know how to react, you see. Didn't seem to know the right thing to do. I realized I was shaking.

David came back from talking to the firemen, and I felt a blanket being gently put around my shoulders. It was the one they'd caught Rose in. He looked at Jack. "Let's go," David said quietly.

Jack nodded, and they led me to my car. Somehow we got in. I don't remember much, but I think I was huddled in the back with my sons and I seem to remember we drove up to the house in silence. Jack and David carried the boys inside, up the front steps and through the huge hall, the only door that was open. I followed, stumbling up the stone steps, gazing blankly at the black-and-white flagstone floor. I remember thinking it was odd to be in the house without Rose tripping down the stairs to greet us, and for a moment I couldn't remember what we were doing there. I stopped still in the middle of the hall. Gazed around. I seemed to have a blanket hanging off my shoulders. . . .

"I'd like to check the boys over, might even give them something to help them sleep," said a voice. It was David, turning to me at the foot of the stairs. "All right with you?"

I stared at him. "Yes. Fine," I whispered.

I watched him carry Max upstairs. Saw him reach out to take Ben's hand at the same time. What was I doing, standing there, at the bottom? Suddenly I came to. "I'll—I'll come with you."

I ran forward and found Ben's other hand and together we took them up the huge staircase, along the corridor at the top, to the bedroom they normally slept in. *Should* have slept in, I thought as I pushed open the door, my mind racing but still, as if it had a blank tape inside it, uncomprehending. I washed their hands and faces in a blur and found clean pajamas, dimly aware I was functioning on automatic pilot as I dipped flannels in hot water, wrung them out, wiped away soot and grime. Max was yawning hugely; Ben, climbing into bed, wide-eyed and pale. Up all night, I thought in panic, with what—nightmares? Horrific visions? But no, because David was even now slipping something tranquil into some warm milk that Joan had just bustled in with, her face white and shocked.

"Poor lambs," she muttered as she put down the tray. "How are they?"

"They're fine, Joan," I whispered, managing to raise a smile for their sake. My throat constricted, my voice began to buckle. "Right as rain after their big adventure, aren't you, boys?"

"We could have died," Ben informed her solemnly, his face a pale mask as he sat bolt upright in bed. "We nearly burned to death in there."

"Did we?" said Max, turning to him, the full horror dawning in his big blue eyes.

"Nonsense," I soothed. "Jack got you out in bags of time, and anyway, the Fire Brigade had just arrived. They'd have got you out of there in a jiffy."

"They couldn't stop the fire," ventured Ben in a tight, high voice. "You saw it, the barn. It was all burning down!"

"Well, letting a building deliberately burn is quite different from getting people out. Of course they'd have got you out if Jack hadn't been there. Heavens, I'd have got you out if Jack hadn't been there!"

"You're shaking, Mummy. And your face is a really funny color," said Max.

"She's cold," said David quickly, making them lie down and tucking them in. "And it's all been a bit of a shock. Now, come on, boys, you've had your milk, Joan will sit with you until you're asleep. Joan?"

She nodded. "Course I will."

"Oh—no." I startled. "I'll do that, David. I'll—"

"You'll do nothing of the sort. I want you downstairs by the fire with a brandy, not sitting up here in the dark thinking terrible thoughts. You can come up and kiss them when you've stopped shaking."

"Can we have the landing light on?" asked Max in a small voice.

"Course you can, duck," said Joan. "And I'll be here at the end of the bed, with my knitting. Till you're fast asleep."

She shooed me out, waving her hand at me, and I suppose I must have looked awful. No good to the boys at all, evidently, since everyone wanted me to go. As I followed David to the door, though, I turned. Held on to the door frame.

"Ben, what were you doing in there?" I asked. "You were supposed to be up at the house, with Granny."

I saw Ben sit up in the dark, in his bed. "You didn't tell us that. We thought Trisha was baby-sitting at the barn as usual, so we just went down there and went to bed. We thought she'd come."

I stared at him, horrified. God—hadn't I told them? Was that right? Had I gone off without telling them where they were sleeping?

"But—but surely . . ." I faltered.

"Come on now," interrupted David gently, taking my arm. "Not now. We can sort it all out in the morning."

I went, twisting my head back briefly to gaze at Ben, before following David, numbly, downstairs.

In the small sitting room a fire was blazing. Jack was sitting beside it, cradling a brandy and staring into the flames. He'd wiped most of the grime off his face, but there was still a dark tidemark round the edge. He reached for the decanter on the table beside him as we came in.

"One for each of you, I presume?"

"Certainly one for Lucy, and a seat here," David pulled the other armchair right up to the fire. "But I'm going on to the hospital now, so I won't. No, hang it. Yes, I will." He poured himself a glass, swirled it around, and drank it down quickly. He stood still for a moment, stared into space, his face white. He looked all in.

"You'll let us know?" I said, moving gratefully to the chair and sitting down. God, my legs were wobbly, I felt like an invalid. "I mean, how she is?"

"Hmm?" David looked blankly at me for a moment, as if he didn't recognize me. "Oh, of course," he said quickly, collecting himself. "And don't worry. Despite her size, Rose is as tough as old boots. She'll be fine."

I nodded and forced a tight smile.

"And don't worry about the boys, either. It's quite clear they didn't inhale anything too dangerous." He put his glass down and made for the door, pausing before he went out. He turned. "The great thing is, though, to talk about it, Lucy. Not pretend it never happened. Particularly with Ben."

I nodded wordlessly back. Couldn't manage anything else. My Ben. My sensitive, owl-eyed Ben.

"I'll be in touch." And with that he went.

A curious stillness seemed to fall on the room as he left; it was as if Jack and I, alone in front of the fire, were in some kind of limbo. As if it hadn't happened. None of it. I looked at the amber liquid someone had put in my hand. Raised it to my lips and sipped it tentatively. Surprisingly, it tasted good. Warm. I took a great gulp and stared into the flames. I saw Jack, running out of them, with Ben in his arms.

"Jack, how can I ever thank you?" I trembled. "Ben and Max, if you hadn't—"

"If I hadn't, the Fire Brigade would have got them out," he interrupted firmly. "They weren't in any great danger, Lucy. The fire hadn't got a proper hold."

I knew this to be as big a lie as I'd just told Ben. I remembered sitting on the grass, stunned and shocked, watching the great arcs of water shoot from the hoses, huge pressurized high-speed jets battling to put out the flames. We hadn't stayed to watch the fight, but I knew it had been in vain. A dark shell no doubt remained, drenched and blackened. All that was left of our home, of our possessions.

"Everything that we owned was in there," I quavered. I took a great slug of brandy, its warm comfort finding its way down fast. "All that we had. Photos, all my pictures of Ned . . ." I put a hand over my eyes, horrified as I realized. "Letters—everything!"

"I know," said Jack quietly, "but that's all you can't replace. Everything else you can."

His face was pale in the circle where he'd washed the soot away, his blue eyes unnaturally bright in the firelight. He'd been in and out of a burning building three times to save lives, and I was talking about possessions.

"Of course it can." I breathed. "Of course it can be replaced. And what do all those things matter, when Rose is in hospital, and Ben and

Max—oh, Jack, I'm sorry." I covered my face with my hands. "How could I even have said that? I—I don't know what's wrong with me. Don't seem able to handle this." I was shaking violently again. "And look at you, all calm and poised and—oh God, I was just so frightened!"

To my horror, tears were streaming down my face, through my fingers, and the shaking was making the blanket fall off my shoulders. In a second he was beside me, kneeling, his arm tight around my shoulders.

"It's fine," he said firmly. "You shouldn't have to handle it. You've had a fright, and you're in shock, that's all."

"My *children!*" I gasped, taking my hands away, all control gone now. "Coming out of those flames! White-faced, in their pajamas, their beds burning upstairs, where—where they'd just slept! Teddies, trains . . ." I could feel my eyes wide and staring as I visualized the horror; saw them running out of their rooms onto the landing, smelling the smoke, seeing the flames lick up the stairs, glancing, terrified, at each other . . .

"And me not there. Me not with them! But, Jack, what were they *doing* there? I left them here with Rose; I did!" My voice rose shrilly.

"Of course you did, my love," he soothed, scooping me off the chair now, pulling me down onto his lap, holding me close to stop the shaking.

"I *didn't* leave them alone; I swear I didn't. I wouldn't do that! And—oh, Jack," my voice dipped low suddenly, "they could have died. They so nearly did!"

"They didn't die, though, did they? They're alive and well and asleep upstairs, OK?" He searched my face with his eyes, gave me a little shake. "OK, Luce?"

I nodded. "OK!" I gasped, finally.

"And so there's no point going over and over it, blaming yourself for something that didn't happen, is there?"

I stared right into the very dark center of his eyes. "No point," I repeated dumbly.

He was stroking my hair off my face now, holding me close, as one would a child. It was so lovely, such a comfort. His warm body close to mine by the fire. I felt I wanted to stay there on his lap forever, curled up like this, and that if I did, everything would be fine. The nightmare might never have happened. He could make it go away and keep everything else at bay, too, this watchful man who did battle in the cause of goodness, who ran through fires in its name. I felt a weight lifting from me and a warm, submissive feeling spread from my stomach to my limbs. My shoulders were steadier now. His face was still close to mine, bright blue eyes alert, checking, concerned, watching me intently. I could almost feel his breath on my face he was so close.

"Are you going to kiss me?" I whispered.

He looked startled. Gave a slight smile. Regarded me quizzically for a moment. "Do you want me to?"

"Very much."

For several seconds we continued to look at each other and neither of us spoke. Then he leaned the last few inches necessary for his lips to meet mine. They were warm and dry, and his arm in the small of my back pulled me gently off his lap and close into him. My head rocked and I could feel my heart pounding against my ribs. At length we drew apart. My arms were round his neck and I looped them over his head, the better to see his face. His eyes searched mine and I dropped my arms to his shoulders again, almost overcome by the intensity of his gaze. I held on tight, and then he drew back, as if to focus, to look at me properly.

"Lucy," he said softly.

That was all. But as we regarded each other, in the firelight, it seemed to me that here was a face I knew so well and yet—I almost hadn't known was there. It was as if I'd been close up to something so large, so huge, I couldn't see it, had been unable to focus. Until now. Until this moment, when he ceased to be the boy I'd known forever, had met in a bar in college, Ned's cousin, a friend to my sons, ceased to be all of that and became a stranger, with whom I longed to be on intimate terms, in a way that would have been unthinkable moments before. I saw his eyes recognize this, too, this need to escape our real selves, to obliterate them with sensation, and in another moment his lips were on mine again. In a silken movement he deftly lifted me off his lap and laid me down on the floor, on the carpet, and then he was beside me, so that we were lying together. As he drew me into his body I arched my back and inadvertently sighed, as if signaling a total openness to all that might happen next. I felt his body harden and respond. When we heard the telephone ringing in the next-door room, our eyes flickered open at each other, alarmed. Interruption would destroy us, now. We needed to be remote, our heads in a whirl, our pasts forgotten, and ordinary sounds would remind us of who we were: Jack and Lucy, down on the rug, by the fire in the sitting room, after a catastrophe. Ridiculous, when you think about it, after all that had happened, the terrors of the night, yet with his hands in my hair, his mouth on mine . . . Still the phone rang, persistently, mercilessly.

"Leave it," I ordered breathlessly, as for a moment we parted. We listened. Motionless, we stared at each other. It wasn't beside us, shrieking and loud, it was in the next room, but nevertheless, it was insistent. It wasn't going to stop.

"We have to get it," said Jack suddenly, drawing away from me and kneeling up. "It might be David."

"Oh! Yes, of course."

I sat up as he left the room. Suddenly I felt very much in the present. Very much on a rucked-up Persian rug in the sitting room at Netherby, my clothes rumpled, my old self, threatening to be shocked, appalled even, by my behavior. I bit my lip and bade my old self down, tried to think straight. My head was spinning incoherently, but through the blur, through the confusion, the only clarity of thought I had was that I wanted him back. I wanted him here, now, beside me, by the fire, making it all go away.

And he was back, a moment later, his footsteps echoing as he smartly crossed the flagstone hall. As he came through the door, though, his face was ashen.

"That was David," he said. "He was phoning from the hospital. Rose died ten minutes ago."

Chapter Twenty-eight

WHEN I AWOKE THE FOLLOWING MORNING, IT WASN'T that I didn't know where I was; it was just that I couldn't work out why. I appeared to be in bed, in the green room. Yes, definitely the green room, at Netherby, I thought, peering sleepily at the faded William Morris wallpaper, but—I struggled up onto my elbows—God, I felt so groggy. Drugged almost. But then . . . yes, of course. Jack had given me something to make me sleep. I stared at the spriggy wallpaper. My mind reeled back. Jack, white-faced, helping me upstairs, up that sweeping staircase, one arm around my shoulders, the other supporting my elbow as I—what, went into shock again? Was that what had happened, why I'd been so weak? Leading me in here, giving me a glass of water, handing me a pill . . . getting me into bed, then pulling the covers up and telling me to sleep. Me, taking the glass with a shaky hand, trying to stop crying, looking at the grim face before me that for some reason, ten minutes ago, I'd been kissing the life out of. Ten minutes before, that is, we'd heard the news that Rose was dead. Ten minutes before, when we'd lain together on the rug, entwined, whilst she'd died of smoke inhalation in a hospital bed.

I stayed like that, propped up on my elbows, the full force of the horror sweeping over me. I gave a sudden shiver, even though it was a warm morning and the sun was streaming through the gap in the heavy linen curtains. When I finally sat up, I realized that, apart from my shoes, I was still wearing my clothes. I swung my legs around out of bed and immediately felt sick. Whether it was the aftereffect of a pill I wasn't used to, or Rose's death, or my home burning to the ground, or perhaps the full implications of my outrageous behavior the night before dawning I don't know, but I ran to the bathroom and threw up.

Slowly, I washed my face, wiped it numbly with a towel. Then I sat on the edge of the bath for a bit. Eventually I got up and tentatively made my way back to the bed, feeling the walls for support. On the bedside table was a photo of Ned. Yes, even here, in the spare room, and for once, I couldn't look at him. I turned it away. Couldn't face him. Ned had had little love for his mother and was no hypocrite, but he would certainly have been horrified by the nature of her death. I stood up slowly, my eyes riveted suddenly by a small gap in the curtains. I knew that if I drew them, I'd see the ruined barn. I knew this was possible from this room. But I couldn't move. Rose was dead, had died in the hospital. This seemed so overwhelming, so colossal, it was all I could do to stand there, wiping sweat from my top lip, trying to comprehend. And then abruptly, from the next-door room, I heard voices. Raised voices, shrill and insistent. The boys. Oh Christ, the *boys*! I flew out onto the landing and darted into their room.

Max was standing at the end of Ben's bed in his Harry Potter pajamas, a cup of milk in each hand. His cheeks were pink with indignation, and he was shouting at Ben, who was pale and wide-eyed, sitting up in bed.

"Mum! Ben says I'm fibbing, but it's true; Joan told me! I went down to get a drink and she told me in the kitchen. Granny's dead, isn't she? Tell him, Mummy!"

"Yes, yes, it's true," I breathed, going toward them both, encircling Max with my arm and drawing him over toward Ben in the bed. I took his hand. "Ben, listen. Granny, very sadly, died last night."

"No!" he yelled, snatching his hand away. "Not in that fire! Not burned to death, that can't be true!" Horror filled his eyes.

"No—no, not like that," I said quickly. "Not burned at all. It was the smoke, you see, and the shock, and her age, too, you know. It was all too much for her. They had to drop her from a window, you saw that, and her heart wouldn't—"

"*No!* I don't believe it. I *won't* believe it! Granny can't be dead; she can't be!"

He was screaming at me now, tears pouring down his cheeks, grief buckling his pale face. Whatever Rose had been to me, she'd been his granny, and though I'd hesitate to prefix that with "beloved" she'd nonetheless invested time and effort in them, and been rewarded with that precious unconditional love only children can bring to a relationship. They didn't judge her as I did. She was their grandmother; ipso facto, they loved her.

I let him cry for a bit, then, as his sobs subsided, tried again. "Ben, listen, darling. I know it's sad, and so sudden," I drew him close, "but older people, grandparents, you know, we have to accept that they die before us."

"But burned to death!" he screamed, pushing me away. "Burned to death, that's awful!"

"No, Ben, that's not true, I told you."

"But he's right; the barn did burn down," insisted Max. "Look!" And with a four-year-old's zeal and enthusiasm for all things dramatic, he ran to the window and swept back the curtain.

I caught my breath. There, on the horizon, was the view I'd avoided from my own bedroom. Perched on the soft, rolling hills that swept up from the lake, where the kingcups gave the fields a golden glow, rose up the jagged, blackened shell of our home, sodden, from the Fire Brigade hoses, and whilst not quite razed to the ground, certainly minus a roof and most of the top floor. At this distance, it was as if the top had been taken off a doll's house, before havoc had been wreaked with a chain saw and a pot of black paint.

"Wow!" breathed Max. "You can still see sofas and tables and everything, 'cept they're all black! But . . . our rooms have gone. Look, Mum. Look, Ben!" He walked to the window as if pulled by a string.

But Ben was not finding it nearly as enthralling as his brother. "I can't bear it," he whispered, clamping clenched fists to his eyes. "Can't bear to think of us in there, of Granny in there, of her struggling to get out, trying to open doors, coughing, crawling along corridors . . ."

"Draw the curtain," I ordered Max.

"But why? I want to—"

"*Now!*"

He hastily obeyed.

"Now listen, Ben—Max, you listen, too." I pulled Max back from the window and put my arms around their thin shoulders on the bed. "What has happened here is," I struggled, "horrendous, yes. And desperately sad. But it is *not* the stuff of nightmares, OK? Granny was old—"

"How old?" demanded Max.

"I don't know, but jolly old."

"Over fifty?"

"Oh yes," I said gratefully.

"God."

"And she *didn't* die a violent death, Ben; she died peacefully. In the hospital, surrounded by her family, and by the people she loved. You are *not* to imagine her crawling around a burning building looking for a way out, because it's simply not true." Even as I said it, I saw Rose, blundering blindly along, one hand over her mouth, blue eyes wide and terrified, or even on her hands and knees as Ben had said, trousers torn, face blackened, gasping for air. "Simply not true!" I lied, shutting my eyes. "You saw her come out alive, and I don't want you rewriting history, OK?"

"OK," they whispered, eyes huge.

I knew from experience that children will believe you if you're insistent enough. You *can* tell them black is white. I remembered Ben, forgetting his lines in a school play once and believing me when I'd said he was absolutely the best onstage because his silent presence was so magnificent. I wasn't sure how well I was doing now, but I had to try to comfort him somehow, try to slice through the terror.

"OK, Ben?" I repeated.

He nodded. "But why us again?" he asked, turning his pale face up to mine.

Max frowned, confused, but I knew what Ben meant. Knew he was talking about his father.

"I don't know," I admitted.

I regarded the white face of my child beside me and felt fury rising up within me like a high-speed elevator. Fury, that once again my precious boy had been damaged. And why had Rose let them go down to the barn alone? What the hell had she been playing at? Why hadn't she put them to bed up here? But now was not the moment. Ben was starting to shiver. I reached for his dressing gown and pulled it around him. "Here, Ben, put your arm in the sleeve, and try to—"

"Can we go home, Mum?" he interrupted, in a small voice.

I stared. Shifted back on the bed to look at him properly. Then glanced quickly out of the crack in the curtain where Max had failed to draw them completely, to the blackened remains beyond. Oh God— how much had this affected him? Had he not completely taken it in?

"Can we?" he repeated.

"He means to London," put in Max.

I swung around and looked at him. "To London?" They both nodded. I caught my breath. "But, darlings, the flat's gone! I sold it; you know that."

"But you could buy it back, couldn't you? Offer him more money? Ask the man who bought it if we can buy it back from him?"

I licked my lips, marveling at their simple faith, their trust in the consummate ability of grown-ups. And of course I'd been hoisted by my own petard. Not a moment ago I'd prided myself on my ability to get them to believe I could fix anything, that black could, quite easily, be white.

"I know," I said suddenly. "We'll go to Lucas and Maisie's."

"Yes!" they both gasped, and for the first time that morning, the dull fear lifted from Ben's eyes.

"Yes, let's go to Lucas and Maisie's. We could live there, couldn't we, Mum?"

I didn't answer that, didn't gainsay it, even though I knew it might not be possible. Because if there was a crumb of comfort on the horizon, by God I'd let them snatch at it. Let them imagine the welcoming arms of their cozy grandparents, the shambolic, chaotic Bohemian house where I'd grown up, where anything went, and where, within a twinkling, Max would be helping Lucas sort screws into boxes in the garden shed, with Ben at the kitchen table, playing Racing Demon with Maisie, shrieking with laughter as they slapped down cards and tore to the finish. Oh no, with the prospect of all that, I wasn't going to pour cold water.

"Can we?" said Ben, clinging to it. "Can we go?"

"I don't see why not," I said carefully, thinking defiantly that we jolly well *would* go, no matter what anyone here said, whatever opposition I encountered, and that once in London—well, we could get rid of the nurse and I could look after Maisie. They wouldn't need a nurse if I was there, and then we could move into the spare rooms on the top floor, couldn't we? Suddenly all things were possible. All things. Because you see, if I could take Ben's mind for one moment from the terror he had the brains to imagine . . . well, I'd move bloody mountains. Do whatever it took to spare him more pain.

"Wait here," I said tersely, "and get dressed. I'll be back."

They hopped off the bed, if not excited, certainly relieved. A plan had been formed.

"We can't!" Ben's face was suddenly panic-stricken again as he stood there, arms outstretched, in his pajamas. All he possessed. Damn.

"Yes, you can." I pulled open a drawer. "Remember, Granny kept these in here, in case you stayed." I dragged out shorts and a T-shirt. "See?"

"Oh yes. She did," Ben said slowly. He fingered the clothes reflectively, remembering Granny again. Nothing could be fixed that rapidly.

"So come on, buck up," I urged, hoping he wouldn't regress too far. "Oh, and hop in the bath first to get rid of the soot. I'll be back in a moment."

I flew into my room and put my shoes on, dressed, already, in all I had in the world, then crept out along the corridor.

It was surely mid-morning, but all was silent. The huge house was deathly quiet as I passed down the long passage, under archways, past a longcase clock that must have stopped, or else someone had failed to wind it, to the top of the sweeping staircase. As I paused for a moment under the domed glass roof that crowned the stairwell, my hand on the polished banister rail, it struck me that it felt more like a mausoleum than ever. But then, that was only fitting, wasn't it? She had been its lifeblood, Rose, its force. It was Archie's house, sure, but only in name. Her tiny presence had been the pulse of the place as she scurried energetically up these corridors, its arteries, raising her less industrious daughters from their rooms, then down to Joan in the kitchen, berating her for preparing cold cuts when there could have been a cottage pie, then off to scold Archie about his smelly Labrador—leaving seething people wherever she went. Running around with a poker, almost, stoking little fires, keeping them going, hustling everyone along, and without her . . . the place seemed to stop.

As I got to the bottom of the stairs, I had an awful feeling that something like a sigh of relief had swept over the house, too. The painted smile of one of the blackamoors who stood sentry at the bottom seemed to confirm this. I glanced away, horrified. No, no, it was an empty, soulless place that I crept through now, I insisted, and when I finally found the shattered remains of her family in the morning room, I knew it to be so.

Archie was slumped in a wing chair by the fireplace, staring into an empty grate, with Pinkie and Lavinia perched on either arm. His eyes were blank and glazed, and he looked about a hundred years old. The girls were talking across him in low voices as he sat numbly between them, staring blankly, his fingers twitching. They stopped talking when I came in, and stood up.

"Lucy," sobbed Pinkie.

I quickly crossed the room to hug them both.

"Pinkie, Lavinia, I'm so sorry," I whispered, holding them both tight.

They nodded, gulping. Their clothes smelled of smoke and I realized nobody had been to bed. Lavinia drew back from me after a while, eyes dry in enormous sockets, hollow with misery and fatigue; Pinkie, her shoulders shaking, sobbed quietly into a spotted hanky of her father's as I hugged her. I looked over her shoulder.

"Archie . . ."

I went across and perched on the arm Pinkie had vacated. His ancient Lab lay protectively across both of his feet. He made as if to rise but couldn't. I got off the arm and crouched down in front of him, the better to see his face. My hand closed over his. He squeezed it.

"She . . . had a good life, you know," he murmured softly. "A full one. Children, grandchildren, the garden, and so on . . . Committees and whatnot. And she wasn't in any great pain, when she went. It was all . . . very peaceful. Quiet. And thank God the lad came. Thank God she saw him."

"Hector? Was Hector there?"

"Lavinia rang him. Came immediately. Up from London. Wouldn't come back here, of course, but—well. They had time together. Alone." He took his eyes off the grate and looked at me directly for the first time, his swimmy brown eyes childlike, bruised, looking for confirmation. "That's important, don't you think?"

"Oh yes. Yes, very," I breathed.

"And she had such sadness, too, of course. Ned, her favorite, you know, always her favorite . . ."

I blanched at this in front of the sisters but nodded, because I did know.

"Yes."

"Never got over that. Never. Thought that the boys, Ned's boys . . . well, thought the world of them, what?" He raised his eyebrows inquiringly, then looked back to the grate.

"Yes, I know," I murmured. His voice was vague, distant, and he seemed confused.

"Filled a gap, I suppose. But she dreamed too much. Didn't know it could never happen . . . would never happen. I couldn't let her have that, however much she'd been hurt. You do see that, don't you, Lucy?" He turned to me again. Eyes wide, appealing. "Wouldn't have been fair. Or proper."

I wasn't sure I did see. Wasn't sure I had a clue what he was talking about, but I kept on nodding.

"Yes, Archie, I see."

"And of course she didn't know, so that was a blessing. Didn't know I wouldn't have it. Died thinking she could. That I'd let it happen."

I glanced desperately at Lavinia for help, but she was standing with her back to the room at the tall floor-to-ceiling windows. She held herself tightly, arms crossed, staring out at the parkland, sunk in her own private misery, Archie's ramblings not reaching her, or her not wanting them to . . .

"But thank God those boys got out. Thank God . . ."

"Yes," I gulped. "Thank God." I knew I'd have my own nightmares about that, be sitting bolt upright in the middle of the night in a muck sweat for years to come, but I blanked it out ruthlessly now. Ben was my priority.

"And, Archie, you know, they're pretty bad, the boys. Ned's boys," I added, in case I needed to penetrate. He glanced up.

"Hmm?"

"Ben and Max. They're—well, Ben is desperately sad and distressed, about Rose and . . . disturbed, almost, about the fire. I'd like to take them away, to my parents', to get them away from it all. Of course I'll be back," I added quickly, lest anyone should think I was deserting a sinking ship, but actually, I almost felt like an interloper here. As if I was intruding on their grief.

"Lucy's right," said Lavinia, turning and coming back from the window. "They must have some space. Little Ben—well, he won't cope."

I looked at her gratefully and Archie nodded.

"Good plan. Make a plan and stick to it, quite right. No need for you to be here. Police have been up already, of course," he glanced at me, "while you were still asleep. Jack gave you a draught, apparently, so we didn't wake you. They believe it was some electrical fault. No funny business or anything, but just some cock-up at the hands of those cowboy builders Rose got in to wire it up. No doubt on the cheap. Always on the cheap . . ." He shook his head wearily. "Anyway. No point going over that now. Her project, her baby. Her baby . . ." His chin wobbled at this, and one corner of his mouth drooped dramatically. A tear trickled down his papery cheek.

Pinkie swooped. "Oh, Daddy, don't!"

They clung to each other as Pinkie sank to her knees beside him, sobbing all the harder. Archie gripped her hands and squeezed his eyes tight shut, grimacing as tears escaped. I watched, helplessly, as Lavinia did, too, arms crossed, her nails digging into her bare arms. She glanced at me. Came quickly across, nodding.

"Go," she whispered, taking my arm and coming with me to the door. "I know where you are if we need you."

"You've got my parents' number?" I asked her. "And my mobile?"

"I have."

We hugged each other hard and I felt how rigid and unyielding her body was.

"Let go, Lavinia," I urged. "You need to let go!"

"Will do," she agreed brightly, drawing back, her tone reminiscent of her mother. "All in good time." She raised her chin. "All in good time."

I squeezed her arm again and then, with one last look at Archie, his chin on his chest, darted gratefully away to get the boys.

I turned left and made for the back corridor, pushing through the green baize door to take the quicker, backstairs route. As I approached the kitchen, I heard Joan and Trisha talking in low voices. Their backs were to me at the sink as they scrubbed potatoes, and it struck me that, although the mood was somber, respectful perhaps, no one was sobbing into their pinny here. No one had their head in their hands at the kitchen table, life was going on, and lunch was being prepared. Yet Joan had worked here for what—thirty years? Their conversation stopped abruptly as they heard my footsteps, but they didn't turn round. Two heads bent industriously over the sink. I hovered guiltily for a second, wondering what they'd been saying. In the silence, I heard voices coming from the gun room, next door. That in itself was unusual. It was

Archie's private room, where he sat alone, in an old leather chair amidst dog baskets and fishing rods and ancient copies of *The Field*, jealously guarding his privacy and his arsenal, snoozing quietly. But Archie was in the morning room. I moved quietly toward the open door and saw David, pacing up and down by the window, seemingly talking to himself. He stopped abruptly the moment he saw me, and glanced warily at someone sitting in the huge leather chair that had its back to me. I couldn't see the occupant.

"Lucy!" He quickly crossed the room and came out to the corridor, shutting the door firmly behind him. "How are you? How are the boys?"

"Awful, David," I gulped. "Well no, perhaps *awful*'s too strong, but Ben's so upset and—oh God, what a ghastly mess!"

I realized I was welling up, and he took my shoulders and held me close for a moment. A moment later he pulled back, holding me at arm's length. His face was terribly drawn and white with fatigue. No sleep for him, either, I imagined.

"Take them away, Lucy. This is no place for them. Not at the moment."

"I'm going to," I breathed. "We're going to my parents'. I'm just going upstairs to get them now and—"

"Good, good," he interrupted, "fast as you can, good plan." His eyes darted warily up and down the corridor, almost to check if anyone was listening. He dropped his voice. "And listen, Lucy, ring when you get there, OK? Not here, on my mobile." He took a pencil and pad from his pocket and scribbled down the number. He tore the page out and gave it to me. "Let me know that you've arrived, hmm?"

"OK," I said slowly, staring at his shattered face. Was it my imagination, or were people behaving strangely? I felt David was being furtive, hurrying me along, almost giving me a gentle push toward the backstairs, or was it just the shock playing tricks with my emotions? He made to go back inside, then paused, his hand on the door.

"And don't worry," he said kindly. "Children are very resilient. Particularly yours. You've done a good job, Lucy. They've been brought up with so much love, they've a wealth of resources to fall back on. They'll be fine."

"Thank you," I said, flooding with relief, so glad he'd said that. So grateful for those few kind words, and not tranquilizers, pressed into my hand for them.

He gave a quick sad smile and went back in. As he made to shut the door, I saw a pair of khaki-clad legs stretched out in front of the leather chair. I recognized the shoes. Jack's shoes. And the top of his copper hair, too, protruding over the back of the chair. So Jack was in there with David, I thought, as I walked slowly away. But he hadn't wanted to be seen. Least of all, by me.

I walked heavily upstairs and a lump came to my throat. I told myself not to think about it. Not to think about last night and what had happened, that it didn't matter. That there were far more cataclysmic events to consider this morning and that, in the scheme of things, kissing Ned's cousin was very small beer. But my mind resolutely refused to behave. It seemed full of Jack and only Jack, his tenderness last night, his kisses, his kindness, so much so that when we drove out of Netherby ten minutes later, I was almost in a dream. I hardly even registered the police car coming up the drive toward me, passing me at speed in the opposite direction. Hardly heard the crunch of gravel as it stopped sharply at Netherby's front door. Gave no thought to the man in a suit, leaping out of the back and dashing up the mountain of stone steps. Didn't stop to consider it at all.

Chapter Twenty-nine

So—why hadn't Jack acknowledged me then? I wondered feverishly, incapable of letting it drop. Why hide? A hazy summer mist threatened to turn to drizzle on the windscreen and I impatiently flicked it away with my wipers. Why hadn't he got up the moment David had said my name, come to the door; why hadn't *he* taken me by the shoulders, reassured me, agreed I was doing the right thing by going to London? Was he really so appalled? So embarrassed? It was almost as if he was hiding behind that chair because I'd thrown myself at him or something, because he was feeling distinctly morning-after-the-ghastly-night-before-ish.

My God—my hand flew to my mouth. Had I thrown myself at him? Christ, maybe I had. Shamefully I recalled my toe-curling opening gambit—"Are you going to kiss me?"—and the blatant surprise on his face. And not just surprise, either, but amusement, I decided, going hot. I cringed. How *could* I have said that, like some pathetic, vapor-sniffing Gothic novel heroine, and to Jack, of all people! Jack, the practiced seducer, the genius of sensuality, the accomplished lover with a girl on each arm, another hanging on his every word—no wonder his eyes had danced so uproariously. No wonder he'd practically guffawed in my face.

And—why now? I wondered desperately. Why was I suddenly so attracted to him now? I breathed in sharply and swerved violently on the A40. *Was* I attracted to him? I gripped the steering wheel as a juggernaut threatened to go up my backside, eyes wide with alarm. Yes, very, I decided, as a piping hot flush washed over me. But—how bizarre, when I'd known him for, well, forever. Why had I never taken such an unreasonable shine to him before? Or had I? I surveyed my past critically, determined to be scrupulously honest. Well, I'd certainly known he was *considered* attractive, but I'd never considered him so myself because—well, he was too flippant. Too wayward. Too flighty. Not a man to be taken seriously. Not a man like Ned, for instance, and besides, he was almost like a brother; it was practically indecent!

But then again, wasn't it true that he'd always had the power to unsettle me? Wasn't it true that a cold look from Jack could rattle my cage, unnerve me, make me feel small? And let's face it, he'd had plenty of opportunity to do that recently. I recalled his censorious eyes following me round London as I'd chased after Charlie in a skirt the size of a belt. God, I'd been so obsessed with that man. Wanted him at all costs, even though he was palpably wrong, just as—well, just as *Jack* was palpably wrong, for crying out loud!

I thumped the wheel in frustration and groaned. Oh, terrific, Lucy, really terrific. Another unsuitable candidate. Talk about the sublime to the downright ridiculous. Another serial philanderer. Look at the way he dropped Trisha like a cup of cold sick. Look at the way he couldn't even face you this morning, tucking himself away behind that chair, unable to conquer his colossal embarrassment. The man has the moral sensibility of an alley cat—he's downright fickle!

Or was it me that was fickle? I asked myself with a sudden secret qualm. Had I become so desperate for a man I'd clutch at anything, even Jack? My reaction to Kit's veiled proposition yesterday came back to haunt me. Unthinkable! I'd stormed indignantly on the way home. So soon after Charlie—why, it was insulting! And yet hours later, there I was, down on a rug, with . . . I swept a bewildered hand through my hair. Glanced in the rearview mirror. Max was nodding off on the backseat, his head on Ben's shoulder. And that was another thing, I thought suddenly. Jack was practically the boys' uncle, another reason for him to avoid me. And naturally he'd thought that through. Thought, Hang on; Lucy and I are friends, related by marriage. The boys adore me, but when I dump her they won't, so do I want to ruin all that? Haven't I got enough women beating a path to my door without that sort of mess on my doorstep? And given the amount of desirable totty around, aren't I actually rather pushed as it is? Hmm . . . no thanks.

I sat up straight, gritting my teeth, flexing my aching shoulders. So. He was finishing it before it had even begun, was he? Dumping me on day one. Of course, quite right and sensible. And that's what I'd be, next time I saw him. Sensible. And distant. Friendly, of course, but retaining perfect sangfroid. Forget it ever happened. Forget Jack. "Jack." I murmured it softly, just as an experiment. A tubful of adrenaline shot up the backs of my legs. My heart gave a foolish skip. I gulped and tried desperately not to think about lying in his arms by the fire, his breath on my neck, his hands in my hair, his—*ooooh* . . . I moaned low, gave a little shudder, and gripped the wheel. Suddenly I shot nervous eyes in the rearview mirror. Ben was watching me.

"All right, my darling?" I gasped, baring my teeth in a parody of a smile.

"Yes, thanks," in a small voice.

"Good, good. Max asleep?"

He looked across. "Almost."

I smiled some more. Ben looked pinched, I thought, as I tried anxiously to study him closer. Stealing glances at him damn nearly put us across the central reservation, though, so I retreated to the slow lane for a bit. Drove more soberly. After a while, I took a deep breath.

"Um, Ben, about last night. You went to bed in the barn, I take it, because you weren't sure where you were sleeping, is that right?"

He stared at me in the mirror, silent.

"And Granny came down and baby-sat down there," I persevered, "presumably because you'd already got into bed and she didn't want to disturb you, is that it? And then, well, what I'm wondering is, when the fire started—"

"Mummy, I really don't want to talk about it." His voice wobbled.

I glanced in the mirror, taken aback. "All right, darling, no. No, fine, of course not," I said quickly. "I was just trying to get the sequence of events in my head. But I can quite see you don't want to talk about it. Yet."

I licked my lips, worried. He seemed so incredibly buttoned up. So tense. Natural, of course, after a terrible shock like that, but why had he gone to bed in the barn, without Trisha? Yes, OK, he'd said he'd thought she was coming down later, but surely he'd have gone and found her, if he was that tired? He wouldn't have told Max to go to bed and then climbed in himself without someone there. No small boy goes to bed voluntarily. He'd have stayed up with the adults, at Netherby, until told to do otherwise, wouldn't he? Something didn't quite ring true here, didn't make sense, but I couldn't probe further. Not yet. Couldn't have that white face turn even paler on me.

After a while I turned on the radio. Hummed along with forced jollity.

"Ben." I smiled into the rearview mirror. "If Max is asleep, why don't you come and sit beside me in the front? Then we can chat."

He hesitated for a moment. "OK."

He undid his belt and clambered over. Snapped himself in.

"So!" I said cheerily. "Lucas and Maisie's for a bit. That's pretty cool, isn't it?"

He smiled and a spot of color came to his cheeks. "Adults don't say cool, Mum. It sounds sad."

"Ah." I nodded. "Sorry."

"So, do they know? Maisie and Lucas? Have you rung them?"

"I have, and they're thrilled to bits, darling."

Sort of true. Kind of. I'd briefly had a word with Maisie, in the ten minutes or so we'd had at Netherby before David had come upstairs to find us, hustling the boys down to the car, which he'd kindly brought round to the back door, then coming back upstairs again, popping his head into my room to see if I was ready. Hovering impatiently in the doorway while I'd been on my mobile to Maisie.

"I'm coming, David," I'd whispered, hand over the mouthpiece. "Literally two minutes."

He'd nodded but hadn't moved. I'd gone back to Maisie. She'd been delighted of course, because she hadn't seen me or the boys for so long, but surprised, too.

"To stay? Why yes, love, of course!"

"Is that OK?" I asked anxiously, briefly turning my back on David, ostensibly pulling the green cover over the bed I'd slept in. "I mean, you haven't still got the nurse? Or a lodger?"

"Neither," she purred happily. "In fact, I'm much, much better. Found a marvelous homoeopathic remedy which works wonders, so I don't need the nurse, and I'm bored with lodgers; they make even more mess than I do. We'd love to have you all, but why so sudden? And for how long?"

"I don't know," I said nervously, gazing out of the window at the blackened ruin on the hill. "Sort of indefinitely, at the moment. There was a fire. At the house. At our house."

Out of the corner of my eye I saw David discreetly move back away from the door into the passage.

"Oh!" She could instantly tell that I couldn't talk or wouldn't talk. "Well, as long as you're all all right," she said hesitantly. "That's the main thing."

"We're fine," I assured her quickly. "But, Maisie, something terrible. Rose is dead."

"Good God!"

There was a long silence. I heard David clear his throat quietly.

"Oh, Lucy darling, how appalling! I don't know what to—" She broke off.

I gave her a moment. Then: "Maisie, I must go now. The boys are waiting."

"Yes, yes, fine," very faintly.

And we'd left it at that. I could imagine her worried face, though, as she put the phone down, saw her huge blue eyes, wide and anxious, as she pulled a hanky from her sleeve, twisted it in her hands, went to find Lucas, to tell him. Saw her hasten out to him in the garden, reading under the lilac tree in his favorite spot, saw him lower his book, worry lines appearing round his eyes. Rose dead. Ghastly. And Lucy in trouble again. Oh dear. Coming home. And they had good cause for concern, too, because—what on earth was I going to do? I couldn't stay with them forever, could I, so where would we live? Would I qualify for a council flat, I wondered, boggling slightly at this. Social security even, or—

"What school am I going to go to, Mum?"

I swallowed. "I'm not sure, darling."

"Not the one in Oxford, then?"

"Um, no. Not that one."

"My old one?" Hopefully.

"Um, still not quite sure. Quite a long way from Burlington Villas, Ben." Crazy. Too far. Out of the catchment area, too.

"A new one then?" he said nervously. "In Westbourne Grove?"

"Haven't really decided." I gripped the wheel hard. Felt hot.

"With a dyslexia bit, like the one in Oxford?"

"Hope so."

"And are we still going to live there forever? At Lucas and Maisie's, I mean?"

More wheel gripping. "Ben, what we're going to do is, we're going to play it by ear. Which is so exciting, isn't it? Not make any firm plans yet, but make plans—oooh, I don't know. In a day or two, say. OK?"

He glanced at me. Gave a worried half smile. "OK."

I breathed out. Finally. But it was a long, shaky breath, and I didn't relax behind the wheel for the rest of the journey. Felt my body tense, as rigid as a board, as we wove our way across London.

MAISIE WAS WAITING AT THE FRONT WINDOW WHEN WE arrived, her sharp eyes guarding the dustbins she'd used to save us a parking space. She hurried out to move them when she saw us. I got out of the car and fell on her, hugging her hard, tears brimming as I blinked into her faded red hair. Maisie. My mum. I hadn't realized how much I'd missed her or what a huge relief it was to be here. I glanced behind her at the recently painted, slightly crooked thin, tall house, with its window boxes crowded with as many weeds as plants, since Maisie entertained all comers. Home. My childhood home, I thought, bursting with the same nostalgia Ben clearly felt for the flat. I smiled and brushed my damp eyes.

"You've painted it pink."

"Apricot, actually, to match my hair, although Lucas says it clashes. What d'you think?"

"Interesting." I smiled, head on one side.

"I thought so, too. Now come on, Ben, Max, my chickens." She bent to hug them. "My, how you've grown in a few short weeks! Just as well, actually, because I need a couple of big strong lads. I'm wrestling with some copper pots I want to sell, but they're covered in gunk and muck, so I thought we'd set to in the garden with the Brasso. Quite a lot of elbow grease is required and your grandpa's got his nose in a book as usual, so I'm relying on you. Come on; come in!" She tossed the empty dustbins effortlessly over the low brick wall and led the way.

"Still got the stall, then?"

"By the skin of my teeth." She grimaced as she hustled us up the brick path, overgrown with nasturtiums and dandelions.

We went through the front door and down the familiar dark passage. It was crowded as usual with stacks of chairs, lamps, books, pots, and baskets, all piled in precarious, tottering pagodas and all, like most things in the house, with dangling price tags, since Maisie oscillated between wanting to fill her stall and not being able to part with her precious wares.

"You boys are in your usual room at the top of the house," she called as she weaved ahead down the hall to the kitchen, expertly avoiding the flotsam. "So take your things up and then come down for cake and tea."

"We don't have any things," said Ben flatly.

Maisie turned, flustered. She looked from Ben to Max. "But of course you don't," she said, rallying. "How exciting! Golly, I wish I could start again from scratch, get rid of all this rubbish. Just think of the fun you'll have buying it all."

"Oh cool!" Max's eyes lit up. "Can we do that tomorrow, Mum? Buy lots of stuff?"

"Er, I think we'll wait and see what the insurance company has to say first," I said nervously. "Why don't you run upstairs and bag your beds, though?"

"And I'll take you on a little spree of my own tomorrow," promised Maisie. "We might even go to that car boot sale in Maida Vale, rummage around and find some old *Beano* albums. Oh, and if you are popping upstairs, you might just look under the pillows." She contrived to look perplexed. "I think I might have left some Smarties up there."

"I'm by the window!"

"No—I am!"

They thundered up, pushing and shoving, happy to be back on familiar territory.

"*Everything's* gone?" whispered Maisie incredulously as she led me into the kitchen. Lucas was settled in an old Windsor chair by the range, reading.

"Everything."

"But you and the boys are all right," said Lucas, standing up and putting his book down, embracing me. I smelled pipe smoke in the folds of his shirt. "And that's all that matters. That's the main thing, eh, love?"

"Exactly," I agreed, raising a weary smile as he patted my back. I felt exhausted suddenly, now that I could relax, now that I was here, and headed gratefully for a chair. Just terribly, terribly tired. I flopped down at the table and a great wave of fatigue broke over me.

Maisie and Lucas bustled around putting the kettle on and getting cake out of clanking tins, exchanging anxious glances over my head. I pretended not to notice and gazed about, mentally ticking off comforting, familiar items; the dresser, bursting with willow pattern china, photos, and grandchildren's drawings. The faded oilcloth on the table. The chipped enamel jug with its fistful of wildflowers. As my aching eyes roved gratefully around, I spotted the book on Lucas's chair, realizing with a jolt that it was the same one Jack had been so engrossed in, except this was the hardback. I recognized the name, Jason Lamont. Slightly trashy I'd have thought for Lucas, hardly the usual Kierkegaard.

The window rattled in its frame as a train went past at the end of the garden, and I smiled as Lucas looked incredulous. It had done that for thirty years, because my father had never quite got round to fixing the catch, yet he still managed to look astonished. I heard someone clatter down the stairs and turned to see Ben, in the hall, picking up my car keys from the table, opening the front door, and heading down the path to the car, probably to get the few remaining books and toys that happily had been in the boot and escaped the fire. All that remained of his possessions. The front door slammed behind him as it always did, because the spring was too strong and Lucas hadn't quite got around to sorting *that* out, either. Lucas managed to look baffled as Maisie grimaced over her teacup. All part of the marriage ritual.

"Good cake," I affirmed, biting into it, astonished I was hungry. But then again, I hadn't eaten for—God, how long? Hours? Days? The recent past seemed such a blur, as if everything were already long ago.

"The usual Dundee, but I might try one of those Nigella ones now the boys are here. They like to help if it's chocolate."

"Help lick the bowl, you mean," I said, grateful we were still talking cakes and not fires or Felloweses yet.

We munched on in silence and I knew they were waiting for me to open up, to gush it all out, tell them in my own time. My throat felt dry, constricted, though, and I knew I'd cry.

I glanced down the passage to the front door. Ben had been gone for quite a while and I began to feel nervous. Presumably he *had* just gone out to the car. He wouldn't go off or anything, would he? I made myself finish my piece of cake, telling myself he'd be back by the time the last crumb had gone. Be back, ringing the bell. Up on the wall, the old school clock ticked away the seconds. The radio was on low, so there was the faint background hum of *The Archers*. I forced the last sultana down and pushed my plate away, quickly got to my feet, knocking my chair over in my haste, just as the doorbell rang.

"Ah!" I breathed, gazing down at my startled parents with a mixture of relief and triumph. "See?"

Lucas picked my chair up in surprise and I saw him shoot a troubled look at Maisie.

"Coming, darling!" I called as the bell went again, with typical eight-year-old impatience.

I marched smartly to the door, and when I opened it, there he was, flanked by a young couple.

The girl was pretty and sweet-looking, with curly blond hair and a pink-and-white complexion, very much in the Fra Angelico mold, and the man, slightly older, tall, slim, wearing a gray suit, and with a narrow, intelligent-looking face. He smiled.

"We found this little chap in the road. I believe he belongs to you?"

"Oh! Thanks." I drew Ben in quickly and grinned. "Playing with the traffic, was he? I'll have the law onto me. Come on, Ben."

"We are the law."

I blanched. Laughed nervously. "Yeah, right."

In the silence, I suddenly realized where I'd seen the man before. In the backseat, being driven fast up the gravel to Netherby, as I left in the opposite direction. Racing up the steps to the front door. I swallowed.

"From Oxford?"

"That's it." The smile was still in place.

"Well—you'd better come in," I flustered, standing back to let them through as Ben ran off down the passage. "Gosh, sorry, if I'd known you wanted to talk to me I'd have stayed on at the house. Archie said it wasn't necessary, that you'd already been and—"

"Oh, quite, and to be honest, it's just a few routine questions. Won't take a minute."

Maisie's anxious face appeared around the kitchen door. "Ben says the police are here."

"It's all right, Maisie, just a few questions. Won't take a moment, apparently."

They smiled down at her apologetically. She responded faintly, shutting the kitchen door.

I led them into the sitting room, removing an old Bakelite telephone from a chair before sitting down, then quickly jumping up to clear piles of books from the threadbare camelback sofa to give them room. I hoped it wouldn't break. One of the legs was very precarious.

"So!" I sank down again. "Any further on? Archie said the fire was probably caused by an electrical fault, dodgy wiring, is that it?"

The man sat on the edge of the sofa, arms resting on his knees, hands clasped. He had an impassive, watchful face and his hazel eyes were trained on me, thoughtful, contemplative.

"Well, no, we think not, now. We think the fire was started deliberately, actually."

"Good God." I sat up, startled. "By who?"

"By a child."

"A *child*!" I stared. Felt the blood drain from my face. "But—but why? Why d'you think that?"

"Because evidence suggests it, Mrs. Fellowes. Comic books wrapped in bundles around matches were found in the garden. Homemade fireworks."

"Fireworks!" I stood up, distressed.

"In a camp, in a nearby copse."

"Jesus."

"And we also have a witness who claims this is so."

"What, you mean, they saw—"

"They saw a child start the fire."

"Who?" I stared in horror. My eyes darted from one face to the other. Both unmoving, impenetrable. "No! Not Ben, Max—they wouldn't!"

"Ben, we believe."

"*Ben!* But—"

"Mrs. Fellowes." He took a large open notebook from a slim leather case on the floor and flipped back a page. "Where were you on the night of the twenty-fourth—yesterday evening? Sit down, please."

I sat, ashen. "I was . . . out."

"Yes, but where? And who were you with?"

"I was in a pub," I whispered. "In Little Burchester."

"Little Burchester. About forty minutes away from Netherby?"

"Yes."

"With a gentleman by the name of . . ." He referred to his pad again, running his finger down to find the spot. "Charles Fletcher?"

"Yes, but only for an hour or so. I left to go home."

"Straight home?"

"No, I went to see a friend."

"And her name?"

"His," I mumbled.

"Sorry?"

"His. Kit Alexander."

"Of Frampton Manor?"

"Yes. I work for him," I added quickly.

"I see." He paused, frowned down again at the italic handwriting that filled the pages of the book. It looked awfully familiar. He glanced up. "But wasn't it your intention, Mrs. Fellowes, to be out for the entire night?"

I swallowed. "Yes."

"Staying the night in the pub? With Mr. Fletcher?"

"Yes," I whispered.

"Who is, I believe, married?"

My mouth opened.

"Mrs. Fellowes? Is he married?"

"Yes, but is there a law against—"

"And you left the children with?" he swept on.

"Well, I left the children with their grandmother!"

"Lady Fellowes?"

"Yes!"

He pursed his lips and frowned. Rubbed his chin thoughtfully with his fingertips. "Lady Fellowes said not. She gave a statement in hospital, before she died, saying that you had never asked her to look after the children. That you'd simply gone off, with your boyfriend, and left them alone at the barn. She said she was hosting a lunch party the following day and had been so engrossed in helping the staff that she'd no idea what you'd done until she glanced up, looked through the kitchen window with the cook, Joan, and saw the barn on fire. She said she raced down there while the staff phoned the Fire Brigade—but the fire had already taken hold. She ran upstairs to the boys' bedrooms—and then got trapped. The staircase began to give way. She found your sons huddled by a window, in Ben's room."

"No! No, that can't be! I would *never* have left them! I asked for Trisha, but she said Trisha was too busy helping with the lunch, so she said she'd do it. Have them up at the house, look after them up there!" My voice was rising hysterically now.

"Was anyone with you?"

"When?" I yelled.

"When Lady Fellowes said that?"

I thought back frantically. "Well—no. No, we were alone." And now she's dead, I thought in panic.

"But Ben could verify it?"

"Well, no, he wasn't there."

"No, but presumably you told him the plan?"

I stared at him. Felt numb.

"Shall I ask him?" He made to get up.

"No! No, don't do that. I—I forgot."

"Forgot to tell him?"

"Yes." I looked down at my hands. Felt my mouth go dry. My throat constrict. "You see," I licked my lips, "I was in such a terrible rush that day. Had to do flowers at the church. Then had to go and meet . . ." I faltered. "Charlie."

"So you forgot."

"Yes," I whispered. "And he got the wrong end of the stick. Ben, I mean. Thought he was sleeping in the barn."

"So . . . they put themselves to bed without an adult? Is that usual, Mrs. Fellowes?"

"No!" I looked up sharply. "No, it's not, and I don't know why! I've asked, but—well, he's too upset to tell me. It's *not* usual—I never leave them!"

"And did your son know where you were?"

I hung my head. "No."

"You didn't tell him?"

"No."

"So, where did you say you were going?"

"I said . . . I would be in London, with a girlfriend. I didn't want to . . . well, hurt him. Say I was seeing . . . a man." I felt desperately hot, the palms of my hands sweaty through my jeans. I clenched my fists.

"I see."

A silence ensued.

"Mrs. Fellowes, I have to persist in asking you whether it's usual for you to leave your children alone at night, as you did last night."

"No, never!" My head jerked up. "And I told you, I *didn't* leave them, Rose said she'd have them. She was lying!"

"And during the day?"

"What?"

"Did you leave them during the day?"

"No," I whispered, aghast. "*No!* Max is only four, for Christ's sake!"

"How about the time," he flipped the notebook open, "he fell in the river . . . could have drowned by all accounts, and was only saved by the quick thinking of Lady Fellowes's nephew, mid-morning, while you were still in bed, or the time Lady Fellowes said she found you drunk, lying comatose on a sofa, smashed bottles on the floor, the children playing with the bits of glass, or the time—"

"Stop; stop!" I gasped. "No! No to all of it! I mean—yes, OK, the first bit, the river, but not like that. Ben did fall in, but comatose on the sofa—that's a blatant lie!"

"So . . . when he fell in the river, did you know where he was?"

"What?"

"Did you know he'd gone off on his own?"

I stared. His eyes were not unkind but focused, direct.

"She told you all this?" I whispered. "In hospital?"

"Wrote it down over the course of a few months. This is her note-book. There are pages of it, Mrs. Fellowes." He flipped through to demonstrate. "Pages and pages. Max asking for Bacardi Breezers at a party. The children left alone for days on end, no food, so coming up to her for meals. Ben withdrawn and traumatized, scrawling obscenities on walls. She said she was worried about them, about their welfare. Began to document the neglect."

"Neglect!"

"We have to verify it, of course, from other members of the family, but we've already done that to a certain extent. Subtly, of course, since they're still in a state of shock. But dates and times have been confirmed, wherever possible. Sometimes, naturally, Lady Fellowes was the sole witness, so it's difficult—"

"Difficult because she's dead!" I shrieked. "And she's lying!"

"Mrs. Fellowes." He cleared his throat. "We've also talked to Ben."

"Ben? When?"

"Just now in the front garden. He was out in the road when we arrived, getting something out of the boot of the car. We just introduced ourselves and had a little chat on the front wall. Nothing scary or intrusive, of course, although we would like to speak to him at length at a later date. But he did confirm he started the fire."

"No! Ben . . . no!" I stood up, trembling. "Why?"

The blond girl shrugged and spoke for the first time. Her voice was soft and silky. "Who knows? But children are driven to do all sorts of things when they're unhappy. It's often for attention, we find."

I swung round to her, my eyes searching her face like headlamps. "Who are you?"

"I'm from Social Services. Mrs. Fellowes, your husband is dead, isn't he?"

"Yes," I whispered, horrified.

"And so you're a one-parent family. We do sympathize. We do know how hard that can be. Nevertheless . . ." She regarded me, shaking before her, hesitated, glanced at the man.

"Mrs. Fellowes," he cleared his throat, "are you here with your parents for the duration?"

"Sorry?"

"I mean, for a while?"

"Yes, yes, we're staying here." I felt numb, in a trance.

"Good." He exchanged glances with his friend and they both got to their feet. He shut the book. I recognized it, with its floral cover. It was one of Rose's journals, from the morning room, one she used to write in, every day, at her desk at the long window, looking out over the parkland. Looking out toward the barn . . . queen of all she surveyed.

"Well, I'm afraid I'll have to advise them to temporarily care for the children," said the woman with the silky voice, picking up her briefcase. "I need to make a report first of course, and we won't make an immediate care order if your parents can act in loco parentis."

"In loco—but I'm not absent!"

"But not effective," she said softly. "I'm sorry, Mrs. Fellowes, but someone has died as a result of your son's actions. That makes him a danger to society. He is underage, but the crime is nevertheless arson. It's also most certainly manslaughter and possibly . . . well. We also believe his actions to be a direct result of yours. The boy's own grandmother was concerned for your sons' safety, keeping carefully documented evidence, even before the fire. I must ask you not to remove your children from this house, Mrs. Fellowes. Not to abduct them in any way, not to take them out of the country, and, for the present, to give your parents full control. We'll go and speak to them now. You'll be visited later on today by the local Social Services, since this is their patch and not mine, and we'll work together on this one. We'll be in touch as soon as a full report has been made. Good day, Mrs. Fellowes."

And leaving me standing there, white-faced and shaking, they departed, to find their way down to Maisie and Lucas, in the kitchen.

Chapter Thirty

WHEN MAISIE FOUND ME SOME TIME LATER, I WAS sitting, cold and rigid in the corner of the room, fists clenched on my knees. She crept in, white-faced, and knelt down beside me, taking my hand.

"Have they gone?" I muttered.

"Yes, they've gone."

"It's not true, Maisie," I whispered, finding her eyes. They were huge and frightened. "I wouldn't leave them alone; you know I wouldn't."

"I know that; I know," she soothed. "It's all been a terrible mistake, and it's all going to be fine."

"It's not going to be fine; they're going to take my children away!" My voice rose to a shrill crescendo. "That's what they said, isn't it? That's what they've just told you; that's what they want to do!"

"No, no, they just said—well," she faltered, fighting for calm, her face buckling, "for us to look after them, at the moment. In the interim. I—well, I couldn't really take it all in, couldn't take in what they were saying, thought it was some sort of nightmare. I kept listening to her voice, watching her face, but couldn't really . . . Something about a care order, because of Rose's death, the fire . . ."

"Oh God, that's not going to happen, is it? Tell me that won't happen!" I shrieked hysterically, standing up now, tears streaming down my face. "They can't do that, can they, Maisie?"

"No, no, of course they can't, darling, of course not!" She reached up and seized my hands, her lip trembling, eyes desperate.

I gazed down at her, kneeling there on the floor, all my terror concentrated on the naked fear in her face.

"You think they can, don't you?" I whispered. "You think they'll take Ben into care, because of what he did. Take out a pen and tick some ghastly box on a form in the Westminster Town Hall—you think they have that power!"

"I—I don't know; I don't know," she wailed, dropping my hands and wringing hers in despair. "I wish Lucas was here. They said such terrible things! Said you left them to spend the night with a married man, in a pub." She looked up at me, very old suddenly, very confused. "Well, I told them that wouldn't be true. Not my Lucy."

I hung my head. "That much was true," I told her, "but, Maisie, I couldn't do it. I met the wife and—oh God, it's a long, awful story, and anyway, it doesn't make me an unfit mother! It doesn't mean I'd leave my children surrounded by homemade fireworks, let them set light to the house!"

"Of course it doesn't," she said staunchly, getting quickly to her feet. "But . . ." Her face fretted into anxious lines again. "Why would she say those things?"

"Rose?"

"Yes, why would she lie? All those things, in that book."

"I don't know!" I wailed, spinning round, shooting my hands into my hair in despair. I paced around the room. "I don't know why she'd do it. Did she hate me so much? Was I such a god-awful daughter-in-law? I mean Christ, she was the one who got me down there in the first place, converted the barn so sumptuously, wanted me right there on her doorstep, so I just don't know why—yes." I suddenly stopped by the bay window. Stared fixedly at the cherry tree in the front garden. "Yes, I do." I swung around to face Maisie. "She wanted my children. Wanted them without me. She wanted them for herself."

"No!" Maisie took a step toward me. "No, she wouldn't be that wicked!"

"She would," I whispered, my mind racing.

"But she was so kind to you, took you in. I *know* Rose; she wouldn't—"

"Oh, but she would, Maisie; she would," I breathed, darting forward and taking her hands, shaking them. Her face was one of mute bewilderment, but my mind was on fire, spinning like a kaleidoscope, shedding scattered shards of light.

"Oh yes, she wanted them all right." I dropped her hands and paced the room again, biting my thumbnail, working it through. "But she wanted them on her terms, up at her house, Netherby, not down at the barn with me. Not separated like that, but in the bosom of her family, without me . . . Yes, her grandsons, to bring up as she saw fit, because, let's face it, that's what she'd wanted all along, why she asked me there in the first place. I knew then I wasn't the glittering attraction; I just didn't know how far she'd go. . . . Ned's boys, you see. Not mine, *Ned's*, and now that she's dead, no one will know the truth. And she was clever, too. Some of the things she wrote in that book *were* true—Max falling in the river—others downright lies, but sprinkled with grains of truth . . . well. They'll think like you, that no one could be so wicked; no one could possibly do that. But I know she could. I know she had it in her." I sank down into the sofa, appalled, exhausted. "I *know* it!"

I thought back to London, when Ned had died. Rose, always on the phone, turning the screw. Pushing me to admit I was cracking up, that I couldn't cope. Couldn't cope with the boys. She'd wanted them then. Wanted custody. Way back then.

Maisie came and sat beside me, her face white, frightened. "Darling, it's too monstrous, too—"

"Ben!" I sat up suddenly, startling my mother with my gasp of inspiration, knocking a lamp over as I got to my feet, but it came to me with absolute clarity.

"Maisie, where's Ben? I must talk to him." I darted out of the room. "This could all be sorted out if I could just get my bloody son to open up, get him to speak!"

"No, Lucy, he's not—"

"I don't care if he's ready or how bloody sensitive he is." I darted into the kitchen. Heard Maisie's voice calling me back. But the kitchen was empty. Deserted. I spun around in terror.

"Maisie, where are the boys? *Ben!*" I bellowed, tearing back into the hall, shrieking up the stairs as I gripped the stair rods. "*Ben!!* Maisie, they haven't taken them, have they? They haven't—"

"Lucy, it's all right." She came running out of the sitting room, colliding with me in the doorway as I rocketed through. She seized my shoulders. "Lucas took them out; it's fine! I tried to tell you, but you're so wound up. It's fine; now calm down!"

"Lucas?"

"Yes!"

We stood staring at each other for a moment. Then I bent my head, put my face in my hands, and sobbed. She put her arms around me. Helplessly I let her guide me into the kitchen, let her sit me down at the table. Her arm was still round my shoulders as I sat, weeping.

"When the police were talking to you," she said quietly, "Ben went very pale and shot out into the back garden. We couldn't find him for a while, but then Lucas found him quivering behind the shed. He's taken them to the park, for ice cream."

"To the park!" I turned my tearstained face to her. "Oh, but he'll watch him, won't he, Maisie? If Ben's worried, you know, scared by the police arriving, and what he's told them, he might . . ." What might he do? Run away? I thought frantically. Would he? It would never, ever have occurred to me before. I couldn't imagine him anywhere except right by my side, with his little brother, but now, with all these cataclysmic events . . . I found I didn't know. Didn't know how my tucked-up boy, who revealed so little, would react. If Lucas's back was turned, buying lollies at the van, given half a chance, would he . . .

"He'll watch him," Maisie assured me fiercely. "Of course he will, and they'll be back in a minute; you can talk to Ben then. Have it out with him."

I nodded.

"And we must stop panicking," she said firmly. "That's not going to get us anywhere. Getting hysterical is not going to help our case."

"No." I looked at her, wide-eyed. Horrified I had a case to answer. We fell silent.

"Maisie, it was probably just a little prank that went wrong, don't you think? The fire starting like that. I mean, surely—"

"Of course it was," she said staunchly. "Little boys and matches, heavens, I remember when your brother was small, he— Oh!"

She stopped as the doorbell rang. We stared at each other.

"Not Lucas," I breathed.

"No, he took a key."

"Oh, Maisie, let's not answer it," I pleaded, holding her arm. "It'll be them again. She said they were coming; let's pretend we're not here. Let's wait for Ben to get back, wait till I've talked to him. Face them when we've got some answers!"

She gazed at me, and I could tell she was tempted. She hesitated, then got up and smoothed down her painter's smock.

"No. No, that's not the way we do things, is it, Luce? Lying and hiding. That's never been our style. Hold your head up and just answer truthfully. It's all going to be fine."

She went down the hall to answer the door. I waited, numbly, at the table. Heard the door open as if in a dream. I could imagine them already, on the step. Young, earnest. Him with a beard; her, no makeup, thick eyebrows, glasses. No children of their own, of course, and no idea of what bringing up two children on your own is actually like, but oh, so full of ideals. Timid-looking, possibly, but don't let that fool you. Brimming with steely determination to right the wrongs of the world. Interviewing mothers much less fortunate than me, in high-rise flats, demanding to know why a child was still in yesterday's filthy nappy or why, at two o'clock, the breakfast things were still on the table, the older children not at school. Why the mother was still in her dressing gown, looking so unkempt, so depressed. And I thought of the times in London when I'd felt myself slipping into that quicksand, conscious I might not actually get up that morning, knowing that might be possible. In Chelsea. Royal Avenue. Because it didn't have to be a tenement flat in Hackney. But I hadn't. I'd gritted my teeth, hauled myself up, put the sandwiches in the lunch boxes, and gone on. Gone on for them, knowing I might have given up if it had just been me. How many times could these people have called then and found me in a heap? Legitimately have had cause to worry about my children? Yet now, four years on, when I'd battled through . . .

If they took the boys, I'd kill myself, I decided quite matter-of-factly. In fact, it came to me with such astonishing clarity, it was quite a comfort. Of course, it was as simple as that. I couldn't go on without the children, so I'd just take some pills or something. Go to sleep. And with that really rather reassuring thought in mind, I braced myself to meet this pair. This duo from the Social Services Department. Braced myself to answer their impertinent, intrusive questions.

I heard Maisie walk back down the corridor with them, her voice muffled. Male voices responded as she opened the kitchen door to show them in. It was Jack and David.

"Oh!" I stood up, relief and confusion flooding through me. Glancing quickly at Maisie's face, I realized she'd already briefed them on the doorstep. Despite the relief, I felt a rush of shame at what they knew, even though I had no cause. I couldn't look at Jack.

"Lucy." David quickly crossed the room and took my hands. "Ghastly for you. I'm so sorry you've had to go through this."

"But—but it won't happen, David, will it?" I babbled. "We all know that. You—you both know me," I dared to look at Jack, "and you both know Ben; you know it couldn't have happened like that. And you'll tell them, won't you, you'll all tell them, Archie, Lavinia, Pinkie, all of you, that what Rose did, what she said—"

"Sit down, Lucy," said Jack gently, interrupting my gibbering and pulling a chair up for me.

I sat and realized I was trembling. I held on to the table, gripped the oilcloth top, as he sat beside me. Maisie and David perched opposite.

"Lucy, what David and I have to tell you." Jack hesitated. "Well, half of it you know already, but the reason why it all happened, I'm not so sure."

"What do I know?" I glanced at David. "I don't know anything! All I know is Rose wanted my children, that she tried to frame me, gave false statements to the police. It's as simple as that!"

Jack nodded. "That much we do know."

"You do?" I gasped. "For sure?"

"Oh, definitely."

"Oh, thank God!" I flopped back in my chair. Stared at him.

"She wanted to discredit you, show you up as an unfit mother. And to that end she kept a detailed log of all the times the children were left alone—"

"But I didn't bloody leave them alone!"

"No, but if they were left in her care, she'd pretend she wasn't consulted. Or if she'd lent you Trisha, she'd call her back unexpectedly to work with Joan in the kitchen, which left the boys alone in the barn."

"Christ! Did she?"

"And then she'd go and get them of course, like the responsible grandmother she was. And write it all down. 'Monday . . . collected boys . . . alone in the barn . . . shameful.' And of course she kept a very close eye on you and Charlie Fletcher."

"But . . . how the hell did she *know* about him? I thought no one knew!"

"Oh, Rose made it her business to know everything. And when you and Charlie met at her party, she couldn't believe her luck. She gleefully tracked your progress, waiting for her chance, waiting for you to spend the night with him, for the affair to get out of hand. And she was delighted when the chance presented itself so fortuitously when you went out, forgetting to tell the boys where they were sleeping. For some reason—and we still don't know why—the boys went to bed on their own. That's when Rose crept down and started the fire."

"*Rose* started it!"

"Oh yes, definitely. In the kitchen, apparently, in a rubbish bin. Just a small fire, you know, with some comics and matches, something the boys could have done, and something she could easily have put out later. And reported to the authorities, in shocked tones."

"Hang on; hang on." I clutched my head. "She *said* she started it? You mean she told you all this?"

David nodded. "Just before she died. Sometime after her previous, fictitious statement to the police."

"Oh!" I seized Lucas's cigarettes on the table and lit one, sucking away at it furiously.

"Anyway, she started the fire, making it look like the boys' doing, but as she was making her way back to Netherby to raise the alarm, she looked back and saw to her horror that the fire had already taken hold. That far from a little smoldering in the kitchen, there was already smoke billowing out of a downstairs window. Horrified, she ran back, and found that the plastic lining of the bin had gone up with a *whoosh* and caught the banisters behind. They were on fire. She panicked, started to throw buckets of water around, but it was no good. The wooden work surfaces and cupboards were burning, smoke was everywhere, and it was out of control. She started running from the sink to the stairs with heavy pails of water, but it did bugger all. Panicking, she ran upstairs, but her foot went through the staircase where the flames were licking through from underneath. She tugged free and stumbled on, but the smoke had got into the bedrooms and she was in such a state, she forgot where the boys' rooms were. In the thick fog, she turned the wrong way, ran along the corridor, opening airing cupboards, your bedroom door, fanning the flames, making it worse."

"But the boys sleep together, at the far end," I breathed.

He nodded. "Exactly. So she had to turn round and go back past the blazing staircase to the other side of the gallery. She found them huddled behind Ben's bed, hands over their mouths, terrified. She grabbed them and ran back with them to the staircase, but by now the fire had really taken hold. It was quite impassable."

"Oh God."

"So Rose, and two small boys, coughing and gasping in their pajamas, simply went backward. They holed up in the boys' bedroom again, huddled behind the bed, with no plan of action, except, apparently, Rose started to pray."

"Christ," I muttered. I put my head in my hands. Imagined the scene. Slowly I looked up, aghast.

"David, are you telling me that that's how badly she wanted custody of my boys? That she'd do that? Go to those lengths?"

David hesitated. "It went wrong, of course, disastrously wrong. But yes, she wanted them at all costs."

"Without me?"

"Well, no, not initially. Initially she wanted you, but she was nervous you wouldn't stay. She spoke to you, Lucy, came down and had it out with you—remember? I picked her up, in the car. She was desperate for you to stay on at the barn, but she wasn't satisfied you would. After all she'd done for you, it seemed you weren't entirely happy. Seemed you might be moving on, taking her precious boys with you. She thought bitterly of all the plans she'd made, all the money she'd spent on the barn, how she'd planned to educate them, the important families she'd introduce them to, circles they'd move in, girls they'd meet when they were older, and now, just on a whim, it seemed, she could lose them. Lose control. Control was so important to Rose. And family, of course, was everything."

"As it is to me, too!"

"Yes, but we're talking family with a capital F here. Ben stood to inherit, Lucy. He was heir to Netherby."

"Ben?"

"Of course. Hector had gone, forever in Archie's eyes; Ned was dead; Ben was the eldest male."

"But . . . not Lavinia?"

"Certainly not," snorted David. "No, no, in the Fellowes family, the females only inherit in absolute *extremis*, if all male lines are totally extinguished. The male line is all. Rose knew that."

"Although what Rose *didn't* know," said Jack quietly, "is that Ben would never inherit anyway. Archie would never have let him."

I stared.

"Why not?" said Maisie.

There was a silence. Jack looked at David. David's eyes turned, slowly, like headlamps, onto me.

"I think you know, don't you, Lucy?"

I didn't, but as I gazed back at him, the wheels of my mind whirred like a propeller starting up. It seemed to me all those shards of light, all those tiny pieces of the kaleidoscope, were spinning, not out of control, but back into place. I gazed at this handsome, elderly face before me . . . at his high brow, his kind mouth, that nose . . . not the eyes, necessarily, too gray, but his hands, definitely. Clasped on the table. So familiar. I nodded, slowly, amazed. Amazed it hadn't occurred to me before.

"Yes, I see," I breathed.

"Why?" Maisie demanded, confused.

"Ben wouldn't inherit," I said slowly, "because he's not a Fellowes." Maisie blinked. "What?"

"He's not a Fellowes," I repeated, dragging my eyes off David's face and turning to her. "Ned wasn't Archie's son."

"Not Archie's son! But—"

"He was my son," said David quietly.

"*Your* son!"

He nodded. I gazed back. Couldn't take my eyes off him now. I was transfixed. He cleared his throat.

"Rose and I, well, we had a long love affair, many years ago, when Archie first started his other life, in London. Ned was the result."

"So the boys . . ."

"Are my grandchildren." His gaze was as steady as mine. Fixed on me. I could hear myself breathing.

"You and Rose!" Maisie gasped.

"Yes, me and Rose." He hesitated. "Or Rose as she was in those days. The most beautiful woman imaginable. And I was potty about her, for a long, long time. Because believe it or not, before the bitterness and resentment set in, she wasn't only very lovely, but full of fun and gaiety, too, damned good company. The life and soul of any party. I'd known her for years, of course, in that vein, at parties, and later as Archie's wife, but when we became close—well, all the fun had gone out of her life. The party was over and she was just very, very sad and lonely. She felt betrayed, you see, used. Archie had used her as a breeding machine, effectively. She'd had the son and heir, and then Lavinia, and he wasn't interested anymore. He'd moved on. To younger models."

"Did Archie know?" I whispered. "About you and Rose?"

"Oh yes." He looked surprised. "He asked me once, over cards, straight out. And I told him straight back."

"Christ! How did he take it?"

"Oh, on the chin. As any chap would. As his due, I think." He rubbed his cheek reflectively. "Shook me slightly, though. Seem to remember I lost that hand." He smiled ruefully, then frowned down into his lap, lost in thought. Looked up. "And he only ever mentioned it once more, after that. Said to me over port one evening, just the two of us, very late, said, 'Glad it was you, David. Saw her going over the edge, eh? Brought her back. Glad you did. Glad it was you. Couldn't face it myself.' "

"Oh!" Couldn't face his own wife. "Too busy with totty in London, I expect," I said angrily.

David shrugged without rancor, unwilling to censure Archie, his friend, and for the first time I felt a sneaking sympathy for Rose. An abandoned wife, expected to see abandonment as her lot. And at her age, and in her milieu, why ever not? Expected to tend the garden, chair committees, be content.

"But . . . Pinkie came later?"

"Oh yes, and was his, definitely his. He saw to that. I think even Archie was slightly peeved at being so comprehensively sidelined, so marginalized, so they had another child, and our affair came to an end. Pinkie saved that marriage, undoubtedly, and look how Archie dotes on her now, spoils her. Oh, she's Archie's all right."

"But . . . he never told Rose he knew about Ned?"

"Lord no. Chap's got his pride. Can't have all the cats coming out of the bag, running round the county, blabbing. No, people suspected of course, because Ned was so different from the rest and they knew of our affair, but nothing was said. And Rose thought she had something on him, you see. A trump card up her sleeve. Had no idea he knew."

I remembered Archie, with tears in his eyes, mumbling by the empty grate, "I couldn't let her have that . . . " Couldn't let Ben inherit, that's what he'd meant. Not when Ned wasn't his son. And yet he'd stood by, watched her take us in, pour money into the barn, known what was on her mind . . .

"And what about Ned?" asked Maisie, quietly. "Did he know?"

David looked at me inquiringly.

"No!" I blanched. "No, I mean, he never said, and—God yes, I'd have known, wouldn't I? He'd have told me. I'm sure he would. And yet . . . well, he always . . ." I hesitated. *Hated* was too strong a word. "He was always so wary of them. Certainly of his mother. And of Archie, too. Distrusted them, almost."

I remembered our wedding, how adamant he'd been that they wouldn't attend. "They've had a damn good crack at messing up most of my life," he'd shouted angrily, "but they're not going to balls up this bit!" And we'd visited them so rarely, in those early days. I'd had to drag him there. . . . I remembered Rose's letter, too, telling me how Ned had rejected her, in his teens. Been repulsed by her. Had he guessed? I wondered.

"And you never . . . ?" I glanced quickly at David.

"No, I never said. It wouldn't have been fair, separating him from his family like that. But I hope I always looked out for him."

"He always liked you," I said truthfully. "Had a lot of time for you, David. Said so, often."

Something flooded David's face at this. Love? Relief? His son, whom he'd watched grow up. Whom he must have been itching to acknowledge, all those years. In the early days of our marriage, I remembered him coming to meet us as we arrived at Netherby, an awkward young couple, in an ancient car, with a baby. David, smiling broadly, shaking Ned's hand, quickly pouring us drinks in the library, keeping the conversation going when Rose swept in, frosty and distant. And at the time I'd just thought—a kindly friend of the family and how lucky they were to have him. A bachelor, who'd rather latched on. But it made sense now, didn't it, I thought with a jolt. Why, they even looked alike, David and Ned. Small, wiry, handsome, and it explained why Ned had so little of the Fellowes character, explained instead his brains, his easy, relaxed manner. All David. I looked across the table at him almost gratefully. Pleased for my boys. Mortimers. Not Felloweses. Felt a guilty rush of relief.

A silence ensued as we were each prey to our own private thoughts. As we digested the lies, the lust, the love, the deceit, and the implacable desire that had unfolded over the years, to end in this.

"So, she told you all this, David?" asked Maisie, eventually.

He nodded. "Yes. At the end, in the hospital. After Hector and the girls had had time with her, Archie came to find me. Took him a while." He grimaced. "I was in the hospital chapel. Said he didn't think she'd got long. That she was asking for me. Asked if I'd like some time with her. I'll never forget the look in his watery old eyes as we stood together in that church, Archie ramrod straight, face muscles twitching, staring up at the vaulted ceiling."

"Remorseful?" I asked.

He sighed. "I don't know. No . . . just very sad, I think. Anyway, I went to her." He paused, and his hand strayed across the table toward Lucas's pack of cigarettes. I shook them out and he took one quickly, lighting it. As he leaned back in his chair and blew the smoke high in the air in a thin stream, I realized his own eyes were watering, too. "Went to her, and sat with her. Stroked her hair, like I used to . . ." He paused, in difficulties now. We all glanced at our hands to give him a moment. He cleared his throat. Went on, calmly. "And . . . well, I had wondered about the fire, you see, so I asked if she had anything to tell me. Anything to do with it. She knew she was dying, knew the fight was over—and she *was* a fighter; that's what I so loved, admired, about her—but she knew she was a sitting duck now. So she stretched out her hand, clasped mine, and told me everything." He gave a wan smile. "I'm no priest, but I imagine that's what absolution does for you. Gives you some sort of comfort. I hope so. At the end, she asked you to forgive her, Lucy. She asked God, too. And then she died in my arms."

I caught my breath, imagining Rose, in a white hospital gown, just another patient, an old lady, dying in her lover's arms. David's gray head bent over her white one, hands clasped, as a deathbed confession unfolded. Rose, asking for redemption. Asking me to forgive her. Really? For trying to take my children? I gulped and stared down at the pattern on the tablecloth. Felt a wave of revulsion. Oh, I don't think so. No, I couldn't do that. Not now, anyway. I'd think about it later, but not when I'd just gone through the most appalling hour of my life.

"But why didn't you tell me all this this morning?" I rounded suddenly on David. "When I was there, at Netherby, saw the pair of you in the gun room—why didn't you tell me then? Why didn't you tell the *police* then? Christ, you could have spared me all of this. I mean, I saw them, roaring up the drive as I was leaving, looking for me, no doubt!"

"Yes, they were," said Jack impassively, "and we knew they were coming. Ten minutes earlier I'd taken a call from the police station, saying they were on their way to interview you. At that stage I didn't have the faintest idea what was going on. David was on the point of telling me, but hadn't, and I got the impression from the police you were in deep trouble. I wanted to give you time, so I simply said I hadn't seen you, which was perfectly true, and why I didn't turn round when you came to the gun room door."

"And I wanted to tell Archie and the girls what Rose had done without the police being there," said David quietly. "Wanted to get rid of them. Which meant seeing you off the premises, since it was you they were after. They took the bait, but I had no idea they'd find you so quickly. I owe you an apology, Lucy, but I'm afraid I made Archie and the girls my priority. I wanted them to hear what Rose had done from me and not some police sergeant."

I thought of Jack and David, going into the morning room, sitting down in front of them, telling Rose's story.

"And were they horrified?"

"Appalled. Couldn't believe it. The girls particularly. Pinkie was in floods. But then, later, they sort of could . . ."

I nodded. "I think we all can sort of believe it, now."

Maisie shook her head, dismayed. Looked down at her hands. There was a silence.

"And do the police know the truth now?" I asked, suddenly fearful again. "Have you told them?"

"I've let them know I have a statement to make—that much has been winging its way down their radio lines, and I'm on my way back to Oxford right now," he glanced at his watch, "to do just that. I just wanted to explain to you first, though. In person."

"Thank you, David," I said gratefully. "And . . . I mean, they'll believe you?" I asked anxiously. "D'you think?"

He smiled. "Don't worry. There was a ward sister behind the curtain, although Rose didn't know it. They have to be on hand in those sorts of circumstances, when it's so near the end. She'd have heard everything."

I nodded. Breathed a sigh of relief. After a while, he sighed, too.

"I must go," he said wearily, setting his hands on his knees and making to get up. He looked very old suddenly. Very tired.

"But what I still don't understand," Maisie stopped him a moment, her fingers on his arm, "is why Ben said he started the fire?"

We all turned at a noise down the hall. The front door slammed. Footsteps came down the passage; then the kitchen door opened. Jack stretched out his hand.

"Let's ask him, shall we?" he said gently. "Because here he is."

Chapter Thirty-one

"Ben?" I got up.

He stood there in the doorway, then came slowly into the room, his dark eyes lowered, glistening. He wouldn't look at me. Down the hall, I saw Lucas quietly shut the front door. Maisie darted her eloquent blue eyes sideways at her husband. He nodded and quickly ushered Max smartly left into the sitting room with his dripping lolly.

"Ben, darling, this is important." I slipped around the table and crouched down beside him. I noticed he still kept a tight hold of Jack's hand. The other one was in a fist by his side. I held the edge of his T-shirt. "Ben . . . why did you tell the police you started the fire?"

"Because I did," he said obstinately, staring at the kitchen floor.

"But that's not true, is it? Granny told David she started it. She lit the fire in the rubbish bin."

"Granny did?" He looked up, startled. "Why?"

"To frighten us, I think, because I was out and—well, complicated reasons, but not to burn the barn down. It just got out of hand. But, Ben—"

"But she said you did it!" he blurted out. "When she ran up to us through the smoke, along the landing, I screamed, 'Granny, the house is on fire!' And she said, 'Yes! Yes, I know; Mummy left the gas on! The kitchen's caught fire!'"

I caught my breath. My God, even then, even with the flames licking up the stairs behind her, she'd sought to implicate me. Even in the middle of a burning building, struggling to rescue her grandsons, she'd found time to get her story straight.

"So why did you say you'd done it?"

"Because I thought you'd go to prison!" he cried, eyes brimming. "I thought they'd think it was such a terrible thing to do, leaving us alone, and with the gas on, that they'd send you to jail, and we wouldn't see you again! So I said it was me, because they don't send children to jail, do they!" He was crying now and his speech coming in bursts, shoulders shaking.

"Oh, darling!" I hugged him. His little body was like rock, though, shuddering but unyielding, and he didn't collapse on my neck. I took his shoulders and held him at arm's length, knowing there was more, that I had to dig deeper.

"But why were you and Max down there in the first place? Didn't Granny say you were sleeping at the house?"

"No, she didn't," he gulped, "and I had an argument with Granny, anyway."

"Why?"

"Because when you'd gone, she came and found us in the garden. Max and I were down at the pond by the greenhouse. We were lying on our tummies feeding the goldfish and she came up and stood right over us. I rolled over on my back to look at her properly. The sun was in my eyes, but she had a funny look on her face, like she'd won a prize or something. She said, 'Well, your mother's really done it this time!' And when I said why, she said that you'd gone out with your boyfriend." He spat the word out bitterly. "And that you were staying the night with him, too. So I got up and said that wasn't true and she was lying, 'cos you didn't have a boyfriend, and she said yes, it was, and I said, 'Well, anyway, Mummy said Trisha's coming down to baby-sit, so we're not staying here with you; we're going home!' " He caught his breath. "And I ran off!"

"He was crying," said a little voice behind us. Max had escaped Lucas's clutches and crept in for some drama.

"I see," I breathed. "And she didn't come after you?"

"No, no one came. We just went to bed. It felt really odd."

"Have you got a boyfriend?" asked Max.

I turned to look at him. Shook my head. "No. No, I haven't. But," I saw Ben glance up, "I *was* going to meet someone that night. That's quite true. But . . . it didn't work out. He wouldn't have been right." I struggled. "For any of us," I whispered.

I was aware of Jack's eyes on me whilst David and Maisie tactfully contemplated the tablecloth.

"You can have boyfriends," went on Max generously. "We don't mind, do we, Ben? But we'd like to know, wouldn't we?" He looked at his brother.

Ben nodded, scuffed his toe. "I think the truth's important," he muttered.

I took a deep breath. Regarded my own shoes.

"And also," piped up Max, "we'd like to be there when you do it. So no door locking or anything, 'cos we're still not sure—"

"I am," snarled Ben.

"No, you're not. You said—"

"Thank you, Max," I broke in wearily, straightening up. "That will do."

I gazed down at Ben. A silence ensued.

"Well," said Maisie, breaking it briskly. She got up and made for a cupboard, squeezing my shoulder tightly as she slipped past me. "I think what we all need now is a very large drink, with plenty of gin, I certainly do, and then some lunch. Lucas and I had planned to make pizzas from scratch, so if you boys want to help throw dough around the kitchen and stick it to the ceiling, you'd better come out to the pantry with me to choose your toppings." She opened a side door and disappeared.

"I'll come!" Max was off like a rabbit.

Ben followed, but at a slower pace. He stopped at the door. Turned. "Sorry, Mum."

"For what?" I swallowed. "Trying to keep me out of prison?"

He shrugged. "Doubting you, I suppose. Like Thomas."

"Hmm?"

"In the Bible."

"Ah." I nodded as he left the room. David and Jack were silent.

"You know," I said, furiously blinking back tears, "I always imagined my elder son might be the one helping me into my zimmer frame at the Twilight Home, bringing me grapes, and turning up my hearing aid. I just didn't expect our roles to reverse quite so quickly."

David smiled kindly. "He's had to grow up fast, Lucy. That's not your fault."

"Some of it must be," I muttered. I sat down, rested my elbows on the table, covered my eyes with my hands. "Oh God, the relief, though.

The relief!" I parted my fingers and gazed through them, wide-eyed. "I can't *tell* you. I feel as if a colossal freezing cold weight has been lifted from my heart. And I can't thank you enough, David." I turned to him. "I really can't. Thank God you *talked* to Rose, got her to spill the beans! God knows where I'd be if you hadn't done that."

He shrugged. "I think the police might have got to the bottom of it one way or another, but you're right. It *is* a relief." He stood up with a great sigh. "And now, I really must go. Reveal all." He clicked his heels, military-style. "I'm away. But, Lucy," he paused at the kitchen door, "I know you think she was a wicked old woman and she got what she deserved, but . . . if you can understand the sort of life she led with Archie . . ."

I followed him silently down the hall, opened the front door for him. I regarded him on the step as he turned to look at me, anxious-eyed, dapper in his tweed suit and yellow tie, turning his Panama with its brigade band in his hands. I didn't want to hurt him.

"I think that you must have loved her very much, David," I said quietly.

He looked down at his shiny brown brogues. Nodded. "Yes. Yes, I did. Never stopped. And blindly, perhaps, but that's how it is, isn't it?" He glanced up ruefully. "And mostly from afar, too, of course, certainly when the marriage resumed, and therefore with my hands tied. So much of what I saw I couldn't interfere in. I just tried to keep an eye on her, tried to be there for her. In the end . . . well, she was too much for me. She got away from me, from my vigilance. My influence. Had I known the way her mind was going . . . well, it goes without saying. You know I would have stopped her."

"Of course." I looked into his kind, sad gray eyes. "And, David, you know, there may come a time when I'll want the boys to know. Not yet, because I think it would all be too much, they've gone through enough, but one day, when they're older, I'll tell them the whole story. As Ben says, I think the truth's important."

He smiled and his eyes brightened for the first time that day. "I'd like that," he said softly.

I realized with a jolt how he must be feeling. With Rose dead. The only one who'd truly loved her. And who mourned her the most, probably, but in silence. As he must have mourned Ned. He glanced down the hall to where they were already making pizzas in a cloud of flour.

"I won't say good-bye, but yes. When you deem the time to be right, Lucy, I'd like that very much."

I reached up and kissed his thin, weathered cheek. "Bye, David."

"Bye, my love. And good luck." He went off down the path.

I watched him go, pensive. Turned to find Jack, standing behind me. "A nice man," I murmured.

"And a good man, too. A rare commodity, these days."

We watched as David got into his car. I was very aware of Jack's presence. Close to me. He cleared his throat.

"Well, I've said my good-byes in the kitchen, Luce. I'll just pop in on Lucas; then I'll be on my way, too."

"Oh! Really?" I turned, panicky. "Where are you going?"

"To collect my car, which for various complicated reasons is still in another part of London, and then . . . I'm not sure."

He regarded me as we stood in the doorway together, his blue eyes steady, clear as the August sky behind him. I wondered what he was thinking. About last night? Surely. Surely we both were. How I'd demanded that kiss and how he'd obliged but—with such a curious look in his eye. I glanced down and scuffed my toe on the doormat. Embarrassed, that was it, I realized with a jolt. That was the curious look I'd yet to pinpoint. Not for himself but for me. As if his kid sister had suddenly behaved badly, taken her dress off at a party, danced starkers on a table.

"Back in a mo . . ." He slid off sideways, into the sitting room.

I heard him joking with Lucas, saw them through the crack in the door. Lucas standing up to embrace him, kiss him on both cheeks in his continental way, Jack responding and picking up the book Lucas was reading, asking if he normally read such tosh. "I mean, look at the cover, Lucas; come on!"

My father roared with laughter. "Lurid, I agree, and quite filthy in parts—had Maisie peering over my shoulder in bed last night with eyes like saucers—but readable tosh, and makes a refreshing change from some highfalutin poetry I know. Certainly makes a change from some of your earnest oeuvres!"

"Earnest oeuvres? Page-turning poetry, mate, that's my line."

And so it went on, the bantering and the teasing, with me listening at the door and thinking, with a sinking heart, that everyone, it seemed, literally everyone—my parents, my children—could behave in this lighthearted, easy manner with this man, whilst the one person who would like to was standing foolishly by, incapable of joining in, because—well, because of some ghastly barrier I'd erected between us. But then, perhaps he was nervous of me, too? Not embarrassed so much as paralyzed with—I hesitated—longing? I knew instinctively this was risible, ridiculous, but nevertheless, my heart gave an exultant kick. Yes, perhaps that was it. I forged on, regardless. After all, he'd done so much for me, I thought eagerly, gently helping me upstairs last night, putting me to bed, hiding his face in the gun room this morning so he could tell the police with impunity he hadn't seen me, and then coming all this way with David to give me the good news, behaving—well. Like a brother, actually, Lucy. Don't get excited. Or even your husband's cousin. But like a lover? I bit my lip. No. And yet that kiss, I thought, as hope resurged. Oh God, that kiss! I rocked in my Docksiders on the doormat. He reappeared, at my elbow.

"Right. I'll be off then."

"Can I come with you?" I gasped wantonly.

He looked surprised. A smile played on his lips. "Of course."

See? Courteous as ever. But quietly amused. Quietly guffawing, actually. I grabbed Maisie's coat from a hook and hid my flushing face as I pretended to look for some keys in the pocket. At it *again*, Lucy. No shame. No, none at all, I realized with a pang as I clutched the keys. I just couldn't help it. Couldn't let him go like this. I dashed down the hall to tell Maisie I was off. She and the boys were engrossed in their flour fog, shrieking with laughter at full volume. They hardly even registered my departure, although . . . were Maisie's eyes just a trifle too averted, her smile too knowing, as she watched me fly back down the hall?

Either way, my feet felt as if they had wings on as I shut the door behind me. I felt reckless now. Exhilarated. My ordeal was over, and I was a normal human being again, one of the multitude, on an ordinary August morning, when the worst crime I could commit would be to make a fool of myself in front of an old friend, not to be had up for neglect before a child probation officer.

I sighed with pleasure as we stepped out into the sunny London streets, white stucco buildings to either side, blue sky above, and beneath my feet pavement, glorious bloody *pave*ment, and . . . and *people*, for God's sake, all around.

"Isn't this wonderful?" I sighed, sniffing the air.

"You mean the carbon monoxide?" He sniffed, too. "Yes, I must say I'm rather partial to it, but then you and I have always been city slickers at heart, haven't we, Luce?" He smiled down.

You and I. Those sweet, delicious words. Totally innocent and innocuous of course, but nonetheless, they felled me. Crashed over my head like a tidal wave.

"Yes!" I gasped, coming up for air. "Yes, definitely. Can't bear the country, actually. All that Mother Nature crap—load of bollocks!"

He looked surprised. I cringed. Oooh . . . too strong, Lucy, too crass. Now you're sounding ignorant and stupid. Why couldn't I get it right? Why was I so nervous? "I mean, no, obviously the country's lovely," I reasoned, "really lovely, with . . . you know, trees and things, but what I meant was—"

"D'you want to get a bus?" he interrupted, a hand on my arm, as one drew up beside us.

"A bus?" I looked at his hand on my arm. Beamed as if he'd offered me a sapphire engagement ring. "Ooh, yes please!"

He shot me a bemused look. "Steady. Not that exciting. But it could take us ages to get a taxi and I can't bear the Tube. Come on; it's a nice big red one, which will have you frothing at the mouth judging by your present demeanor, and we can even go upstairs. If you're a good girl I'll buy you some sweets when we get off, too, no end of treats." He hustled me aboard and jumped on behind me. I clambered upstairs, giggling breathlessly, stupidly.

"Any idea where we're going?" As if it mattered.

"Of course. Come on, right down the front. You can pretend to drive."

I laughed some more, ridiculously happy and high as a kite as I swung down the top aisle in front of him like a big kid, a hand grabbing at each pole. This was better. This was fine. He'd got the merry banter going and we could hide behind it, in the lurching conviviality of a London bus, until we found our feet. As we sat down on the front seat, though, my mouth dried. All the merry banter dropped off me and dribbled through the grooved wooden floor below. It was so long since I'd been on a bus and I'd forgotten how small the seats were, how incredibly squished we'd be. Our legs—bottoms, actually—pressing together, really quite hard. I gulped. Heavens. I leaned forward and gripped the handrail. No. Silly position. All sort of bent double. I couldn't lean back, though; it would look unsure, uncool.

London rumbled past beneath us, and leaning forward at a ridiculous angle, I concentrated hard. Concentrated on the meandering crowds ebbing and flowing, bathed in the glorious summer sunshine, pretty girls in short skirts, dapper men in city suits, jackets over shoulders, dodging and jostling on the pavements, all with quick eyes, a purpose. Darting into delicatessens to seize a sandwich and a latte, into bookshops for a quick browse, talking urgently into their mobiles, all at the double, and all seen through the leaves of rustling plane trees, which brushed the window, their pale lacy leaves fanning out and flickering against a clear blue sky. I sighed with pleasure, despite my discomfort.

Jack shifted slightly to give me more room. "A very big sigh. Happy to be back?"

I smiled and sat back, determined to be sensible. To get a grip. "Very. Although to tell you the truth, half an hour ago my worst nightmare was about to unfold and my boys were going to be ripped from my clutches, so right now I'd be happy to be anywhere. A Russian salt mine would do nicely; north face of the Eiger, splendid. But—no, it is nice to be back. I may be shallow and urban, may have failed miserably to commune with nature, but this feels like home to me. The boys feel it, too, I know." I gazed down. "Not that I have anywhere to house them in this splendid city, of course, but I refuse to think about that just yet. We'll stay with Maisie and Lucas for a bit."

"That's not quite true, you know," said Jack slowly.

My tummy, unaccountably, turned over. "Sorry?"

"Well, contrary to what you think, you're not as church-mouse poor as you may believe."

"I'm not?" I looked at him, startled, as the bus lurched round a corner.

"Well, where d'you think Rose got all the money to do that sumptuous barn conversion? To buy all that elegant Conran furniture that went up in flames?"

"Out of her own pocket, I presumed."

"And so did I. Which is mighty magnanimous when you think about it. Particularly since she and Archie were strapped for cash and bellyaching about trivial things like reglazing the greenhouse and planting a few shrubs. But then of course, we all knew you were a different matter. You and the boys were her cause. She had an absolute mission to keep you there at all costs, so one assumed she just found the money, somehow. And so she did. In Ned's trust fund."

I stared. "What?"

"Were you aware that he had a trust fund?"

"Well, yes. Yes, I was. I think it would have amounted to something when he was thirty-five, the theory being that that was when he'd need it most—mortgages, school fees, et cetera—but, Jack, Ned *died*. So I didn't think . . . I mean, I assumed . . ."

"It wouldn't come to fruition?"

"Well, no."

"And no one told you otherwise?"

I flushed. God, I'd been so lax. Hadn't even thought to ask. Wouldn't even have known *who* to ask. But then, it had been the last thing on my mind at the time.

"How old would Ned have been this summer?"

"Thirty-five."

"Exactly. And that fact occurred to me, too, recently, as Rose was charging around buying up Harrods, so I checked with my mother."

"Your mother?"

"Archie's sister. She's a trustee."

"Oh! Yes, of course."

"You knew?"

"David told me."

"Ah. Well, what you may not know is that she spends much of her time jetting around Cap Ferrat, so she wasn't in a position to lay her hands on any documents when I rang her a while back. Last week, though, she was back for a friend's funeral, so I bullied her into going through all her drawers in Lowndes Square. She finally found the trust contract at the bottom of her desk. The funds were to be made available *regardless* of Ned's death, and were to be, and I quote, 'bequeathed to his immediate family and dependents.' "

"Oh!" I sat up. "That's us!"

"Or her."

"Who?"

"Rose."

"You mean—"

"That's how she chose to interpret it. Rose—who incidentally was a trustee herself; there were four of them—knew that you were unaware of the terms and managed to get her hands on the money. She only needed three out of the four signatures to achieve it, and that she did. Now admittedly, she spent it on you and the boys—which would be her fallback position if anything was queried—but I think 'immediate family and dependents' was, frankly, more directed at you."

"Of course it bloody was! Good grief, running around spending our money—Jesus, Jack, it gets worse! *She* gets worse."

"Except that from her point of view, she probably reasoned that since the money was bequeathed by Archie's father, she was just as entitled to it, as an in-law, as you were. And you know what they say. Where there's a will there's a relative."

"But surely the other trustees—I mean your mother was abroad, sure, and Rose signed for herself—but she must have got the other two, whoever they were, to agree?"

"The aunts." He grinned. "Cynthia and Violet. And of course Violet didn't have a clue what was going on. Signed with a flourish, I should think, thrilled to bits to be let loose with a fountain pen, probably added some hearts and smiley faces, too. But it was Cynthia who originally alerted me. She came to find me in the study one day in quite a state—wringing her hands, stomping up and down in filthy wellies, a tiara strung round her neck on a piece of binder twine—said she'd been worried about it for some time. Rose had evidently got her and Violet to sign a piece of paper which she hadn't much liked the look of. To do with Ned's inheritance, she thought, but she wasn't entirely sure, because Rose hadn't let her read the whole document. What Rose had promised, though, in measured tones, with those steely blue eyes of hers, was that if Cynthia *didn't* sign, she could say good-bye to her precious herd of cattle. That they would no longer be accommodated at Netherby, and would find themselves at the market."

"God, what a—" I bit my lip.

"Quite. It also explains why the aunts took to wearing their jewelry at all times. They were convinced Rose was after that, too. Went to bed in it, apparently."

We were traveling toward the park now. Behind forbidding iron railings, acres of soft, warm green spread away from us, in the distance.

"So, is there . . ." I hesitated.

"Any left? Well, it's taken a fair battering obviously, courtesy of the luxurious barn, et cetera, but there's enough. Enough for you to put down a lump sum and take out a mortgage, for instance. Get a flat for you and the boys."

"Really?" I breathed. "But," I frowned, "maybe it should be saved? You know, for the boys. Perhaps it should stay intact, for when they're older. Maybe that's what Ned would have wanted?"

He shrugged. "Maybe. That's another possibility, but it's there, if you need it. And frankly, I don't think Ned would have wanted you to struggle."

"No." I inched forward to the edge of the seat. Gripped the handrail again. "No, he wouldn't. He never mentioned it, you know," I said quietly. "I mean, I knew it was there, was aware of it, but vaguely. It wasn't discussed. Almost as if he was ashamed of it. Ashamed to be privileged."

He smiled. "Very Ned. The Trustafarian tag was hardly his style, was it?"

"No. It wasn't."

As we trundled down Kensington Church Street I plunged deep into thought. Yes, how marvelous. Wonderful, in fact. Enough money to start again, in a flat, here, in London. Of course it was wonderful, but—I stole a sidelong glance at Jack. "You and the boys." That's what he'd said. Now why should that make me feel flat? Deflated? Why not elated, thrilled to bits to be solvent, self-sufficient again? A woman of means, for God's sake? I swallowed. Because—oh, I don't know. Because here I was, still on my own again, somehow. Pathetic, but I couldn't help it. Should be ecstatic, but . . .

"Yes, you and Lavinia will both be women of property," he mused beside me.

"Lavinia?" I came to.

"Oh yes, didn't I say? Now that the male line has been totally exhausted, she really will get Netherby." He smiled. "I spoke to her about it this morning, actually. And despite her mother's death, she couldn't resist a little skip of excitement, a quick clasping of hands. No more handsome rectories, you see."

"You mean—"

"Well, she doesn't have to get married now, does she? And I don't think she ever wanted to, really. She's constitutionally unsuited to it, would bully some poor chap to an early grave. No, it was the thought of having no stately pile that was driving her to all those dates. Fear of ending up in a cottage in the village, beholden to whoever was at the big house, like the aunts. Now, when Archie dies, she'll be mistress of Netherby. In fact, *before* Archie dies, if you ask me. Oh, she'll run that place like an oiled watch, take over where Rose left off, hold the reins very firmly. Archie and Pinkie can revert to babyhood again, stick their thumbs in their mouths and let her run the whole show."

I smiled, nodding. "She'll love it. Although actually, don't be so sure about there being no man beside her. A certain Roddy Taylor set her pulse racing the other day, and he was only Mock Tudor."

"Roddy?" He raised an eyebrow. "Nice chap. I was at school with him. Wouldn't be bullied by her, either." He sighed. "Ah well, there you go; maybe Netherby will be a proper family home again. Filled with little Taylors. Rose will be spinning in her grave."

"And Archie?"

"Oh, as long as he sees out his days there, I shouldn't think he gives a toss."

I smiled. "I'm pleased for her, for Lavinia. She'll certainly do a better job than Hector would. Ned, too, for that matter; he wouldn't have wanted it. Although . . . maybe she'll offer it to Hector? When Archie dies?"

"She's already said as much, but Hector turned it down flat." Jack's mouth twitched. "No, apparently he and Rozanna are setting up in a cottage in Cornwall. In a picturesque rural idyll on the north coast, well away from prying eyes, but with their painting and their *lurve* to keep them warm."

I grinned. "Good for them. And good for Lavinia. She's the best man for the job."

"Quite, just as it's a crying shame Princess Anne will never be queen—could show that soppy brother of hers a thing or two—no, this is the best result. And I'll bet she'll make the place sing for its supper, too. There won't be massive debts and holes in the roof and disorganized, gratuitous guided tours but proper pay-a-tenner-at-the-door tours, tearooms, souvenir shops, corporate events in the park. And why not? Better than relying on trust funds to buoy it up."

"She'll be in heaven." I imagined her, striding around the grounds right now, hands in her cardy pockets, pearls swinging, heart pounding excitedly, making plans, always marginalized by her mother but not now, trying decorously to hide her glee but with a broad smile brimming, whilst Archie and Pinkie languished in the shade of the huge umbrella on the terrace, feet up in their Lloyd Loom chairs, gazing on, happy to let her take the reins.

"She'll be kind to the aunts, too. She always had a soft spot for them. Let them move back in. Look after them a bit."

"No doubt. She sent her love, by the way, Lavinia. When she heard what Rose had done, she was horrified. Said she'd like to come up and talk to you. Sort out a few things, apologize for her mother."

"She doesn't have to do that," I said slowly, "but I'd like to see her, anyway. I don't want," I struggled, "well, I don't want to cut the boys off entirely. One day, I think I'll tell them about David, but Netherby's still their grandparents' home. I don't want to sever the connections with Lavinia and Pinkie." I turned for reassurance. "D'you think that's right?"

"I do," he said after a moment's thought. "But I also think you'll find things will take their own shape. Things have a habit of falling into place by themselves. Ben and Max will make up their own minds about where they want to go, where they think their roots are, whom they want to see, and whom they regard as their grandparents and aunts and uncles. I would just tell them the truth at an age when they can take it on board, and let nature take its course. Here we are. We need to get off here."

I glanced up, surprised. We were in Chelsea now, right down by the river. The sun was dappling the water black and blue, and colorful barges were bobbing jauntily at its edge. On the other side of the road, the glinting windows of tall brownstone buildings with ornate balconies and the odd blue plaque dotted here and there gazed imperiously across to the more modern power station opposite. I followed Jack downstairs. He jumped off ahead of me and set off across the main road at a pace. In my haste to follow, I forgot to look left and had to sidestep a lorry, flushing as it sounded its horn and swept past me. Thanks, Jack, I thought, jogging to catch up. On the other side of the road, he marched a few hundred yards farther on, then turned smartly left down a little backstreet. He strode on past a pub, an entirely retrograde step in my view, then swung a right down another little side street until—

"God, what's the flaming rush?" I yelled, stopping and holding my side. "You're going at a million miles an hour, Jack, and anyway, where are you going? What are we doing here?"

He stopped, just ahead of me. Turned. "Oh, didn't I say? This is where I left my car. Over there."

I peered farther ahead to where he was pointing and realized where we were. Cheyne Walk, or its environs. One of its many tributaries, anyway, and at the end of the road was his bright red Mercedes. It was parked outside the pretty blue mews house, the one with the cascading window boxes full of lobelia. The one with the equally pretty French girl inside. My tummy churned. I even remembered her name. Pascale. This was Pascale's house.

Chapter Thirty-two

"YOU . . . LEFT YOUR CAR HERE?"

He walked toward it. "Yup. Often do. Makes sense."

Of course it did. Perfect sense. No doubt there was a convenient parking permit to be borrowed. A handy little ticket to tuck cozily in the windscreen as they snuggled together upstairs. I swallowed and glanced around in panic, desperately wanting that bus to still be there, to be able to jump back on it, trundle on down the river, but it was probably halfway to Hammersmith by now. He strode on.

"Um, Jack," I called after him, "look, I was thinking. Now I'm here, I might, you know, peel off. Do some shopping or, um, go and see Teresa." I tried to sound cheerful, willing my disappointment not to show.

He turned, looked surprised. "You're not coming in?"

I breathed deeply. "Probably not. On balance."

"Oh." He looked disappointed. "I wanted to show you around."

I blinked. "Around Pascale's house?"

He frowned. "Pascale's? This isn't Pascale's house; this is my house."

"*Your* house!" I stared. Looked up at the pale blue façade. "You *live* here?"

"Well no, not yet, but I intend to, soon. It's only just been finished. Only just got rid of the builders." He took a key out of his pocket.

"But hang on—I thought, well, when I picked you up that day, you didn't say it was *your* house!"

"You didn't ask."

"Yes, but—I mean . . ." I gazed up again, astonished. "Well, bloody hell, Jack!"

"What?"

"Well, I mean, bloody *hell!*" I waved my arm around, speechless. "I mean, look at it! It's three stories high, for God's sake! A delightful little mews house in the heart of old Chelsea, in a cutesy bijou street full of media luvvies—must have cost a flaming *fortune*! And on a *lecturer's* salary?" I gaped. Closed my mouth. Pursed my lips. "Have you been selling your body? Become a proper gigolo?"

He grinned. "Nope."

"OK," I said slowly, "so . . . don't tell me. No, don't tell me, Jack; don't tell me." I put a finger to each temple in mock concentration. "The poetry. That's it. You've wowed the literary world with your latest offering and they've made you Poet Laureate. They're all fawning around you and you've sold your sex scandals to the newspapers."

"Wrong again."

I dropped the fingers, frowned. Then I smiled. Nodded knowingly. "Oh, right, yes, OK, I've got it. Silly me, of course. A *trust* fund. Another terribly convenient Fellowes trust fund, lurking in some long-forgotten family vault just waiting until you turned—oooh, what would it be now, Jack, thirty-six and a half? Golly, I bet the great unwashed wished they could turn up nest eggs like you Felloweses can, eh?"

"Like *you* can, you mean."

I flushed. "Yes, well, that's the children's. And I may not touch it."

"Jolly noble." He grinned. "But no, I'm afraid I'm not as fortunate as you, Lucy. My personal inheritance, such as it is, is being squandered, probably as we speak, by my dear mama, liberally, and I hope joyfully, on the gaming tables of the South of France. And good luck to her, I say." He paused, turned before going up the path. "But heavens, how impudent of you to inquire as to how I have the means." He raised an eyebrow in mock surprise. "How frightfully forward."

"Well, gosh, *sorry*, Jack, but the last time I visited your gaff it was a two-room, fourth-floor affair in Earls Court, with pigeons in the rafters and mice behind the fridge. As I recall, we sank a bottle of plonk that didn't require the services of a corkscrew and spent the evening trying to tape up the windows with Elastoplast. How come you've migrated to a poofy little place like this!" I boggled at the designer window boxes, the symmetrical bay trees standing sentry by the door.

"I had no idea my penury was so apparent," he mused. "How distressing. And you're quite right," he conceded with a sigh as we reached the door. "This isn't my house at all."

"Aha!" I pounced. "I knew it wasn't! It's Pascale's, isn't it?" I stepped hurriedly back off the doorstep.

"No, it's not bloody Pascale's," he said, taking my arm as he opened the door, "and stop backing away. It's actually Jason Lamont's."

"Jason who?"

He ushered me in and I gazed around, marveling as we stood in a pretty cream hallway, light and bright with coir matting, walls covered with prints and watercolors. An archway led off to an equally sunny sitting room with sandy wooden floors, pale green sofas, and dusty rose curtains, whilst another arch led down some steps and on to an airy kitchen, beyond which a garden beckoned.

"Jason Lamont," he said as he marched off kitchenward. "God, it's stuffy in here." I followed at a slower pace, wondering why the name was so familiar.

"He's a writer," Jack informed me helpfully as he made for the French windows. With one hand he reached up to unbolt them and with the other delved into a box on the kitchen island, which seemed to contain about a dozen identical books. He plucked one out and tossed it to me. "Here!"

"Oh!" I caught it. Just. Stared at the cover. Red, with a black cross on it, splattered, in a puddle. Very dramatic. "Oh. Hang on." I turned it over. "This is the one you and Lucas were both reading. And Archie, too."

"Quite right, except I was reading the paperback. Which isn't out yet."

I frowned up at him, puzzled. "Isn't . . . ?" But he was busy propping the doors open to get some air. I glanced down again. Slowly opened the cover, and read the flyleaf:

Jason Lamont was born in Oxford. Little more is known about him, save that he is unprolific and has a penchant for fly fishing, the former, quite possibly, being a direct result of the latter. He lives in London, with his conscience.

Suddenly it dawned. "It's you," I said quietly, looking up. "You're Jason Lamont."

He grinned. "Good name, don't you think? Catchy title, too."

I looked again. *Devices and Desires.*

"I know this book," I said slowly, turning it over in my hands. "The hardback was a bestseller last year. And now they're making a film out of it, with Tom Cruise and Julia—"

"Roberts, that's it," he said, stuffing his hands in his pockets, grinning broadly now. "Pretty girl. Nice teeth. Met her in Cannes last summer. Smarter than she looks."

He strolled out into his leafy garden, humming. His back was turned deliberately to me, since, despite the nonchalance, he was clearly unable to keep a huge smile at bay.

I, in turn, seemed unable to retrieve my jaw. I stared at his back. "God, you sneaky . . ."

I stood stock still for a moment, watching as he studiously arranged some teak chairs around a small table in the middle of the lawn. Carefully brushed leaves off a pile of books that had been left out. Then I came to. Hastened after him.

"Jesus Christ, Jack! Jason bloody *Lamont*! Why didn't you tell me?"

"Oh, come on, Luce." He squinted up at the sun, purporting to do more chair arranging, looking for shade. "Not much point having a nom de plume if everyone knows who you are. Much more fun to be incognito, and actually, *so* much more fun watching everyone read the thing and pass comment, not knowing it's you they're insulting or flattering. So delightfully partisan, somehow." He grinned. "Too much sex was Rose's sniffy pronouncement as she read the last page and tossed it to Archie, who a few days later growled, 'Not enough!' And anyway, on a more serious note, I wasn't entirely sure how penning a trashy blockbuster would go down with the powers-that-be at the university or, more to the point, my extremely highbrow and literary poetry publishers. Didn't know if I'd be out on my arse. Actually, I needn't have worried. My poetry editor thinks it's highly amusing. Thinks it might actually help sell the poems, give the punters the flip side of the coin, so to speak. Hope so." He scratched his chin thoughtfully and gazed down the garden. "Got a slim volume coming out in September. Not that it'll impinge on anyone's consciousness, except a few loyal stalwarts who read the *TLS*, but you never know. That's my real pride and joy."

"But God, Jack—that's fantastic!"

"What, the poetry?" He turned, eyes shining.

"No! I mean yes, of course, but . . . you know, the *film* deal! The

Tom Cruise bit. The bestseller, God—amazing! So," I swung around the garden, waving my arms incredulously at the tasteful leafy enclosure, "that's how come you bought all this?"

He shrugged. Thrust his hands in his pockets. "That's how come. I needed somewhere to live, and it was about time. My flat, as you so eloquently pointed out, was a disaster area and getting beyond a joke. Damp garret walls may be gritty and artistic, but they were giving me pneumonia. The money was suddenly in the bank and this came up for sale. It was in the right location, so—"

"For what?"

He paused, ran a hand through his hair. "Hmm?"

"Right location for what?"

He turned and narrowed his eyes down the garden to the wisteria-clad wall at the bottom. "Oh, I don't know."

"For Pascale?" I said suddenly. "Is she close by?"

"Pascale *again*?" He threw back his head and gave a hoot of laughter. "Pascale's my decorator."

"Your *decorator*!"

"Or should I say—because I know she'd prefer it—my interior designer. She did this place up for me, right down to the last lick of paint, the penultimate cushion, the final tieback. I didn't have a clue, and didn't care, either, couldn't be less interested—except for what goes on the walls and in the bookcases—and she came recommended by a friend. I just gave her a 'light and airy' brief and let her get on with it." He glanced back into the house. "She's done quite well, don't you think? D'you like it?" He sounded almost anxious.

"Oh yes!" I breathed, gazing back, too, into the creamy kitchen, admiring the pale, bleached cabinets, the bright Turkish rugs on the wooden floor. "God—yes, it's lovely." I was warming to Pascale, too, now that I knew she was just the decorator. Clever girl. Pretty, too, I thought charitably, nice eyes, and—

"Oh!" I swung abruptly back to Jack. "You kissed her!"

"Didn't."

"Bloody did! Yes, no, *sorry*, Jack, you did. When I picked you up, you know, that day when I'd been—"

"With Charlie," he said grimly.

"Well yes, OK. You two were hanging out of an upstairs window like a couple of lovebirds, billing and cooing and looking like you'd just—"

"Made love? Excellent. Excellent news. That was entirely the impression I intended to give. In fact, we'd just been choosing the carpets for the bedrooms."

I stared. "But why would you . . ."

"Want to make it look like a love nest?" His blue eyes widened. "Why, because that's where you'd just emerged from, my dear Lucy. All tousled and rumpled, tumbling from the steamy, sensual arms of your panting red-hot tiger lover. I couldn't let the side down, now could I? Couldn't let you think I'd merely been comparing the Axminster with the Wilton all morning? Feeling the pile?"

I stared, confused. "But no—hang on; you *did* kiss her," I persisted obstinately. "I remember."

He pecked the air. "Like that?" He raised an eyebrow.

"Well . . ."

"Oh, undoubtedly. Yes, I did, well spotted. And three times, too, on the cheeks. Very French, our Pascale, and very flirty, but not my type. A decorative decorator, but lacking in substance between the ears, if that doesn't sound too unchivalrous."

He looked at me. His blue eyes were steady yet vibrant in the sunlight. Challenging almost. The color of a Devon sky. For a moment I couldn't breathe.

"Now . . . why would you want to do that, Jack?"

"Do what, Lucy?"

"Make me think she was your lover?"

"Oh." He scratched the back of his head thoughtfully. Scuffed his toe on the grass. "To make you jealous, I suppose. Didn't work, did it?" He grinned down at the daisies.

"But why?" I persisted. I stepped forward. We were close now. Very close. His eyes came up from the grass to meet mine.

"You still need to know?"

"Yes," I breathed. "I need to know."

The silence that followed was highly charged. At length he cleared his throat. Went on in a low voice.

"Well, I should have thought that was perfectly obvious. I love you,

Lucy. I've always loved you." He shook his head slowly. Looked bemused. "Surely you know that?" He regarded me gently, his eyes soft. Vulnerable, even. I knew at once it was the voice of truth and not experience.

"No," I whispered. "I didn't know that. Why would I? God, how long? I mean—God, Jack, *always*?" I was stunned. So stunned, I sat down, on a convenient chair, my legs buckling.

He pulled up another and straddled it backward. "Pretty much," he decided thoughtfully. "I mean, what am I saying? Yes, right from the beginning, certainly. Right from day one."

"Day *one*! But you never said!"

"No, quite right, never said. No chance, really." He scratched his ear sheepishly. "That bastard Ned got in before me, didn't he?" He narrowed his eyes past me. "And that was so unlike him, actually. So untrue to form. To get in quick." He folded his arms across the top of the chair, rested his chin on them, and smiled ruefully. "The deal was, you see, in those days, that when we went out together, on the pull, I'd commandeer the bar and give the girls the eye as they lined up for their spritzers, then give them a bit of banter. His job was merely to organize a couple more bar stools and follow through with some more intelligent chat. Mention Kant. Nietzsche. That sort of thing." He smiled. "April fourth. Remember? Remember where we met you, Luce?"

"Of course I do," I said slowly. "In the college bar, a sixties night or something . . ."

"Exactly, a sixties night. And there we were, Ned and I, propping up the bar as usual, but eschewing any groovy clothes because we didn't want to look complete nerds—Ned had a token kipper tie on as I recall—trying to look like we were too cool to breathe, when in you walked. On your own. A confident, stunning hippie. In a long blue antique silk dress, which rippled as you walked across the room, and with that sheet of long blond hair down your back, flowers in your hair, beads—you didn't care. Nothing halfhearted about your style. You asked the barman for an orange juice remember?"

"Of course I remember," I whispered. I was staring at him, stunned. He loved me. He'd *always* loved me.

"And then Ned, in a very un-Ned-like way, blushing madly, butted in and offered to buy it for you. I couldn't bloody believe it. He'd only ever organized bar stools in the past, never offered to buy the drinks.

Anyway, we spent the next hour or so chatting at the bar, the three of us, remember?"

I nodded. Couldn't take my eyes off him.

"And then you said you had to go. Your flatmate was cooking supper or something. And I was on the point of coolly offering my services when Ned played a blinder and suggested he walk you back to your house. Well, I waited, teeth gnashing, and half an hour later he returned. He walked up to the bar, in that typically thoughtful way he had, with that wry look on his face, hands deep in his pockets, staring at the ground, and stopped in front of me. When he looked up, his eyes were alight. On fire. 'All right mate?' I said nonchalantly, terrified. 'Slip her one did you, you bastard?' He looked straight at me. Eyes still shining. 'You know, Jack,' he said quietly, 'I've just met the girl I'm going to marry.' "

I gulped. Inspected my nails.

"And I roared, of course, theatrically. Clapped him on the back, said he was a romantic fool but more power to his elbow or some such rot, but actually, I wanted to hit him. And be sick. It was the first time, you see, that I'd ever felt anything with any certainty." He frowned down at the grass. "When you stood beside us, that night . . . I can still remember very clearly the impact you had on me. How I felt when you looked at me with your clear, frank green eyes. How my heart buckled up when you smiled, talked so naturally—so like Maisie, now I know her—and so unaffectedly. And I remember thinking, with resounding clarity, *Yes. I could spend the rest of my life with this girl.*"

I held my breath. Couldn't utter. There was a silence. He shifted in his chair. A regrouping gesture.

"So, Ned and I, we went back to our respective student houses and I hoped, prayed, that he'd forget. Not bother to get in touch with you. But the next day . . . there you were. Walking to a lecture with him. Having coffee with him in the window of that steamy café we used to go to. And then I kept seeing you both, in town, in bookshops, in the library even, working together quietly, heads almost touching over books, me feeling hollow inside as I walked past and, 'Oh, hi, Jack!' as you glanced up. And then a year later, you were married. It was all over."

"And you were our best man," I whispered.

"I was."

I had a sudden glimpse of him standing next to Ned in church, two straight backs in dark morning coats, side by side, as I walked up the aisle with Lucas. . . . And then at the lunch, afterward, in Lucas and Maisie's back garden. My mind flew back to that sunny, happy day, the garden full of jasmine and lobelia, a long trestle table covered in white linen, strewn with white roses and poppies. Ned, beside me, and opposite . . . Jack. The only Fellowes present, with Jess beside him, the bridesmaid, in sexy black lace, flirting outrageously, Jack peering ostentatiously down her cleavage. Then Jack, standing up, after we'd eaten Maisie's salmon—no, no *Jack's* salmon, because Jack had caught it, given it as a present—getting to his feet and banging his spoon on the table for quiet. Tall, handsome, copper-haired, smiling, a glass of champagne in hand, a fierce light in his blue eyes, making us all laugh.

"You made a speech," I breathed. "About—"

"About how a lucky bastard had got in before me." He smiled wryly. "About how I was pipped to the post. I did. Exactly. And everyone thought, How chivalrous. How sweet."

I stared, astonished. Licked my lips. "But, Jack," I struggled, "no one would have known. I mean . . . it never showed. I didn't know, not for one moment! You never gave an inkling."

"Of course not; how could I? Last thing I wanted was to look like some love-struck git who fancied his cousin's wife. Especially since Ned was my best mate, too." He narrowed his eyes thoughtfully. "Yes. Good. Glad it didn't show. Always wondered. Nice to escape with a few tattered shreds of pride."

"And Hannah!" I remembered suddenly. "You escaped with Hannah, too, from that wedding. My old schoolfriend, who you treated to an alfresco bonk in Regents Park. We all heard about it."

"Ah, true. Hannah. Excellent smoke screen. The ultimate red herring. Nice girl. Big tits."

"But, Jack . . ." I struggled, "so *many* women! Before, during, after. I mean, surely one of them—"

"So many, but never the right one," he interrupted brusquely. "I flitted, Lucy. I couldn't have you, so I tried as many other varieties as possible. And very pleasurable it was, too. And I was nothing if not optimistic, either. I kept thinking one might eventually match up, might cut the mustard. They didn't, but I plowed on regardless, filling in time between haircuts." He shrugged. "I suppose, in days of yore, I might have galloped off to the Crusades, murdered a few heathens, got you out of my system that way, but instead, I wrote poetry and bonked pretty women." He shifted in his chair and grinned. "D'you know what John Betjeman said when he was interviewed before he died? When asked if he had any regrets, he lisped, 'Not enough sex.'" Jack threw back his head and gave a hoot of laughter. "Not a complaint this poet will be able to get away with, I fear, and totally reprehensible of course, but . . . come on, Luce. What was I supposed to do? Pick one at random and marry her regardless, even though I didn't love her? Settle down in Putney with the requisite number of children in order to talk schools at dinner parties?"

"No, but—"

"Not one of them, to my mind, Lucy, came close to you. Not one." He looked at me steadily. It seemed to me the garden went very still for a moment. The trees stopped their rustling; the birds paused in their singing.

"And then when Ned died—" he went on.

"Yes, when Ned died," I broke in, "exactly! Even then, much later . . . you never came to me in that way. You never showed your hand, Jack; I never knew!"

"I couldn't, Lucy. You weren't ready. I kept thinking you nearly were, that it wouldn't be long, but your grief was . . . so huge. So magnificent. So . . . humbling. Seeing you sob at that kitchen table, night after night, there was no point at which I could have said, 'Ah well, never mind, Luce. Ned's gone, but I've always fancied you, so how's about it?' And how could I compete with a ghost? A ghost I loved and mourned, too?" He paused. "Particularly since . . . you blamed yourself."

I glanced down at my hands. "I told you, didn't I?" I said softly. "You were the one person I told. Before Charlie."

"You told Charlie?"

"Yes, but . . ." I shook my head dismissively, "for different reasons. To help him."

I thought back to that night when I'd confessed to Jack, over the contents of a wine box, crying, raving, insisting that *I'd* done it, *I'd* bloody killed Ned. Pacing round the flat like a madwoman, possessed,

plastered, staggering, beside myself. I hadn't forgotten he'd seen me like
that. But I'd shut it out of my mind. As one can.

"And that made you ill, Luce; you know that, don't you? The grief,
and then the ridiculous guilt. So unfounded. You let go of the reins, for
a bit."

"That's tactful," I said wryly. "Let go of the reins, Christ, I went do-
bleeding-lally. And everyone was brilliant. You, Jess, Teresa, my parents, the children—God, the children. I'll never forget Ben, one
Sunday lunchtime: 'Mummy, shall I choose some clothes for you? Instead of that dressing gown?' " I shuddered.

"And then you rallied. Made a decision not to go down that route."

I nodded. "I did. And I got it together. I polished up my act, and
then . . . "

"Then?" He was watching me intently.

"Well. Then I met Charlie."

He nodded down at the grass.

"*Saw* Charlie," I corrected myself. "Saw him in the street. And that
was it."

Jack continued to contemplate the lawn. "Lucy, at the risk of sounding like an amateur psychiatrist, would you like to tell me about that?"

I sighed. "About Charlie? I don't know."

"Yes, you do."

Something in his tone made me look up. I met his eye. Glanced
away again. "Yes. OK. I do know." I paused. "I was attracted to him for
obvious reasons. Sexy, gorgeous, handsome, etc, but . . . there was more
to it than that. And Jess was quite wrong, incidentally. She thought I
wanted him because I couldn't have him, because he was unavailable,
but no. No, it was the opposite."

"You wanted him because he was married."

"I think so."

"And a father."

"That, too. A married man with a child. It was what I'd lost, you
see. I didn't want anything else. That's what I'd had, what had gone,
and I wanted the same again. That'll do nicely, I thought, plucking him
off the shelf. One of those. He was irresistible. Awful." I shuddered.

Jack shook his head. "Not really. This amateur psychiatrist would
say it made perfect sense."

"Yes, but all the time . . . Oh, Jack—God, if I'd known . . ."

"What, that I was waiting in the wings?"

"Yes, I—"

"Oh, come *on!*" He got to his feet. Turned away, thrust his hands in his pockets. "Don't make me laugh, Luce; it wouldn't have made any difference! What—the ultimate single guy? Jack the lad, Jack who couldn't commit to lunch, let alone a lifetime? Who was about as far from a reliable husband and father figure as one could possibly get? Please don't tell me that if you'd known the lie of the land you'd have been round at my place, gagging for me like you were for Charlie. Please don't tell me that!"

"No, no, I'm sure I wouldn't have. And yet . . ."

"What?" He swung back.

"Well, things have a way of coming full circle, don't they? Of coming around naturally, don't you think? It's almost as if I had to go through all that. The grief, the guilt, the—yes, all right, say it, Lucy, the depression—and then afterward, as I came up for air, I remember feeling so elated. So high, so . . . *crazy* . . . as I chased around after Charlie. As if I could do anything. It was another kind of madness. The high after the low."

"And now? At the top of the circle? Where the two lines meet?"

"Now." I spread my hands carefully on the wooden table. "Now you're all I want, Jack. All I want." I looked up.

We regarded each other in that long, leafy walled garden, and it seemed to me his eyes devoured every fiber of my being. And mine his. My heart swelled. How well I knew him, really, I marveled as I explored his face, his eyes, his mouth, and how strange that only recently I'd known myself to be in love with him. Or was that so? Wasn't it true that he'd always had the capacity to rattle me? To force me to reevaluate myself, view myself from unflattering angles, often with guilt and shame? Why, then, if I hadn't cared? Why, if it hadn't been bound up with love?

I looked at him now as he stood before me, arms rigid as he gripped the back of a chair, leaning forward, intent, watching my every movement. Yes, so much I'd seen of him, but so little I'd known, understood. The strings of girls, the wayward life, all, as he said, hugely enjoyable, but if I'd really stopped to think about it—not Jack. Not in keeping. He wasn't a shallow man. I knew that; his poetry told me that. God, literary reviewers told me that in column inches every Sunday, so why hadn't I spotted it? Spotted that something was missing? A huge gaping hole in his life, a void, which he wrote about constantly but couldn't fill?

One of the books on the table was his; I knew it well. Recognized it. His first slim volume of poems, published just after we'd all left university, to boozy, enthusiastic acclaim, at a party in an Oxford pub. I went cold as I remembered the dedication. How we'd teased him. I opened it now, looked at the flyleaf. *"To the one that got away."*

My mouth dried. "Jack . . . I'm so sorry."

"Don't be."

"So stupid. No idea."

"Just as well. You were married. A married woman."

He grinned and I gave a weak smile in response.

"And, Jack, this house." I sat up, glanced around. "I mean, was it—"

"For the boys. And you, of course, but mostly for Ben, so he could go back to school. Be amongst friends, have the security he needs."

I appeared to have a lump the size of an Elgin marble in my throat. I also appeared to have stopped breathing. I stood up.

"To . . . live here? With you?"

He straightened up from the chair. Scratched his head awkwardly. "Well, yes. With me. Sorry. You see, I suppose what I'm asking, in a fairly cack-handed and inarticulate way, particularly since I'm supposed to have a way with words, albeit written ones, is whether," he licked his lips, "whether you'd do me the honor of becoming my wife."

"Your wife!"

"Quite a step, I grant you," he went on hurriedly, "and an impulsive one at that, some would say rash even, but . . . not me. No, not me. I've waited nine years, you see."

Nine years. As he gazed at me, I felt the heavens crash in on my head. Felt suffused with a sensation I knew from past experience to be happiness but also felt the pure, white pain of lost time, exploding behind my eyes.

"I missed out the first time by being too slow, and I've waited and watched you ever since—hopefully not too intrusively—but now I need to show my hand. Can't hold back any longer. Lucy, you look so shocked. I'd hoped, imagined, that you might feel, well . . ."

I walked round the table and took his hands. His eyes were anxious, but I couldn't speak, couldn't reassure him. I felt totally overwhelmed as tears, I think of relief, inexplicably choked my throat. You see, I'd never expected happiness to come like this again. It was something I'd once had, had never cherished enough, and had never expected to have back again.

"Yes," I breathed when I could. "Yes, Jack, I do. You were right to hope and imagine, I do feel the same. I love you. I know that now and I think—well, I think I've known for some time."

"So . . ."

"So," I took a deep breath, "to answer your question, yes. I will marry you. But you're quite wrong. The honor would be all mine. All mine."

We stood for a moment, smiling at each other. Then he took me in his arms and kissed me in the middle of that leafy London garden, its high walls protectively around us, under the gaze of a pure blue sky. And as he did, I felt my soul wander out of its cell. As I stood in the sunshine, with his lips on mine, his arms tight around me, my bones loosening and turning to liquid as I melted into him, a feeling flooded through me that I felt, in all consciousness, had a pretty good claim to be called pure joy. When we finally parted and had panted into each other's necks a bit, he stepped back, took my face carefully in his hands. Cradled it. Every nerve in my body crackled; every sinew creaked. I could feel his breath on my face, could see the desire streaming out of his eyes. Our hearts pounded together, thumping away in proximity.

"In the end," he whispered, his eyes searching my face, "I went for the pale blue Axminster."

"Did you?" I gasped.

"I did. It's a short, tufted pile, and I'm told it's very hard-wearing."

"Excellent news."

"It's what the salesman coyly called Top of the Range, but I believe the expenditure will pay dividends. I believe it has longevity. Would you like to see it?"

"Nothing," I murmured as he took my hand and led me back toward the house, "would give me greater pleasure."